THE CLOSE

Jane Casey was born and brought up in Dublin. A former editor, she has written twelve crime novels for adults and three for teenagers. Her books have been international bestsellers, critically acclaimed for their realism and accuracy. The Maeve Kerrigan series has been nominated for many awards: in 2015 Jane won the Mary Higgins Clark Award for *The Stranger You Know* and Irish Crime Novel of the Year for *After the Fire*. In 2019, *Cruel Acts* was chosen as Irish Crime Novel of the Year at the Irish Book Awards. It was a *Sunday Times* bestseller. *The Killing Kind* was a Richard and Judy Book Club pick in 2021, and is being adapted for television. Jane lives in southwest London with her husband, who is a criminal barrister, and their two children.

🐦 @JaneCaseyAuthor
f JaneCaseyAuthor
📷 JaneCaseyAuthor

Also by Jane Casey

The Close

JANE CASEY

HarperCollins*Publishers*

HarperCollins*Publishers* Ltd
1 London Bridge Street,
London SE1 9GF

www.harpercollins.co.uk

HarperCollins*Publishers*
Macken House,
39/40 Mayor Street Upper,
Dublin 1
D01 C9W8
Ireland

First published by HarperCollins*Publishers* 2023
1

A catalogue record for this book is available from the British Library

ISBN: 978-0-00-840497-0 (HB)
ISBN: 978-0-00-840498-7 (TPB)

Typeset in Sabon LT Std by Palimpsest Book Production Ltd,
Falkirk, Stirlingshire

Printed and bound in the UK using 100%
Renewable Electricity by CPI Group (UK) Ltd

For Sarah Law, with love

We walk the path in innocence because we do not know what is at its end.

Robert Macfarlane
Underland

1

All murder investigations were different and yet all of them began the same way, at least for me: standing in silence near a body, trying to catch the faintest echo of what had happened. Sometimes the air still vibrated with violence and high emotion, and sometimes the silence was empty. It was a habit that I kept to myself, but one that reminded me of the fundamental truth: this was more than a job. Someone's life had been ended too soon. Finding out who had done it, and why, was my duty.

Silence could be hard to come by, however, depending on the crime scene and who else was there. Currently, I was battling to hear anything over the hum of conversation from uniformed officers and scene-of-crime specialists and, inevitably, my colleague, Detective Constable Georgia Shaw, who talked as if she was paid by the word. I tuned back in just in time to hear, 'So he was in the driver's seat, but I mean, clearly, he didn't drive here, did he? Because he was already dead from what Dr Early said. With the rigor, and everything.'

The body was slumped, half of it inside a bright blue BMW sportscar, half lolling through the open door. One arm dangled. Dr Early, bright-eyed and brisk, had demonstrated with a quick swing that it hung loose.

'He would have been in full rigor when they moved him to the driver's seat. You can see he's not in the correct position to have been driving. The angle of his legs is all wrong and his feet wouldn't have been near the pedals. I'd guess he was curled up and they were able to slide him into the seat all right but they needed to move his arm to close the door.' She had straightened up with a shrug. 'You can break rigor, but you can't make it come back again.'

'So we were supposed to think he was killed in the car?' I said. 'And assume it happened here?'

'Your guess is as good as mine.' Dr Early had returned to her examination, probing the bloody mess on the top of the victim's head, where someone had hit him with enough force to smash his skull.

The victim: Hassan Dawoud, a doctor, aged thirty-four. And where we stood was the car park of the big, sprawling London hospital where he had worked. It was just after five on a clear June morning, the light delicate but with the promise of heat later on. The nearest hospital building was a triumph of Sixties brutalism in stained concrete, with aluminium-framed windows that flared brightly as the early sun caught them. Behind them, hundreds of onlookers, I guessed, attracted by the fuss of a murder investigation in full swing. We had taped off half of the car park, which sent the hospital authorities into a tizzy: people would be coming to appointments and to visit their loved ones and to visit A&E and the car park was already inadequate. Without access to parking, the hospital simply could not function. The sooner we took our dead body and went, the better, they had strongly implied.

'Do you want to talk to Liz St John? She's keen to get home,' Georgia said.

'Who is that? Oh – the woman who found the body?' My first instinct was to tell Georgia to do it. I spent a lot of time trying to give her jobs that she couldn't get wrong. In truth my reluctance had more to do with the motivation I'd been

2

struggling to find lately. I had seen the woman already, sitting in the back of a police car with the door open, a blanket around her shoulders, her eyes wide with the kind of stare that saw nothing. *Make an effort*, I told myself. 'I'll speak to her. They're ready to move the body, if you don't mind looking after that.'

'Of course.' Georgia sounded keen and competent, and at least one of those things was true. She was getting a lot better, I reminded myself. I still found myself checking up on her, but nine times out of ten she'd got everything right. It was really just the thought of the tenth time that kept me on edge.

And speaking of being on edge, Liz St John was doing a fair impression of someone who had reached that state some time ago. She was holding a cup of tea, probably not the first one she'd been given. Her other hand was heavily bandaged.

'Mrs St John? I'm DS Maeve Kerrigan. I understand you found the body.'

She nodded. 'I didn't know – I said to the police when they came, I had no idea. I would never have opened the door if I'd known.'

'You opened the car door?'

A convulsive nod. She was thin and pretty usually, I guessed, though tiredness had put bags under her eyes and dulled her skin. Fair hair, fat diamond stud earrings, another few carats on her fingers and a Mulberry bag at her feet. A well-off woman who had blundered into her worst nightmare. She was staring at me with matching interest, seeing, I supposed, someone whose life was nothing like her own. I was wearing a dark trouser suit with a plain white top underneath, minimal jewellery, minimal make-up. I was tall and striking enough to attract attention but I tried to look neutral when I was at work. What was routine to me was shocking to her, and I reminded myself to be gentle with her.

'Go back to the start. Why were you at the hospital?'

3

'I was chopping carrots for the children's tea. Batons.' She half-laughed. 'They don't even like carrots, you know. They wouldn't have eaten them.'

'And you cut your hand,' I prompted. I wanted to get her out of there before the body was moved. It was behind screens but there were things you didn't need to hear, never mind see.

'We have these knives – they're Japanese. Very expensive. They're far too sharp. I must have been distracted and I sliced into my hand.' She grimaced. 'I had to wait for Hughie – my husband – to come home before I could go to the hospital. To mind the children. So I was quite late getting here, and then it was a four-hour wait. They made me have an X-ray – anyway, they were nice to me. I was worried that I was wasting everyone's time by coming here, but . . .' she trailed off, lifting her hand, showing me the bandages.

'What time did you leave the emergency department?'

'Coming up on two in the morning. It was still busy.'

'It's always busy,' I said, with feeling.

'Yes. Anyway, I came out here and the parking machine was broken.' She gestured in that general direction. 'There was a notice on it. Coins only. No notes. I mean, who carries that much change? And the amount they charge for parking . . . well, I didn't have it. I was short two pounds. Everything was closed and there was no one around. I was stuck and Hughie was at home with the kids so I couldn't get him to come and rescue me. I knew the receptionists wouldn't be able to give me change but I thought I might find someone to help. I was about to go back into the building when I saw the car.'

'Hassan Dawoud's car.'

She nodded.

'Why did you go over to it? Was there something about it that attracted your attention?'

She looked surprised. 'I know – knew him. He's my next-door neighbour.'

4

I blinked. 'Wow.'

'Quite a coincidence.' She frowned. 'Except, not really. Lots of doctors live around where we are, and it's the closest A&E to us. It wasn't a surprise to see someone I knew. I didn't think anything of it except, "Oh good, Hassan will help me." The windows are tinted but I could see him in the driver's seat.'

'So you went over.'

'And knocked on the window. When he didn't look up, I opened the door. And he fell out.' She swallowed convulsively. 'I thought he was ill. I thought – well, I don't know. But then his cap came off and I saw his head.'

'It must have been a shock.'

'A total shock. I was almost sick.' She shut her eyes, and I saw a glint of sweat across her forehead as if the nausea had returned. 'Hassan means handsome, did you know that? Someone at playgroup told me. He was terrifically handsome. Beautiful, really. Seeing him like that was a *nightmare*.'

'Did you touch him?'

'I sort of caught him when he flopped out. I checked for a pulse, but he was cold.' She shuddered. 'Maybe I shouldn't have touched him, but I didn't know.'

It was a pain, forensically speaking. I hoped she didn't know what I was thinking. 'We'll need to get a sample of your DNA, if that's all right.'

'Of course. Anything.'

'Was Hassan married?' I had noticed a platinum ring on his hand.

'Yes. Last year. They seemed happy.' She bit her lip. 'Most of the time, anyway.'

'What do you mean?'

'There were arguments now and then. Breaking china. Shouting.' Her eyes slid up to mine. 'It's not that I'm nosy. I couldn't help hearing, when we had the back doors open. It gets so hot in the kitchen. Late at night – when they'd been partying – there were rows.'

5

'Violent ones?'

'I don't know. I can't say.' Instant regret, common to witnesses who felt they had said too much. She looked down at the tea. 'This is cold and disgusting. Could you take it away?'

I took the cup out of her hand and put it on the roof of the car. 'Go back to Mr Dawoud's marriage. Tell me about his wife.'

'His – oh, no. No. Sorry. I've misled you. Hassan didn't have a wife. He had a husband. Cameron. But he's away.' She shivered. 'So it couldn't have been him who did this. Could it?'

2

'I told you all of this before. We had a good marriage.' Cameron Grant Dawoud sat with his hands clasped in front of him on the table, pressed tightly together. A tremor ran through his body every few moments: a physical manifestation of the grief that had left him red-eyed and puffy-faced. He was big, his muscles well-defined, his shoulders straining the cotton of his T-shirt. He was thirty-six, I knew, but his sandy hair was thinning across the back of his head already. The sun had burned him pink across the bridge of his nose and the upper part of his arms. He had come straight to meet us when he got back to London, pausing only to get his solicitor to join him.

I was reserving my opinion of Cameron Dawoud.

'Did you ever argue?' Beside me, Georgia was taking a confident lead with questioning him.

'Of course.'

'Of course?' she repeated, her eyebrows raised as if she was surprised. *Don't overplay it, Georgia.*

He shrugged. 'I'm not going to try to tell you we didn't fight now and then. That would be unrealistic.'

It would have been a lie, too, I thought.

'Was it physical?' Georgia said. 'When you argued?'

'No.'

'Was there damage to property?'

'No.'

'Neither of you ever got angry enough to throw things?'

'I said no.' His jaw was clenched.

'That's not what we've heard,' Georgia said cheerfully and I saw his eyelids flicker as he thought about who might have come up with a different version of events.

'You must be talking about Liz.'

'What makes you say that?' Georgia hopped on what he'd said as if it was evidence of wrongdoing and he sighed.

'I know she found him – you told me that much – so I suppose you've been talking to her.' He rubbed his eyes. 'You can't have had time to talk to anyone else, really. What is it – twelve hours since he was found? Less than that? And I presume you want to start with me since I'm his husband.'

He was no idiot, I thought, and he was easily out-thinking my junior colleague.

'What difference does it make if Liz told us?' My voice was quiet. It was almost the first thing I'd said in the whole interview and Georgia looked around as if she had forgotten I was there. She was enjoying herself, and I was not. I wished I was somewhere else, and looked down at my notebook to hide the thought from the man I was supposed to be interviewing.

'It doesn't make any difference, really. Except that she was mistaken.' He shrugged. 'I don't know why she would say that we fought. She seems like a perfectly nice woman, but I can't say I know her well enough to judge her as a witness.'

'Did you ever call the police? Either of you?' I was the last person to judge them if they hadn't involved the police, given that I hadn't called for help myself when I'd stumbled into a relationship with a man who won arguments with his fists.

'Absolutely not. And you can check that quite easily, can't you?' He glared at me, his brow furrowed. 'Why are you

8

wasting your time on this? It's hardly a big deal that we argued. That's what adults do from time to time, kids. Life isn't one long honeymoon, no matter how much you love each other.'

'But you hadn't been married very long,' Georgia pointed out. 'Still in the honeymoon period.'

'It was almost a year.' His voice broke and he hung his head for a moment. 'We'd been together for four years before that.'

'Why did you decide to get married after all that time?'

'Because we could,' he snapped. Then, in a gentler tone, 'Because we wanted to make a permanent commitment to one another, I suppose. We both felt marriage was for life. We didn't have anything to prove – everyone who knew us knew we were completely devoted to one another.'

'What did you argue about?' I asked. Cameron turned his attention to me again, his forehead furrowed.

'All kinds of things. Who hadn't loaded the dishwasher properly. Who was supposed to pick up the meat from the butcher. Who didn't water the garden.'

'Was that all?'

A flicker of irritation. 'Sorry to disappoint you. Hassan liked to let off steam that way. He'd pick a fight over something small and we'd argue for ten minutes and then he'd make it up to me over a whole weekend.' He sounded more Scottish when he was upset, I thought, which was the sort of giveaway that could be useful. 'Were you hoping for some juicy details of infidelity? I presume you think that we weren't faithful to one another because we're gay. You're assuming we wouldn't play by heterosexual rules.'

'I'm not assuming anything,' I said. 'Some people have open marriages. Some people have affairs. Some people are faithful to one another. I'm sorry to ask about anything so personal but I have to.'

'Don't pretend you don't enjoy it.'

9

Cameron's solicitor shifted in his chair, a small but meaningful movement and Cameron pressed his clasped hands to his forehead, mastering himself.

'Of course I understand. You have to find out if I had a motive to kill him. Even though I couldn't have killed him because I was away. Which you know.'

Cameron Dawoud had been competing at a windsurfing competition in Pwllheli, in North Wales, when his husband's skull was fractured.

'I wasn't going to ask about your relationship and whether you were both faithful.' *Yet.* 'I was more interested in arguments about money.'

He gave a short huff of surprise. 'We weren't exactly short of cash, if that's what you mean. Hassan was a consultant, which means he got paid a decent amount of money, even for his NHS work. He spent half the time working for the NHS and half of the time for Havenview Hospital, which is private. He was a kidney specialist. People respected him. He earned a lot and he spent money on things he liked. Same as me, if it comes to that.'

'What do you do?' Georgia asked.

'I'm an accountant.'

'Do you work for a particular company?'

'I'm self-employed. I have a decent client list.' He managed a grotesque kind of smile. 'You know where we live right? You know we couldn't have afforded a five-bed house in a nice part of London if we weren't doing all right.'

'Appearances can be deceiving,' Georgia observed. 'You could have been managing a lot of debt.'

'Could have been. But we weren't. You're welcome to go through our financial records and I'm sure you will.' His eyes were steely. 'I was in charge of the financial side of things, as you'd expect. Hassan knew what he had to spend and he was careful about it. We didn't argue about it. We argued about stupid little things because that was how we were. And then

10

we made up. There was no lasting damage. No resentment. No motive, from your point of view.'

I'll be the judge of that, I thought.

'Did anyone wish him harm?' Georgia asked, and Cameron laughed, without humour.

'Well, clearly they did. But if you're asking if I was aware of someone wanting to kill him, then no.'

It was hard to tell whether Cameron despised us because we were women or because he thought we were asking all the wrong questions, but I could tell he hadn't formed a very good opinion of us. I tried to think of something to say that would cut through his defences and prove that we were on his side, really, assuming that he wasn't his husband's killer. My head remained stubbornly empty of anything useful. Beside me, Georgia cleared her throat.

'What I'm asking is if he had any enemies.'

'No. He was on good terms with his family. He didn't get on with all of his colleagues but we're not talking about anything disciplinary. He was just a very determined, focused person and he didn't like anyone saying no to him. If he couldn't get what he wanted by asking, or charming someone, then he shouted. That annoyed some people.' He pinched the bridge of his nose, fighting for composure. 'All I can think is that someone killed him because they hated what he was. I think they killed him because he was married to a man and they loathed that. There are plenty of people who think that way, believe me. And some of them are prepared to act on it.'

I let Georgia scurry away after the interview on the pretext that I wanted to tidy up the interview room. The last thing I wanted was a full discussion of where we had both gone wrong in handling Cameron Dawoud. I should have played a bigger part when it became clear that she wasn't able for him, and I had let her fail instead. To teach her a lesson, she had undoubtedly assumed.

11

It's not that I didn't want to help you. I couldn't.

It was all too close to home, that was the trouble. All much too reminiscent of the experiences I should have been able to leave behind when my last relationship ended in the most dramatic way possible.

When I left the empty room I stood in the corridor and closed my eyes for a moment. There was work to do, and plenty of it, and conversations I needed to have, and for that I needed energy. Unfortunately, I was all out.

The sound of a door opening brought me back to where I was and what I should be doing, a feeling that only intensified when I clocked the tall figure sauntering towards me: Detective Inspector Josh Derwent at his most urbane, and therefore dangerous.

'That didn't go too well, did it, Maeve?'

'You were watching?'

'On the monitor.' He brushed a thread from the sleeve of his jacket.

Of course he was entitled to watch any interviews I did; I was a DS and he was my DI. Supervision was part of his job.

For anyone else, that would have been the whole story.

'Why?'

'Curious.'

'About what? The case?' I hesitated. 'How Georgia was doing?'

'No, angel. Not her.'

I rolled my eyes, not even attempting to hide my irritation as I set off down the corridor. I didn't know why I had expected anything different. Josh Derwent was an HR disaster, a walking liability who had done multiple training courses in professional behaviour. The courses had achieved nothing except that now he was aware of when he was breaking the rules, and how, and exactly how much trouble he would be in if I complained.

I didn't complain. I had learned not to mind, mostly, and

to recognise that the way he challenged me was a sign that he cared. No one was more annoying; no one knew me better. If I found him irritating, very often it was because he was right about something and I had to admit I was wrong. Just as often it was the other way round. I'd trained him to listen to me, some of the time. He was my boss, my landlord, my friend. And, currently, he was my problem.

'Give me a break.'

He fell into step beside me, with the kind of easy stride that told me I needn't bother trying to outpace him. 'What happened to you in there?'

My grip tightened on my notes. 'What do you mean?'

'You let him get away with not answering half your questions. He called you homophobic—'

'He did not.'

'—and so you let him avoid talking about whether they were faithful to one another. That's not like you.'

'It was a first interview and he's not officially a suspect.'

'Of course he's a suspect.'

'He wasn't even there.'

'Uh-huh. Pretty convenient for him to be five and a half hours away from where his husband was being murdered, don't you think?'

'I do,' I allowed. 'But I also think it would have made it quite difficult for him to bash his husband's head in.'

'He could have hired someone. You heard him. Money wasn't an issue.'

I pressed the button for the lift with maximum force, as if that would make it come quicker. 'It's not easy to find someone to carry out a murder for you.'

'Not easy, but not impossible.' He turned to face me, leaning his shoulder against the wall, his hands in his pockets. 'What about the domestic violence angle?'

'What about it?'

'There were a few questions you could have done with

13

asking. Who was the aggressor? Did they ever get counselling? What kind of injuries are we talking about?'

'I can find all of that out. In fact, he's not the best person to ask if he was the one who was handy with his fists. Hassan Dawoud was slightly built. Cameron is a tank. I'm not assuming he was the aggressor but if he was, we're more likely to hear about it from Hassan's friends or colleagues.'

He leaned towards me. 'You went somewhere else the second Georgia brought it up.'

'I don't know what you're talking about.'

'Yes, you do,' he said softly. 'And you know why I'm saying it.'

Without thinking I raised a hand to the collarbone that my boyfriend had broken the previous summer, then let it fall when I realised what I was doing. The challenge in Derwent's eyes softened to pity, and that was almost worse. I felt my throat tighten.

'You're jumping to conclusions. I didn't know enough to take Cameron Dawoud on. He was pure granite and he wasn't going to give us anything unless he had to. All we had was a sketchy story from the neighbour. Once I've followed it up with her and confirmed it with their friends or relatives or anyone Hassan might have confided in, I'll go back to Cameron with it. At the moment I don't know enough to know when he's lying to me, but I will.'

'*You* didn't tell anyone.' Derwent's voice was silky. 'What makes you think Hassan did?'

I felt the colour wash into my face. 'This isn't about me and I don't know why you keep bringing it up. It's old news. I'm over it.'

'I wonder . . .'

'What?'

'I wonder if you really believe that.' Derwent straightened up, dropping the inquisition abruptly. 'And I wonder if now is the right time to ask you something.'

'What?'

'If you'd do something . . . unusual with me. It would involve going away. A complete change of scene.'

'For work?'

He looked affronted. 'Of course for work.'

Of course. Derwent had a partner, Melissa, and even if he hadn't, he would have a bit more subtlety than that. Flustered, I said the first thing that came to mind.

'Going away – for how long?'

'Don't know.'

'Then no. I would say no.'

'Then I won't ask you.'

At that moment the lift doors slid open and I shot into it. He stood in the hallway, watching me, his expression unreadable. He never took no for an answer if it was something he really wanted, I thought.

It was as if he'd heard me. 'I won't ask you *now*, anyway. Some other time.'

I had my hand on the button to keep the doors open. 'Are you getting in?'

'No. I'll take the stairs.'

The doors closed and I felt my shoulders drop, somewhere between relief and dismay. I knew Derwent well enough to be certain the conversation wasn't over.

3

The Dawouds lived in a secluded, tree-lined road a couple of miles from the hospital as the crow flew, but it might as well have been another planet. Detached houses were set back from the road, with expensive cars parked on the driveways. Somewhere children screamed, a thin noise that was happiness rather than horror. There were discordant notes: the police officer standing on the pavement outside the first house in the street, and the police tape strung across the gateway, and the Metropolitan Police Forensic Service vans parked along the road, and several bunches of flowers propped against the hedge.

'We're not releasing the house until Kev is happy,' Georgia told me, preparing to step into her paper suit. I was doing the same, tucking my hair back under the hood.

'Did he tell you if he'd found anything?'

'No.' She bit her lip. 'He'd probably have told you.'

'Kev and I go way back.' I gave her a reassuring smile; there had been a time when I had envied other police officers their easy confidence with the crime scene technician. 'He tells me all sorts of things he shouldn't.'

Kev Cox was a wizard who had a sixth sense about where he might find DNA or blood spatter or a careless fingerprint.

No one was better at reading a crime scene than him. So when I found him in the kitchen of the big, empty house, and saw the set of his shoulders, my heart sank.

'Nothing?'

'Not so far.' He looked up from his clipboard and shrugged. 'It could be your crime scene. I'm not ruling it out.'

'Go on.'

His face puckered with frustration behind his mask. 'Just a few things that don't add up, like we found his mobile phone on the kitchen table. I'd expect him to have taken it with him if he was leaving the house for any length of time – it's second nature now, isn't it?'

'You have to make an effort to go out without it,' I agreed. 'Unless you want to be untraceable. But it's a shame we won't have cell-site analysis to tell us where he went.'

'It makes me think that he was dead before he left here but there's nowhere with obvious blood spatter, and nowhere that's too clean. Look at this.' He pointed to the marble work surface on the kitchen counter. 'Crumbs. Fingerprints everywhere. Smudges on the window. The cleaner comes on Fridays, I'm told, and no one did much cleaning in her absence.'

'So no one mopped up a puddle of blood.'

'Nope. I found a smudge – one smudge – on the back door.'

'Inside or outside?'

'Outside.' He shrugged. 'Could belong to our guy. Could belong to someone letting themselves into the back garden to make a getaway. Could be a gardening injury from a few days ago. There wasn't much of it.'

'Hmm.' I went across to look out at the garden, realising that it wasn't overlooked to the rear. Tall trees and shrubs lined the walls, adding to the impression of privacy that was the greatest luxury London could offer. The house itself was like something from a magazine, all brass detailing and restrained good taste. Parquet floors, expensive sofas, a high-end kitchen with designer stools at the breakfast bar: the ideal home for a pair of well-heeled professionals, even if it was on the large side for two. I made a note to ask Cameron if he and his husband had been thinking about having children. He would know I was seeking a motive, but it was still worth asking. 'What's that at the end of the garden?'

'A home gym.' Kev came to join me. 'I've got a couple of techs in there, don't worry. They haven't found anything. The flooring out there is rubberised but it's soft and absorbent, not wipe-clean. If there was blood, it would stain.'

'Right.' I stepped out onto the patio, careful to avoid making contact with the door. An expensive barbecue sat under a canvas cover. Big sofas bracketed a fire pit. The overall air of affluence persisted.

'Nice place for a summer party.' Kev winced as a scream tore the air from the garden next to us. 'Except for that, obviously.'

I had jumped too. The scream came again and ended in a happy gurgle before a toddler's voice was raised in outrage. 'Mummy. Mummy!'

'Isn't it bedtime?' I said to Kev, who rolled his eyes.

'Goes right through your head, doesn't it.'

The house beside the Dawouds would belong to Liz St John, I thought, and it looked just as expensive and desirable as my victim's house. Money couldn't buy you peace and quiet, but it could definitely make you think you were entitled to it.

A rustle at the door was Georgia stepping out gingerly on the metal footplates Kev had laid across the patio.

'Anything?'

'No.' I pointed discreetly at the house next door. 'That's the only house that would have line-of-sight on the garden. We should talk to her again.'

'She didn't mention seeing anything.'

'She might not have thought it was relevant. And she might have a cleaner or a housekeeper or gardener or someone else we don't know about. They could be a witness.'

'Assuming anything happened here,' Georgia said.

'We have to start somewhere. Do you mind going round to talk to her?'

She looked surprised. 'Don't you want to do that?'

'I'm sure you can manage it,' I said, and watched her go with mixed emotions. I'd spoken to Liz St John at the hospital, I thought. I'd done my bit. If Georgia still needed me to hold her hand on a straightforward interview, she was in the wrong job.

You should still have gone with her.

I ignored the nagging voice of my conscience and turned back to Kev. 'Where did Hassan keep the car?'

'In the garage. Left of the front door. I've had a preliminary look.' He brightened. 'The floor is polished concrete. Very good surface for footprints. The place is immaculate. I think it's worth spending a bit of time on it.'

I nodded. 'Can I walk through the rest of the house?'

'Be my guest. If you find anything, let me know.' He headed off in the direction of the garage, his usual cheerful whistling modulating to a minor key. Frustration didn't sit well with him.

I started at the back of the garden, scanning the gym from the door to avoid getting in the way. It was equipped with expensive kit: a Peloton bike, a massive treadmill, a rowing machine and stacks of weights. The back wall was mirrored, doubling the crime scene technicians who were crawling around the floor and delicately swabbing near-invisible smudges on the walls. I glanced at myself automatically: tall, anonymous in protective gear. Dead-eyed.

I turned away and strode back to the house, pausing for a second at the door to get an impression of the place. It was as Kev had said: nothing out of place, nothing remarkable. Every room was tidy but not too tidy, clean but not excessively so. As I walked around I noticed the floors were in need of a vacuum here and there, and the mirror in the en-suite bathroom was splashed with water stains. If someone had cleaned up a crime scene they could never have recreated the lived-in feel of the place. Nothing jangled with that unsettling vibration I'd come to recognise as the aftermath of violence. Nothing jarred.

Georgia was loitering outside when I came out of the front door. 'Anything interesting?'

'Not really. What about Liz?'

She shrugged. 'She was fine. Made me feel like a scruff. I should have left my protective suit on so I didn't make the place dirty.'

'House proud, is she?'

'You'd never know two little kids live there. You could eat your dinner off the floor.'

'Did she see anything next door?'

'No, but I'd say she's too preoccupied with herself to notice much. And the kids make noise all the time. You know how it is – you have the bifold doors open because the rooflights make the kitchen so hot when the sun is shining and suddenly you realise how much sound carries. Hassan used to complain about it, she said, but poor little Nell went through agonies when she was teething.'

It was a pitch-perfect imitation of Liz's drawl and I grinned appreciatively. 'Such a nightmare with the rooflights. I suppose she didn't notice anyone calling next door? A delivery, even?'

'She didn't say. Why? Do you think someone burgled the house?'

'No,' I said, surprised. 'Nothing so dramatic. I just want to know if there was a point when Hassan stopped answering the door. The blood on the back door is inconclusive. If nothing happened in this house, I want to work out when he was here and when he went out.'

'That would be helpful.'

I sighed. 'Let's face it, any facts at all would be helpful. So far all that we really know for sure is that Hassan Dawoud is dead.'

4

The weather was beautiful the following day, through the office window. Small, bright-edged clouds slipped away overhead, racing east in a bright blue sky. Pigeons whirled on the air, weightless and lovely from a distance. Where they found a window ledge the males strutted and preened, balls of confident fluff as fat as full-blown peonies. Beautiful, if you didn't look at their rheumy eyes and mutilated feet.

I shouldn't have noticed any of it.

I stared out of the window at the sharp green growth on the trees, the wind flipping the leaves like a croupier turning cards, and wished I had nothing else to do but let the summer day pass into evening, and evening deepen to night before my eyes.

The Dawoud case needed my attention. I couldn't leave it up to Georgia even though she had been picking up the slack, taking on tasks that I should have dealt with myself, and all without complaint or asking for praise. Georgia was becoming a useful member of the team, just as I was turning into a dead weight.

Yet another email slid into my inbox. I read the subject line and fought back a yawn: counsel with a question about an upcoming trial. It would be an easy one to answer, only needing a quick check of the file, but lassitude pressed down on the back of my neck like a heavy hand.

If my best friend, Liv, had been at work, she would have noticed that something wasn't right – she would have noticed it before I was even aware of how I was feeling. She would have taken me out for a drink and interrogated me gently but inexorably until I faced up to reality. But Liv was off on maternity leave, utterly besotted with her plump, cheerful baby. And of the others who might notice . . . I scanned the other desks. The usual suspects: Chris Pettifer on the phone, leaning back with one arm propped behind his head, his belly domed under a straining shirt. Colin Vale, his lips moving as he read through a report, blinking fast behind his thick glasses, his cycle jacket hung carefully over the back of his chair, ready for his perilous trip home. Pete Belcott was sending messages from his personal mobile phone, his face flushed and somehow unwholesome: a dating app, I thought, or just some straight-forward sexting. He licked his lips as I watched, his tongue working at the corners of his mouth, and I wished I could unsee it. A few other detectives were scattered around the room, all of them hard at work, none of them remotely inter-ested in me or my problems.

And if they had been, I would have been horrified, I reminded myself. I sighed as I dragged my eyes back to the screen in front of me and clicked on the email. It was a model of brisk communication, as I'd expected from that particular lawyer, and the question was as straightforward as I'd antic-ipated. I sighed again, and yawned, and looked vacantly around the office once more, and jumped as I realised I'd been under surveillance all along.

There was a meeting going on inside DCI Una Burt's glass-walled office; the murmur of voices had been a constant from behind the closed door since I got to work. I had failed to notice two things: that Derwent was at the meeting, and that he had managed to find a seat commanding a perfect view of my desk. The office was lined with blinds for privacy, but most of them were crooked and one had fallen down altogether, leaving a large gap. That was where he had chosen to place himself. He was sitting with his legs stretched out in front of him and crossed at the ankle, which was typical; he liked to take up as much space as possible. Also typical were the arms folded across his chest, and the straight-browed glare he was giving me that said more clearly than words: *I know you've been doing the bare minimum to get by, and not even that today, and if you think it's good enough you've got another think coming.*

I forced myself to concentrate on answering the email, taking great care to get the details right. I checked it twice, sent it, and looked back to reassure myself that Derwent was no longer watching.

He hadn't moved a muscle: his whole focus was on me. At that moment, Una Burt must have said something to him because he turned his head towards her desk and spoke. It was impossible to guess what he was saying, but his expression wasn't encouraging.

Maybe the bad mood wasn't entirely because of me.

The gaps in the blinds offered me a tantalising glimpse of the other people at the meeting. A man in a dark suit, balding and bespectacled. A woman in a fuchsia jacket, her fair hair cut into a bob that was designed to project competence rather than style. There was something familiar about her although all I could see was the back of her head; I frowned, trying to place her. There was a fifth person. I rolled my chair back a few inches to get a better view: Assistant Commissioner Simon Grayton, the mayor's pet, appointed to a newly created position with a brief to transform the Met into a modern police force, whatever that meant. He wasn't particularly popular with the ordinary coppers who actually policed London, but he was well-spoken and accomplished in management speak. He had the power to shut down our entire team, if he wanted to, and I couldn't imagine why Una Burt had taken the risk of allowing Josh Derwent anywhere near him. There was almost no chance Derwent would get through a whole meeting without saying something unforgivably offensive – in fact, even now he was sitting up and leaning forward, responding to the woman. Her shoulders were up around her ears, her head shaking as she listened to him speak.

Oh shit.

I was half glad that it was nothing to do with me, and half disappointed, and that in itself was a surprise. It was so long since I'd felt the jolt of curiosity that I'd almost forgotten what it was like. I wanted to be in the meeting, not outside it, and it was months since I'd cared about anything like that.

Derwent had stopped talking but he looked as if he was far from finished with whatever he'd been saying. The woman was holding forth now, jabbing a finger in his direction, and the balding man had leaned over to put a supportive or quelling hand on her chair. A professional relationship, I thought, even if it was a close one, or he'd have made physical contact with her.

I wished I could see Una Burt's face – would she back Derwent up or hang him out to dry? And what did Simon Grayton make of it? Why was he even there?

For a moment, I felt like the old me. The fog in my brain seemed to have cleared.

Una's office door opened. The man in glasses came out first and stood to one side, one hand supporting his elbow as he pressed a finger to his lips. He was younger than I'd thought, prematurely aged by stress, and behind his glasses his eyes were worried.

'—I'll be honest with you, I haven't heard one thing from you or from *him* that made me think you'll make any effort whatsoever to stop this from happening to someone else. And it makes me wonder if you'd care more if you had different victims.' The woman sounded as if she was on her last nerve

24

as she burst out of the office like a cork out of a bottle. The *him* she'd mentioned was undoubtedly Josh Derwent. Well, his charm either worked on you or it didn't; there was no middle ground.

That was assuming he was bothering to use his charm, of course.

'Now, I don't think—' Simon Grayton began, his tone emollient.

'You can't say that—' Una Burt, shrill in contrast with the assistant commissioner. And over the top of both of them, far too audibly, Josh Derwent, his voice sharp enough to cut steel.

'What you want us to do isn't possible.'

'Why not?' she demanded. 'I thought you had the answer.'

'That's not what I said. I had one suggestion, but there are no guarantees it would work. And besides, that approach requires an enormous commitment of manpower and resources, and we have other priorities.'

'More important people to worry about?'

'Don't put words in my mouth,' he snapped.

'If it's resources,' Simon Grayton said smoothly, 'then I can assure you, there's no issue with funding this enquiry. I'll make sure you have what you need.'

'The question is how we can help,' Una Burt said. 'All of the options are on the table. And it is a top priority for us, I can promise you, Mrs Jacques.'

Her name was the prompt I'd needed: Rula Jacques, the mayor's right-hand woman, a fixer to her fingernails. The media made a big deal out of the fact that she was unelected and answered to no one except the mayor, who was widely thought to be under her thumb. Rula by name, ruler by nature, the headlines said. Such a shame she wasn't good enough at playing the political game to run for office herself, they murmured with what might have sounded like sympathy if it hadn't been edged with contempt. She was a short woman in person, broad across the hips, and her look-at-me clothing choices felt like deliberate defiance of other people's expectations. A brilliant strategist, she had guided the mayor throughout his political career, and he owed her a lot.

So pissing her off was pretty much unthinkable, considering that the mayor could punish the Met any time he liked.

Derwent didn't seem to have got the message. He stood in the doorway, glowering down at Mrs Jacques.

'We have to operate inside the law. We can't pile in and arrest anyone and everyone who might have some involvement in this . . . situation.'

'Crime. You can call it a crime.' Rula Jacques was shaking, I noticed, her movements uncoordinated as she plucked at her bag and settled a necklace at her throat. She was holding back tears with a dam of anger.

'Evidence is the issue,' he said softly, and there was a touch of compassion in the way he looked at her, though I suspected you'd have to know him very well to spot it. 'We don't have any. All we have are your suspicions—'

'That's not quite all.'

'No.' He made a small movement with his shoulders that I knew to be frustration: not with her, but with the situation that meant that he couldn't help her.

'Mrs Jacques, we will do all we can.' Simon Grayton bowed, an oddly formal movement.

'Inspector Derwent and I will come up with some other ideas,' Una Burt added, with a meaningful side-eye in his direction.

'Let me walk you to the lift.' Grayton steered Rula Jacques away, the nameless functionary trotting behind them.

Derwent didn't miss a beat, turning towards me before the door had closed fully behind them. His expression was thunderous. I quailed. *Not now. Not here. Not in front of everyone.*

'Josh. Where are you going?' Una Burt sounded like a particularly brisk dog trainer. 'I think we have rather a lot to talk about, don't we?'

26

He stopped and I wondered if this was the moment where he would slip into downright mutiny, and if so what the consequences would be.

'Come on. My office, please.'

A muscle flexed in his jaw. With a visible effort, he made himself turn back and walked past Una Burt silently. She followed him, and shut the office door with a firm hand.

5

Hassan Dawoud's handsome face stared at me in moody black and white from the centre of the noticeboard that stood in the corner of the office. Georgia had commandeered it for our use; she was a visual person and it helped her to lay everything out. Dawoud's features were a perfect mixture of strength and delicacy: thick eyebrows, long lashes surrounding dark eyes, a straight nose and square jaw, a softly curved mouth and elegantly cut cheekbones. He had had the sort of face that made you look twice.

I knew better than to read much into a single photograph, or to think that a personality could be interpreted through genetic good fortune, but I also knew that life could be very kind to wealthy, privileged people who happened to be beautiful.

'Do you think he was spoilt?'

'Yeah.' Georgia was leafing through pictures, her hair swinging in a golden bell that hid her face. 'I think he was probably a bit of a nightmare.'

'Based on what?'

She tossed her hair back to look at me, just a trace of hurt in the angle of her eyebrows. Hurt that I was asking her to back up what she'd said with facts, which was Georgia all over. We needed facts, I felt like telling her, because feelings didn't stand up in court, but she should know that. 'Based on what his colleagues said. He was popular with patients and a bit of a hassle for the admin staff. He did his job well and he expected everyone else to do the same. He didn't quite do the bare minimum but the impression I got was that he wouldn't put himself out for anyone else by staying late or taking on extra work.'

'Not the kind of thing that gets you killed, as a rule.'

Georgia began sticking pictures up in neat rows: the car in the car park, the body slumped sideways, ghostly fingerprints on the door handle highlighted in powder.

'These match Liz St John.'

'Makes sense,' I said. 'What about the inside of the car?'

'Wiped. So was the door handle. There wasn't so much as a smudge apart from hers.'

Close-ups of the body came next, the photographer getting closer and closer until it was a series of fragments: the victim's face, his skin waxy; his hands in his lap, the fingers loosely curled; his feet awkwardly twisted in the footwell as if someone had stuffed him into the driver's seat. He wore a dark T-shirt and running shorts over leggings. His legs and arms were slender.

'Was he a runner?'

'Long distance.'

'Was he training for the marathon?'

'Not this year, apparently. He had some trouble with injuries and fitting in the training, given his work commitments, so he didn't bother with it but he still did a fair bit.'

'He looks like a runner.'

She dropped her voice so only I could hear her. 'Josh runs marathons, doesn't he?'

'I believe so.' I didn't want to talk about Derwent.

'He's built more like Cameron than Hassan. Pure muscle.'

Shut up, Georgia. 'So maybe our victim was in his gym before he was killed.'

29

'Maybe he went somewhere for a run and his running partner hit him over the head with a brick.'

'His trainers were spotless. They've gone off for forensics, but they didn't look as if he'd been running in them.' I tapped the end of my pen against my mouth. 'It bothers me that he was at the hospital. Were we supposed to think he drove himself there and then died in the car?'

'I don't know.' Georgia stepped back. 'The pathologist's absolutely certain that he wasn't killed in the car. Whatever hit him was moving fast and hit him on the left side of the head above the ear. But she did say that the way the blood was pooled around his legs made her think he was placed in the car very shortly after he died. She said he would have been there for a few hours. She thinks he was killed at least twelve hours before he was found.'

'Do we have pictures of the house?'

'Loads of them.' She slid the stack across the table to me and I started shuffling through them, wondering what I was looking for.

'We asked Cameron to look through these, didn't we? Was anything out of place?'

'No.'

'And the forensic search didn't turn up any other traces of blood?'

'Nothing so far.'

'And no one saw anything. Did you make any progress on the deliveries?'

She pulled a face. 'I'll get on to that.'

With an effort, I held back the sarcastic remark that I really wanted to make. What had she been doing for the last twenty-four hours?

What had *I* been doing, if it came to that?

'I would. Did he go anywhere?'

'Not as far as anyone can say. And you know the phone is no use because he left it in the kitchen.'

I sighed. 'My guess is that he was killed near the car because moving the body would have been the risky bit. Do we know when his car left his house?'

'No. I asked Liz but she said Hassan came and went at odd hours as a rule and she tended to tune it out. You know how a sound like that turns into background noise.'

I nodded.

'On the other hand, we know when it arrived at the hospital because it pinged the car park's ANPR. He had a sensor in his car to raise the barriers.'

I perked up. 'Do we have CCTV?'

'Not really.'

I unperked. 'Why not?'

'The camera on the parking barrier is focused on the number plate and the place where the car was parked is under trees. You can see them here, look.' She pointed at the pictures on the noticeboard. A row of lime trees had been planted along the car park wall. 'They did a good job of screening the driver. All we can see is a man in dark clothes and a black cap. We picked him up going through the pedestrian gate here.'

Georgia had stuck up a floorplan of the hospital layout, and traced a line from the car to the gate. She added a picture beside it, a still from the CCTV.

'This is our suspect. The timing is right – about ten minutes after the car entered the car park.'

'Is that really the best image?' I didn't try to hide the dismay in my voice.

'That's it.'

The quality was terrible, and that wasn't the only problem. Our suspect had his head down, a hoodie pulled up over the cap and his hands in his pockets. He had on dark tracksuit bottoms and trainers. His clothes were baggy but he seemed lean – fit, but not muscle-bound like Cameron.

'I can't even see any logos on his clothes or trainers.'

31

'There isn't anything that would help us to identify him. Completely generic clothing.'

'Is he white?'

'He could be,' Georgia said carefully. 'But that's just a guess, if I'm honest. You can see a little of his face but it's in shadow. He could be IC2 or IC4.'

'Witnesses?'

She shook her head slowly. 'We have boards up. We're appealing for information. So far, nothing useful. It was a busy night in A&E, but the rest of the hospital was fairly quiet. Not that many people come and go at that time except for emergencies and people going to the maternity wing.'

'We need to check CCTV for the area. See if we can pick up where he went next.'

'Already on it. Unfortunately the streets around the hospital are mainly residential so there aren't many premises with their own cameras.' She quailed at the look on my face. 'We're checking though. What else?'

What else? My mind was blank. I collected myself. This was familiar territory, after all. 'We need a motive.'

'There isn't one.'

'There must be. Why are people murdered?' I ticked it off on my fingers. 'Who they are. What they have. What they do. We need to think about who Hassan was, and what he did.'

'For a living, you mean?'

'Maybe. Yes. But not just that he was a doctor.' The fact that he had been left at the hospital bothered me a lot. Was it a message? Or designed to mislead us? If he'd been killed at the house why not leave him there instead of moving the body? 'We need to find out where our victim went on Tuesday. We need to go through his bank accounts. We need to download his phone and any other tech he had. We need to find out if the hospital was significant – if he was put there because the motive for murder was something to do with the hospital – or if he was dumped there for some other reason. If his

32

neighbour hadn't found him, the car might have gone unnoticed for a while. Cameron was only due back today.'

'Dawoud had two days off work in his diary.'

'Had he? Why?'

'Don't know.'

'Next time we talk to Cameron we can ask him if he knew his husband was taking time off while he was away. In the meantime there's a lot of work to do.'

'Isn't there always?'

'What I would really like,' I said slowly, 'is a scene and a motive.'

'And an ID on the driver.'

'And a pony of my very own.'

Georgia giggled. 'And a man who's good in bed and can cook.'

'Let's not aim for the impossible,' I said, and turned around to find Derwent standing behind me, unsmiling.

'You two. The meeting room. Now.'

6

The meeting room was crowded by the time we got there so Georgia and I had to settle for standing at the back. I leaned against the wall and checked the time surreptitiously. Almost the end of the working day. If I tried to sneak out Derwent would spot me immediately. That was probably the reason he had left me and Georgia until last when he was rounding up what seemed like every other detective in the building.

He was at the front of the room, his hands in his pockets, the scowl firmly in place as Una Burt fussed through her papers beside him. No one would ever have guessed that they did the same job, I mused, or that Una was senior to him, a detective chief inspector acting up to replace our upwardly mobile superintendent. Una was short and bustling, her clothes chosen for practical purposes rather than because they did anything for her appearance. Today her blouse was khaki silk, if you were being kind, or snot-coloured polyester if you wanted to be accurate, and it made her skin look grey. Derwent had shed his suit jacket and turned his shirt sleeves up, but his tie was immaculate, the shirt unrumpled despite the long day, his shoes buffed to a soft shine. He was a perfectionist in all things, whereas Una prioritised work over just about everything. I doubted there was one opinion they shared aside from their commitment to the job.

'So, the reason we've called you all in here is because we have a challenging investigation to take on. You'll all have noticed Rula Jacques here this morning, and Assistant Commissioner Grayton, so you'll have gathered this is something that deserves our full attention.' Una Burt hesitated, which wasn't like her. 'It's not our usual kind of thing. We react, as a rule, whereas this is a proactive kind of investigation. It's an opportunity that I hope some of you will take on.'

Silence in the room. We were all experienced enough to know that if you were getting the hard sell about an investigation being an opportunity and a challenge and a priority for the bosses then it was likely to be a massive pain in the arse, as well as a potential career-killer.

Burt turned expectantly. 'Josh? Do you want to jump in here?'

Less than anything, his face said. 'Get the lights, Pete, would you?'

The room went dim and Derwent poked at the laptop in front of him. The screen on the wall lit up on a photograph of a man. It looked like a mugshot or an ID picture, but he was looking away from the camera, his eyes focused on something to his left. His hair was cropped and he was thin, almost gaunt, the bones of his shoulders visible under the thin fabric of his T-shirt. His face was wrinkled but I couldn't decide if that was age or exposure; I wouldn't have been able to speculate on his age within twenty years.

'This is Davy Bidwell. He was found dead in a house in Acton four months ago. He would have been thirty-three years old.'

'Drug addict?' Belcott guessed, and Derwent looked irritated at the interruption.

'No. Other problems, but not that.' He regrouped. 'His body was discovered when the council were checking for a gas leak in the property. No one had reported him missing. The local CID team investigated and I think they did a reasonable job. There was no sign of violence at the time of death. Cause of death couldn't be determined because of the condition of the body, but the pathologist suggested he would have weighed less than ninety pounds at the time of his death.'

'How tall was he?' a woman at the front asked, scribbling notes.

'My height.' Derwent let the two words hang in the air for a moment, not needing to say that he weighed twice that. Davy had been skin and bones.

'What was he doing there?' I asked. 'Was it his house?'

'Not his house. It was a derelict property, boarded up, and the owners are overseas – the original investigation concluded that he had made his own way to the property and had broken in, seeking shelter. From the appearance of the remains' – Derwent flicked to the next image, which was not Sight of the Week and generated a little hum of reaction from the room – 'he had been there for some time. There's a degree of mummification. The OIC did try to narrow it down and concluded most likely he had found his way in there during the very cold weather in December. His clothes—' Derwent broke off and shook his head, angry with the huskiness in his voice that gave away his emotions. He cleared his throat and flicked to the next slide, which consisted of a stained anorak laid flat on a white surface.

'He was inadequately dressed for cold weather. He wore this anorak which came from Open Air Warehouse, a brand that stopped production nineteen years ago. In addition he had a pair of jeans, a long-sleeved cotton shirt and a pair of sports socks. All of the items of clothing showed signs of wear and tear. There was a pair of trainers beside the window that was probably his point of entry. The OIC's theory was that he took them off in case he made the carpet dirty.'

The images slipped onto the screen and away, lingering in

my mind like retina burn. The clothes, stiff with dirt and decay. The socks, black on the soles. The trainers, worn and filthy. The carpet which was fit only for a skip, that he had been so careful not to mark.

'Was he homeless?' The woman at the front, young and keen, new. Vidya Long, I thought. I had said hello to her on her first day and then forgotten about her completely.

'He certainly doesn't seem to have had anywhere to go but he wasn't known to any homeless services. And he wasn't supposed to be homeless. Davy was a vulnerable adult. He had learning disabilities and he had struggled with independent living. He had mental health difficulties – depression, paranoia, dissociation. He had lost contact with his immediate family, and they hadn't seen him for a couple of years before his body was found, despite their best efforts.'

'Where was he supposed to be?'

'The last address he resided at officially was here.' A map filled the screen: a neat loop of little boxes. A railway line ran down behind one side of the loop, a row of black stitches on a green quilt. 'This is Jellicoe Close in a little place called West Idleford. It's a nice little town and this is a nice little place to live. Davy Bidwell moved here from his sheltered accommodation in Cheltenham two years ago. The staff in Cheltenham weren't happy about it but there was nothing they could do to stop him. He was determined to leave. When he arrived in Jellicoe Close he lived in number 7, this house.' Derwent tapped it. 'The woman who lives here is named Judy Thwaites. She told the detectives who spoke to her after Davy's body was found that Davy had spent a few days with her and then moved on. She said he made friends with someone who gave him a job on a farm and that was where he was living. Judy was a nice lady, according to the officers who interviewed her. She liked to help people. She thought she was doing Davy a favour by giving him a place to stay and an address to use. She said she didn't realise the difficulties Davy had with his mental health and he was an adult, so she didn't know where to start with raising the alarm. He was still using her address for official correspondence but she didn't have a forwarding address for him. That's where the trail went cold.'

'So he went to work on this farm, didn't like it, wandered off, made it to London, got hypothermia and died in a derelict house,' Chris Pettifer said. 'Sad story. No foul play.'

'Couple of details you should know before you make that call,' Derwent said quietly. A pathologist's diagram appeared on the screen, an outline of a man littered with annotations. 'He had recent and not-so-recent fractures. Three broken ribs in various stages of healing. His left wrist, which wasn't set properly. His left scapula. He was missing three teeth and two were broken.'

'Poor bugger,' Pettifer said softly, and there was a murmur of agreement.

'Secondly, Rula Jacques is married to a man named Charles Bidwell,' Una Burt said from the shadows. 'Charles is Davy's brother. Rula pushed the original investigation as far as she could. She wants someone to be held responsible for what happened to her brother-in-law.'

Someone groaned, and I could understand it. Grieving people found consolation in *something being done*, and Rula was in a position to insist that we took action, whether it was appropriate or not. It would probably have been wise to keep my opinion to myself, but I couldn't let it go.

'Chris is right. He died of natural causes. He was obviously treated terribly and someone should be prosecuted for the abuse he suffered. That's a problem for the police wherever this farm is, not for us.'

'We have been allocated the job of finding out what happened.' Una Burt looked down the room at me and gave a little helpless shrug. 'We don't have a choice about this.'

'What does she want us to do?' Belcott demanded. 'Bring him back to life?'

38

'She wants us to watch Judy Thwaites.' Derwent went to the door and switched the lights back on.

'Surveillance?' Georgia looked sceptical. 'We're supposed to park a van in the middle of the cul de sac and hope no one notices us?'

'No. There's a plan,' Derwent said tightly. 'But it involves committing to an unknown number of weeks being resident in Jellicoe Close, undercover. I need two volunteers who would make a convincing couple for several weeks.'

'Several?' I couldn't help asking.

'Not more than eight. Starting in a week.'

'Potentially running into the school holidays?' Colin Vale's eyebrows shot up. 'My wife would kill me. I can't say it's not tempting to escape, though.'

'But why? Just because Judy is the last fixed point we have for him?' I was still trying to work out the logic, and failing.

'She's convinced that Judy – or someone close to her – is involved in the exploitation of vulnerable individuals. She wants us to find out where Davy went after he left Jellicoe Close and she wants us to stop it happening again.'

'Why should it happen again?' I asked. 'What makes her think this isn't a one-off?'

'Because at least three other vulnerable adults have been resident for a time at number 7, Jellicoe Close in the last six years.' Derwent closed his laptop with a savage swipe of his hand. 'And no one seems to know where they are.'

7

I had wanted to get home but when I reached my flat I wrinkled my nose. The air was overheated and stale, because no one had come or gone all day while I was at work: dead space. The cereal bowl still sat in the sink, half-full of cloudy water. There was a mug of tea on the counter, the top puckered with a skin of milk. I stared at it for a while, remembering that I'd made it, not remembering why I'd left it there without drinking it. That happened, from time to time: lost moments that I couldn't recover. Trauma, I gathered, could have that effect, and I hated it. The bruises had faded, the bones had mended and still the harm my ex-boyfriend had done ran through me like dark veins in marble. I wanted to be better – I willed myself to feel better – but these days it felt as if every turn I took led to a dead end.

The next day was Friday. I had a day off, even though I'd protested about the amount of work there was to do on the Dawoud case.

'Take it,' Una Burt had ordered, drowning me out. 'You look tired.'

There was something particularly annoying about being told I looked tired when I was doing my best to keep myself looking as if I was on top of things. The truth was that I *was*

40

tired, but it was the kind of tiredness that didn't respond to sleep. Just as well, really, because as usual I woke up at six, my bedroom hot, the bedclothes creased and damp with sweat.

I threw myself into domestic activities. I washed the dishes, with extra-hot water and plenty of washing-up liquid, as if that would make up for leaving the place in a mess the previous day. I took out the ironing board and meticulously pressed the clothes I would wear the following week. Look the part and I would feel the part, or at least that was the theory. Look as if I was in control and no one would guess the truth.

I changed the bedclothes and opened every window. I mopped and swept and vacuumed, plumping pillows and cushions.

When I was finished with housework I stayed in the flat, finding reasons not to leave, pottering around aimlessly. I should go out for a run or even a walk . . . I should call my parents . . . I should arrange to meet a friend or trawl a dating website for a last-minute night out. But there was always tomorrow, or the next day. I wasn't back at work until Monday. That was ages away.

Food shopping was one thing I should do; I did not, and I didn't regret it until the evening when I was foraging in the kitchen for something to eat. I was hungry but bored by the very thought of it; I wanted to eat but it didn't matter if it was sweet or savoury. There had to be something that required no effort and tasted OK.

I ended up on the sofa in the living room, a bag of slightly stale popcorn resting on my stomach. I wasn't hungry enough to eat it after all, I'd discovered, and yet I couldn't make myself get up and put it in the bin. I was watching a documentary about wolves without really taking it in, my thoughts fragmented and incoherent.

I should eat something . . . Rula Jacques was very angry . . . if it all comes down on Derwent he might end up leaving the team . . . Stupid of him . . . The popcorn isn't that bad,

if you ignore how chewy it is . . . what a lot of effort it takes
to raise a wolf cub . . . I should have done better with the
interview the other day and I knew it at the time, and what
was worse, Georgia knew it too . . . Rula Jacques wrote a
speech for the mayor about institutional racism in the Met
that had annoyed a lot of people, and she didn't care . . . but
she didn't seem intimidating. She was upset . . . Derwent has
that effect on people . . . winter is hard on wolves . . . God,
I have to do it all again on Monday . . . but at least there's
the weekend and I can enjoy myself, if I can think of anything
to do . . .

Car.

Not all that unusual, I thought. People came and went.
Some of them made a meal of parking on the narrow street.
Some of them revved their engines as if they were particularly
irritated.

Curiosity brought me to my feet. I peered down at the
street, where headlights were still shining: the car had squeezed
into a tiny space. I recognised the vehicle at the same moment
as the lights switched off, and the driver shoved his door
open.

'Oh no.' I said it aloud. Derwent couldn't have heard me,
but he looked up as if he had. He saw me straight away and
glowered, then pointed meaningfully at the front door as he
started towards it.

Even if he hadn't noticed me, I thought, trudging down the
stairs, he would just have let himself in with the key he retained
as my landlord. And if I complained, he would have reminded
me that key had probably saved my life the previous summer.

He was looking away from me when I opened the door,
frowning down the street at something in the distance.

'What are you doing here?'

Unhurriedly, he turned back and looked me up and down,
the disapproval palpable. 'Can I come in?'

'Can I stop you?'

42

His eyebrows twitched together. 'It's your place.'

'You've made it very clear ever since I moved in that it's your place. Is this about work?'

'Yes.' He paused for a second. 'And no.'

Yes was enough to allow him inside, but I didn't like the sound of no.

'Then you'd better come up.' I stepped back, brushing a few stray crumbs of popcorn off my T-shirt. He watched them fall to the floor, his mouth tight with disapproval, and that was why I had done it.

'Cup of tea?'

'No, thanks.' He took the stairs two at a time and I followed more slowly, giving him time to look around. Everything tidy, everything in its place, as if on some level I'd known he would be coming over.

'All in order?'

He gave me a dark look from the doorway of the bathroom. 'Do you think I'm checking up on you?'

'Am I wrong?'

'No.' He slung his jacket on the newel post at the top of the stairs. 'Maybe I will have tea.'

'You just want to see what's in the fridge.'

'I can guess. Takeaway containers and a few things that used to be green that you bought with the best of intentions.'

'No, actually. I cleaned it out earlier.'

He opened the fridge door. We both looked at the empty (but clean) shelves, and the absolute lack of anything fresh.

'I haven't been shopping this week,' I began, hearing the defensive note in my voice, and his face softened for a blink-and-you'd-miss-it moment. Then he was back to business.

'We need to talk.' Without asking, he went into the sitting room and flung himself down on the sofa, one arm thrown over his eyes as he stretched uninhibitedly.

I stepped over his legs and sat primly on the small armchair in the corner. 'Tired?'

43

'A bit.' He moved the arm so it was behind his head and he could look at me. 'Long day.'

'Aren't they all?' I clasped my hands around my knee, sitting bolt upright. *He* could sprawl but I wasn't going to. 'I can't imagine why you'd make it longer by detouring to see me on your way home.'

'I need to talk to you and I didn't want to do it at work.' He paused for a second. 'What's up?'

I tilted my head a few degrees to the left, puzzled. 'What do you mean?'

'That's what I thought.'

'I'm lost,' I said. 'What did you think?'

'That I wouldn't get anywhere with you.' He sighed. 'Look, Maeve, you're not yourself.'

'I'm fine.'

'I might not be the right person to talk to but if I can help . . .'

'Help with what?'

'You've been through a lot in the last year.'

'A lot' included lying, bleeding and unconscious, in the room where we were sitting, and a trial where I was the victim rather than the investigating officer. I blinked, composed.

'That's going to leave a mark,' Derwent went on.

'Of course.'

'And you miss Liv.'

'Of course,' I said again, my voice softer.

'I know it's been hard.'

The tell-tale burn of tears at the back of my eyes made me tense up. I folded my arms and pinched the soft skin above my elbows, where he couldn't see it.

'We all go through hard times. And I'm busy at the moment. Lots on my plate.'

He raised his eyebrows politely. 'You can cope with hard work, as a rule.'

'Yes. I didn't say I couldn't cope.'

44

He sat up at that and leaned forward. 'Look, Maeve, most people wouldn't notice, but I know you better than that. I wouldn't be having this conversation with anyone else at work if they were working the way you are. You're operating at the same level as everyone else, and that's not like you.'

I cleared my throat. 'That's a typically back-handed compliment from you. You're basically saying I'm not usually this shit.'

'That's exactly what I'm saying. But if you don't want to talk to me about it, I'm not going to force you to.' Abruptly he changed tack. 'Why haven't you volunteered for the surveillance job?'

Wrong-footed, I blurted out the truth. 'I – I don't want to do it.'

'Why not?'

He and Una had laid out the scenario: a house across the street belonging to someone who genuinely needed a dog-sitter at the last minute. Two detectives, posing as a couple. A holiday, paid, with nothing to do but wait for something to happen.

Too good to be true.

'It sounds like the kind of job that's going to go wrong, if you must know. Rula Jacques has expectations that we can find out what happened to her brother-in-law, and get enough evidence to lock up whoever was responsible, *if* they committed a crime, which we don't honestly know. I don't know which moron came up with the surveillance plan but it feels like a massive commitment and probably a total waste of time.'

His eyebrows lifted. 'It was my idea.'

'Oh.' I folded my arms more tightly. 'Well, you had to suggest something.'

'I think it could work.'

'How?'

'If the right people are involved. If you were involved, Maeve, I know you'd get the neighbours to trust you. You'd

45

get Judy to trust you. You'd find out everything about what happened to Davy and they wouldn't even spot what you were doing. And if we did manage to stop them from doing the same thing all over again – if we managed to rescue some of the other people who might be being exploited right now – wouldn't that be worth your time?'

'Yes, but I have other work to do.'

'The Dawoud case?'

'Yes.'

'You can work long-distance. Tell Georgia what to do. You don't need to be in the office for that.'

'You just don't care about it because it's not your murder.'

'True. But it looks straightforward enough.'

'Does it?'

'Yeah.' He reclined again, his hands locked behind his head, elbows wide as he stretched. 'And don't try to tell me you think it's the crime of the century either. You're going through the motions, Maeve, and you know it.'

'That's not fair.'

'Not to Cameron Dawoud it's not, no. Don't you think he deserves someone investigating the murder who really cares about what happened to his husband?'

I couldn't sit there and listen to him any more. I jumped up and went to the window, nettled. 'I thought you were convinced Cameron was guilty?'

He smirked. 'Yeah, I am. But someone has to prove it. Is it going to be you?'

'I'll do my job,' I said stiffly, and he was on his feet too, fast as a hunting cheetah.

'Not with your whole heart, the way you usually do.' He took another step, crowding me whether he knew it or not. 'You need a reset, Maeve. A fresh start.'

'Isn't it more that I'm ideal for this job because I don't have any dependants. No children. No pets,' I said, unable to keep the bitterness out of my voice. 'No annual leave booked.'

'So? You have fewer commitments than other people on the team. That's not why I want you to do it instead of the others who put themselves forward.'

'Which was who?'

'Georgia. Vidya. Pete Belcott.'

I gave a shocked laugh. 'You wouldn't send him.'

'Not with you.' He paused. 'Not with *anyone*.'

'It could be a good opportunity for Vidya.'

'No.' That steady look again, the one that saw through me. 'I want you. So does Una.'

'I doubt she has an opinion either way.'

'She most certainly does.'

I wasn't going to change my mind. 'No. Thanks but no thanks.'

He looked down, adjusting his watch strap, suddenly and uncharacteristically awkward. 'Is it because of me?'

'You?'

'I thought – maybe it was that you didn't want to spend that much time around me.'

'Not at all. I didn't even know you were going.'

A glint. 'I already asked you.'

'Not properly. I didn't even think—'

'This case needs a senior officer. Rula insisted. And we'd do a good job.'

'It's not that—'

'We might even have fun.' He moved towards the door and paused, looking back at me with an unreadable expression on his face. 'I'll let you think about it.'

And he was gone. I was halfway through shaking my head in amazement at his audacity when he put his head back into the room.

'Just so you know, Maeve, if you say no . . . I'm definitely going to take it personally.'

47

8

'Let me get this straight,' Liv said. 'He wants you to move in with him—'

'So we can share the surveillance.'

'For *weeks*. And the cover story is that you're his *girlfriend*?' Her voice had risen from the murmur she'd used for the rest of the conversation and I heard a tiny, sleepy protest followed by tender shushing. 'Sorry about that. I'm sitting on the floor of the nursery.'

'Won't Sonny go to sleep on his own?'

'We're working on that.' More shushing. 'But seriously, his *girlfriend*?'

'We're supposed to be house-sitting for the homeowner – she's best friends with one of the local cops and he sounded her out to see if she'd mind us using her house. The story he told her is that we're hoping to catch a prolific burglar.' I ran a hand through my hair, lifting it off the back of my neck. 'She's genuinely looking for someone to do it, too. She's an academic and she's been invited to the US for a lecture series. She needs to be away for most of the summer and she needs someone to live in and look after her dog. The cover story is perfect.'

'You could go on your own.'

'That's what I thought, but Una thinks it's too dangerous.'

'You could not go as a couple.'

'We would be *pretending* to be a couple, in public. It looks less suspicious than a pair of friends happening to move in together. At least, that's what Josh said.'

'It makes me think this is just an excuse for him to get you on your own for a few weeks.'

'And do what?'

'Well, you know it's not my area of expertise and I'm hazy on the details, but I'd assume it involves his penis and you in some combination.'

'*Liv!* He's got a partner. A serious one. And even if he didn't, he's my boss. And I wouldn't. You know that.'

'I don't know anything.' Amusement sweetened her voice. 'Anything could happen. This is Josh we're talking about. He's pretty irresistible.'

'Completely resistible,' I said. 'Utterly. I know him far too well. The tricks have no effect on me.'

'Of course not.'

'Anyway, you know what he's like. It's probably mind games. He's probably waiting for me to say I want to do it so he can tell me he's picked someone else.'

'Did he tell you that you were the only one who could possibly do it?'

'How did you know?'

'Flattery is step one. Did he make any threats?'

'No, not really.'

'Emotional blackmail?'

I sighed. 'Of course.'

'Then we know he's serious.' She chuckled. 'Maybe he really does think you're the best person for the job.'

'I think he wants—' I broke off. How much did I want Liv to know about my state of mind?

'He wants what?'

'To make sure I'm OK.'

'Why wouldn't you be OK?'

'Oh, you know. It's been a tough few months.'

'You've had tough times before.'

'Yes. I mean, I'm fine.'

'Fine?' Liv repeated. 'Oh dear.'

'I'm just tired.' I lay down on the sofa, my legs stretched out across it, then realised I was snuggling into the still-warm hollow Derwent had left. I sat up again, feeling disorientated, as if I'd woken up from a vivid dream. I'd rung Liv right after he left, before I'd thought about what I was going to say, desperate to get her opinion on what Derwent was suggesting. The flat still seemed to be full of his presence. 'He's under a lot of pressure to be seen to do something. It's one of those cases that's all suspicion and no evidence.'

'Why isn't it the usual kind of surveillance job? Weeks in the back of a van eating takeaways, in regular shifts?'

'Because of the location. It's too quiet. Lots of families, lots of retired people, and absolutely nowhere to hide unless you have a good reason for being there. They thought about putting in the usual kind of surveillance teams and couldn't make it work. We need to be able to get close to the suspects and we can't do that from the back of a van.'

If I was honest, the location was one of the things that tempted me. Derwent had shown me photos of the town on his phone before I left work on Thursday. West Idleford was a sweet little slice of commuter heaven in the home counties: it had a train station with a low brick station building and a wooden fence, straight out of a toy trainset. It lay in a valley surrounded by rolling tree-covered hills and farmland. There were two primary schools and one secondary school, a cricket pitch, a couple of steepled churches, a library, a doctor's surgery and some shops for essentials and luxury fripperies. It was a world away from the heat and noise of London. Another world, another life – and I hadn't thought about it before but now I wanted a break from my usual existence, quite passionately.

'So are you going to do it?'

'If I don't he'll get Georgia to take my place. Or Vidya Long.'

'I don't know her.'

'She's new,' I said. 'Not a patch on you, but keen.'

'And how would you feel about him taking either of them?'

The urge to lie was instant but pointless. Liv would spot it in a heartbeat.

'Not pleased, obviously.'

'He knows how to manipulate you, doesn't he? What if you called his bluff and he ended up doing this surveillance with Georgia?'

I sighed. 'She's a lot better than she was, you know. She's far more interested in work and less bothered about flirting with every man she comes across.'

'Really?'

'I think she's met someone and it's calmed her down.' I rubbed my eyes. 'Maybe she would be the better choice to do this.'

'But he came to you.'

'First, yes. He gave me the first refusal on this amazing once-in-a-lifetime opportunity.'

'Is that how he put it?'

'No. He was really . . .' I trailed off.

'Persuasive?'

'No. Diffident.'

'Interesting tactic.'

'You think it was a tactic?'

'Isn't everything, with him?' Her tone changed to a more businesslike one. 'What would you miss out on?'

'Work?' The Dawoud case was on my mind. 'I don't have anything too pressing except for a doctor who was killed and dumped in his car.'

'I saw that case in the paper! Tell me all about it. I'm dying of boredom here.'

I imagined Liv sitting cross-legged beside the cot, one hand on Sonny's stomach. If she was wearing tracksuit bottoms and a T-shirt, they would be colour-coordinated and perfectly fitted. Not for her the bedraggled new-mother look.

'We have no leads. No motive. His husband is grieving and touchy.'

'Doesn't mean he's innocent.'

'I'm aware of that.'

'OK. Sorry.'

I bit my lip. 'No, I'm sorry. I shouldn't have snapped. But it's not all that exciting, believe me.'

'You don't sound as if you're one hundred per cent pre-occupied with this case, Maeve,' Liv said carefully. 'And that's not like you.'

I admired the technique; she had circled back to me and my state of mind without triggering my defences. I'd seen her do it in interviews, more than once. I should have been on my guard.

'I'm giving it everything I've got.'

'And how much is that? You know I've been worried about you for a while. You might be a bit . . . burnt out.'

'I'm fine.'

'Yeah, fine. That word again.' Liv sighed. 'I have to go, Maeve. If you want my advice, you should do it. Go and play house with Josh Derwent. Get away from it all. Do something different. But don't do him.'

'If I do this, and it's a big if, I promise not to do anything stupid with Josh Derwent.'

I meant it, too.

9

'You think you'll do it?' Una Burt's eyebrows shot up. 'I told him you'd say no. What are you going to do about your other jobs?'

'I've worked outside the office before. As long as I get to see anything important and I keep in touch with the others, I should be able to manage. I'll have access to my emails, won't I? I'll just be at the other end of the phone.'

'It sounds as if you've made up your mind.'

In fact I had gone back and forth on it all weekend. I'd brushed my teeth the night before as a definite yes, gone to sleep as a firm no, and woken before the dawn to weigh up whether it was a good idea or not, for hours.

But I couldn't stand to dither about it any longer. I had to make a decision and stick to it.

'I want to do it.'

'Well, if you're sure.' She went to the door of her office. 'Josh?'

His demeanour was very much best-behaviour as he stepped into the room. His darkest suit, his whitest shirt, his hair parade-ground neat. All dog, no wolf. He shut the door behind him and turned around, already talking.

'Look, I didn't get a chance to explain it properly the other night. I'm sure I can convince you it's a good idea, Maeve, if you just let me talk to you—'

'She said yes.' Una Burt's voice was dry as dust. She sat behind her desk and started shuffling papers. 'She's happy to do it.'

'Happy is possibly an exaggeration,' I began, cautious, but Derwent was talking again. With a qualm I recognised the triumph in his voice, overlaid with a veneer of professionalism for Una Burt's benefit.

'So we need to prepare.'

'Agreed,' Burt said. She slid a folder across the table. 'That's what I got from the previous OIC.'

Derwent was flipping through the folder, frowning.

'I talked to her this morning.' Burt leaned back in her hideous but fully ergonomic chair. 'According to her, they did everything they could. She thinks Rula Jacques won't give up until someone is in custody.'

'That's awkward,' Derwent observed, his attention wholly absorbed by whatever he was reading.

'She wished you luck. You'll be the one who breaks it to Rula Jacques if you can't put a case together.'

That brought his head up. 'Seriously? Rula doesn't like me.'

'Then you have nothing to lose. Whereas I do.'

'That promotion is so close you can feel it.'

Burt looked down at her desk, trying to hide that he'd hit the mark. She had been waiting for her promotion for a long time. 'Acting up' was one thing; it was another to be left to do a job that wasn't officially hers, with all of the negatives and few of the positives.

'Don't worry. I'm sure I can charm Mrs Jacques if I try.' He slapped the file on the edge of the desk. 'Thanks for getting hold of this.'

It wasn't often that I got to see Una Burt looking disarmed. 'You're welcome.'

'How long have we got?' I asked.

'The neighbour is booked to leave in a week's time. She has a usual house-sitter but the woman's mother had a heart attack so she had to drop out, which is very lucky.'

'Isn't it,' I murmured, not catching Derwent's eye. Unlucky for the house-sitter's mother. Too bad. Move on.

'The timing couldn't be better,' Burt went on. 'We can let the neighbours think you're friends of the house-sitter. We get you in, you find out what you can, and then write a report that makes us look as if we took Mrs Jacques' complaint seriously.'

'We are taking it seriously,' Derwent pointed out. 'Maeve and I are giving up a lot to do this.'

'A few weeks on holiday in an idyllic village, right in the middle of a heatwave? You're breaking my heart.' Burt reached out to pick up her desk phone, stopping with her hand on the handset. 'If you've got the file, I think we're finished here.'

Dismissed.

My instinct was to run away – what had I committed to? – but Derwent stepped in front of me as soon as we left Una Burt's office.

'A week. That doesn't give us a lot of time.'

'Time for what?'

'Gathering background information. Working out our cover stories. And . . .'

'And what?'

His gaze started at my feet and worked up, slowly, assessing me.

'And *what*?'

'Don't take this the wrong way.' He took my arm. 'You're going to need some work.'

I must have walked from Una Burt's office to the meeting room, but I was so blind with rage that I was barely aware of it. My only coherent thought was that I would tell him what I thought of him and then go back to Una Burt to tell her I'd changed my mind, and I wouldn't feel bad about it either.

Derwent shut the door behind us. I turned around, hands on my hips, and glared at him. He settled himself against the door, his expression expectant.

'Are you trying to suggest that I need a makeover because otherwise it wouldn't be plausible that I could be your girl-friend?'

'You're so hard on yourself, Kerrigan. You're quite decent looking. Very nearly up to my standards.'

'You—' I broke off because I recognised the light in his eyes: he was enjoying the hell out of this and getting angry was just playing his game. 'Then what did you mean?'

'You look like a copper. Not your clothes – they're easy to change. It's the way you carry yourself. You look at people as if you have a right to judge them. Most people miss what's going on around them. You have to look as if you're not paying attention. You can't stare at people as if you could take them in a fight.'

'That is not how I look at people!'

He matched my outraged tone mockingly. 'You're doing it right now!'

'You're provoking me.'

'Yeah, I am.' He grinned. 'Just keep it in mind, OK? You don't want to look as if you're patrolling the place. It's a small community and we'll stick out anyway. You'll be attracting plenty of attention, believe me, so you need to look as if you don't mind it. Start from now. Loosen up. Let your hair down.'

'Literally?' I kept my hair tied back at work, always.

'Why not? And while you're at it, don't be so guarded all the time. You're constantly on the defensive with me.'

'That's because you're always on the attack.'

'I am not.'

'You know you are.'

'OK,' he said, as if it wasn't – almost as if he was hurt.

56

'What about you?' I countered. 'You look like what you are too. I'd guess you were a police officer no matter what you were doing or wearing.'

'I get a lot more leeway than you do. Men who look as if they wouldn't mind a fight are ten a penny. Women, not so much.' Before I could argue the point, he held up the file. 'I think we should go through this together.'

It seemed like a reasonable suggestion. He put the file on the table, slid off his jacket and threw it over the back of a chair. 'You too.' He indicated my jacket. 'Take it off.'

'I can read while I'm fully dressed.'

'Give me strength. I'm not asking you to strip to your knickers. Just take it off,' he snapped, rolling up his sleeves. Patience wasn't one of his virtues at the best of times. I unbuttoned my suit jacket, feeling as if I was taking off armour, and shrugged it off, but stood holding it in front of me.

'This isn't going to work unless you trust me,' he said.

'I – I do trust you.'

'Then stop behaving as if I'm a threat. It can't look like work, but it *is* work. I know it and you know it. Bear that in mind and get on with the job, which in this case is looking as if you actually like me.'

He pulled out a chair and sat down, flipping open the file. I couldn't shake the feeling that it was a trap, somehow, but I moved to sit beside him.

He leaned his elbow on the back of the chair I'd left empty between us and pointed at it. 'What's wrong with this one?'

It's too close to you. I didn't say the words but what I was thinking was written on my face and he grinned.

'Some girlfriend you'd be.'

'Look, it's difficult.'

'I know. That's why you have to start practising now. It has to look natural. This' – he indicated the chair again – 'is a professional distance. We have to look as if we're in a relationship. Now try again.'

57

I shifted across to the chair that had been between us, hesitating only a fraction before I settled near enough to him that our elbows were touching.

'Closer.' His attention was apparently focused on the first page of the file.

I shuffled over an inch.

'Closer.'

I caught the undertone in his voice. 'Are you laughing at me?'

'Yes. I am.' He turned and looked at me, and it was unusual for me to get the full beam from such a small distance. I felt the eye contact as physically as if I'd touched a live wire. 'This is the most ridiculous situation we could be in, and the best way to get through it is to laugh about it. Stop overthinking it. Forget it's me. What would you do if we were really going out? Where would you sit?'

I edged over another inch, so that our thighs were touching. It was the most natural thing in the world for him to move his arm so I was leaning against him, with his arm on the back of the chair behind me, so that we could both look at the page at the same time—

I didn't notice him moving until I felt something touch my arm: a fingertip. He traced a line down from my shoulder in a way that was unhurried, and to me unbearably intimate. I flinched.

'What are you doing?'

'Reading,' he said, wounded.

'You know what I mean.' My face was hot.

'Fuck's sake, Kerrigan, you'd think you'd never been out with anyone in your life. This is what people do when they're in a relationship. They touch one another.'

'Not in public.'

'Yes, in public,' he insisted. 'Look, this is a two-person job because it's full-time, from the beginning, and if one of us needs to leave for any reason we can still keep up the surveillance, plus it's safer to work as a pair. We need to be a couple because otherwise people would think it was weird that two friends were sharing a house-sitting job. We'd look like what we are, and make the suspects wary, and we'd wreck our chance to find out what's going on.'

'So you said the other night.'

'Yes. Well. Look at me, Maeve. Properly look, as if you'd never met me before. What would you make of me?'

I gave him the kind of up-and-down scrutiny that he liked to give women, but instead of minding he sat up a little straighter, turning towards me so I could get a better look. He was tanned, his hair a shade or two lighter than in mid-winter, thanks to running many miles outside every week. His thigh pressed against mine, all lean muscle, as were the fore-arms he had revealed by rolling up his shirt sleeves. He was broad in the shoulder and fit as a butcher's dog. I rarely looked at him as a physical entity; I was far more concerned with what was going on behind his eyes than how blue they were, as a rule, but even I had to admit he was an attractive man.

Until he opened his mouth, I reminded myself.

'What do you see?'

'My boss. What am I meant to see?'

'Someone who can handle himself in a fight. Someone who likes women. Someone who can take his pick of the best.'

Every now and then he still managed to surprise me. 'Wow. You don't have a low opinion of yourself, do you?'

He shrugged. 'Experience tells me I can get whoever I want. Usually.'

'Right.'

'And if I wanted you, I could have you.'

I gasped. 'That is—'

He spoke over me as if I hadn't said anything. 'And if we were really in a relationship, I'd never take my hands off you.'

I swallowed. The famous Derwent charm at full power and just for a moment, it almost worked, before he ruined it.

'I'd be reasserting ownership constantly to warn off anyone who thought about trying it on with you. Which they will, if you drop the attitude. You don't realise how intimidating you are.' He looked back at the file for a moment before he added, as an afterthought, 'But you look all right apart from that.'

'Thanks,' I said acidly.

'People will believe in us as a couple if we act the right way. They'll believe I might be jealous. If I look as if I'm watching everyone around us, they'll assume you're the reason for that. It will help if I do things like put my hand on the back of your neck when we're walking down the street together, or touch the small of your back—'

'Absolutely not.'

His eyebrows snapped together. 'Would you prefer me to put my hand on your arse?'

I laughed in spite of myself. 'No, but—'

The chair shot backwards as he stood up. 'If you agree to do this job, you have to be all in, Kerrigan. You can't go halfway and stop. All or nothing. Decide if it's what you want before I come back.'

He went out of the room, banging the door so loudly that I jumped.

Yes, he would be possessive with his girlfriends, and it would be a good reason for him to glower at anyone we encountered. I took down my hair, shaking it out slowly, thinking about the kind of woman who chose to be in a relationship with an alpha male like Derwent. Not someone who presented much of a challenge to him. Not someone who questioned his authority.

It didn't come naturally to me to behave that way, but maybe that was the point. It would be easier to act a part than to be myself with Derwent.

And I could do with a break from being me, all things considered.

10

The sun streamed into the car, easily defeating the air conditioning. I turned it off and slid my window down instead, propping my arm on the sill and letting the wind blow through my hair. My T-shirt was sticking to my back and I hoped I wasn't looking as sweaty as I felt. The forecast was for a prolonged heatwave, day after day of cloudless skies and soaring temperatures. London was no place to enjoy hot weather, with its sticky streets and crowded neighbourhoods, the smell of rubbish and grilling meat that hung in the air and the constant singsong of sirens in the night.

'You're so lucky,' Georgia said bitterly, 'going off to live in the country with the most attractive man in the Met.'

'You're so lucky,' Liv said down the phone, 'leaving all your responsibilities behind to have an adventure.'

'You're so lucky,' Pete Belcott groused in the kitchen at work, 'getting to drop all your cases to go on holidays.'

I had put my mug down with a clink. 'I'm not dropping my cases. I'm working. I'll just be out of the office, that's all.'

'I'd take it.'

'But I wouldn't take you,' Derwent had said, filling the doorway, his expression forbidding. 'Not even if what was needed was a gay couple. I'd take Chris instead.'

Chris Pettifer had been sitting reading the paper at the small table in the corner. He raised his coffee cup in a silent salute, not looking up.

'Why wouldn't you take me?' Belcott asked.

'First of all, I've always fancied Chris.'

'Mutual,' Chris said through a mouthful of muffin.

'And secondly, he's not lazy. If I needed someone to sit on his arse watching TV, you'd be the first on my list.'

'We all know why you're taking *her*,' Belcott said with a vicious twist on the final word.

'Why is that?' Derwent's voice was pure ice.

Belcott stared at him, his face red, his instincts for self-preservation just about getting between him and saying what he was thinking.

'Maeve is the best person for the job,' Derwent said, when it became apparent that Belcott wasn't going to reply. 'She's proved herself over and over again. If you ever do anything of note – and if I don't die of shock – I'll put some opportunities your way.'

He walked off, leaving a very awkward atmosphere in the small kitchen. I had taken a great interest in finding fresh milk in our tiny fridge, while Pettifer chuckled to himself. I was usually able to stand up for myself but on this occasion I felt embarrassed and tongue-tied. When I turned to leave the kitchen Belcott was in my way. The hostility in his face made me shiver. Derwent was the one who had told him he was lazy, but I was the one who would get the blame.

I had bought enormous sunglasses and tiny shorts, on Georgia's advice, but I wore them with trainers rather than the heeled sandals she'd suggested, because I wasn't prepared to trade fashion for the ability to move with ease. Derwent had nodded in unsmiling approval when I came out of the flat, lugging my bags. I wondered fleetingly if he was nervous about what we were doing. He was lifting the bags into the boot of his car, grim-faced.

'Is everything OK, guv?'

'Yeah.'

'You don't seem very cheerful.'

'I'm having the time of my life.' He slammed the boot. 'From now on, don't call me anything but my name. No sir, no boss, no guv. This is where it starts.'

'Right.' That was what I'd intended, I wanted to say, but instead I focused on getting into the car and putting on my seatbelt. Tension was cascading off him in almost visible waves as he sat behind the steering wheel and started the engine. For the first few minutes of driving his shoulders were up around his ears and the muscles in his arms were taut like piano wire from how hard he was gripping the wheel.

We were a mile away from the flat before he spoke again.

'I didn't like saying goodbye to Thomas.'

'Oh, I see.' I did, too. Thomas was the son of Derwent's girlfriend, Melissa. He worshipped Derwent and in return Derwent loved him with a fierce, uncompromising protectiveness that couldn't have been stronger if the boy had been his own son.

'He's going to miss me.'

'Of course he is. But you can phone him.'

'It's not the same.'

'How does Melissa feel about you being away?'

A shrug as we drew up at the end of a long line of cars waiting at a contraflow. Then, clipped, 'She understands.'

She had to understand, I guessed. She had no choice about what he did or didn't do. At least in this case, it wasn't entirely Derwent's own choice to be away. I should count myself lucky that I was travelling north trapped in a car with the Incredible Sulk rather than Chris Pettifer, who would be eating something unspeakable, or Pete Belcott, who would undoubtedly have been peering covertly at the mile of thigh exposed by my shorts.

As I thought it, I glanced sideways at Derwent, to discover

he was looking at my legs. He looked away again immediately, his ears tinged with red, which was something I had never, ever seen before. I hadn't been aware shame was even in his repertoire of emotions. I reached down and picked up my bag, rummaging through it aimlessly, then sat with it on my knee as if I'd forgotten it was there. I doubted he was fooled, but by mutual agreement neither of us said anything about it.

We inched onwards, the satnav informing us that the time to our destination was increasing as the traffic ahead of us got steadily worse and worse.

The car was the only thing that moved in the heatstruck landscape: limp leaves hanging from still trees, stunned sheep crowded into narrow bars of shadow, birds pinned to the fields like cut-out paper shapes. The wind buffeted my hair, wrapping it around my face and throat, until I couldn't bear it any more and wrestled it into a messy ponytail.

'Are you nervous?'

It was the first thing he'd said for ages. 'No. Not yet. I feel as if I've prepared well enough for it.'

Hours of research. Hours of meetings with other officers on different task forces, who made no secret of their relief that we had ended up taking on this job instead of them. Hours of looking at photographs and reading statements and trying to make sense of the scant facts we had to play with. And hours of pretending to be Josh Derwent's girlfriend, complete with a shopping trip for clothes and make-up.

'You need to look softer,' Georgia had said, which meant a lot of smudgy eyeliner and a lip tint that made my mouth look bruised, or as if it had just been kissed if you believed the packaging.

What I had discovered was that it took a surprising amount of courage to look softer, let alone to be softer – to let my guard down. And Derwent had been kind, after the first day when he had established he was in charge. If it was a dance,

I was to let him lead. I was more used to being an equal partner, despite the difference in our job titles and level of experience. I knew I would mind the drop in status until I got used to it.

The other thing that we had to get used to was a change of name. Our names had been in the news enough that a casual internet search brought up article after article where we were mentioned separately or together. Detective Inspector Josh Derwent had become plain old Josh Derham and instead of Detective Sergeant Maeve Kerrigan I was now Maeve Kernaghan, in the unlikely event that anyone needed to know our surnames. The names were close enough that if either of us stumbled we might get away with it. The less we changed, the easier it was to avoid mistakes. It wasn't sophisticated but it was enough to thwart someone's casual curiosity, and that would probably do. We didn't do social media, Derwent had said firmly, if anyone asked. He didn't have time for it and I was to say I was on a digital detox.

'Better than trying to fake it.'

The farmland began to give way to houses with tall hedges, set well back from the road, their names written on the gate-posts. Then came smaller houses that were closer together, the gardens less sheltered from view, showing off bird tables and swings and slides, paddling pools gleaming blue in the hot sunshine. Finally there was a sign announcing a drop in the speed limit and 'Welcome to West Idleford'.

'We're here,' I said unnecessarily, and Derwent slowed to a crawl, dawdling through the outskirts of the small town. The houses gave way to rows of cottages, a post-war estate, the secondary school . . . it was one thing to study photographs and maps of Idleford and another to find it springing to life around us, complete with people going about their day. Families clustered on the green, pushing children on swings, queuing for ice cream from a van that was parked in a space that was supposed to be for disabled users. I turned my head to glare as we drove past, then remembered that I wasn't supposed to be noticing that kind of transgression and whipped back to face front. If I'd thought Derwent would miss it, the curl at the corners of his mouth told me he'd noticed, and moreover that he thought it was hilarious.

The train station came next, and a parade of shops, and then before I was ready we had turned left. The road led to another wide expanse of green grass with a halo of 1930s cul de sacs radiating off it. There were six in total, all named after Royal Navy admirals for no reason that I could understand, and we were heading for Jellicoe Close.

'What number is the house?'

'Three,' I said, and heard the tension in my voice. Stage fright, pure and simple. As the car moved up the road I was aware of people moving in the gardens, of a man washing his car, of a pair of Lycra-clad cyclists preparing to set off on a long ride, but I couldn't look at any of them. The sound of my heart pounding filled my ears, and I swallowed, dry-mouthed, as I dropped my sunglasses down from the top of my head so I could hide behind them. Derwent swung into an empty space just outside the house, parking with a hint of showing off in the way he handled the car. He turned the engine off and the silence was far too loud. I drew the band off my ponytail and fluffed out my hair, stretching as if it had been a long drive (it had) and I was pleased to arrive at our destination (not exactly).

Derwent put his hand on my bare leg, and the hours of practice meant I managed not to squeak in outrage, or jump, or pull away, or any of the other reactions I'd given him before. I looked up to discover he was smiling at me.

'It's all right.'

'Of course it is.'

His hand tightened on my knee for a moment. 'Remember, whatever happens, it's just work.'

'I know that. I'm not likely to forget.'

'Smile,' he said calmly. 'It'll help. It's physiologically proven that you can't smile and feel nervous at the same time.'

I grinned at him, feeling the nerves wane a little. 'Well, as long as it's physiologically proven. Do you think they're watching us?'

'Of course. Nothing this interesting has happened here in weeks. They'll stare at us and we can stare back. It's normal to be curious. But remember, we have the advantage. We know all of these people already.'

We did. We had pleasantly chatty dossiers on the inhabitants of the close, written by Vanessa Underwood, the academic whose house we were borrowing. I looked past Derwent and saw a pair of women standing on either side of a low hedge. One was holding a pair of old-fashioned garden shears. Her hair was a steel-grey helmet. Ruth Otis, I thought, who had a husband named Alan. She was an enormous gossip. She spent most of her time with her neighbour, Judy Thwaites. And that was Judy herself on the other side of the hedge, a blonde in acid-yellow capri pants and a teal vest top.

She teaches aerobics and dance classes at the community centre. You never see her without her face on. Ruth told me she's a year older than her – but she looks at least ten years younger. Very friendly; she will want to know everything about you but just because she likes people, not because she wants to use it against you, unlike Ruth . . .

And the two men tinkering with their bikes and eyeing us covertly would be Mike Knox and Rhys Vonn, the fathers of families who lived at 9 and 6 Jellicoe Close respectively. And the man washing his car, who had been polishing the same wing mirror since we'd parked, was Stephen Bollivant, who lived at number 4, on his own except for a large dog.

Number 1 is empty and has been since I moved in . . . number 2 is Fleur and Brian Nolan who got married three years ago. Fleur is desperate for a baby and they've been

67

having IVF for ages . . . Number 5 is Mrs Holding and her son Gary, who's her carer. Gillian has dementia and sometimes goes wandering. You'll know her straight away, she always wears a nightie and men's shoes . . .

'Come on,' Derwent said, opening his car door. 'Time to let the dogs see the rabbit.'

'Am I the rabbit in this scenario?'

'Absolutely,' he said easily. 'I promise you, no one is going to be looking at me.'

He wasn't particularly interested in staring at the woman; there would be a better time for that and anyway, he didn't want to rush it. She wasn't entirely his type, he'd thought at first glance, despite the obvious points in her favour, but the way she deferred to her companion piqued his interest. It was the man who held his attention though as the two of them came to stand at the front of the car together, staring around themselves as if they'd never been anywhere so interesting in their lives.

He looked away, pretending to be distracted by what he was doing, because he was good at operating on different levels, keeping his thoughts hidden. What was it that made the man so intriguing? This stranger had an air about him, that was what it was – he was vibrating with potential for damage and it was a thrill to be so near it, like a cliff edge calling him to step into the air, or an electric fence that he might feel compelled to reach out and touch. The new arrival was standing quite still but there was something about him that was taut, as if he was under tight control, like a strung bow, or a dog straining against a short lead.

The dog. That was why they were here. Vanessa was going away and they were coming to look after the dog, friends of her usual dog-sitter, stepping in to help out. Everyone in Jellicoe Close knew about it. The old women had been speculating for days.

He busied himself because no one should guess that he was fascinated by the newcomers.

No one should notice him measuring himself against the man,

guessing at his strength, wondering where his weak points were – because he would have weak points, even if he kept them well hidden. Everyone did.

11

The front door swung open as we walked up the short drive to the house; Vanessa Underwood was one of the many people who had been watching our arrival, in her case from the privacy of her own home. *Our* home for the next few weeks, I reminded myself, and looked at it with interest.

'Welcome! Thank you for coming.' She stepped out onto the porch, which was mantled with a sweet-smelling canopy of jasmine, starry white flowers against dark green leaves. She was a slim woman with a cheerful freckled face and large, red-rimmed glasses. Mid-forties, with dark hair that was uncompromisingly threaded with silver, she wore a black-and-white striped top and black trousers that had an unexpected drape across the front. I would have guessed she was an architect or designer but academic worked too.

'It's a pleasure,' I started to say, only to be interrupted by a shriek from Vanessa.

'Pippin, no!'

Instinctively, Derwent dropped into a crouch to field a small brown-and-white dog who had shot out through the open front door. He hooked a finger in the dog's collar. 'Hang on, where are you off to?'

The dog stood on its hind legs and paddled the air with

its front paws, desperate to get away. It had outsized triangular ears that it seemed to have borrowed from some other dog.

'Pippin, you are such an escape artist.' There was an edge of tension to Vanessa's voice under the easy good humour. 'Can you get him back inside? My taxi should be here soon and I need to show you where everything is.'

Derwent picked the dog up and tucked it under his arm like a rugby ball. The dog's little legs stuck out, completely still now as it looked up into Derwent's face. 'No wriggling,' he said sternly.

'Oh, he'll probably listen to you,' Vanessa said. 'He loves men.'

'How old is Pippin?' I asked.

'Four.' Vanessa ran a hand through her hair, looking anxious. 'He's calmed down a lot, really he has. He's so much better about running away than he used to be. But I don't let him out at the front because people do drive too fast around here and I'd hate for anything to happen to him.'

'Not as much as we would,' I said, and stroked the top of his head gingerly. It was like warm velvet. The little dog blinked and swiped his tongue over his nose. 'Is he a Jack Russell?'

'He's a bit Jack Russell and a bit a few other things. Probably some corgi in there, given his diva personality.' Vanessa's forehead corrugated with worry. 'I hate leaving him behind.'

'We'll look after him,' Derwent said with a reassuring amount of confidence. 'Why don't you show us the ropes?'

'Of course. Come on.'

The hallway was wider than I'd expected. It was mostly full of suitcases, but it was light and pleasant, with stairs on the right along with the entrance to the living room. A door at the end led to the kitchen, where the sunlight was dazzlingly bright. Some challengingly phallic ceramics stood on the hall table and a mobile hung from the ceiling, the elements made from folded tin suspended on wires. Vanessa, I guessed, was an art lover.

'The house was built in the 1930s. This whole estate was, and most of the houses haven't changed that much at the front. You'll notice the differences more at the back – some people have extended and some haven't. I did the kitchen two years ago. Do be careful of the front door, because the latch doesn't always hold. You have to make sure you've closed it properly.' She ushered us into the living room, which had originally been divided into two and was decorated in cream and blue. Where the dining table would have been, there was an enormous desk, and the back of the room was lined with books. There were two sofas in the front part of the room, though the one nearer the window seemed to get more use than the other, and when Derwent put the dog down he jumped onto that sofa, triumphant. The television was angled towards it. Every inch of wall that wasn't covered in bookshelves held framed art: felted circles, delicately sliced paper, smudgy abstract oils, and over the fireplace a truly graphic watercolour of a nude that I decided I simply wouldn't see. Derwent was looking around, his hands in his pockets, his expression neutral.

Even though we were inside and out of earshot of the neighbours, Vanessa dropped her voice. 'The house is on a hill – you'll have noticed you had to walk up the drive. It means this bay window essentially gives you a view of the whole street which I thought would be useful for you.'

'Very,' I said, casually working out our line of sight to Judy's house. Only the shrubs in front of the window threatened the view. 'Can we cut back the bushes in the front garden?'

'I wish you would. They're so overgrown. The gardening tools are in the shed at the end of the garden. And if you could mow the lawn?' She looked at Derwent hopefully.

'Nothing I enjoy more.' He came to stand next to me. 'Thank you for letting us do this, Vanessa. It's a big help.'

'Of course. Anything I can do. Anything at all. I can't bear burglars. So awful to be a victim of crime in your own home.'

73

'What else should we know? What are the downsides?' he asked.

'If you can see the neighbours, they can see you.' Vanessa blushed. 'When I moved in first I didn't have any bedroom curtains and I quite liked it because the house faces south-east and you can let the dawn wake you up. It didn't occur to me that anyone had noticed until Ruth told me her husband kept finding excuses to stay up late so he could watch me going to bed. I couldn't look either of them in the eye for months. I slept in the spare room until the new curtains arrived.'

Derwent glanced at me and I knew what he was thinking: we would have to be careful to act as a couple in the house, not just when we were outside it. I blushed, which was at least in character for my new role.

'There are only two bedrooms upstairs – that's all I need. I turned the little room into a walk-in wardrobe. Some people convert the loft but I couldn't think why I would need to. So the kitchen is here . . .' Vanessa led us down the hall into a very modern kitchen that ran the width of the house. A dining table and chairs took up one side of the room, with dark green kitchen units on the other. A wall of glass doors formed the back of the house and a low, comfortable sofa was positioned so Vanessa could sit and look out at the garden.

'Lovely,' Derwent said. 'That's what you get when you move out of London. A proper garden.'

'The railway line runs behind it – there's an embankment. But the trains aren't very frequent. You can walk along behind the houses all the way along the railway line and then if you keep going there's a public footpath that takes you to the Holmwood.'

'The what?' I asked.

She laughed. 'It's just a fancy name for a bit of wilderness but it's the best place to walk Pippin because it's fenced. There's another footpath that goes to it around the other way, through the cul de sac. It cuts between number 5 and number 6 – you can't miss it. There's a lake, lots of trees – you have to keep him on the lead though, because once he gets into the undergrowth he gets terribly excited about rabbits and you'll never see him again.' Vanessa blinked at us. 'I have tried to work on recall but he's absolutely useless.'

'That is very surprising.' Derwent tickled the little dog under the chin. Pippin stayed at his feet, staring up at him, one paw on his foot. 'He seems so intelligent.'

'Oh, he is. It's a deliberate choice. He really is a pain,' Vanessa said lovingly. 'But worth it.'

Both of us made noises as if we agreed.

There was time to have an in-depth discussion about dog food and snacks, Pippin's bedtime routine and the street's WhatsApp group before the taxi beeped outside, sending Pippin into orbit. He ran up and down the hallway barking hysterically.

'Oh no, he'll get out. I wonder – maybe I should—'

As Pippin skittered past me into the kitchen I reached out and shut the door, which was glass, so we had a grandstand view of him skidding to a halt and realising he'd been trapped. He rushed back and stood with his front paws on the door, whimpering, his black eyes shining with emotion.

'I want to kiss him goodbye,' Vanessa wailed, and I kept my hand on the door handle.

'Better not. We don't want him getting out.'

'No. No. Of course not.' Vanessa crouched and flattened her palm against the glass. Pippin bared white, very pointed teeth at it. 'I hope he'll forgive me for abandoning him.'

'He'll have a wonderful time,' I said, as Derwent picked up the suitcases and headed out of the front door, taking the direct route to get rid of her. 'We all will.'

Vanessa turned to me and I caught a glimpse of the incisive mind behind the fussing.

'Do you think anything will happen?'

'I don't know.'

'I don't like to think you're wasting your time, but I don't want to believe there's anything to worry about. It seems impossible, doesn't it?'

I nodded. 'This is a nice place.'

'The reason I decided to live here was because I felt nothing bad could happen here.' She sighed. 'But I suppose bad things can happen anywhere.'

'Unfortunately that's true.' I smiled. 'But it's our job to stop it.'

Vanessa looked back to where Pippin was watching, sitting down now with his ears at half mast. 'I hope everything will be all right.'

I wasn't sure if she was talking about our job or the dog.

The house seemed very quiet once the taxi was gone. Derwent shut the front door and stood in the hall, his arms folded, silently brooding.

'What are you thinking?' I asked, half expecting him to dodge the question.

'Just that it's up to us now, whatever happens.'

The two of us, on our own together, in a house that we were sharing. We spent a lot of time together usually, but with other people around, or on the other end of the phone asking for an update on where we had been and where we were going. No one was going to check up on us now unless we made contact with them. We had stepped out of our usual lives, cut off from all of our usual stresses as well as the consolations. We had total freedom to handle the case as we saw fit, from that moment on, but that freedom came with a daunting weight of responsibility.

'It's like being on a desert island, isn't it?'

A flash of amusement lit up his face. 'With the benefits of indoor plumbing.'

'It's a lovely house.'

'Seems to be. Some of the decor is a bit much.'

'The ceramic penises?'

'They are knobs, aren't they? I thought they just looked like them but no. That one's got bollocks.' He shook his head. 'She needs therapy. Mind you, we couldn't have designed a better place for surveillance than the sitting room.'

'You'll have to take charge of the dog. He seems to like you.' I looked at the small figure, pressed so close to the kitchen door that his breath was fogging the glass. 'I mean, I say dog. He's more of a furry rocket with a death wish.'

He was surprised into laughing, and there was something in his expression that it took me a moment to read: relief.

Because I had made a joke? Had I not been making jokes?

'Do you want to check out the rooms upstairs?' I said, more or less at random.

There was the briefest of hesitations, so split second that I wondered if I'd imagined it. 'After you.'

I ran up, ignoring the piteous whining from the kitchen where Pippin was keen to let us know he was pining to death. Derwent followed more slowly, taking a tour of the spare room and bathroom before he came to join me in the large, pale-pink bedroom at the front. It wasn't until he was standing beside me, both of us contemplating the wide expanse of the art deco-style bed, that I remembered we weren't at a crime scene and this wasn't like any of the other times we had stood in a bedroom together, and that if you were Josh Derwent you were probably having to suppress the memory of a thousand other bedrooms, and women you seduced as easily as clicking your fingers.

As if he had heard what I was thinking he turned away abruptly, clearing his throat. 'You'd better have this room.'

'Thanks.' It was beautifully decorated with a set of furniture that matched the bed in style, although the bed was an ultra-plush king-size modern one that looked blissfully comfortable, and the dressing table, wardrobe and bedside tables were proper antiques. The art was all photographic but landscapes rather than anything eye-wateringly explicit, thankfully. Vanessa kept that kind of art where everyone could see it, for reasons that were probably Freudian.

'I'll take the spare room,' Derwent said. 'It's smaller, but it's all right.'

'As long as no one guesses we aren't sharing a room.'

'Good point.' He moved to the window and leaned on the sill, looking out. 'I'll strip here every night with the curtains open and the lights on.'

'They'll be selling tickets.' I looked over his shoulder to where the two women opposite were staring up at us with undisguised curiosity. 'Look, you're not even taking any clothes off and they're fascinated.'

'Should I wave?'

'That very much depends on which body part you were thinking of waving.'

A glance over his shoulder, full of warm amusement and that hint of relief again: I hadn't imagined it. I stepped closer to him and slid my arms around his waist, leaning my cheek against his broad back.

'For the benefit of the audience.'

He covered my hands with one of his and we stood like that for a long moment. I closed my eyes so I could listen to the birds in the trees and the slow rhythm of his breathing.

'Maeve. If the bed in the spare room isn't comfortable—'

'It will be.'

'But if it's not.'

'Well, there are two sofas downstairs.' I disentangled myself from him and stepped away. 'One of them is bound to suit.'

12

From: maeve.kerrigan@met.police.uk
To: georgia.shaw@met.police.uk
Subject: Hassan DAWOUD

Hi Georgia,

Just wondering if there are any developments I should know about. Can you send me notes/transcripts of any interviews you do? Are you planning on speaking to Cameron Dawoud again? If you do, can you ask him who paid for the house? Did he have a pre-nup with Hassan? Were they equal contributors to the household budget or was Hassan the main earner? I'd like to push him on the finances because he was touchy about it when we interviewed him and I don't think he answered those questions adequately.

Did you manage to track down any friends of the couple? I really want to know more about their arguments. Again, I think he was far too defensive when we spoke to him about that.

I'd also like to know if there were any professional issues affecting Hassan at the time of his death – any outstanding complaints, any patients or their families who blamed him for poor outcomes. It bothers me that he was dumped at the hospital.

Are we still waiting for Kev Cox to give us a proper report on the house and the car?

Have we had the pathologist's report back yet?

Is there any news on the CCTV from the hospital car park and the surrounding area? Do you have any idea of where our suspect went after leaving the hospital? Did we recover any video? I'd like to see him moving. Those stills aren't really helping.

Maeve

From: georgia.shaw@met.police.uk
To: maeve.kerrigan@met.police.uk
Subject: re: Hassan DAWOUD

Hi! I thought you would be far too busy to think about the Dawoud case! How's everything going? Have you settled in yet? It must be so weird to be settling into domestic bliss with Josh Derwent.

So, I've attached the video we recovered from the hospital car park. The best image was the still we grabbed from it – you really don't get much more of a view when he's moving. I'm also looking for dashcam footage as well as other sources of CCTV. Someone must have seen him! The only other thing I'm thinking is that he might have changed his clothes as he was leaving the hospital, if he found somewhere out of sight of CCTV. I'm looking for anyone who might be him. At least, I'm not looking. Colin Vale is the one who gets to scour the CCTV we've collected.

I'm still waiting for the full reports from the SOCOs and the pathologist. I rang to chase them and Dr Early is just waiting on some results from the blood chemistry but she was really confident about the time of death being twelve to fifteen hours before the body was found, given the rigor and livor mortis, and she said the cause of death was a single blow from something heavy. She did note that there were some small abrasions on the body, but she said she couldn't tell if it was perimortem damage or from someone moving the body immediately post-mortem. They weren't defensive injuries.

I'm seeing Cameron again tomorrow. I'll try to do a better job of getting him to trust me. He gave me a few names of people who were friends of them both, plus I've got into Hassan's phone and I have a few other people to contact who Cameron didn't know or didn't suggest. I don't want to assume he's being helpful, you know?

One thing – there was a WhatsApp conversation on the phone that was all deleted except for the last message. It was unread. I'm guessing it was quite an intense conversation because the last message was 'next time I see you I'll be in you' which I assume is a sex thing. No name saved with the number except a full stop – no contact details, nothing. The number is out of use. I'm thinking secret lover. That would give us a good motive, wouldn't it?

I hope it's going OK. Remember, if in doubt, stare at Josh and bat your eyelashes. It works every time.

Georgia

From: maeve.kerrigan@met.police.uk
To: georgia.shaw@met.police.uk
Subject: re: re: Hassan DAWOUD

That CCTV from the hospital is absolutely shocking quality. What's the point in having cameras if you can barely see anything? But it's helpful to get a sense of how he carries himself. I think he is older than our initial guess – mid-thirties or even forties. I like the thought that he might have changed his clothes. Look for someone wearing those generic trainers. They never think of changing their shoes and socks.

Thanks for asking about the house and everything. So far so good.

Do remember to send me the SOCO and pathologists' reports when you get them. And the interview transcripts. The GMC might be able to help with any information about complaints. You should also get hold of bank statements and a mortgage statement – get as much information as you can before you speak to Cameron. If he was worried about them splitting up, that might have given him a motive. The WhatsApp message you found is really interesting but hold it back until we find out a bit more about it. Is the phone number out of use or is the phone just switched off? Can we find out if it was registered to anyone? When was the last message sent?

I'm sorry I'm not there. If you want to check anything with me, call me. I've got my phone with me. I might not be able to talk freely, obviously, but it's better than nothing. Let's set up a phone call to run through everything in the next couple of days. That's easier than pinging emails back and forth.

Don't let Cameron rattle you when you interview him. Tell Una Burt you don't want Pete in there. I'm not saying he's homophobic but he definitely isn't at ease around gay people. Pettifer is far better than you'd think. You can learn a lot from him. He lies in wait and lets them come to him. You wouldn't think it would work but he always gets his target in the end.

Maeve

13

I didn't have the classic where-am-I moment the following morning when I woke up; I knew where I was before I had even opened my eyes to see the pale-pink bedroom glowing with morning sunlight. I sat up in bed, trying not to catch my eye in the dressing table mirror, and listened. Scuffling came from the bottom of the stairs, along with an ear-splitting yelp that interrupted the steady stream of pleasant abuse that had woken me.

'I know you're not in the harness properly but that's because you wouldn't put your feet where they were supposed to go. That's not my problem, is it? You can waddle the whole way if you don't want me to fix it for you, you stupid animal. What sort of idiot . . . that's better, isn't it? Maybe you could try listening to me next time instead of . . . no, come back, you don't have your lead on yet. If you think I'm opening the door when you're not on the lead, you must think I'm a fool. Shut up. No, *shut up*. You'll wake her up.'

'I'm awake.' I came out onto the landing. Pippin barked joyfully and Derwent twisted to look up at me. He was wearing running shorts and a London Marathon finishers' T-shirt.

'Morning.'

'Isn't it a bit early for a walk?'

'I want to take him out before it gets too hot.'

I rubbed the sleep out of one eye. 'Did Vanessa say we should do that?'

'It's just what you do if you're a good dog owner. Not that this is a good dog. You're not, are you?'

Pippin did a pirouette of sheer joy.

'If you can wait a couple of minutes, I'll come with you.' I felt wide awake and excited, keen to get on with the job.

'You don't have to. You can go back to bed if you like.'

'I'm up now.'

He checked his watch. 'You've got two minutes. It'll take me that long to finish getting ready and put the lead on this twat.'

In fact, it took me five minutes to get ready, wriggling into leggings and a T-shirt at the same time as brushing my teeth and hair and smearing on some sunscreen. I came downstairs with my trainers in my hand to find Pippin and Derwent continuing their battle of wills.

'Do you want me to hold him?'

'I can manage.' He said it through gritted teeth. 'Get up, you absolute bastard. This is not the time for tickling your tummy.'

Pippin rotated on the small of his back, legs splayed in the air, his expression beatific. Derwent dropped to his knees, his jaw set in an expression I recognised. Pippin was not going to win this one.

'Right. Ready?' He was breathing hard when he stood up, victorious.

'What it reminded me of,' I said, tying my laces, 'was when you get two tramps fighting in an alleyway. No one keeps their dignity.'

'No one asked you.' He looked down to where Pippin was sitting angelically at his feet. 'I'm not doing that every morning.'

'I think the dog might be the one who decides that. It looks as if he enjoyed it.'

85

'Just for that, you can bring the poo bags.' He opened the front door and the two of them disappeared down the drive as I scrambled to pick up keys and the bags and a bottle of water.

Jellicoe Close was quiet at that time, the curtains drawn in all of the upstairs windows, no sign of anyone stirring. Every driveway had a car parked in it. I was careful not to stare at Judy's house, but Derwent let his gaze skim over it as he put his sunglasses on.

'Anything?'

He shook his head, a tiny movement that no one except me would have noticed. 'Ready?'

'Ready.'

We walked down the middle of the cul de sac, Pippin's claws loud on the tarmac. Long shadows stretched across the road and I shivered at the chill when we passed out of the sunshine, but it wasn't unpleasant. The morning air was fresh and tiny birds flitted over our heads, winging from one shrub to another. Every few paces the dog veered sideways to investigate an enticing smell, or a suspicious scuffling sound that proved to be a squirrel, and every time it interrupted the steady rhythm of our progress. The fourth time it happened, Derwent stopped.

'Don't fuck about, Pippin. I said I was taking you for a walk, not that I was prepared to stand around while you commune with someone else's piss.'

'You have to let him go at his own pace. Vanessa said—' I broke off, distracted.

He looked at me quickly. 'OK?'

I turned towards him. 'There's someone up there. Behind me. In the house at the end of the cul de sac, number 5.' *Mrs Holding and her son, Gary . . .* 'Someone is standing in the window.'

Slowly, casually, he looked past me. 'I don't see anyone.'

'There was someone. I saw them.' The pale oval of a face,

a figure standing still, something nightmarish and unnatural about the way they stood stiffly, arms held out from their sides. I shivered, rubbing my arms. 'They must have ducked back through the curtains. If I had to guess, it was Mrs Holding.'

'She's the one with dementia, isn't she? Even so . . .' He took a step closer to me, and took hold of my hand, as if it came naturally. Palm to palm; we had held hands before, when we were trying to provoke a reaction from someone who was watching me, but it had felt strange then.

And now?

The hairs were standing up on the back of my neck, but that was the shock of realising we were being watched, not to mention the cool of the early morning. It couldn't have been because every nerve ending in my hand was signalling urgently that it was touching Josh Derwent's hand, or the sheer thrill of physical contact. Of course he had opinions about hand-holding and I thought of him chiding me the previous week: *never interlaced fingers in public, Maeve, that's for teenagers*. What about in private, I had asked, amused, and he'd looked at me and said, *at times*, which had sent me off on a highly unprofessional train of thought.

His eyes were hidden behind the sunglasses, but the corners of his mouth curved upwards, as if he was able to hear what I was thinking. When he spoke, though, it was to the dog.

'Get a move on, Pippin, or we'll go home.'

Reluctantly, the small animal allowed himself to move an inch or two away from the smell that was holding him captive, and then another couple of steps, and at last we were on the move, heading for the narrow path that led between two houses at the end of the cul de sac. As we approached number 5 I was able to stare at it for longer, scanning the windows for any movement, any twitch of the curtains, anything out of place. There was nothing at all. The house was silent and still.

My imagination.

Someone had been there, I thought stubbornly. I didn't invent things. I wasn't, as a rule, nervous.

Derwent held my hand gently but deliberately, and I waited for him to let go as we disappeared from view down the pathway between the houses, but he didn't loosen his grip. We walked in companionable silence, shoulder to shoulder, avoiding the nettles that flourished on either side of the path. I stepped over a broken beer bottle, the air still sweetly brackish from where the liquid had spilled.

'A good night ruined.'

'Not necessarily.' Derwent pointed. 'Looks as if someone had some fun, anyway.'

A few steps further down the path a foil packet was caught in the long grass, ripped open. I looked around for the condom that had been inside it but, used or unused, it was nowhere to be seen.

'I have to keep reminding myself this isn't a crime scene.'

'That we know of.'

I rolled my eyes. 'All right. If it is a crime scene, we've just hoofed through it. I'd like to see you explain that to Kev Cox.'

'Yeah, well, obviously it's only teenagers.' He was distracted by some graffiti on the wall, a tag that was repeated five or six times. 'What does that say? "Tow"? "Tox"?'

'Something like that.'

'This must be where you come to rebel around here.' He looked around. 'It's sheltered, isn't it? One streetlight on a pretty long stretch of pavement, trees blocking the view from the houses. You could get up to anything you liked here and no one would know.'

'No cigarette butts. There would have been cigarette butts in my day, but they all vape now.'

'In my day there would have been porn mags.'

'Of course there would,' I said quietly.

'A short walk was an education, believe me.'

'That explains a lot.'

We had arrived at a green-painted metal gate.

'The Holmwood, I presume.' Derwent reached out to open it but the dog shot through the bars then doubled back, entwining his lead in the gate and barking hysterically when he discovered he was trapped.

'Genuinely, I have never met a stupider dog,' Derwent told him, crouching to disentangle him. The sound of quick footsteps coming towards us made me turn, to see a man in very brief shorts and a sleeveless top running at a steady pace. He had a German shepherd on a long lead, the dog's tongue lolling pinkly as it ran ahead of him. Derwent got Pippin free just in time and swung the gate open for the runner who flashed past us in unsmiling silence.

'Any time, mate,' Derwent called after him, his voice loaded with sarcasm. 'No need to say thank you.'

'Please don't pick a fight with our new next-door neighbour.'

'Him?'

'Stephen Bollivant,' I said, passing through the gate myself. 'Didn't you recognise him?'

'Obviously not. Did Vanessa say he was a wanker?'

'She said he was quiet and shy.'

'Shy.' Derwent snorted. 'That must be why he wasn't able to say thank you.'

'You're just annoyed because he has a proper dog and you have a walking liability who is currently rolling in . . . yes, I think that's fox shit.'

'For fuck's sake.'

'Three out of ten for situational awareness so far.'

He glowered at me, as if it was my fault that Pippin was wearing a thin layer of reeking black excrement. 'I don't remember inviting you to join us.'

'But aren't you glad I came?' I relented. 'Look, if you want to get some actual exercise, I'll walk Pippin on the way back. You can have a run.'

'Really?'

'Yes, really.' The path had widened, the ground underfoot dark and rich and firm. The early light speared through gaps in the tree canopy, shafts of pure gold in the dense greenery of the forest. A breeze stirred the leaves overhead with a noise like running water, and I felt my spirits lift. For once, we weren't on our way to a crime scene or a body. There was nothing frightening in these particular woods, on this particular day. 'I'd like to.'

'Thanks. Let's see if we can make a bit more progress first.' Derwent looked down. 'Why don't you show us this lake, sunshine? Make yourself useful.'

Pippin surged away, heading downhill, and we fell into step beside one another again. Derwent was humming under his breath, his stride matching mine, and the day stretched out ahead of us, full of potential, empty of irritating duties.

You're so lucky, everyone had said.

Maybe they were right.

14

Climbing back up the hill an hour later, on my own, with a dog that was going to need extensive hosing before he was allowed into the pristine house, I was a little less in love with the Holmwood. We had discovered it was a steep-sided valley so dense with ancient woodland that you couldn't see more than twenty or thirty feet into the trees. The paths were well worn and clearly marked, leading us down from the top of the valley to the lake that lay at the bottom of it. The water was pockmarked with rings where fish rose to lip at the clouds of tiny flies hanging above the surface. Dense reeds circled the lake, and at one end a small, battered boathouse stood on stilts over the water. It was peaceful, except for other dog walkers and runners. Pippin yearned to fight every dog that we encountered, and Derwent sulked about not getting to overtake the runners who steamed past us, and eventually, at the far end of the lake, I gave in.

'Go on. I'm taking this lunatic home. Neither of you are good company this morning.'

'Thanks.' To my surprise, he dropped a kiss on my cheek before he disappeared, his long stride taking him out of my sight in moments. I turned and trudged along the lakeside, back up the path we had strolled down earlier. It was a lot harder in reverse, and perhaps there was an easier way but I wasn't prepared to dive down any of the inviting paths that led into the woods when I was by myself. The air was warmer now, even under the trees, with real heat where the sun broke through the leaves. My T-shirt was damp with sweat and I was out of breath.

'Come on, Pippin. Nearly there.'

The little dog had stopped, tired out. He looked up at me hopefully.

'Not in a million years when you smell like that, my friend.'

At last, the gate, and the high walls on either side of the narrow path, which had a different feel to it when I was on my own. The walls hid the long gardens that belonged to numbers 5 and 6, Jellicoe Close. The garden of number 5 was a wilderness of overgrown trees choked with ivy and bindweed, while number 6 had tall leylandii all along the boundary wall. I could understand the wish to block out the noise from pedestrians, and the desire for privacy, but the evergreen trees were a dense screen that felt impenetrable.

Anything could happen here . . .

A child shouted on the other side of the wall, very close to me, and I jumped out of my skin before I reminded myself that the house belonged to the Vonns – Rhys and Nicola – and their two children were seven and fourteen. If I had to guess, it was the seven-year-old who had just discovered a snail on her slide and had to tell everyone about it. Thea, I thought.

I hustled Pippin through the gap and into the Close itself, to discover that while we had been out, the neighbours had come to life. A teenage schoolgirl was standing on the pavement, carrying her blazer. She was tall, with red-gold hair that glowed in the sunshine. As I watched a sturdy boy ran out of number 9 and joined her, his hair wet from the shower. They walked off together, settling their school bags on their backs, serious in their Monday-morning demeanour. The car in the driveway of number 9 hummed into life, reversing into the road before it purred away. Mike Knox, I reminded myself. One of the cyclists from the previous day.

It was like walking out on a stage full of actors, all busily playing their parts, while I shuffled through the scene feeling out of place and self-conscious.

But of course I had Pippin with me, and he was an old hand.

'Hello, little Pip. What've you been rolling in, then?' Alan Otis was standing by his garden gate, his belly straining the buttons on his shirt. A bucket-shaped sunhat hooded his eyes in shade, but his white, even false teeth gleamed with artificial perfection in the sunlight.

'Please don't tell Vanessa I let that happen the first time I took him out. He was just so quick. I couldn't stop him.'

'Oh, I know what he's like. Greased lightning. We used to look after him for Vanessa sometimes, you know, when she was busy. Had to say we couldn't do it any more. Ruth – that's my wife – she was always worried he'd run off and get hit by a car.'

'I'm terrified,' I admitted. 'But I hope we'll do a good job.' I introduced myself and Alan squeezed my hand between both of his, which was an unnecessarily intimate experience, I felt.

'We saw you arrive. You and your er . . .'

I correctly identified that I was supposed to explain the relationship. 'Josh? He's my boyfriend.'

'Boyfriend.' Alan sniffed. 'He should get a ring on your finger, miss, instead of wasting his time being a boyfriend.'

'Oh, plenty of time for that.' I looked down at my feet, blushing, and pulled the lead through my fingers. 'We haven't been together that long.'

'I wouldn't let the grass grow under my feet.' Another flash of the teeth. 'Ruth and I were engaged one month after I met her and we're married fifty years next spring.'

I murmured something congratulatory.

'So how long are you two going to be hanging around here?'

'A few weeks. Vanessa has work commitments overseas.'

'She's a high-flier. Intellectual, you know.'

'So I hear.'

'What about you? Are you an academic?'

I shook my head, wide-eyed. 'I'm not even working at the moment. Between jobs.'

'What do you do usually?'

'I used to work for a travel agent.'

Alan whistled, producing a thin noise that made Pippin's ears twitch. 'Glamorous.'

'It really wasn't! I was stuck behind a desk watching other people go away on amazing holidays.'

'And your fella? What does he do?'

'He's a security consultant.'

'What does that mean?'

'I don't really know.' I giggled at my own ignorance. 'He generally works from home, apart from site visits.'

'How did he get into that, then?'

'He was in the army.' No word of a lie.

'Was he? That makes sense. Posture, you know. They never lose it.'

'Like ballet dancers,' I said seriously. Alan gave a bark of surprised laughter.

'I wouldn't know anything about that.'

Feeling fairly confident that I had established my airhead credentials well enough, I said goodbye to him and dragged Pippin off to his date with the outside tap. He loudly deplored the entire experience, whining and barking at the hose.

'You would think I was torturing you,' I said through clenched teeth. 'Maybe there's a lesson here about not rolling in fox crap.'

'Ignore him,' said a male voice from behind me. 'That's what Vanessa does too.'

'Pippin was just telling me she runs him a bubble bath.' I turned to find a dark-haired man at the foot of the drive. He was thin, his shirtsleeves rolled back to show off sinewy arms. A fringe flopped into his eyes over expensive designer glasses with horn frames. His jaw was harshly cut, and even at that early hour there was a hint of shadow on it.

'Brian. I'm next door in number 2.' He jerked a thumb in that direction. 'I thought I'd come over and introduce myself.'

'Maeve,' I said. 'I'd offer to shake hands, but unless you want to smell like wet dog, I wouldn't advise it.'

He laughed. 'I'll let you off. Is that an Irish name?'

'It is. My parents are Irish.'

'Mine too.' He grinned at me as if he was pleased to find we had something in common. 'At least we dodged being named something no one can spell.'

'You'd be surprised how often I get emails addressed to "Mauve",' I said with feeling.

'Brian?' A woman in a tightly belted linen dress was standing at the bottom of their drive. 'I thought you were running late.'

'I am, I am.' There was just a hint of impatience in his voice, and none at all in his face when he turned back to me. 'Well, Maeve, it's nice to meet you. This is my wife, Fleur. Also my conscience, it seems.'

I waved. Rigid disapproval was her response.

Fleur and Brian Nolan who got married three years ago . . . Fleur is desperate for a baby and they've been having IVF for ages . . .

I could find it in myself to be nice to poor Fleur, I thought, even if I didn't get much back.

'It's lovely to meet you,' I said. 'This is such a friendly neighbourhood.'

'It can be. Brian, you'd really better go. You've got that meeting, remember.'

'I'm gone.' He jogged to his car, a high-end Audi, and swung out of his drive at a speed that was on the sharp end of safe.

Fleur watched him go. Her face was set in a miserable expression. They seemed comically at odds in terms of their personality. The torture of IVF's hope and despair cycle could break up the strongest couple, I knew, and the cracks were definitely showing if Fleur couldn't even pin on a brave face in front of a stranger.

'We're looking after . . .' I trailed off, because Fleur had turned away and was walking back into the house without any further acknowledgement of me. I would work on her, I decided. Hadn't Derwent said I was good at talking to people?

Pippin got my attention by shaking water droplets all over my legs and I took him inside, where he demanded breakfast before curling up in his bed in the corner of the kitchen, his head jammed up his bottom.

'I'll hold your calls,' I said, and went to have a shower. Afterwards I drew the curtains, catching Alan's eye as he tinkered with a lawnmower. He'd chosen a mid-lawn location that allowed him to keep our bedroom window under observation, I noticed. He gave me a wave and pointed to his left, where Derwent was deep in conversation with one of the cyclists from the previous day. They were both standing with their arms folded across their chests, their legs spread wide, trying to outdo the other in terms of manliness. It looked very cheerful and friendly. Derwent said goodbye and jogged over to the house to begin a complicated series of stretches against the front wall. His skin was glowing golden in the morning light. A small, unworthy part of me hoped Fleur was near enough to observe him.

As if I would even consider *making a play for Brian, quite frankly, when I have* that *to look at.*

At least, that's what I would think if I was really the character I was playing.

'It's just work,' I said out loud, and went to make breakfast.

He hadn't expected them to be up so early. Getting to know their schedule was key. Too soon to say if they would stick to it. The previous evening they had carried in their bags (he'd enjoyed watching her leaning to reach the back of the boot, up on tiptoe, the muscles taut in her calves and thighs) and unpacked, he guessed, and that had taken most of the evening. A familiar moped had buzzed into the cul de sac around eight: a delivery from Ruby Murray's, the best curry house in the area. She had come to the door to get it, smiling at something the delivery guy said to her and tucking her hair behind her ear, which made him think that she might be shy, possibly. She had tipped well, the delivery man skipping away down the drive with a cheerful wave. He liked that. He liked the idea that she was kind.

Kindness was a weakness that could be exploited.

She was pretty but it was the docile quality she had that appealed to him most – a diffidence that he hungered to exploit.

For most of the evening the man had sprawled on the sofa with the blue light of the television holding his attention. She had been in the kitchen, he assumed, but he hadn't gone to look. There would be time for that. Besides, he knew that anticipation was worth savouring.

That was all very well. But the shock of seeing them in the morning had been a rush. He had kept his head, he thought, despite the surprise.

Oh. There you are. And you're perfect.

That was the first thought that had flashed into his mind when he saw her.

But then there was him. A challenge, no doubt about it.

That made it almost better; he would get a particular thrill from outwitting him. He had mental power the other man couldn't imagine. Discipline. Planning. Execution. When he was ready, the other man wouldn't be able to stop him. She had been on her own in the woods, and he knew a lot about moving through the woods. He could be close enough to someone to touch their shadow and they'd never know he was there.

His hands were shaking now, the fingertips tingling as adrenalin flooded his system. He clenched his fists, half hating the sensation, half relishing it. He was desperate to relieve the feelings that were building up inside him, but he had self-control. It didn't come easy, but nothing worth having does.

15

'So what are we doing today?'

'Shopping for food.' Derwent poked his spoon into the bowl of cornflakes in front of him. 'This is a shit breakfast.'

I sat down at the table, at a safe distance. 'What's wrong? I thought exercise was supposed to give you endorphins.'

'I ran into Rhys Vonn on my way back.' He pulled a face. 'I don't like him.'

'In a professional sense or a personal one?'

'Don't know yet. Something about him gave me the creeps.'

Vonn was tall and fit-looking, but he had luminous white skin to go with his red hair; it would be entirely like Derwent to take against him for the unforgivable crime of being ginger, or for having a beard, or for wearing head-to-toe Lycra and cycling everywhere, or for being his physical equal. The ways to annoy Derwent were more or less infinite.

'What were you talking about?'

'He was asking me to play football on Saturday for his five-a-side team. They're short a player. Just a local league game.'

'So? Presumably you said yes.'

'I didn't have much choice. He implied I might not be fit enough.'

'Well, you couldn't let that go.'

He winced. 'He manipulated me, didn't he?'

'Completely and totally. Don't you like football?' I had hazy memories of him taking part in a Met tournament a couple of years before, which had involved a lot of boasting.

'I hate all team games.'

'Worried about letting other people down?'

'Absolutely fucking not.' He looked at me, outraged. 'Oh, you were joking.'

'I was. What's the problem?'

'You're penalised if you try too hard.'

'Allow me to translate that into English – you foul the other players and get sent off.'

'Sometimes.' He pushed the bowl away from him. 'I should have said no.'

'We all have to do things we don't want to for work,' I said primly. 'Come on. It won't be that bad. I'll come and watch.'

'That is all I need.'

By the time we parked at the supermarket, Derwent had recovered what passed for his temper.

'I'm doing the lion's share of the cooking, so I'm picking most of what we buy. I've seen the rubbish you like and I'm not eating it.'

'You're basing that opinion on an incomplete picture,' I protested. 'I eat good food too. And I'm not sure I want you to do most of the cooking. I'm not keen on no carbs, my-body-is-a-temple stuff.'

'You've never eaten anything I've cooked. I'm good at it.'

Or no one dared to tell him he wasn't. 'OK, OK. But I can cook a few things.'

'Spaghetti Bolognese.'

'That's one,' I admitted. 'But only one. I've been working on it. I've got at least six meal options I can do without thinking about it.'

'All right. You can do a couple of dinners a week.'

'Thanks.' I hadn't intended to volunteer for any cooking duties, and I couldn't help feeling I'd been outmanoeuvred. A woman was getting out of a grey Range Rover in front of us, her fair hair swinging in a ponytail. She was clutching a mobile phone and talking to herself as she organised her shopping bags and a trolley. 'Hey, that's the car that was parked in front of the Vonns' house. That must be Nicola.'

'Good spot. Bear it in mind. We need to look as if we usually shop together.'

'I know,' I said patiently. 'We've discussed this a hundred times. I know what I'm doing.'

It was no surprise whatsoever that Derwent took ownership of the trolley, and also no surprise that he disapproved of most of the things I put in it. There were three or four things that united us: a hatred of peanut butter, a preference for thick-sliced bread and apricot jam. The rest was pure attrition.

'You can't give Pippin that food,' I pointed out in the dog-food section as Derwent fitted a tray of tins into the end of the trolley. 'He gets special food because he's been neutered. It stops him getting fat.'

Derwent examined the bag of dry food I'd handed him. 'Diet food for eunuchs. What a miserable way to live. Fair enough, he can't have his balls, but let him have his meaty chunks.'

'Vanessa would never forgive us. Anyway, you're into healthy eating. Why are you suddenly trying to feed the dog canine fast food?'

'I feel sorry for him.'

'Because of his balls?'

'You wouldn't understand.' He took the tins out though, and replaced them with the bag, shaking his head sorrowfully.

'I knew you'd end up bonding with Pippin. You have a lot in common.'

'I can assure you I still have my testicles.'

An elderly lady who had been creaking past paused to gaze at us in horror, then hurried away.

I sighed. 'If you could just . . . not. We'll get kicked out.'

'I'm trying to make friends.'

'I think she was afraid you were going to whip them out.'

'Not in the supermarket. Maybe later, if you play your cards right.'

'I'd rather look at Pippin's.'

'Those days are gone. Unless you can find the specimen jar.'

'I suppose we're not allowed snacks,' I said in the crisp aisle.

'No, you should definitely buy some. As many as you want.' He was reversing down the aisle, scanning the shelves. 'I was going to get some chocolate too.'

'Why?' I was suspicious.

'PMT.'

'You get PMT? That would explain a lot, actually.'

'No. You do.' His eyes were bright with mischief.

'I do not.'

'Oh, you absolutely do.'

'You have no idea about my menstrual cycle.'

'Five days before you get your period, you start eating even more crap than usual. Anything salty or sweet is fair game and you get incredibly grumpy if your blood sugar gets too low. That's when I pretend I've missed lunch so we can stop at a petrol station and you can stock up. Three days before, all your tops are suddenly too tight across the chest. I worry about getting pinged in the eye with a rogue button. Two days before, you're at your most dangerous and literally anything can set you off. Just before it, you're always distracted and spacey. And then on day one you always feel like shit and take painkillers whenever you think I'm not looking.'

'When did you work this out?'

'Years ago.'

It was uncannily accurate. I walked away instead of saying anything, colourful products blurring as I moved past them. He caught up with me two aisles over.

'Are you angry?'

'I'm not sure what I am.' I felt exposed, embarrassed, and above all else surprised that he'd noticed any of it.

'It's not a big deal.' He coasted on the trolley for a few metres like a teenager, looking back at me to see if I was amused. 'It's not as if you complain.'

'I wouldn't.'

'I know.' He abandoned the trolley and came to stand in front of me, putting his hands in his pockets, sheepish. 'We're together a lot. I can't help it. I notice things.'

'Yeah.' I couldn't look at him. 'Like how tight my tops are.'

'Like when you're in pain and you're pretending you're fine,' he said softly.

To my horror, I felt tears welling in my eyes.

'What are we – six days before? Over-emotional. Right on cue.'

I sniffed. 'Bog off, Josh.'

'Seriously, I spend more time with you than just about anyone else. You must notice things about me.'

'I try not to think about you.'

He stood still for a second, absorbing the implications, then nodded. 'I see.'

'No, you don't—' I stopped. Impossible to tell him I knew him better than almost anyone, and mostly didn't feel as if I knew him at all. 'Look, can we just forget it?'

'Of course.'

We finished the shopping in awkward silence.

I had to hand it to us. We couldn't have done a better job of looking like a real couple if we'd tried.

Back in the car park, I was loading bags into the boot when I heard Derwent greeting someone. I turned to see Nicola Vonn, her trolley piled high with bags. She paused, looking dazed, as if he'd roused her from a trance. Up close she was very attractive, with clear tanned skin dusted with freckles and big grey eyes. She was too thin, though, her cheekbones hollow and her neck corded with tendons.

'Oh – you're Vanessa's house-sitters.'

'That's right.' He leaned past me to shake her hand. 'Josh. This is Maeve.'

She smiled at me but her eyes were unfocused and I doubted she would remember my name. With an effort she said, 'I hear you're playing football with my husband on Saturday. He's very competitive. Just so you know. He plays to win.'

'So do I,' Derwent said.

'It's not fun when they lose.'

What did *that* mean, I wondered. Beside me, Derwent was very still, and our response seemed to wake her up to the fact that she'd said something troubling. She laughed as if it had been a joke.

'I'm so busy at the moment. Camilla – my eldest – she's in a play at school this week, and I've been helping with the rehearsals. There isn't a speck of food in the house and I think the cleaner's going to go on strike when she sees the state of the bathrooms.'

Derwent smiled. 'In that case, we'd better not keep you.'

'Yes.' She didn't move. 'You could come to the play, if you wanted. It's a fundraiser, for the school – I'm supposed to be selling tickets but I've only managed to convince a few of the neighbours to go. I was just going to pay for the last couple myself. I've been carrying them around in my bag for weeks.'

'We love the theatre,' I said. 'Don't we?'

'Very much so,' Derwent said. 'What's the show?'

'They're doing *A Midsummer Night's Dream*.' Nicola was digging in her bag. She came up with a handful of crumpled paper. 'These are twenty pounds each, but you get a ticket for the raffle too.'

'Wonderful,' I said, and watched Derwent hand over the cash, standing so close to her that it looked as if he was doing a drug deal. I presumed Una Burt would sign off on it as a legitimate expense. It wasn't specifically connected with our investigation, but then it wasn't unconnected either. We needed to be involved with the community, invisible, and not obviously focused on Judy Thwaites.

'It's on Friday,' she said. 'In the school grounds. An outdoor performance. If it doesn't rain, I mean. And if it does rain we're just supposed to put up umbrellas and sit through it. I shouldn't have said anything about the play. It'll probably be awful.'

'I'm sure it will be wonderful.'

'Well. Yes. Maybe.' She put a hand up, seeming surprised to discover her hair was in a ponytail.

'We'll see you there,' Derwent said gently, and she pulled herself together enough to say goodbye and return to her car.

'No smell of alcohol on her breath.'

'I wondered why you were invading her personal space like that,' I said.

'Why else?'

'She's an attractive woman.'

He snorted. 'She's mental. Or on drugs.'

'Or both,' I suggested. 'Do you think she should be driving?'

'Nope.'

We watched her pull out of the car park, swinging onto the wrong side of the road and over-correcting with a jerk.

'I hope she'll make it home safely.'

'At least it's not far. She should be fine if she doesn't meet any cyclists.'

'Like her husband?'

'I told you there was something off about him.'

'You did. Your famous insight strikes again.' The words sat between us like a solid, unwieldy lump. I squirmed. 'Look, when I said I never thought about you, that's not really true. I—'

He turned his back on me and opened the driver's door, getting into the car before he paused for a second, one hand on the door handle. 'Why don't we never talk about it again.'

16

'So, how's it going?' Georgia sounded chirpy, as if I'd rung her for a gossip rather than a work call. Before I could answer, Derwent pulled a saucepan out of a cupboard, dislodging a heap of baking trays that slid onto the floor with a clatter. 'What was *that*?'

'Josh cooking dinner.'

'He can *cook*? Oh my God. He really is the perfect man.'

'Georgia—' I snatched up the phone, torn between muting her and running out of the kitchen, and while I was deciding what to do she carried on, every syllable clear and distinctly audible.

'We were just talking about that though, remember? About how you never find one who's good in bed and in the kitchen?'

Derwent raised his eyebrows politely as I finally managed to silence her. I gathered up my notes.

'I think I'll take this call in the sitting room.'

'Seems like a good idea,' he said.

I hurried down the hall, my face hot. 'Georgia, you were on speakerphone.'

'Oh.' Then, '*Oh, shit*. Did he hear me?'

'Yep.'

'I don't even remember what I *said*,' she wailed.

'Well, Josh will never forget it.' I sat on one of the sofas and fanned my notes out on the coffee table. 'But never mind. I've said worse.'

'Have you?'

'Probably.'

'Well, now that I've humiliated myself, how are things? Are you settling in?'

'It's fine. Everyone is very welcoming. I'm going for afternoon tea with one of the neighbours tomorrow. Ruth sent Alan over to invite me.'

'Working hard,' Georgia teased, and I sighed.

'It's really difficult. I keep thinking I'm going to put my foot in it. And the woman who's invited me over is sharp as a tack. She's an incredible interrogator. I'll have to be on my guard.'

'You'll do fine.'

'Hope so.' Back to business. 'So, thank you for forwarding on the forensic report and the other material. I've been reading through them this afternoon.'

'And what did you think?'

That we were in trouble, I thought. 'Am I right in thinking that there wasn't a single trace of blood in the victim's home except for that one smudge on the outside of the back door that Kev found on his second sweep?'

'That's all there was.'

'Can we check with Cameron whether Dawoud might have injured himself somehow in the gym or the garden on a previous occasion? I don't like that we're relying on a single two-millimetre trace of blood to establish that we've found the crime scene, especially if we can't tie it in to the day in question.'

'Absolutely.' She was writing it down, I was relieved to hear. *Let's not rely too much on your memory, Georgia . . .*

'Was the garage floor swept and mopped after the car was moved? Can Kev check specifically for tyre marks?'

'Yes, but why?'

'If someone mopped the floor after the car was moved to the hospital car park, we know that the killer or an accomplice was the one who took it out of the house, not Hassan. It ties the murder to the house.'

'Oh, I should have thought of that.'

'He said there was a partial footprint on the garage floor – do we have any idea of the size? Would it fit the driver we've got on CCTV? Or could it have been Hassan who left it there?'

'OK . . .' Georgia was scribbling madly. 'Kev did say it looked like a trainer.'

'He said it was a rubberised sole, *like* a trainer. That doesn't mean it *was* a trainer.'

'You sound like a defence brief.'

'One day, with any luck, we'll be going through this in front of a jury. Kev's too experienced to be definite about anything he doesn't know for sure, so he's not going to say it's definitely a trainer. But at the same time, don't get tunnel vision. Don't count someone out because they were wearing a – a—'

'Deck shoe?' Georgia suggested.

'That kind of thing exactly.' I flipped through the report. 'And the blanket from the back seat of the car – can we ask Cameron about it?'

'What about it?'

'Whether it came from the house, was it usually kept in the car – anything, really. I think he was probably under the blanket on his way to the hospital. If it came from inside the house, again, that means he was likely to have been killed in the house or garden. If it was always in the car, he could have been anywhere at all when he died.'

'Sure thing. Kev said he thought the back of the driver's seat had been lowered and raised again because it was left in a position that wasn't how Hassan usually had it – no wear and tear on the mechanism. He said it would have been relatively easy to move the body from the back to the front that way.'

'So no one saw a thing.'

'Exactly.'

'The financial documents . . .' I slid them out and glanced through them again, with a whistle. 'We're in the wrong job.'

'I know! I need to chat up some accountants.'

'That mortgage is hefty.'

'Yeah, but they could afford it.'

'Just about. They were gambling on being able to maintain that income, weren't they? If Dawoud was running into professional difficulties, that might have been an issue for them.'

'You mean the brothers who were suing him for negligence after their mother died?'

'The Arnolds. We need to trace them and find out if they have alibis. They're a close-knit family and they were clearly furious with him. And we should see if any of them might be a match for our driver. And we should find out if they had a chance of winning their case.'

'Yeah, I'm waiting to talk to the other consultant in the department – Dmitri Stefanidis. He's giving me the runaround. His secretary is definitely stalling me.'

'Well, he'd be busy. His workload has doubled.'

'That's true. Did you see the life insurance policies?'

'I did. It'll set Cameron up nicely.'

'That's a good motive.'

'One of the best,' I agreed. 'Unfortunately motive isn't as important as evidence. There's still nothing to link Cameron to the murder. But one thing did occur to me. Cameron presumably kept a close eye on what they were both spending. He might have spotted some unusual expenditure – hotel rooms, meals out, gifts – and realised that Hassan was having an affair.'

'Clever,' Georgia said. 'If he could find it, we could find it.'

'That's what I thought. It's worth spending some time going

back through Hassan's bank accounts. Anything that gives us a lead on who the lover was would be a help.'

'You know, I liked Cameron a lot more this time when I interviewed him. I felt the shock was wearing off a bit and he was less angry, more sad. He said he hadn't been sleeping.'

'Guilty conscience?'

'Maybe. He looked rough. I didn't mention the message I found from the mystery lover. I'm not looking forward to breaking that news, if he didn't know.'

'Never fun,' I agreed.

'You were right about Chris being a good interviewer. He got him talking – loads of stuff about their life together, the neighbours, his job. I don't think I'd have got so much out of him.'

'Watch and learn. Chris taught me a lot of what I know. That's how we all get better at the job.'

'You were always good.'

'I really wasn't. And I still get plenty of things wrong.'

'Not the way I do.' She sounded wistful. I found myself wishing I could see the expression on her face.

'You're doing fine. This is hardly standard operating procedure for a murder investigation. Just keep asking for help where and when you can. And next time maybe we could do this over Facetime.'

'Oh yes, I really want to see the house.'

I spared a glance for the picture over the fireplace. I would need to find a room that was free of sexually charged artwork or I dreaded to think what Georgia would say about it.

'What else did Cameron tell you? Anything surprising?'

'Hmm. Nothing really.' She started to laugh. 'Except that he and Hassan found Liz St John a bit much. She seems like quite a fussy neighbour. I checked up and she actually made a noise complaint about them to the council when they had a party that ran late. Cameron said they called her the tiger mother because she was so obsessed with her kids, but she

110

was always good for a spare teabag. They generally got on fine – went round for a barbecue, drinks parties, that kind of thing, but they weren't close friends.'

'Liz thought they were, didn't she?'

'Very different feeling on the other side of the hedge.' Georgia sighed. 'You know if Liz was the one who'd been murdered neither Cameron nor Hassan would have known a thing about her usual routine, whereas she knew a fair bit about the two of them coming and going.'

'Luckily for us.' And that was about the only bit of luck we'd had so far, I reflected, as I said goodbye to Georgia. I put the phone down on the table and sniffed the air, trying to gauge whether dinner was imminent. It smelled amazing, I had to admit, and I was absolutely starving.

Some movement caught my attention out of the corner of my eye and I turned to look at the road. A bird, I thought, gliding low in the evening shadows, or someone walking past the house. But if it was a pedestrian they'd been moving quickly, because I hadn't been in time to see them.

What had I said to Derwent? Three out of ten for situational awareness?

'I'd give you a round zero for that one,' I said out loud, and got up to see if I could speed up dinner before I died of malnutrition.

17

Derwent and I had agreed that it was important not to make our interest in Judy and her son too obvious. On the other hand, it was vital that we didn't avoid her; that would be more suspicious than going out of our way to make friends. The next morning I glanced out of my bedroom window to see Derwent in Judy's front garden, rehanging her bird feeders under her close supervision. She was holding Pippin's lead but the little dog was lying down, his head on his paws, as if he had enough experience of this particular situation to know that his walk was going to be indefinitely delayed.

When Derwent and Pippin finally got back, half an hour after I would have expected them, I was waiting in the kitchen.

'How was Judy?'

'Thorough.' He shook his head. 'She could give the Spanish Inquisition pointers.'

'From this side of the road it didn't look as if she was having to get out the thumb-screws,' I said. 'You seemed to be having a lovely time.'

'Oh, it was quite enjoyable, or it would have been if I hadn't been concentrating so hard on remembering the details of where we met and how we got together.'

My blood ran cold. 'Please tell me you stuck to the story. I've got tea with Ruth this afternoon and I need to make sure what I say is the same as what you've told Judy. If they start comparing notes and our stories don't match up, we're in trouble.'

'I'm pretty sure I did. I told her I fell for you the first time I met you, but it took you a lot longer to appreciate my good points.'

'Of course you did. You keep your good points well hidden, in fairness to me.'

'That's not what Judy thinks. But she agreed with me that sometimes women are very obtuse about knowing what they want.'

I rolled my eyes. 'Women, eh?'

'She thinks we look good together.'

'How flattering. What else did she find out about you?'

'That I was in the army. The places I went. What I did after that – the non-police version.' He folded his arms. 'The basics.'

'You never talk about that kind of thing with me.'

'I told you she was good.' He shuddered. 'I feel as if I've been turned inside out.'

I dropped some bread into the toaster. 'While she was busy finding out everything about you, what did you find out about her?'

'Not a huge amount. But I did tell her you were very keen to help out with her charitable work.'

'*Did* you?' I turned to glower at him.

'Yeah, well, you're better at that kind of thing than I am.'

'What kind of thing do you mean? Senior aerobics at the leisure centre?'

He laughed. 'Definitely that. No, I meant you're better at talking to people and finding out things about them. It comes naturally to you.'

'Flattery will get you one piece of toast.' I dropped it onto a plate and handed it to him. 'You can organise your own jam. What did you sign me up to do?'

'Nothing *too* bad.' He was employing his most persuasive

tone, which made me suspicious, and I was right, because later that morning I found myself standing in the back room of the Little Paws charity shop, wishing for better gloves than the very thin, fragile ones I was wearing, as Judy handed me a collection of bulging plastic bags.

'I'm not going to lie to you, dear, we do get some odd bits and pieces in with the donations. I think sometimes people forget what's going to the bin and what's for the charity shop, so you get some extraordinary things. I had a nappy once – a full one, sadly. Disgusting. And someone's takeaway.' She cackled. 'Puts you off your food, really it does.'

'I'm not sure I want to look in these,' I said, trying to guess the contents of the bags from the shapes they were making.

'What you need to do is divide things into sellable and not sellable piles. We do tell them not to bother with broken or damaged things because no one is going to buy them, really, are they? Sometimes I wonder what sort of houses these people live in. Did you have a look around the shop to see what I mean about the things we can sell?'

I nodded. I had spent a happy ten minutes browsing through the miscellaneous knitted items and ornaments, knick-knacks and frankly incredible amateur art that was the core stock of Little Paws. It was hard to find an animal type that wasn't taken care of in the charity sector, but Little Paws had found their niche by focusing on gerbils and hamsters.

'And the odd chinchilla, but that's really more of an interest of the founder than an official thing,' Judy had confided in me as she drove me to the shop. 'Cats and dogs get all the attention, don't they? And donkeys. Hamsters and gerbils are more seen as *disposable*.'

'I was never allowed a hamster when I was a child,' I had said wistfully and truthfully; my mother had taken a strong line on rodents.

'Well, you see, there it is. They're not just for children. No pet should be for a child, should it? A little living thing.'

114

I thought of Davy Bidwell and literally had to bite my tongue to stop myself from asking her how she felt about humans, specifically.

'You're quite an animal lover, aren't you?' I said instead. 'Feeding the birds, helping out here.'

'Well, I do try to help where I can. I help the old folk at the community centre.' A cackle. 'I'm older than some of them.'

'You're only as old as you feel.' I held up a china kitten. 'This looks OK.'

'That'll go,' Judy said. 'It should have a pair, though. One with a ball of wool and one with a fish. Have a look.'

I went through the rest of the bag, discovering that it mostly consisted of old pairs of tights and a few crumpled paperbacks. 'Maybe the other one broke.'

'Probably.' She held out her hand. 'I'll take the kitten.'

'Have you always done a lot for charity?'

'Since my son Tom left home.' She dusted her hands off on her jeans, which were pale pink and fitted. 'I suppose it gives me something to do. I like to be useful.'

A son. There was absolutely no reference to Tom in the files I'd read on the previous investigation into Davy Bidwell's death. I cursed the previous investigators thoroughly and silently, and set out to find out what I could. 'It must be lonely without him.'

'Sometimes. You know how it is. He comes to visit quite often.'

'Hopefully I'll get to meet him then.'

'Oh, you'll see him.' I couldn't tell from Judy's tone whether she thought that would be a pleasant experience for me or not. 'Anyway, since my husband died and Tom left home I've been on my own, and I like people, so I find things to do that mean I can have a bit of a chat with someone. Loneliness is a killer.'

'How did your husband . . .' I trailed off as if I wasn't sure how to finish the sentence. I was trying to come across as casually curious.

'Dropped dead on holidays. One minute he was fine, the next gone. Twenty-three years ago.'

'I'm so sorry.'

'Well, it was a long time ago.' She flashed me a bright smile. 'We carry on, don't we?'

'Did you ever think of marrying again?'

'No. Glad to be done with it, to be honest with you. I like my freedom.'

'What about taking in a lodger?' I said. 'Maybe that would be good company for you.'

'Ah, but I like to be free to foster.' She was digging through a box energetically, pausing to examine what looked like a defunct TV aerial.

'Er . . . not children?'

'Hamsters.'

'Of course.' I was beginning to feel desperate.

'And I do sometimes have people staying with me. Incurables.' She laughed. 'That's what we used to call them. "Mentally deficient", that kind of thing. I know we're not supposed to say it any more but I can never remember the right words. It changes all the time and I lose track. They stay with me sometimes, when they have nowhere else to go. It's nice to be able to help, isn't it?'

'I imagine so. Why don't they have anywhere else to go?'

'Well, their families don't want them, do they?' She folded a cardigan with neat, sharp movements. 'Or they don't have any families. Sad, really. It's all right when they're children – hard on the parents, but they get looked after. Once they grow up, if their parents are gone, where do they go? Out of sight, out of mind, that's how it is for a lot of them. They're not all easy to deal with, but you have to have patience, don't you?'

'I'd find it very hard.'

116

'Well, it's not for everyone, but I do what I can.' She patted my arm. 'When you're my age you'll know the world is full of pain. Whatever we can do to make it easier for other people is worth the effort. And it's only now and then, so I really don't mind.'

'Where do they go after they stay with you?' I asked in an off hand way but actually it was the key question: if she knew what happened to the men after they left her home, she was guilty of a whole rake of serious charges that ran all the way up to modern slavery and murder.

'No idea, love. My son sorts it all out. He's got a friend who takes them. I look after them for a few days or weeks. They go on to wherever they're headed next. And that's all I know.' She made her way over to the tiny kitchenette. 'Cuppa?'

I let her divert us into a discussion about hot drinks while I carried on sorting through junk, on autopilot. If Judy didn't know where the men ended up, she might actually not be worth charging with anything. I'd be lying if I said I was disappointed. I'd come to like Judy, with her coral lipstick and big earrings and larger-than-life personality. I wouldn't mind at all if, in the end, she was free to carry on feeding her birds and gossiping and helping disadvantaged gerbils to her heart's content. But I thought about Davy Bidwell's poor wasted body and I wanted, very much, to find out more about Tom Thwaites and his helpful, hospitable friend.

18

Later that day I faced my toughest test so far: afternoon tea with the Otises. I crossed the road feeling highly self-conscious, carrying a dish covered with a tea towel, trying to remember all the details of our cover story. Ruth Otis had her front door open before I reached the halfway point.

'What have you got there?'

'Strawberries.' I handed her the bowl. 'From the garden.'

'Oh.' She peered under the cloth. 'Well, they do look nice, I suppose.'

'They taste even better. I had a few when I was picking them.'

'You didn't have to bring anything.' She looked up at me, her small eyes suspicious. 'I did plenty of baking for today.'

'I'm sure you did. It's just that I didn't want to come empty-handed, but I'm not a baker, I'm afraid.'

She reached out and grasped my hand with cool, plump fingers. 'No. Too warm-blooded. You can't have hot hands and bake decent pastry. Come on.'

Suddenly self-conscious about the temperature of my extremities, I followed her into the house, which was unmodernised. The two main rooms downstairs had been kept as a separate sitting room and dim, crowded dining room, and there was a small, dark galley kitchen at the back. Despite the heat of the day Ruth was wearing a long-sleeved floral dress and tights.

'We thought we'd eat outside.' She was wheezing with the exertion of carrying the bowl of strawberries, and I wondered if her heart was all right. 'Alan's out there already.'

'Great,' I said with more enthusiasm than I felt, for two reasons. I didn't want to be outside in case it inhibited Ruth from spilling everything she knew about the neighbours, and I'd changed into a white top that was cut lower than I'd realised after I'd showered the charity-shop mustiness away. Derwent had studiously avoided commenting on it, which made me more uncomfortable about the inches of cleavage on display rather than less so. Alan was going to be delighted.

'I'm sorry your young man couldn't come to tea.'

'He's got to work, I'm afraid.' I resisted the urge to make a crack about her calling him young. That was the sort of thing the real me would do; the ideal girlfriend I was playing wouldn't dream of it.

'What did you say he does?'

'He's a security consultant?' I made it a question. 'I don't really understand what he does, to be honest with you.'

'No. Well, they don't always want to talk about their work, do they?' She poured boiling water into an ornate teapot that was standing on a tray with sugar, a jug of milk, bone-handled cutlery and a stack of dainty plates. 'You could carry this out for me. Send Alan in to get the rest.'

The sunshine was like a slap in the face after the dark kitchen. Dazzled, it took me a moment to navigate the step and locate Alan. He was sitting under a tree, reading a newspaper at an elderly metal table, the white paint peeling off it in fingernail-like half-moons. The garden was longer than Vanessa's. Bright flowerbeds edged an immaculate lawn, and there were large, leafy trees for shade. A birdbath stood in the middle of the lawn, and a fountain bubbled in a rockery at the end. It reminded me of my parents' garden: formal and somehow dated. My parents had had the same garden furniture for thirty years too.

I slid the tray onto the table. 'This is beautiful. Do you do it all yourself?'

'All my own work.' He got up and paused to ease his back. 'Getting a bit much for me, now, truth be told, but I keep going. I get a bit of help for the heavy stuff, you know. Planting and that.'

'Do you help out with Judy's garden?' I followed him back into the house and accepted the cake stand he handed me. Ruth was rummaging in the fridge.

'Judy doesn't care about gardens. She's got a great big hot tub out there and a load of decking and gravel. Low maintenance, she says. Not a bit of shade. On a day like today you could fry eggs out there.'

'Is she here?' I whispered and Alan shook his head.

'Hairdressers. She goes every week at this time.'

'Then I can say I prefer trees and grass,' I said truthfully.

'Well, me too. But she likes to sunbathe.'

'Who? Judy?' Ruth had emerged from the fridge. 'Terrible, it is. She sits out there in a skimpy bikini whenever the sun comes out. Cooks herself.'

'You don't know where to look,' Alan agreed.

I bet you do know where to look, actually, Alan.

'Oh,' I said. 'I see. Does she live on her own?'

'Except for her son, Tom. He comes and goes. Spends the night now and then.'

'What does he do for a living?' I asked casually.

'I don't know,' Ruth said vaguely. 'This and that, you know.'

'He's a difficult customer,' Alan said. 'Always has been. She used to worry about him. Then we thought he'd settled down, didn't we?'

'Yes. We had high hopes when he got married. But he has a knack for getting into trouble. He always gravitates towards the wrong people. He's got some not so nice friends.' Ruth took the cling film off a bowl of cream. 'Not what she deserves, you know. Having a son like that.'

I would have liked to know more about the friends, but I forced myself to take it slowly. The last thing I wanted to do was arouse Ruth's suspicions. If she thought Derwent and I weren't who we said we were, it would be all over for us.

'Does she have any other family?'

'No.'

'So it's just her in the house?' I was pushing it, I thought. Even an arch gossip like Ruth would get suspicious eventually if I kept asking questions like that.

'At the moment. She sometimes has people staying with her. Unfortunates,' Ruth mouthed. 'I couldn't do it, but she has a lot of patience with them.'

'Oh really? Where do they come from?'

'Oh, you know . . .' Ruth's attention fell on a plate of scones that was sitting on the kitchen counter. They were oozing cream and jam. 'The cream is going to go runny if we don't get a move on.'

I filed out obediently with the cake stand, admiring the coffee cake that was resting on it. 'You've gone to so much trouble.'

'Well, we like to be welcoming, don't we, Alan?' Ruth sat down with a sigh of relief that was echoed by the air rushing out of the foam cushion underneath her. 'Now tell us all about yourself, dear. Where did you say you were from?'

I recognised that there was a price to be paid for the cakes and tea, and proceeded to pay it. We moved from my Irish background and childhood in London and my parents' jobs to Derwent, seamlessly.

'So you met . . .'

'We were set up by a friend of mine. Una. She works with Josh. She's actually his boss, so he has to do what she says.'

'And was it love at first sight?'

'Well, it was something at first sight. He makes a strong first impression.' If only they knew what that impression had been. I remembered vividly that I hadn't liked him at all. I certainly hadn't trusted him; I had been intimidated and unsettled by him, unsure how to cope with the force of his personality and the way he liked to challenge me. But then he'd been hiding his redeeming features very effectively at the time.

'You're a beautiful couple. You'll have lovely children.'

I choked on my tea. 'We're not really at that stage yet.'

'You don't want to wait around too long, my love. You'd be surprised. It gets harder and harder to conceive the older you get. Once you're in your thirties—'

'Leave her alone, love. They're just having fun practising at the moment, isn't that right, Maeve?'

Thank God Derwent hadn't come with me so I didn't have to avoid catching his eye. 'You know how it is, Alan. We're still in the early stages, really.'

'Don't hang around, that's all. Easy to think you've got forever but you want to get married and have a bit of time to yourselves before you start having babies and lose your figure,' Ruth said comfortably. 'We were married eighteen months before we had Charles, and Ann came along two years after him. So it all worked out perfectly for us, you see.'

I had already heard rather too much about Charles and Ann and I was keen to get the conversation back to Judy Thwaites. 'This seems like a lovely place to bring up children. Were they friends with . . . Tom, was it?'

'He's older,' Ruth said. 'You know how it is at that age. A couple of years is a lifetime. But we were happy enough that they weren't close.' A significant look passed between her and her husband. 'The teenagers are a bit wild at the moment. We hear them late at night, don't we, Alan?'

'They like to go drinking in the lane.'

'The one that leads down to the Holmwood?'

122

'That's the one. All the kids round here go down there.' Alan pulled a face. 'But they're decent for the most part. They go to the tennis club too. Play cricket and so forth. The school is good. That's what brings the parents here.'

'I met Nicola Vonn at the shops yesterday.'

'Ah, Nicola.' Ruth was cutting the coffee cake with exquisite care.

'She seems nice.'

'Neurotic,' she said with some satisfaction. 'If you shook her, she'd rattle. Always at the doctor getting a new prescription.'

'That's a shame.'

'Well, if you were married to him . . .' She trailed off.

None of my business. Nothing to do with our case. I leaned forward. 'What do you mean?'

'Always out on his bike. No help with the children. Leaves everything to her. And you know he barely works. He made a fortune in the City and now he spends his days managing his money, or so he says. The rest of the time he's messing about at the gym or going out with Mike Knox.'

'Is that all? So he's not a very attentive husband?'

'Well, you never know, of course.' She sipped her tea. 'But you hear things. Everyone has a different standard for what's acceptable, don't they.'

I blinked, not having to feign confusion this time. 'I don't really know what you mean.'

'Better not to say.' She leaned in. 'And then there's Brian.'

'Brian?'

'And Fleur. A lot going on there.'

'Fleur seems quite . . . possessive.'

'Well, she would want to be. Just keep an eye on how he behaves around the ladies.'

'Goodness,' I said. 'He seemed very friendly to me.'

'He would. To you.' Ruth sniffed. 'He won't be when it comes to your Josh.'

I could imagine that my Josh wouldn't warm to Brian either.

'Have you seen the Holdings yet?' Alan asked. 'Gillian and her son Gary. Poor Gillian is lost in her own world.'

'Dementia.' Ruth shot Alan another look. 'I worry about Alan getting it, but he keeps saying he's fine.'

'I am fine, for God's sake, woman. Stop fussing. Anyway, Gillian Holding isn't fine. You have to keep an eye out for her in case she wanders.'

'We will.' I sipped my tea. This counted as obscuring my interest in Judy, but I was also enjoying Ruth's insights into the secrets of Jellicoe Close. 'Is Gary the only carer looking after her?'

'Supposedly. But I don't think he does very much caring.' Ruth's mouth was tight with disapproval. 'He seems to spend all his time on his computer in the front room. He's always there, in the dark, all hours of the day and night. No wonder he doesn't notice her coming and going. And she's become very frail. I wonder if he's feeding her properly.'

'It can be difficult,' I said diplomatically, making a mental note to find out more. 'Very hard on Gary too, if he's the only carer. How old is he?'

'Thirty-something by now, I should think. But no girlfriends. Or boyfriends, actually, if it comes to that. It wouldn't be a problem if Gary fetched up with a boy on his arm but no. Nothing. He's never had anyone. No friends, either.'

'That's so sad.'

'It's a waste. And more to the point, a waste of a good education. He went to a very expensive school and then he got a place at Cambridge, but he didn't stick it out. They got rid of him.'

'Why?' I asked.

Alan made a noise which proved to be a gentle snore. Ruth sighed. 'He does doze off these days.'

'The sun is very hot. Let him sleep,' I said. 'You were saying about Gary? He was asked to leave Cambridge?'

'It was drugs, I think. Gillian never said directly, but we all thought it was drugs. He was always an odd boy. Very withdrawn. Not normal.' Ruth shuddered delicately. 'He goes out late at night – I see him sometimes, skulking around after dark.'

'It might be his only chance for any exercise,' I said, and she smiled.

'You're very naive, aren't you? Always thinking the best of people.'

'I like to think most people are basically good.' I wondered if I was laying it on too thick.

Ruth threw her head back and hooted derisively. 'Oh, when you've seen as much as we have, you'll change your tune, I promise you. People are capable of all kinds of bad behaviour, and some of them hide it better than others.'

19

'What did Ruth talk to you about?'

'Our sex life, mainly.'

'Really?' Derwent turned over the lemon sole he was frying, concentrating on the pan. Pippin was sitting at his feet, drooling hopefully, and I was perching on the kitchen counter. 'I hope you told them it was excellent.'

'I made no complaints. Just so you know, Ruth thinks we should start trying for a baby sooner rather than later. I'm not getting any younger.'

I'd expected him to laugh, but he didn't. The muscles around his eyes tightened a fraction, but that could have been because of the hot air rising from the frying pan.

'What did you find out about the neighbours?'

'What didn't I find out? She went through just about everyone in the cul de sac and assassinated their characters, but in the vaguest of terms. She doesn't like your pal Rhys Vonn.'

'Ruth's opinions are spot on. Why not?'

'Nicola is a basket case and Ruth blames him for being a crappy husband and father, despite being richer than God. She said something about everyone having different limits.'

'She said that?'

I thought for a second. 'No. She said, "Different standards for what's acceptable".'

Derwent twirled the spatula he was holding, considering it. 'Bum sex?'

'Not right now, thank you.'

He grinned. 'That's my kind of joke.'

'We're spending too much time together.'

'Please tell me you found out something about Judy Thwaites after all that. Did they say anything about the son?'

'He's in the middle of a mid-life crisis according to Ruth. He's in his fifties but he drives a fast car and is rude to Ruth. Ruth is very cat's-bum-mouth about Tom.'

Derwent swore under his breath. 'Why are we only finding out about Tom and his mates now? I don't want to sound like Rula Jacques but they did a shit job on investigating Davy's death. We'll have to find out more about him. I'll email Colin. Does this Tom visit often?'

'Every couple of weeks. He'll be at the summer barbecue, Ruth thought. Everyone in Jellicoe Close goes. They have it on the big green. All the different roads join in – each one has their own patch of grass. It sounds quite sweet.'

'I can't wait.' Derwent poked the fish. 'Did they say where he lives?'

'No. They just said that he was trouble.'

'Then I'll look forward to making his acquaintance. What else?'

'She confirmed that Judy sometimes has vulnerable people staying with her but I didn't get any further with that.'

'I suppose you were busy talking about shagging.'

'Not as much as Alan was hoping I would.' I kicked my heels against the cupboard. 'Hey, what happens if we run across some other kind of crime while we're here?'

Derwent put down the spatula and turned to face me. 'No.'

'What do you mean, no?'

'I mean don't complicate things. You're like a radar station scanning for illegal activity. We're not here to solve every problem in Jellicoe Close.'

'No, I know that.' My heels thudded into the cupboard again, twice, before he sighed.

'What is it?'

'As well as generally not liking Rhys Vonn, Ruth said something about his older daughter going missing. The one in the play. Camilla. She disappeared for a couple of days last year and wouldn't say where she'd been. But get this, the Vonns didn't want to involve the police.'

'That's interesting.'

'That's what I thought. The school made a fuss about her not turning up and then she was back and that was the end of it.'

Derwent was frowning. 'I'm troubled by the Vonns.'

'We'll get a closer look at them on Friday. At the play,' I reminded him.

'Oh yeah. The play. I can't wait. What else?'

'Brian – you know, Brian and Fleur from number 2 – is possibly unfaithful, but it might just be Ruth's nasty mind.'

Derwent slid the fish onto the plates with a flourish. 'Could you drain the broccoli?'

I jumped down and picked up the saucepan, reversing into him by accident as I stepped back to avoid Pippin who was everywhere underfoot.

'Careful.' Derwent turned me towards the sink. '*Can* you drain the broccoli, I should have said.'

'You got in my way.' I waited until the boiling water had sunk into the plughole with a gurgle. 'Basically if you listen to Ruth, no one in Jellicoe Close has a happy relationship except for her and Alan.'

'And us.'

'Well, that's depressing.'

There was a tiny pause. 'Why?'

'Do I have to remind you we're pretending to be madly in

128

love? Plus Alan has a constantly wandering eye.' I sighed. 'I'm beginning to think real love doesn't exist. Except for you and Melissa, I suppose.'

He had been spooning mashed potato onto the plates but he stopped so he could glower at me. Some people had boundaries; Derwent had electric fences. I took an involuntary step back.

'I didn't mean—'

'I know what you meant.'

'Sorry. Really. I shouldn't have said it. For one thing, we're supposed to be involved in one of the all-time great romances. Talking about your actual partner doesn't seem like a good idea.'

'Probably not.' He looked down, deep misery in the set of his mouth, and I realised with a pang of guilt that he was unhappy and I hadn't spotted it, which made me think he'd taken care to hide it from me. I'd been so caught up with my own problems lately that I hadn't even wondered if he had anything to worry about. He and Melissa had argued in the past about *his* past, and life was complicated for both of them, but they had stayed together. I had always assumed they were devoted to one another, though I'd never actually asked.

'Is everything OK?' I moved towards him and he stepped away smartly.

'Let's eat before it goes cold or Pippin steals it. Tell me what other depravity is going on in this harmless small town according to Ruth and Alan.'

The fences were up again. I didn't push it. We stayed with safe subjects over dinner, and afterwards I cleared the table, then opened my laptop.

'What are you doing?'

'Working?' I looked up. 'Georgia is keeping me in the loop on the Dawoud case.'

'Any reason you can't do that in the sitting room?'

'No, I suppose not.'

'It's just that if we're supposed to be – what was it? One of the all-time great romances – I think we should be in the same room.'

I gathered up my computer and phone and followed him into the sitting room, averting my eyes from the painting over the fireplace. In the soft lamplight it looked even more intimate: blushing, rounded thighs and tender skin.

'A lovely alcohol-free beer, because we're on duty but we're supposed to look as if we're not.' He set it down in front of me, then sat on the sofa, leaning back, remote control in his hand. A brief scan of the world outside and he returned his attention to the television, or so it might have seemed if you'd been looking in from outside. I knew he was aware of every leaf that fluttered outside the window, which reminded me of whatever movement I'd half-seen the day before. Nothing worth telling him about, I thought, and wondered why it had unsettled me so much.

This was a perfect opportunity to try to coax him into talking about his relationship, but talking about Melissa would be a quick way to ruin the evening, too. Patience, I counselled myself, and knew it was at least half cowardice. I shuffled closer to him and elbowed him. 'Arm.'

'So loving. So romantic.' He stretched his arm out along the back of the sofa so I could lean against him. I wriggled.

'I can't get comfortable.'

'If you've got scabies, we can probably swing by the pharmacy tomorrow.'

'I do not have scabies,' I said with dignity. 'I'm trying to find a way of sitting on this sofa that looks lovey-dovey, like I'm trained to.'

'I don't remember coaching you to behave as if you have an itchy and highly infectious skin disease.'

'I'm doing my best. If you'd chosen Georgia instead of me she'd be straddling you around now.'

130

I could feel him laughing quietly. 'Then how would I see the TV? Oh – Pippin, for God's sake.'

The dog had jumped up on the sofa beside him and was spinning in tiny, concentrated circles.

'His claws are so sharp,' Derwent complained, edging towards me. 'He's taking up the whole fucking sofa.'

'This is ridiculous. There's room for all three of us. Just sit properly.'

'As if I'm the problem here . . .' He tightened his arm around me, though, gathering me in so I could curl up against him.

'That's better.'

'Go on. Get on with work. I'll keep an eye on the road.'

I opened the files Georgia had sent me that day and settled down to read. It should have felt strange to be tucked up on the sofa with Josh Derwent, but after the first couple of sentences I was lost in concentration, barely aware of his breath stirring my hair or the slow, measured movement as he lifted his bottle of beer to his mouth. It was the television erupting into sirens that made me look up.

'Seriously? *Traffic Cops?* And does it have to be that loud? It's like being in the car with them.'

'It's my favourite.' He turned the volume down by one. 'I've seen this episide before. You're going to love the final pursuit.'

I went back to my reading, hopping back and forth between the documents and the email I was preparing to send Georgia. I didn't notice that Derwent was reading over my shoulder until he said, 'What's that?'

'Oh – Georgia's notes from an interview with one of Dawoud's colleagues. Another consultant at the hospital. His name is Dmitri Stefanidis. She finally got to talk to him today.'

'"DS – HD c/less",' Derwent read out, looking pained. 'Was she taking notes in crayon? What use is that?'

'I asked her for the notes. I don't think she realised it would be helpful to add a bit of context. What I suspect this means

131

is that Stefanidis thought Hassan Dawoud was careless. There was an open investigation into a patient who died – his family wanted to know if the treatment he'd received was appropriate. Dawoud was still practising though.'

'"HD s-abs, over-pr, arr.".' Derwent snorted. 'How are you supposed to decode this crap?'

'Luckily I speak Georgia. Dawoud was self-absorbed and over-privileged, Stefanidis thought. And arrogant. Stefanidis thought his colleague was a liability and didn't like working with him. But would he be so rude about him if he was responsible for killing him?'

'Never discount the double-bluff.'

'No.' I felt as if I was missing a key piece of information. You did get the full picture from Georgia but it came as a bag of jigsaw-puzzle pieces. I opened the next file.

'Witness statements?'

'Are you bored or something? Watch your programme.'

Sulking, Derwent eased himself down a few inches, spreading his legs to compensate, and I found myself squashed against the end of the sofa. My first instinct was to complain; my second was to see what he thought. He was good at this, after all.

'These are witness statements from the delivery drivers who called to Dawoud's house that day. The last one tried to deliver something at . . . let's see . . . 3.06 p.m.' I was speed-reading. 'He says he left a card. I wonder if we retrieved that from the house. If Dawoud had already left, the card should have been there.'

'What's the significance of the delivery time?'

'I'm trying to pin down a time of death to give us some idea of where he was when he died. At the moment we haven't nailed down either.'

'What are the options?'

'The house is the obvious place for him to be attacked, but there's no evidence of it at all.'

'What about his phone? Does that help to narrow down your time of death?'

'The last time he looked at it was about half an hour after the final delivery. Then he didn't pick up any more messages or take any calls or use the internet.'

'*After* the delivery?'

I nodded.

'Are you getting cell-site analysis for the phone?'

'We will, but it was sitting on the kitchen island when we searched the house. Either he left it there or the killer did.'

'Why would he leave it?'

'If he was meeting someone somewhere dodgy and he was afraid it might get nicked? Or if Cameron had some way of keeping an eye on where he was? All those find-my-phone apps are a jealous husband's best friend.'

'What if he was up to something illegal? He had a gym at his house so he was into his appearance, or his husband is. They have a big disposable income, Dawoud was over-privileged – it wouldn't shock me if he was into drugs of some kind or other.'

'He was a doctor.'

'So? Doesn't mean he didn't like to look a certain way, or that he wouldn't want his husband to look a certain way. Cameron's a big lad. There aren't many people who can keep up that kind of bulk without some help from pharmaceuticals.'

'I'd forgotten you'd seen him,' I said, and blushed, because the reason Derwent had been watching the interview was because he'd been checking up on me.

'He wouldn't want to source anything illegal through the proper channels. Get Georgia to find out if there were any signs of drug use at the PM. She could ask Cameron if he ever used any muscle-building drugs or if they were into chemsex parties. Dawoud could have been picking up some GHB and speed for the weekend. He'll kick off about her being homophobic but it's worth considering.'

'You're a genius.'

'Hardly.' He said it in a distracted way, his focus on the window rather than me or the TV.

'What's up?'

'Someone walked past the house.'

'It's not illegal.'

'That's his fourth time going past.'

'Description?' I kept my eyes on the screen, feeling distinctly unsettled, glad of Derwent's solid presence beside me. On the television a uniformed officer smashed a car window and dived in to drag out the driver, for no reason that I could see except that he wanted to show off for the cameras.

'White male, dark hair, thin build, bad posture. No one I've seen before.'

'Could be Gary Holding. Ruth said he wanders around at night.'

'The creepy son?'

'The full-time carer,' I said. 'I think it's the only time he feels he can leave her. People with dementia don't always sleep that much. It's possible she has a couple of hours in the evening where she's definitely out for the count and he can go out.'

'Or he likes looking in windows.' Derwent looked at me. 'Want to give him something to stare at?'

'I think he's seen quite enough,' I said firmly, and started typing my email to Georgia.

He walked along the railway embankment behind the houses as if he had the right to be there, because being furtive would attract attention. No one would remember seeing him, if they even looked out of their windows. Most of them never seemed to pay any attention to what was happening behind their houses, especially in the blue light before full, dark night, when people put lamps on and turned the world outside into a mystery.

He counted the houses: the first abandoned, overgrown, the garden parched from the summer heat. Paint had flaked on the ground where someone tried to get in through the locked back door, and he frowned. It wasn't him. He wouldn't make that kind of a mess. He made a note to take a closer look but not now, not when he had something else urgent on his mind. The next house had washing hanging on the line, stirring a little in the evening breeze. Lacy knickers and a matching bra beside a pair of boring pyjamas with a teddy on the front: green light, red light. In the upstairs bathroom, behind frosted glass, a peachy silhouette moved; she was getting into the shower. Another time, he might have stayed to watch, even though it held no novelty for him. This time he wasn't interested, but he took the mild frisson he felt and added it to the sharper hunger that was driving him.

And here was his target, the glass extension that gave him a perfect view into the kitchen, where the lights were on but – *fuck* – there was no one home. Not even the dog, the bane of his life, worse than any security light or alarm system. Nothing moved. His mood flipped from pleasant anticipation to rage, pure and simple. He moved back the way he had come, focused this time on the ground at his feet, where invisible hazards lurked in the twilight, especially when he was moving fast enough to raise his heart rate. He rounded the corner into the cul de sac and walked up the pavement, conscious of keeping his hands loose and relaxed instead of balled into fists. His back was wet with sweat, and under his arms.

They were sitting in the front room with the curtains pulled back, as if they *wanted* him to see them, watching television, though she had her computer on her lap. His arm was around her, pulling her against him. It was a controlling position, a dominant one, and as he thought that the man said something that made her laugh and duck her head, her cheeks flushed, as if she was embarrassed or aroused. The man reached for his drink and leaned back, a smug, stupid grin on his face, his attention on the television.

In the shadows outside, he tasted blood and realised he had chewed the side of his tongue, frustration and desire and rage making him lose control of himself.

There was someone coming towards him, he noticed with an electric thrill of fear, and he picked up his pace, made eye contact, smiled pleasantly, walked away, even though he would have given anything to stay.

20

Gardening wasn't one of my life skills but I wasn't prepared to admit that to Derwent. While he went out for a run the next day – because he was training hard in advance of the football match – he left me to tackle the enormous shrub that was brooding in the corner of Vanessa's front garden.

'What do you want me to do with it?'

'A little layering, maybe a fringe.' He looked up at me from where he was kneeling to tie his laces. 'Just hack a few chunks out of it so we can see the street properly.'

Easier said than done, it transpired. I had secateurs and a pruning saw and no idea how to handle the job. The shrub contained clouds of tiny mites that all seemed determined to find a refuge up my nose, and I was hot, and I hated the plant and Derwent more or less equally. I cut off what seemed like a vast pile of branches and took a step back to see that it looked exactly the same as before. If anything, taking some of the weight out of it had made the rest bushier.

A thud and a muttered curse from the front garden next door caught my attention.

'Are you OK?' I peered through the leaves to see Stephen Bollivant trying to lift a large rectangular item wrapped in layers of bubble wrap. Because of its width it had slid out of his grasp to balance on one point, and he was straining to get a better grip on it. 'Can I help?'

'Yeah. Thanks.' He waited while I dropped the pruning saw and jogged around to support one side of the package. The muscles in his arms were taut with effort and a patch of sweat darkened his polo shirt between the shoulder blades, which I understood as soon as I lifted my side.

'Wow, this is heavy.'

'It's a mirror. Very old. I just hope I haven't damaged the gilt.' He was running a hand over the bubble wrap on the corner, testing the edges to see if there was any give in it.

'Do you want to unwrap it to check?'

'Not if it's bad news. I'm taking it to a client's house. I shouldn't have tried to move it on my own but my usual guy isn't free this morning and I thought I could get it into the van by myself.'

I looked around to see a small blue Ford Transit parked at the kerb. 'That van? I'll give you a hand.'

He looked surprised but muttered, 'Thanks.'

He was shy, I remembered, as for the next couple of minutes we manoeuvred the mirror in silence, apart from an occasional mumbled command from him. I eyed him covertly. He had fair hair and grey eyes and the kind of complexion that flushed easily, despite his tan. The van was spotless. It was equipped with fabric webbing to hold the contents securely in place, like a removals lorry. He spent a long time tightening the straps and testing the buckles to make sure the mirror wouldn't move as he drove.

'Bit late to be careful.' He jumped out of the van. 'But it would be stupid to crack the glass on a two-mile journey now if it survived the fall earlier.'

'It looks as if you did a good job of wrapping it up. You might have got away with it.'

'Hope so.' He ran a hand over his head, worried. 'The frame would be a pain to repair but I could do it if it's just cracked.

The glass is the original and it's literally irreplaceable. If that went, I'd have to charge them a tenth of what they've agreed to pay, and that's assuming they'd want it.'

'I see why you were so concerned with securing it.'

'Yeah.' He looked at me, uncertain. 'Er. Thanks for the help . . .'

'Sorry, I should have introduced myself. I'm Maeve. House-sitting for Vanessa. Is this you?' I gestured at the side of the van where gold script read Bollivant Antiques.

'Yes. My business. Stephen.'

'Nice to meet you.' I smiled. 'Do you have a shop to go with the van?'

'I work from home. I keep anything portable here. Large items go into storage until they're needed.'

'Needed?'

'I work mainly with professional interior designers who know what they want. I source things for them on commission and buy the odd item on spec if I like it.'

'Wow. That's amazing.'

'It's a living.' He gave me an awkward half-smile to take the edge off his words.

'You must love antiques.'

'I do.' He looked down at his feet, unable to maintain eye contact. 'I started out looking for things when I was a teenager at car boot sales and in charity shops. I made a couple of lucky buys and that was it. Hooked.'

'Will you be able to unload the mirror at the other end? Because if it's just a couple of miles away I could come along.' I shoved my hands in the pockets of my shorts and stood on the side of one foot, the picture of diffidence. 'I really want any excuse at all to stop gardening.'

'Is that what you were doing?' He turned to look at the shrub.

'More like vandalism. Vanessa said I could cut it back a bit and I thought I'd give it a go, but it's so hot today.' I fanned myself with a limp hand.

'Moving furniture is much less effort.' There was a hint of humour in his voice for the first time.

I laughed. 'Maybe not, on reflection.'

'Well, it's very kind of you but there should be people at the other end who can help me.' He hesitated. 'There is actually one more piece in the house that I'd like to take. It's not heavy but it's fragile – a two-person job.'

'Lead the way.' I followed him into the house. If I hadn't known he was in the business, I would have thought it was slightly over-furnished, but it didn't have the junk-shop feel I'd expected. He hurried me past the sitting room so I had just enough time to form a lightning impression of a room filled with gilt-framed paintings and Chinese porcelain, the warm glow of mahogany and the soft patina of brass. The walls were painted dark colours – blues, greens and a rich purple – and the air was scented with proper beeswax furniture polish. In the hallway, paintings were stacked against the walls five or six deep and I edged past, careful not to kick anything. The kitchen was a large room but old-fashioned in style, with a scrubbed pine table at the centre and a mismatched collection of dressers displaying a great number of plates in various sizes and colours. A navy-blue Aga stood against one wall. I thought it would be a cosy space in winter. Currently the back door was closed, slightly to my relief, since the German shepherd was lying on the lawn. The dog looked friendly enough but it was a lot bigger than Pippin, and I was in its home.

'This is the piece I want to move.' Bollivant indicated a long bubble-wrapped package that was lying on the floor.

'What is it?'

'It's a candelabrum on a stand. Over seven feet.'

'Wow. The place you're furnishing must be a Gothic mansion.'

'Pretty much. It's owned by a rock star.' He flashed a surprisingly charming smile at me. 'He hasn't got much taste but his decorator does.'

'And it pays the bills,' I said.

'Very much so.' He lifted the wider end of the package. 'It's light but it's really annoying to move. If you could take the base . . .'

I helped to manoeuvre the package through the house and out of the front door, which involved negotiating a fairly awkward turn by the stairs. The bubble wrap was slippery under my fingers and I was petrified I'd drop the candelabrum or whack it into a door frame. Whatever the rock star was paying, I was unlikely to be able to match it on my salary. When it was safely lodged in the back of the van, and tied in place like the mirror, I heaved a sigh of relief.

'Don't take this the wrong way but that's far too much stress for a Thursday morning.'

He smiled to himself as he slammed the van doors. 'And I was just about to offer you a job.'

'Putting the new neighbour to work already?' Rhys Vonn's voice was loud, and I hadn't heard him approaching so I jumped out of my skin. Stephen's voice was toneless when he replied, but I had the impression he was furious.

'She was just helping me out.'

'I bet she was.' Rhys was buckling his cycle helmet. He grinned at me. 'Wish I could think of a way for you to help *me* out.'

I tilted my head to one side like a confused dog. 'I don't mind helping anyone who needs it, but I thought you didn't work? I mean, that's what I've heard.'

'Who's been talking about me behind my back?' He was laughing.

I glanced across at Ruth and Alan's house and then bit my lip as I looked back at him. 'I – I shouldn't say.'

'Don't worry, sweetheart. I can guess. What did you have her doing for you, Steve? Polishing your brasses? Dusting your knobs?'

Bollivant's face was flaming. 'Moving some furniture.'

'A likely story.'

'What's going on?' Mike Knox was wheeling his bike down his drive. He crossed the road, nodded to me and said, 'Hello, Stephen. All right?'

'Not bad.' It was a mutter. I suddenly felt very sorry for Stephen, who was staring at the ground. Mike Knox was taller than Rhys and had dark hair that was turning silver at the temples. He was more reserved but in his own way I thought he was as confident as his louder neighbour. He saw me looking at his bike.

'You probably think none of us do any work around here. I've got a day off – staff training.'

'It's a lovely day for a bike ride. Are you going far?'

'Just an easy fifty k,' Rhys said casually. 'There or thereabouts. Not too many hills either.'

'Easy,' I repeated, not having to pretend to look appalled. 'I'd die.'

'You get used to it. You should come out with us sometime. You could borrow Nicola's bike. She never uses it any more.'

'I'd like that,' I lied.

'And I'd like to watch you.' His eyes went from my face to my feet and back again, slowly and insolently. I managed not to shudder, but it was close.

'Come on.' Mike checked his watch. 'We'd better get a move on if I'm going to be back in time to do the school run.'

The two men cycled off, Rhys staring at me for a little too long as he went past.

'Don't let him upset you.'

I'd almost forgotten Stephen was there. His face was red but this time I thought it was anger rather than awkwardness.

'Who? Rhys? He didn't, really.'

'He's a *shit*.' The words slid out from between clenched teeth. 'Stay away from him.'

'Why?'

Stephen didn't take the bait. He was watching a figure

jogging out of the lane that led to the Holmwood: Derwent, returning.

'I'd better get a move on.' He felt for his van keys. 'Thanks for the help. Good luck with the gardening.'

He whipped into the van and shut the door on me halfway through my goodbye. The engine started immediately and he drove away at speed.

'All right?' Derwent had crossed the road. His top was soaking but he picked up the front of it to wipe his face.

I cringed. 'Don't come near me.'

He held out his arms. 'Come on, bring it in. Sweat doesn't smell when it's fresh.'

'Whoever told you that was lying.'

He grinned. 'What did I miss?'

'I've decided I don't like Rhys Vonn either, and I'm not too sure about Mike Knox.' I told him about the bike riders and his expression darkened as he leaned into a stretch.

'Wankers. What about him?' He nodded at Stephen Bollivant's house. 'What were you doing with him?'

'Helping with some furniture he was moving from his house to his van.'

'You should know better than that.'

'What's that supposed to mean?'

'I'm going to have a shower and then we can have a little talk about Ted Bundy. It's a classic move. "Oh, I can't carry this furniture. If only there was someone to help me." I knew he was up to something from the way he ran off as soon as I showed up.'

'Stephen Bollivant is not a serial killer,' I protested. 'He's just shy.'

Derwent shook his head. 'They said that sort of thing about Bundy too.'

143

21

I walked the short distance into West Idleford town centre with Pippin in the afternoon, despite the heat, and did a survey of the local shops. There was a grocery store that was heavy on luxury goods and light on the basics. I bought a strawberry ice cream from their extensive display of Italian gelato, and a dog ice cream for Pippin. We sat and ate them on a bench with varying degrees of dignity. Most of the other shops sold designer clothing, wine or lighting. Every second commercial space was a beauty salon or a hairdresser's; grooming was clearly very important. I could do with a pedicure, I thought, wiggling my toes inside my trainers. I would have to give in and wear sandals at some stage and I couldn't go out with naked toenails; it wouldn't match my image at all. After the ice cream I allowed myself a solid twenty-minute think about the Dawoud case which got me not very much further. Hassan Dawoud's life was still a mystery to me and until I understood him, I suspected I wasn't going to be able to make sense of his death.

Still in a thoughtful mood, I gathered up Pippin and began to make my way back, stopping off in the pharmacy for some Epsom salts. The route took me past the library, a pretty round building with Doric columns supporting a small portico. Two people were struggling through the doorway: an older woman and a younger man who was taking most of her weight. I spotted brown lace-up brogues on the woman's feet. A floral-patterned nightie stuck out from under the unseasonably warm cardigan she wore. Gillian Holding, I guessed, which meant the man with her must be Gary. I thought of Derwent's description of the man he'd seen walking past the house the previous night. Dark hair with a receding hairline, slim build. Bad posture, Derwent had said, but it was hard to tell since he was leaning towards his mother solicitously.

I drifted across the road and tied Pippin up in the shade of the portico, beside a water bowl the library staff had left out for passing dogs. He drank noisily and then sat down, looking as if he was glad of a rest. I pushed open the door and stepped into the cool, surprisingly large room that smelled of old books and modern technology. Bookshelves stood in spokes around a central table with computers on it. There was an area of low, comfortable seating near the librarian's desk and Gillian Holding was sitting there while her son dealt with the librarian. Gillian's hands were folded on her lap, her fingers working anxiously around one another. Her hair was iron grey and hadn't been brushed that day, I thought, noticing the way it stuck out at odd angles. I sat down on the adjoining sofa and picked up one of the newspapers from the table, trying to appear as if I was absorbed in it.

'Did she enjoy the last ones?' the librarian was asking. She held a handful of audiobooks that she was shuffling through as she spoke.

'It's hard to tell. She listened to this one – the George Eliot – but I don't know if it was just because she liked the narrator's voice.' Gary Holding had a slow, deep voice himself. It sounded rusty, as if he rarely got the chance to speak. 'It used to be a favourite of hers. Maybe there was some familiarity to it.'

'I'm glad she listened to it anyway.' The librarian was a smart fair-haired woman in her fifties with a brisk manner. 'I've set aside a couple that I thought she would like –

145

Persuasion, which is such a beautiful story, and a Georgette Heyer that's very amusing. It's actually one of my favourites.'

If that was intended to seed a conversation, it fell on stony ground. Gary shrugged without enthusiasm. 'Worth a try, I suppose.'

'I could see if the narrator of *Middlemarch* has recorded any other audiobooks, in case it was the voice . . .'

'Don't go to any trouble.' He shifted his weight, as if he was suppressing impatience. 'I don't know if she takes any of it in really. It's just better than silence. She doesn't like having the television on any more.'

'Don't blame her. Load of rubbish on it most of the time. Or depressing ads. Nothing but funerals and life insurance and charities looking for money to spend on more TV ads. Give me a good book any day.' The librarian laughed. 'I would say that, though, wouldn't I?'

He checked his watch. 'I should be getting her back home. She doesn't like being out for too long.'

'I'll just get the books sorted out for you.'

The librarian took the library card he handed her and headed off to the office behind the desk. I thought she was extraordinarily patient and that Gary Holding was downright rude. He didn't seem shy, unlike Stephen Bollivant – more irritable, as if he had somewhere better to be. He turned away and picked a book off the shelf, losing himself in it immediately.

I glanced around to see Mrs Holding disappearing through the door. I gave a yelp, jumped up and hurried after her. I had thought she was barely able to walk but she was moving with considerable speed, her shoes slapping the pavement, loose on her feet. When I caught up with her I hesitated. It wasn't exactly appropriate to grab hold of her. I settled for stepping in front of her.

'I think your son is waiting for you in the library. Shall we go back and find him?'

'No.' She spoke with vigour, her eyes fixed on the middle

146

distance rather than me. A smell rose from her clothes: the old-dog odour of the homeless, as if what she wore had got damp and dried on her body many times. The nightie was stained down the front with something greenish. It didn't look as if the spill had happened recently. 'I need to go home.'

'I'm sure Gary will take you there. Actually, we can go together. I'm living in Jellicoe Close at the moment, minding a dog for one of your neighbours – Vanessa?' I was gabbling, desperately hoping Gary Holding would appear, the rest of my attention on his mother. She was trying to get past me while I walked backwards. How long did it take to put a book back on the shelf and walk outside? He must have heard me. 'I've got to get the dog. He's tied up at the library. Why don't you come back with me to get him?'

'I need to go home,' she said. 'It's too dangerous if no one is there.'

'I'm sure the house is locked up very safely.'

'I need to watch out for the devil.'

'The devil,' I repeated. 'Well, I think—'

'He has a human face and a human form that hides him from everyone but me.' Her voice was a mutter. 'I know him. I see him. I see what he does.'

Gary Holding emerged into the sunlight at last, shading his eyes. He was looking in the wrong direction. His stomach was domed under his faded Metallica T-shirt despite his arms and legs being like sticks. I raised a hand and waved, trying to attract his attention.

'What does the devil do?' I asked, trying to hold Gillian's interest. If she was talking to me, she wasn't walking off.

'He takes the girl into the shadows to hurt her.'

That got my attention. 'The girl?'

'From . . .' she shook her head. 'I can't . . . but I know her. He wants her.' Her hand found my arm and gripped it with surprising strength. Her fingernails were long and filthy. 'He wants to *consume* her. I have to keep watch.'

'At the window,' I guessed.

Gary had finally spotted his mother. He walked after us, not hurrying.

'Yessss.' She sounded relieved.

'And that's why you don't like the television any more.'

'I have to watch.' She released her grip on me as Gary approached.

'Sorry. My mother wanders off.' He took hold of her arm and she went limp, all her weight on him. 'For God's sake, stand up.' To me, he said, 'She does this. She won't cooperate.' Up close Gary had patchy stubble on his cheeks and neck where he hadn't bothered to shave properly. His nostrils flared when he talked and he had the pallor of someone who spent most of their time indoors.

'She said she wanted to go home. She said she has to watch for someone?'

He looked bored. 'That's what she says all the time. It's rubbish. She's anxious about everything now but there's no reason for it, so she constructs these narratives to explain it. Apparently it's not uncommon in dementia sufferers. The trouble is that she sounds quite lucid a lot of the time. It's only if you know her that you realise it's total rubbish.'

'She said there was one person in particular—'

'The devil? I haven't seen him, I'm afraid. Although depending on the day it might be me. It might even be you.'

'Oh,' I said. 'Oh well. I'm heading back to Jellicoe Close. We could walk together.'

He seemed discomfited. 'How did you know we live there?'

I introduced myself properly. 'Ruth told me about your mum.'

'I bet she did.'

'Bitch,' Gillian Holding spat, which shocked me. 'And the other one.'

'Alan?'

'She means Judy. They never got on.' He shook his head.

148

'Sorry if I should have recognised you. I don't always. I have a bit of face blindness. If I see someone out of context, forget it.'

'It can be difficult,' I said diplomatically. 'If I can just run back and get Pippin . . .'

'You'll catch up. We won't be making much progress.'

He was really, truly uncharming, I thought, jogging back to where Pippin was sleeping, his head on his paws. Gary couldn't have many opportunities to talk to people but he was acting as if I was imposing myself on him.

Which I was, admittedly. I dragged a not-totally-compliant Pippin along the pavement until we were beside the Holdings again.

'Should I walk on this side, Mrs Holding? You can lean on me if you want.'

'She won't. She only leans on me.' Gary talked about her as if she couldn't hear him. 'Passive resistance. It's annoying.'

'Do you have any help with her?'

'No.'

'Could the GP help arrange something? It's a lot for you to do by yourself.'

'He'd want to put her in a home. We'd have to sell the house to pay for it.'

And you'd end up with nothing, and nowhere to live, I filled in silently. Worth the effort to look after her for a bit longer, maybe. What would I do in the same situation?

Get a job, came the answer. If Gary was trapped, it was a prison of his own making. But what I said was, 'You can't look after her all the time.'

'I do though.' Almost to himself, he said, 'You don't know what you can do until you have to.'

'Does she sleep well?'

'No.'

'When do you get out by yourself?'

'I don't.' He looked past his mother so he could see me, a

149

sardonic expression on his face. 'You ask a lot of questions, don't you?'

'Sorry. I sound really nosy.' I gave a little laugh. 'I thought I saw you last night, walking up and down in the street.'

'Not me,' he said easily. 'I was at home all night.'

'We don't like nosy people,' Gillian announced. 'We don't like people who poke their noses into our business.'

'Sometimes they're trying to help though,' I tried.

'They can fuck off.'

Gary laughed softly. 'That told you, didn't it?'

'I'm sorry. I didn't mean to pry.'

'No, you probably didn't.' He sighed. 'We get a lot of do-gooders trying to help. Ruth is always sniffing around. She loves seeing Mum like this. She always envied her – Mum is younger and she used to be beautiful, if you can imagine that. After my dad died, and when I came back from university, Ruth was always coming round. She said she was there to help but I always thought she was just soaking up the misery. I'm glad Mum doesn't really know what's going on any more. I try to make sure she gets dressed and washes and everything but it's hard. She doesn't want to, a lot of the time, and I get tired.'

'I'm sure you do,' I said with real sympathy.

'She doesn't like wearing shoes because they hurt her feet but she'll wear Dad's old ones. She insisted on wearing the cardigan today. I do my best.' He rubbed his eyes. 'I don't know why I'm telling you all this. You're a good listener.'

'I do understand, a bit. We went through the same thing with my grandmother,' I lied. A large part of my time as a response officer had involved locating vulnerable dementia patients who had wandered away from their homes. I knew very well the strain that carers experienced.

We were turning into Jellicoe Close now, and both Pippin and Mrs Holding picked up their pace. Mrs Holding was murmuring something under her breath, over and over again.

150

'What's she saying?'

'"It's not safe. It's not safe."' He sighed. 'The usual.'

'It's not,' she said clearly. 'She should go away.'

'Does she mean me?'

The hand landed on my arm again, her nails digging into my skin. She was looking straight at me, her eyes bright. 'Go. Now. If you stay, you'll be sorry.'

'Mrs Holding—' I began, but the brief moment of lucidity was gone. She began singing something, her breathing laboured.

Gary sighed again. 'Come on, Mother. Let's get you home.'

I watched their halting progress up the street, and despite the warmth of the day, I shivered. Maybe it was because I knew there was something dark underlying the expensive perfection of West Idleford, but I couldn't discount Gillian Holding's words as easily as her son did.

He would have liked a bit more time to prepare before he got so close to her, but one of his skills – along with self-discipline – was knowing when to take advantage of an unexpected opportunity. Some of the things he'd got away with amazed him. It made him feel as if he was meant to be doing these things, as if it belonged to some kind of cosmic pattern. God's plan.

Bullshit, he thought, but it amused him to imagine everything was all preordained: there wasn't a culture in history that didn't believe in some kind of fate or great all-knowing being pulling the strings. The latest version was the belief that all life was a computer simulation, which just showed the extreme limitations of the human imagination: swap out computers for the Greek gods and it's the same thing all over again. From mountain-dwelling deities to a handful of wires in a few millennia, but the instinct to worship was the same, the driving desire to hand over responsibility for his mistakes to something that he couldn't understand, something bigger and wiser than he could possibly imagine.

And sometimes he did feel as if something was moving him, as if he was powerless to resist. Right and wrong didn't have any meaning any more. There was what he wanted and what stood in his way. There was winning and losing.

And he didn't lose.

22

I was already bolt upright by the time I realised I was awake. My heart was thumping in response to the adrenalin flooding into my body. A thin sheen of sweat glossed my skin. A dream, I rationalised, but I wasn't convinced that was right and I knew I wouldn't sleep until I had checked it out properly. I pushed back the covers. Pippin was barking downstairs, muffled behind the door, but that wasn't unusual. I'd noticed I was starting to tune it out. He was campaigning to be allowed to sleep with Derwent, so far without success.

Then the sound that had disturbed me came again: three loud knocks on the front door, hollow-sounding blows made with the side of a fist. Pippin got louder, furious. I put the light on and grabbed a sweatshirt as I squinted at the clock on my phone – four minutes past two.

Derwent had been faster than me to get moving. I heard him rattle down the stairs while I was pulling the sweatshirt over my head, and I reached the upstairs hallway at the same time as he opened the front door.

'Sorry to bother you.' The voice was strained and I didn't realise who it was until I crept down a few steps, crouching so I could see the person at the door. Gary Holding's face was white and his hair was all over the place. His clothes were rumpled, as if he had been sleeping in them.

'What's going on?' Derwent demanded.

'It's my m-mother.'

I came down another step and he noticed me. He leaned sideways, cutting Derwent out of the conversation.

'I know it's the middle of the night but you said you didn't mind helping. It's Mum. She's g-gone. I've tried to look in the usual places but there's no sign of her.'

'I'll help you look for her.'

'We both will.' Derwent sidestepped so he was very firmly between me and Gary Holding again. 'How long has she been gone?'

'I was asleep. I don't know when she got out.'

It wasn't my imagination: Gary was sulky when he spoke to Derwent. Intimidated, I assumed. Being woken up in the middle of the night hadn't done much for Derwent's mood, and I knew the expression that would be on his face as a result.

'Is anyone else looking for her?' Derwent asked. 'The police?'

'I haven't called them yet.'

'You should. And see if you can get anyone else to help search for her. Three of us won't be much good if you don't know how far she's gone or when she left.'

'Was she on foot?' I asked.

'Yes, I keep the car keys locked away. She hasn't tried to drive anywhere for a couple of years but you never know. She doesn't have a licence any more, obviously.'

'Where does she like to go?'

He looked woebegone. 'She could be anywhere, really. The shops . . . she likes the woods, too.'

'She won't be easy to find if she's in the woods,' Derwent said. 'Look, you really need to let the police know. She's a high-risk missing person – they'll try to respond quickly. If you're lucky they might be able to get a helicopter to take a pass over the woods.'

Gary quailed. 'Do you think it will come to that?'

'I don't know. This has happened before, hasn't it? How did that end?'

'She turned up. She usually makes her way home.'

So why are you on our doorstep? I could practically hear Derwent thinking it.

'I just don't want to cause unnecessary trouble,' Gary was bleating.

'Go and call the police. Tell them everything you've told us. We'll meet you outside in ten minutes. Knock on doors – the more the merrier.'

'Couldn't we just keep this between us?' Gary passed his tongue over his lips, blinking rapidly. 'I'm sure we could manage—'

'What about the street WhatsApp group?' I said helpfully. 'If you don't want to knock on doors I could put a message on it and see if anyone responds.'

'Good idea, Maeve. See you in ten minutes, Gary. Or five. Five would be better.' Derwent shut the door on Gary's protests. He turned to glare at me. I opened my eyes wide.

'What did I do?'

'You made him think you were nice.'

'I am nice.'

'Too nice.' Derwent shook his head. 'As if I was going to let him wander around alone with you in the dark. Is his mother even missing? This is probably an excuse to be alone with you. She's probably tied up in her bedroom. Or his.'

'Josh!'

'It would make sense, though, wouldn't it?'

I was writing the message for the WhatsApp group. 'You're going to have to be careful. You sounded like a cop when you were talking to Gary.'

'That's because I'd quite like to turn him over. I bet his computers are worth a look.'

'Now who's looking for other crimes? But seriously, keep

an eye on what you're saying and how you're saying it. We have to blend in.'

'If this woman is in danger, and the local force can't send a unit straight away . . .'

'Then we're it. I know. But be subtle about it. I'm going to get dressed.' I pulled the sweatshirt down over my pyjama shorts as I made my way back up the stairs, aware that Derwent was right behind me.

'Wear something you can tuck into your socks, and a top with long sleeves,' he said. 'If we have to go hacking through the undergrowth in the Holmwood you'll be cut to ribbons.'

'I'll see what I can find.'

'And as an added bonus it might put Gary off.'

A collection of people had gathered at the centre of the cul de sac when we came out, carrying torches and our phones, and I was surprised to see how many people had responded to the WhatsApp message. Rhys Vonn was there in a hoodie and tracksuit bottoms, jumping from foot to foot with an excess of energy. Mike Knox looked aloof beside him, a still point in the melee. Judy was standing with Alan, who was wearing a very extrovert paisley dressing gown that was threatening to fall open at any moment. I couldn't imagine what either of them thought they could contribute, but Alan at least was probably on a fact-gathering mission. Ruth wouldn't want to miss any of the drama but she couldn't pretend she was fit enough to search the area. Judy was wearing a fluorescent tabard and carrying a first-aid kit. Brian and Fleur were standing a little distance from the main group. Brian raised his hand and smiled when he saw us making our way towards them, unaware that Fleur was scowling at him.

'One of your fans?' Derwent said out of the corner of his mouth.

I pretended to cough to hide what I was saying. 'Fleur.'

'Ah.'

Stephen Bollivant's dog was straining at the end of its lead, causing him to curse and take a couple of involuntary steps down the road.

'That dog looks useful,' Derwent observed. 'Has he caught her scent?'

'He's not looking for her yet.' Effort was making Stephen sound breathless. 'He just wants to go for a run.'

'Typical. I didn't even bother bringing Pippin. If we were looking for a sausage roll, he might be helpful, but otherwise he'll just get in the way.'

Stephen gave him a tight smile. 'Klaus might be more of a liability than anything but I didn't want to leave him behind.'

Rhys Vonn clapped his hands. 'Who's in charge?' He was clearly about to volunteer, but Brian stepped forward.

'We should split up into groups. We need a map of the area that we can divide into sections and search methodically.'

'You sound as if you know what you're doing,' Derwent said. I picked up an undertone of relief that he wasn't going to have to take charge.

'I used to volunteer with mountain rescue when I lived in the US.' He put out his hand. 'Brian.'

'Good to meet you. Josh.'

'This isn't exactly mountain terrain,' Rhys Vonn began, and walked into a glower from Derwent that made him fall silent.

'Right, Brian's in charge,' Derwent said. 'What about the police?'

'They'll send someone as soon as they can.' Gary held out his hands, helpless. 'They're overstretched, the lady said.'

'Underfunded. They closed the police station here four years ago.' Alan sniffed. 'We're sitting ducks for burglars and the like.'

'First things first,' Brian said. 'Are we absolutely certain Mrs Holding isn't in the house?'

'I looked. There isn't really anywhere she could be,' Gary said.

'We could look again.' That was Derwent and I shot him a warning glance; he was drawing attention to himself.

'Maybe you could do it?' Brian was looking at Judy and Alan, who nodded self-importantly.

'Good idea.'

'I'm first-aid trained,' Judy said, rattling the box. 'I used to be a nurse. If she needs any treatment I can help.'

'I don't think—' Gary began.

'It's a good idea.' Rhys Vonn had been quiet for long enough. 'No harm in making sure, Gary. She could be in your garden. You have no idea where she is, you said. You don't know when she left.'

'No, but—'

'We need to look everywhere.' He rolled on the balls of his feet, chewing a tiny piece of gum, and I wondered if he'd taken the coke to wake himself up or if it was a standard Thursday night around the Vonns' house.

'Organise into pairs,' Brian said, and instantly there was a hubbub as everyone started to discuss it animatedly.

I hadn't been aware of him moving but Gary was beside me. 'Maeve, we could look together. I think that would be very sensible. I think we'd have a good chance of finding her.' His eyes were wide, too much white showing, and I noticed he was trembling with tension, or excitement, or both.

I wouldn't walk to my front door with you. I hoped revulsion wasn't showing on my face.

Derwent cupped his hands around his mouth and yelled, 'Shut up.' When a slightly shocked silence fell, he said, 'This isn't about picking your favourite person for a night-time stroll. This is about making the best use of our resources. The Holmwood is a likely place for her to be, so we need a couple of teams to go there.' He pointed at Stephen Bollivant. 'You know it, don't you? And I've been running there for the past couple of days. We could go together.'

'I know it well too,' Mike Knox said.

'We can cover the south end,' Rhys suggested. 'You two and the dog can do the north. It's more overgrown.'

Derwent nodded. 'Brian?'

'I want to search around the lake. I'll go with Mike and Rhys.'

'Brian,' Fleur began, grabbing at his arm, but he shook her off.

'You and Maeve should go together – Fleur, isn't it?' Derwent said. 'Check around this area. The back gardens. There's that path that runs around behind the houses, isn't there?'

'She said something about the shadows when I saw her earlier,' I said. 'She was worried about what she could see from her house.'

'Don't blame her.' Rhys laughed loudly. 'You never know what you'll come across around here.'

'What about me?' Gary's voice quavered. 'What should I do?'

'You need to stay here until the cops come. You're the point of contact for them.' Derwent turned away, dismissing him, and I saw a look of absolute fury cross Gary's face.

'You know, if we do find your mother she might not want to come with us,' I said, remembering how she had behaved outside the library. 'If you could stay here, we can call you and get you to come to wherever she is. If you're searching too we might not be able to get hold of you.'

'Good point,' Mike Knox said and I smiled at him, grateful for the support.

'OK.' Brian had his phone in his hands. 'We've got a map of the area. Let's all make sure we know where we're going.'

Everyone clustered around to see the map on the tiny screen, discussing it with their search partners. I didn't attempt to make conversation with Fleur. She was standing on her own and looked as if she was on the verge of tears.

I wasn't *that* bad.

159

'Keep in contact with one another and with Gary,' Brian said. 'Don't wander away from your search partner. If you see anything like clothing or any kind of clue, let us all know.'

'Use the street's WhatsApp group,' Mike said. 'Then we'll all see it.'

'Does everyone know what they have to do?' Brian said, looking around. 'Yes? Then let's get going.'

23

As the search groups headed off in different directions, Fleur and I were left standing in silence, staring at one another.

'Where do you want to start?' I asked, given that she was on home territory.

She shrugged. 'No idea, really. Where do you think?'

'Well, we've got to cover the whole area around Jellicoe Close. There's the pathway behind the houses, isn't there? And the gardens. We could start with the front gardens.'

'If you want.'

She was entirely listless, as if she didn't see the point in the search.

'Do you have a torch?'

'Yeah.' She showed me a small torch that was going to be slightly more useful than a flickering candle, but only just. Mine would be as bright as stadium lights in comparison.

'Great,' I said. 'I was going to suggest we share out the gardens between us but on second thoughts let's look together. Two sets of eyes are better than one.'

She shrugged and turned to walk beside me. I shortened my stride, trying to match hers, and only succeeded in clashing elbows.

'Sorry.'

'It's OK.'

'Are *you* OK?' I asked, abandoning subtlety. 'I know it's the middle of the night, but—'

'I don't mind that.' She sighed. 'It's fine. It's nothing.'

'I just thought – if I'd done something wrong—'

'You?' She gave a loud, theatrical laugh. 'It's not about you, I promise.'

Then why are you being such a bitch? I relieved my feelings by gripping my torch so hard that the rubberised casing creaked in protest. 'OK. Let's start here, then.'

The garden of number 1 was hugely overgrown and full of spider's webs, which I discovered by walking into one. Fleur helped me to brush the strands of the web out of my hair as I rubbed my face.

'That is just the worst thing.' I was shuddering.

'This place hasn't been touched for a long time.' Fleur seemed to have brightened up a bit now that something bad had happened to me. 'No one has lived here for ages and ages. I don't know who owns it. The back garden is even worse.'

I winced, pulling my sweatshirt sleeve over my hand to protect it from some enormous thistles. 'I should have worn gardening gloves.'

Fleur stepped on the thistles, tramping them down so I could shine my torch into the hollow beyond them in the dark shade of a vast hydrangea.

'Thanks. That's really helpful.'

'I'm not sure it is. She couldn't have got past the thistles without breaking the stems.'

She was right and yet I'd been on searches that ended in much more unlikely places, where people had squirrelled their way into impossible holes and corners. The last place you'd think to look was the best place to hide, after all. Unfortunately I couldn't tell Fleur that without giving myself away.

'Let's just search everywhere. Then when they come back and ask, we can be absolutely sure we haven't missed her.'

Silence from Fleur, which I took to be disagreement, but she moved around the garden beside me and helped to hold back branches. When I stepped on a paving stone that tipped so that I pitched forward, she grabbed my arm and supported me until I had my balance.

'Careful.'

'I'm trying to be. This place is boobytrapped.'

'Our house was like this when we bought it.'

'Really?' The second house in the close was neat now, the grass mowed to velvety fuzz, the driveway weed-free and power-hosed to an antiseptic standard of cleanliness.

'We put everything into it.' She gave another laugh, this one just as forced. 'Our forever home.'

'I'm not a big believer in the concept of a forever home.' I was peering behind a rainwater butt. 'Places suit you for different times in your life. If a house isn't working for you any more, you should move on.'

'Where do you live usually?'

'In a flat in London.'

'Renting?'

'Josh owns it.' *And doesn't live there but let's gloss over that.*

'You should get yourself some equity in the place. Don't pay rent to your boyfriend. If you break up, he's made money off your relationship and you'll have nothing to show for it as well as nowhere to go.'

'OK.' She was right but it was an uncompromisingly trans-actional view of relationships. I tried to imagine negotiating a share in the equity of a boyfriend's home in the first flush of romantic passion, and failed. Then again, I didn't have a brick of property to call my own. Maybe if I had treated my relationships as business deals I would have done better. 'It's a tough conversation to have though. Most people don't want to think about breaking up when they're moving in together.'

'Most people need to think again. Money and love don't

163

go together.' She shrugged. 'If your boyfriend – Josh, is it? – doesn't want to cut you in on the flat then you shouldn't stay in a relationship with him. It's a good test of whether he's using you or if he really cares about you and wants the best for you.'

'That hadn't even occurred to me,' I said truthfully.

'Women aren't supposed to be businesslike about money and they always get screwed.'

'Always?'

She rolled her eyes and walked away. I followed her obediently to the next garden, which was hers and clearly empty.

By mutual silent consent we confined our conversation to the search and whether there was something behind that car (there wasn't) and actually whose car was that (it belonged to Judy's son Tom, which caught my attention).

I played my torch over the back of it, memorising the licence plate. It was a silver-grey Mercedes estate, two years old, muddy around the wheels but high end.

'I thought he was coming next weekend.'

'He probably is. He drops by now and then. He travels a lot for work so he's always spending the night here and then leaving early in the morning.'

'What does he do?'

'No idea. I just see the car. He blocked Brian in once so we had to knock on the door and Judy was a fucking pain about it. She didn't want to wake him up to move it.' Fleur snorted. 'These men and their overprotective mothers. It's no wonder none of them behave like grown-ups.'

'Is Brian's mum like that?'

She rolled her eyes. 'You wouldn't believe it. I'm the devil incarnate because I make him iron his own shirts and cook the occasional meal.'

'Classic Irish mother.'

'That's what he says. He says she can't help it.'

'I'm not sure they try,' I said, thinking of my own brother

Dec and how my mother fussed over him. He could do no wrong. 'Is he nice? Tom?'

Fleur shrugged. 'I didn't think so but he's probably not at his best when he's half-dressed and half-asleep. I notice he hasn't turned out for the search party. Maybe Judy decided not to wake him up.'

'He might have been more use than Judy. She's not what you'd call robust, is she?'

A snort. 'Tougher than she looks. And she's fitter than me. She walks in the woods every day and goes swimming at the health centre and she does dance classes. She's always on the go.' Fleur pulled at her top, suddenly self-conscious. 'If you're thinking I could do with some of that myself, you're not wrong. I spend too much time sitting at a desk.'

'Don't we all?' I said it without thinking, and she frowned. 'Do you work?'

'Oh – not at the moment.' I dropped my voice. 'We should keep it down. Some of the kids are probably still asleep.'

We moved on to number 3.

'You need to cut this back.' She indicated the monster shrub that had defeated me the previous day. I couldn't quite manage to channel my upbeat undercover personality and gave a sigh instead.

'Gardening is not my thing.'

'I don't imagine that's a problem for your boyfriend. Presumably you have other . . . talents. Skills.'

'What do you mean by that?' A question you ask when you know exactly what the other person means but you can't believe they said it. I couldn't miss what she was implying even if I tried.

'You should know that it doesn't last when it's all about sex. No matter how much you fancy each other, that wears off eventually. Then you're left with one another.' She sniffed. 'There's no guarantee he'll still be interested when he doesn't want to shag you any more.'

165

It was a bitchy remark that was designed to put me off making further conversation, and having delivered it Fleur didn't hang around. She had moved on to Stephen Bollivant's house, and I followed, searching through the remaining gardens in heavy silence.

The front gardens were relatively easy to search. The path that ran behind the houses was another matter, when we trudged around to where it began behind number 9. The plants on either side were overgrown and I soon ran into trouble with long, trailing brambles that caught at my skin and clothes in the darkness. I stopped as sharp hooks buried themselves in my hair.

'Hold on – I'm stuck.'

Fleur ploughed on, ignoring me. I had given her my torch because she had taken the lead as we started down the path. Now I watched her disappear around the corner, the light blinking out as thoroughly as if she had switched it off. I had Fleur's torch but the light it cast was so feeble that I prioritised having both hands free, shoving it into my pocket and relying on the moonlight. The night was clear and warm, the air full of the scent of flowering plants in the gardens and along the path. In other circumstances I might even have liked being out there in the dark. While I struggled with the brambles I was aware of tiny movements around me as small animals carried out their nocturnal business: there would be rats, whatever about cuter mammals. Something ran over my foot and I caught back a scream. With an effort, and the sacrifice of some hair, I yanked myself free and moved on, taking care to avoid the brambles as best I could.

The backs of the houses were fascinating to me, private worlds that gave me a new idea of the people who lived there. I wasn't sure I would have liked the path being there if I lived permanently in Jellicoe Close. It was a good reminder that the back of our house wasn't necessarily private. We would need to maintain our cover there as well as in the sitting room, I thought, and wondered what that would entail. How did you cook romantically? As if you can't keep your hands off one another, I imagined Derwent saying, and blushed at the very thought.

I kept expecting to see Fleur, or at the very least the torch-light reflecting back off the undergrowth, but as I pressed on around the U-shaped path there was nothing ahead of me but soft darkness.

I crossed the path that led down to the Holmwood, looking down it for a long moment in the hope that I might see Derwent on his way back, but it seemed deserted. It would be very nice to have him around, I acknowledged, shivering despite the warm air. I plunged into the second part of the route behind the houses, making better progress on this side. It was fenced in properly because of the railway embankment that rose up on my right, and that had kept the brambles under control.

A sound behind me caught my attention. I stopped to listen, holding my breath. Another sound, a branch breaking, I thought. Someone or something on the path. My eyes were wide as I peered into the darkness, but I couldn't see anyone. I opened my mouth to call out in case it was Gillian Holding, or one of the other searchers, but some instinct made me hold the words back. Gillian shuffled in her oversized shoes. The sounds behind me had been stealthy.

Someone didn't want me to know they were there.

I had the sense that they had stopped too, that they were waiting for me to move. The hairs stood up on my arms and I wished I had pepper spray or better yet, my extendable baton. I itched to summon reinforcements on the radio that was currently sitting in my flat.

Could it be Gary? I swallowed, genuinely uneasy, and angry too. If this was a joke it wasn't my idea of funny. I looked around and saw a gap in the fencing to my right. I squeezed through it, shoving nettles out of my face, squirming into the heart of a large bush with as little noise as possible. My clothes were dark and the branches of the bush swung heavy with leaves. I would be invisible, just about, unless the person knew where to look for me.

The seconds stretched out as I stayed still. My muscles began complaining and I fervently wished to scratch the exact centre of my back where an insect had bitten me. I was just beginning to wonder if I'd overreacted – if I hadn't, in fact, heard anything behind me, and my imagination had created the entire situation – when a figure materialised on the path. Stepping softly but swiftly, a man moved past me and disappeared into the distance. I had the impression of dark clothing and an athletic, soundless stride, but between the branches and the fence he had been hidden from me as effectively as I had hidden myself.

A stark choice presented itself to me. Maeve Kernaghan, dog-sitter, would not have taken any chances. She would have scurried to safety, preferably by finding her boyfriend and hiding behind him. DS Maeve Kerrigan, on the other hand, wanted very badly to find out who was lurking in the shadows at that time in the morning, quite obviously up to no good. Nothing to do with our case, Derwent would probably have said, and he might have been right – but Tom Thwaites's car was parked near his mother's house. What if he was suspicious about the new arrivals in Jellicoe Close, and wanted a closer look? I shivered. All I knew about him was that he was unpopular with the neighbours and the type to fall in with a bad crowd. He liked the finer things in life, as evidenced by his car. He was implicated in a very unpleasant crime. And he wouldn't be very happy if he knew what we were doing in West Idleford.

Enough was enough; I was going to have to do something to try to take control of the situation. Hiding in a bush and waiting to be rescued wasn't going to cut it. If I went along the path, I might run into him, but I wasn't armed and I didn't know where Derwent was and I'd been in enough fights to know the odds wouldn't be in my favour. What I needed was to be able to identify this man, first and foremost, and then I could worry about arresting him. I was on a slope that led up to the railway line. If I ran up there, I could get a good view of the area and possibly make better time than the stranger sidling along the overgrown path.

But what if he found Fleur while he was looking for me?

There was nothing I could do about that, cold hard reason suggested. I didn't want her to come to harm but she would make an excellent distraction for him, and if he was occupied with fighting her I might have a chance against him. Plus I would be quick if I heard a scuffle up ahead. She wasn't on her own, even if she thought she'd left me behind.

I shot out of the shelter of the bush that had hidden me so effectively and crossed the open ground that led to the top of the slope, where there was very little cover. I moved as quickly as I could, crouching, and went fast and low over the wall at the top so I was facing the railway line. I had intended to run along it. As train stations went, Idleford was quiet to the point of torpor. Even at busy times there were two trains an hour. Tucked away as it was at the end of a branch line, there was no need for any train to pass through after hours either. There wouldn't be any traffic on the line until six at the earliest.

Even so, the sight of a figure standing in the middle of the line gave me a jolt of pure fear, not on my own account this time, but for the woman who stood there, her nightgown hanging off her shoulders like a shroud.

I had found Gillian Holding.

24

She was standing perfectly still, her hands dangling by her sides, facing away from me, and as far as I could tell she wasn't aware that I was there. My first instinct was to call out to her but I thought better of it. I didn't want to scare her. I definitely didn't want to have to chase after her along the unlit railway line that stretched into the distance, to tree-lined infinity; one of us would break an ankle on the loose stones between the sleepers.

First things first. I took out my phone and tapped out a quick message to Derwent, telling him where I was and what was happening, that I couldn't call him because I was afraid of making any noise but that I needed back-up. The relief when he replied made me weak: I had been half-convinced that he would be somewhere with bad reception and I would be on my own.

Hold tight. 999 on the way.

That Mrs Holding had decided to trespass on the railway line was good news; it doubled the chances of a police response since technically this was now British Transport Police's problem. Or rather mine until they turned up, I reminded myself, stepping warily onto the line. I hadn't told Derwent *why* I couldn't make noise, letting him assume that it was because I was afraid of scaring Mrs Holding, and that was part of the story but it wasn't the whole thing by any means. I was keeping one eye on the area to the left of the railway line, where I had last seen the man who followed me. If Gillian Holding screamed, or ran, it could attract his attention, which was something else to worry about. Technically I wasn't alone any more but I didn't feel at all sure that he would be put off once he realised he was facing the combined might of me and an elderly dementia sufferer.

On the other hand, Gillian Holding needed help. I couldn't stand around waiting for us both to be rescued. I walked slowly towards her, humming under my breath to announce my presence. She turned her head to one side, listening, but otherwise she didn't move.

'Mrs Holding? It's Maeve. We met yesterday, do you remember? At the library, and then we walked back here together. You'd been listening to some books, I think. *Middlemarch* . . .' I was rambling, hoping that my tone of voice would reassure her. 'Do you think you could come with me? This way?'

I put my hand under her elbow, gently, anticipating that she might lash out. She came with me though, docile and calm, still lost in her own world like a sleepwalker. Her skin was icy. I guided her to the side of the embankment where there was a small brick structure. She sat on it and I stood next to her, stripping off my sweatshirt.

'You're cold, aren't you? Let's warm you up.' I wrapped the sweatshirt around her shoulders. She didn't seem to notice, but she didn't shrug it off either. She was staring into space, her mouth working.

'Is that any better?' I crouched, trying to make eye contact with her. 'What's going on, Gillian? Is everything all right? Where were you going?'

171

'Get away.' She made a movement, pointing down the railway.

'You wanted to get away? From what?'

'This place.' She plucked at the material of her nightgown, fretful. 'You know. The evil.'

'The evil?' I repeated. 'What do you mean by that?'

'No one listens. But I see. I see a lot.'

'From your house? What do you see?'

'I see them together. It's not right. He shouldn't. But he does. They all do. Disgusting. They're all disgusting.' She was speaking with real vehemence. 'William's always bothering me. Even when I'm asleep. He thinks I don't know but I do.'

'William?'

'My husband.'

'Gary's father?'

'Of course Gary's father. Who did you think I meant?'

Gary had said his father was dead. I adjusted my level of interest accordingly.

She tilted her head. 'William is not a bad person, of course. Not like the other one. But obsessed. They all are.'

'Who is the other one?'

'The one I call the devil. He smiles and smiles.' She closed her eyes, her face twisted as if she was in pain. 'As if I can't see him for what he really is. He knows I saw him. He knows. He looked up and he saw me watching and I saw him. I saw him.'

She was getting more and more upset, her body racked with deep shudders. I put my arm around her and rubbed her arms to get her circulation going.

'It's all right. Everything is going to be fine, Mrs Holding.'

She looked straight at me, her eyes wide and alert instead of vacantly staring as before. 'I think he's going to try to kill me. You'll remember, won't you? If I die. You'll know.'

Gary had said she sounded lucid but what she said was rubbish. I looked back at her and thought, *but I believe her* . . .

'Who is it, Mrs Holding? Who threatened you?'

'Mum!' The shout came from behind me, and I turned to see Gary running along the side of the railway track towards us. A group of the searchers straggled behind him in ones and twos and I picked them out as they got nearer: Stephen Bollivant on his own, still towed by his dog, Derwent steadily overhauling them with Brian Nolan keeping pace by his side, Rhys Vonn and Mike Knox a fair distance back with another man in dark clothes, a man I didn't recognise. A second shout came from the other side and I saw a couple of officers jogging down the tracks from the direction of the station, torches in hand, high-vis jackets gleaming.

'Here they are,' I said cheerfully, and turned back to see that Mrs Holding's face was grey. Her eyes were wide and fixed. She gasped and swayed, and I was just in time to catch her as she fell.

'I should have known you'd sniff her out. Better than a blood-hound. We should have stuck a lead on you and let you have your head.'

'Thanks,' I said drily, lacing my fingers around the steaming mug Derwent had handed me.

By mutual consent we had slid away from the neighbours as soon as we decently could. Gillian Holding and her son had gone to hospital in an ambulance so she could be treated for hypothermia, against Gary's objections.

'She needs to get home and get to bed,' he said to the kind but firm paramedics.

'We want to get her checked over. She's got a nasty cut on her leg,' the older of the two said. 'You won't be long, I don't think.'

'She needs to get some rest.'

I thought Gary was on the verge of tears. I went across to him.

'I think it would be a good idea for them to take her, Gary.

We don't know what happened to her, do we? A doctor should have a look at her.'

His face was a picture of misery. 'I don't like her going into the hospital.'

'You can come with her,' the paramedic said cheerfully. 'Hop up in the back. You can reassure her on the way to the hospital.'

Gary had hopped, still reluctant but bowing to the inevitable. As the ambulance swung out of Jellicoe Close there was a definite lift in the overall mood.

'That's a job well done.' Rhys Vonn stretched, looking smug. 'All back to mine? I think we deserve a drink after all that.'

Stephen Bollivant was already moving towards his house, dragged there by Klaus. 'Not for me.'

'Typical wet blanket.' Vonn turned to Derwent. 'You won't let me down.'

Derwent had shaken his head. 'It's nearly dawn.'

'Come for a cooked breakfast then.' Vonn slapped him on the back, hard. 'The rest of us can have Buck's Fizz or Bloody Marys and you can be boring with your bacon and eggs.'

'I need to get some rest. And Maeve is dead on her feet.'

I was tired; at that very moment I was yawning so widely my jaw cracked.

'All right. I see that. I bet you can't wait to get her back to bed,' Vonn said to Derwent with a snigger. I couldn't see Josh's face but with some satisfaction I watched Vonn's grin disappear.

'I'll come, Rhys,' Mike Knox said. 'Anyone else?'

Brian nodded, as did the man I hadn't recognised. Derwent had informed me in a mutter that he was Tom Thwaites, who had joined the search party after I'd gone. He was stocky and balding, unshaven to the point that I wondered if he was growing a beard, and I didn't find him particularly intimidating until he glanced at me. I saw nothing in his eyes but emptiness. I'd noticed the same vacancy in murderers I'd locked up: a profound absence that you recognised when you saw it, instantly, as evil.

But he had taken the time to search for Gillian Holding, I reminded myself. That wasn't evil.

His eyes had passed over me but now they returned to my face with a sharper kind of interest, and all reason fled away. On instinct I moved, putting as much space as possible between me and Tom Thwaites, and bumped into Brian.

'Where's Fleur?'

He looked uneasy. 'She . . . er . . . went home.'

'With my torch.' Leaving me at the mercy of whoever had been following me. I was glad I'd found Gillian, of course, but I was frustrated that I had missed out on identifying the man who had been lurking on the path, and my irritation made me curt.

'I'm sorry about that. I'll drop it back to you.' He pulled a face. 'I think she was tired, you know? She hasn't been sleeping all that well lately.'

'She left you on your own, Maeve?' Derwent came to stand beside me, looming over Brian. 'What was the thinking behind that?'

'You'd have to ask her.' Brian shrugged. 'No harm done.'

I agreed that it had all worked out all right and we had headed back to the house. Now I was curled up on the kitchen sofa, tired but too strung out to sleep. Derwent was roaming around restlessly, in the same condition.

'So Fleur fucked off, did she?'

'We didn't exactly get on.' I pulled a face. 'She's touchy.'

'She has a face like a slapped arse.'

'That too.'

'Brian is all right though.' Derwent picked up an envelope and studied it. 'You wonder why people like that get together. Where's the appeal?'

'Maybe she's changed. People do. They start off in the same place and grow apart. It happens all the time.'

He frowned, and said nothing.

I stretched. 'What about you? How was the search?'

'Annoying. I couldn't exactly take charge. I had to let them make suggestions.'

'Awful for you.'

'Well, it is when they're idiots.' He dragged out a chair from the kitchen table and sat in it moodily. 'Bollivant was quiet but he's growing on me. He speaks when he has something to say. Rhys Vonn goes on and on. Constant ear piss. I can't stand him.'

'Did you all stay together?'

'No. Everyone went their own way after a while.' He sighed. 'No one listens. They all set off on their own wild goose chases.'

'When did you pick up Tom Thwaites?'

'He was loitering around outside when I got to the Holdings' house to collect Gary.'

'Just hanging around?'

'He said he was looking for his mum. Why?'

I told him about the man on the path and he listened with a deepening frown on his face. 'You didn't tell me.'

'I didn't have the chance,' I protested. 'I noticed someone behind me, I hid, I tried to circle round to get a good view of him and I found Gillian Holding. Then I texted you.'

'But you didn't say you were in danger.'

'I don't know that I was,' I said slowly. 'All that happened was that he came up behind me and he was moving as if he didn't want anyone to hear him. Maybe I was nervy because of the circumstances. Maybe it was completely innocent.'

'Or maybe it wasn't. You thought something was off.'

I nodded.

'Well, you were probably right. You have good instincts, as a rule. It's a shame that it doesn't stop you blundering into trouble.'

'For a second there I thought you were going to pay me a compliment that didn't come with a sting in the tail.'

176

'Stop putting yourself in harm's way then.' He leaned forward, elbows on his knees, serious now. 'I can't be everywhere, Maeve. You know better than anyone that we're in danger here, all the time. If we get found out, the kind of people we're dealing with won't think twice about getting rid of us. They're already in a load of trouble. If Judy and Tom are part of a conspiracy to take advantage of vulnerable people, they'll be looking at significant sentences. More to the point, they'll be working with some very bad people indeed. We've already picked up on that, haven't we? Ruth and Alan warned you Tom was in with a bad crowd.'

'I know.'

'So I don't like that someone was following you, given that it could have been one of Tom's pals. When did you notice them?'

'As I said, right before I saw Gillian Holding. After everyone you were with had split up.'

'Fuck. And you really didn't see this person in any detail?'

'It was a man in dark clothes. That's all I can tell you.' I quailed at the expression on his face. 'I did try to see.'

'I know.'

'I've been thinking about what Gillian Holding said to me.' I had told him about it while the kettle was boiling. 'This person who threatened to kill her. It could have been the man who was walking on the path. Maybe he wasn't after me at all. He could have been trying to find her before anyone else did. It was a golden opportunity to deal with her and make it look like an accident.'

'That's a possibility,' Derwent said slowly.

'And when you all turned up together and she fainted . . . everyone assumed it was because of hypothermia, but I think she was scared.'

'He was there?'

'Or she thought he was.'

'That's the trouble. She's not what you'd call a reliable witness.'

'And they were all there. I don't know who she meant.'

'"He smiles and smiles". That sounds like Rhys Vonn.'

'Or Brian,' I said, thinking about the men. 'Or Mike Knox – he doesn't talk a lot but he has a really striking smile, with his beard being so dark.'

'Stephen Bollivant has that nervous grin.'

I shook my head. 'The truth is it could have been any of them.'

Taking advantage of opportunities. That was what he was good at, as a rule. Making a move when everyone else was still thinking it through. Taking a risk and dealing with the consequences. It was what made him great, what made him unstoppable.

But not this fucking time, apparently. He hadn't been able to turn the situation to his advantage, not at all. He had an open goal but he'd kicked the ball wide.

He walked down through the woods in the soft grey light of the morning, unable to sit still even though he was operating right at the limits of exhaustion, his vision skipping, his head ringing as if there was a swarm of bees inside it. He had tried everything that usually gave him a lift and all that had happened was that he'd made it impossible to rest. The jitters were bad, bad, bad. He needed something to make him feel better: to fuck someone, to hurt someone. To put everything back in the right order, with him at the top of the pile.

He kept playing it back in his mind to pinpoint the moment where it had all gone to shit.

Right at the start, he thought. Right when the new guy had come out of his house, swaggering like he was in charge. In fairness, the golden opportunity had only just appeared before him – the old woman out of the house, unaccounted for, at risk of the kind of accident that would be easy to set up so no one could suspect he had anything to do with harming her – and there was that smug fucker, Josh, throwing his weight around, making it impossible to think or do anything except fall into line. He'd been ordering everyone around. Natural leadership, they called it, when it was someone like Josh. No one did what *he* said when he told them to, unless he'd given them reason to be scared of what would happen if they didn't. That was why he liked them biddable, demure, compliant. He found himself thinking about Josh's girl-friend again, imagining himself taking her off him. She might cry but she wouldn't fight.

If he had only been able to get to the old bitch first – but the dimwit bimbo had got in the way. He would pay her back for that one day, when he got the chance. Teach Josh a lesson as well. Fuck up their lives, both of them, good and proper. He kicked a rotten log that splintered into dank shards.

Down below him, by the lake, someone moved into view: a girl in school uniform. She was wearing her blazer, her arms folded across her chest because it was a colder morning than some lately, the sun hiding away. He had told her to be there at six and it was five to, but there she was, nice and early, the way he'd trained her to be.

She was waiting for him.

She knew how lucky she was. *She* appreciated him.

He picked up his pace.

25

As I came downstairs, Derwent whistled. 'Wow, you look . . . tired.'

'Thanks, Josh. Really. That's kind.' I checked in the hall mirror, seeing the hollows under my eyes that no amount of concealer could disguise. 'Unlike some people I'm not good at napping.'

Derwent grinned. 'It's a skill.'

He had spent the afternoon sprawling on one of the sofas in the sitting room with Pippin in the crook of his arm, both of them blissfully asleep. I had retreated to my bedroom, which proved to conduct sound from the sitting room with remarkable efficiency. The regular snores from downstairs had become more and more annoying as time passed. Even with the curtains drawn and a pillow pressed against either ear I hadn't been able to sleep until I tipped into sudden dreamless darkness a couple of minutes before the alarm went off. Now my head felt as if it was stuffed with old rags. I had showered, and changed into a pretty broderie anglaise dress, and had done my hair with extreme concentration and the help of a YouTube tutorial, and had applied Georgia-standard make-up. None of it had made me feel any better.

181

'Don't worry. At least you have an excuse to fall asleep at the play.'

'I'm not going to fall asleep,' I snapped. 'I love *A Midsummer Night's Dream*. I studied it for GCSE.'

'Oh, even better. What will make your day is a load of schoolkids murdering Shakespeare for a couple of hours. Have you ever been to a school play?'

'According to Ruth the school is famous for its plays. They do this every year and it's the high point of the summer term. Everyone around here goes.'

'Which is why we're going.'

'Exactly.' I looked at him, neat in a polo shirt and jeans. 'I see you dressed up.'

'This is the local smart-casual uniform. I'm just trying to fit in.' He held out his arm. 'Come on. We'd better get going. It would be a shame if we missed the kick-off.'

'Curtain up.'

'Yeah. That.'

Idleford Park School had all the trappings of an expensive independent school. The main building was a high Gothic Victorian mansion with sleek modern additions to the left and right that announced themselves as the sports complex and the library building. It was set in a wide expanse of parkland, complete with a grassy hollow known as the amphitheatre where the play was due to be performed. Derwent parked the car between a long, low Bentley and a brand-new Range Rover.

'So this is a state school?'

'Technically,' I said. 'But the house prices around here ensure that it's mainly very well-heeled parents who can afford to send their kids here and they've done a huge amount of fund-raising to give the school the best possible facilities. It's over-subscribed, apparently.'

'Why don't they just send them to posh private schools?'

'Oxbridge. State school applicants have an advantage. These kids will be competing with inner-city ones who don't even have a proper school library, let alone a swimming pool or all-weather lacrosse pitches, but they count the same for the universities' purposes.'

Derwent pulled a face. 'Everyone's equal but some are more equal than others.'

We walked across the grass towards a pair of smiling uniformed girls who were checking tickets and doling out programmes. Derwent had been right about what he was wearing: every man was dressed in some version of polo shirt and trousers, although some wore suede loafers without a trace of irony. I was glad Derwent had skipped that particular detail. The women wore summer dresses and strappy sandals, toned arms on display. I felt seriously lacking in both highlights and diamonds, and held on to Derwent's hand a little more tightly than I might have otherwise. He glanced at me and smiled to himself.

Dubious though I was about the school, the amphitheatre didn't disappoint. The grassy bowl was lit with solar lanterns stuck into the ground in rows, tiny lights that shed a warm glow on the grass and looked like stars as the light faded overhead.

Ruth had explained the layout to me.

'They've built a stage out of one end of the hollow and there are proper seats facing it, where it's flat. That's where Alan and I always sit, because I'm really too stiff these days to sit on the ground, but if you bring a blanket you can sit on the slopes at the side. People bring picnics and so on. There's a sound system so you won't miss anything and I think it's rather nice on a warm summer night. Romantic.'

'Those days are long gone, aren't they?' Alan had said cheerfully, and I saw a faint shadow touch his wife's face, but it was gone the next second. Behind Ruth's stolid exterior beat a dreamer's heart.

183

The school hadn't missed any opportunities to make money from the evening. By the entrance to the theatre there was a large gazebo hung with bunting. A sign pointed to it: CHAMPAGNE BAR. It was besieged, the crowd six-deep.

'You were lucky to be able to buy a cup of tea at events in my school,' I said.

'And it came in a little bendy polystyrene cup.' Derwent shook his head. 'I thought I was too young for "it wasn't like this in my day".'

'Oh no, you're definitely old enough for that.'

The slopes at the side were crowded and a hum of conversation rose up along with the soft thunk of champagne corks popping and the occasional gale of laughter.

'We're a bit tight for space,' a uniformed girl said to us, enunciating beautifully through a mouthful of expensive orthodontics. 'Are you OK to go on the top row?'

'Definitely,' Derwent said firmly. 'Lead the way.' To me, he muttered, 'You get a better view and something to lean against.'

I followed him to a position at the base of a tree. He spread out the picnic blanket he had been carrying and a cloud of Pippin's hair rose from it. I watched it float across the theatre on the evening breeze, drifting into people's picnics, and winced.

'Lowering the tone already.'

'Just sit down and pretend it's nothing to do with us.' He threw the programmes down next to me. 'I'm going to get us some drinks. Back in a second.'

It would take him ages, I thought, sitting up with my arms hugging my knees and looking around. There were the Knoxes, on the other side of the grassy bowl. Alice Knox was unpacking box after box of Tupperware, laying it all out in front of her family. The boys were shoving one another, fighting over something. I tried to remember their names: Brody was the younger one and then the older one was . . . something like a dog's name, I had thought. Tip, that was it. They were stolid boys, taking after their mother who was distinctly unathletic, with short legs, narrow shoulders and wide hips.

I spotted Alan and Ruth next, near the front, draped in blankets against the so far non-existent evening chill. They were sharing a thermos of something steaming and looking very pleased with themselves. The Vonns were in prime position near the stage, Camilla having a starring role. Rhys was waving at people in the crowd, acting as if they'd come to see him. I felt uneasy, watching him. Camilla's sister, Thea, was sitting with her head leaning against her mother's shoulder. I wondered if she was looking for support or offering it to Nicola. The woman looked drawn, the light finding shadows in the hollows of her skull.

'Here, take this.' Derwent held a glass in front of my face.

'That was quick,' I said, surprised.

'Bar presence. You've got it or you don't.' He sat down and clinked glasses with me. 'This is better than working, isn't it?'

'If Pete Belcott could see us now . . .'

'Don't talk about him.' He nudged me. 'There's Judy, look, down near Alan and Ruth. I don't see her son.'

'I can't imagine this is his kind of night out.'

He looked around, outwardly casual, taking it all in. 'I saw Mike Knox at the bar. He seems like a good guy.'

I was amused. 'He *seems* like it but you're not going to commit to saying he is.'

'Trust no one and you won't be disappointed.'

'How good are you at making friends, would you say?'

Derwent shrugged. 'I don't trust people with too many friends. They're always trying to hide from themselves in a crowd.'

'That's bleak, even for you.'

'I just don't need a lot of other people.' He looked at me. 'I have everyone I need.'

A lone flute began to play somewhere off stage, a haunting melody that made the buzz of conversation dwindle to silence.

185

A violin joined it, and a cello, the sound swelling as one instrument after another began to play. The stage lights dimmed and six dancers darted on, each carrying a light, each wearing a different colour of gauzy dress and matching ballet shoes: sugar almond pink, icy blue, silver grey, sea green, soft lilac and palest yellow. They spun gracefully, weaving patterns of light in the darkness, as invisible figures in black filled the previously empty stage with what proved to be painted trees and flowers when the lights went up: the forest materialising out of nowhere. A girl was standing with her face in her hands, sobbing, the folds of her skirt graceful around her slender legs. On the other side of the stage, two young men stood face to face in crisp white shirts and chinos but with bare feet, glaring as if they each wanted to kill the other. Two more actors strolled onto the stage, dressed as older men in suits and ties.

'Full of vexation come I, with complaint against my child, my daughter Hermia.'

The boy had sprayed his hair grey and was affecting a quavering old-man voice which got a ripple of laughter from the audience. He was confident as he laid out the first of the love triangles I remembered from studying the play at school, Hermia forced to choose between Lysander and Demetrius. Hermia was played by Camilla, looking ravishingly pretty with strawberry-blonde hair loose around her shoulders and a sweetly distraught expression on her face. And she was good, I realised as she engaged in the quickfire banter between the lovers and jealous Helena, who was dark and earnest and had impeccable comic timing.

Not your average school play. I settled back and prepared to enjoy it. I did, too, except that I couldn't help wondering about a few minor mysteries.

'Tip Knox is in the same year as Camilla,' I said under cover of the applause at the end of the first act. 'Why isn't he in the show?'

'No talent? No interest? No time?'

'The standards are high.' I was reading the programme. 'Huh. Mike Knox helped with rehearsals. Maybe that put Tip off.'

'You don't think they're a happy family?'

'Do you? Look at them.'

Mike Knox was the odd one out in that family and he seemed determined to make that clear to anyone who glanced in their direction, sitting on the very edge of their picnic rug with his back to his wife. Tip was hunched over his phone, his attention on the screen. Brody seemed to be asleep. Alice was fidgeting as if she was trying to get comfortable.

Music began to play: the next act was about to begin, putting an end to our conversation. Ignoring the whirling dancers on stage, cavorting around donkey-headed Bottom, I stared across at the Knoxes. Mike was focused on the stage, taut with tension. Even if he had helped with the production, it seemed odd to me that he was so absorbed in it, so capti-vated by the actors on stage to the exclusion of everything else. But on reflection, I didn't know much about him. I only thought of him as an adjunct to his louder friend, Rhys.

At the interval I was standing in a queue by the row of Portaloos when someone nudged my arm.

'Thanks for minding us a place.' Judy Thwaites, grinning up at me ingratiatingly, with Ruth in tow. 'The queue's so long we'd have been there forever.'

'I'm not sure we should barge in,' Ruth said softly, but Judy laughed.

'No one minds, do they? Age has its privilege.'

'I think I'll go to the end of the queue.'

Judy grabbed hold of Ruth's sleeve and steered her back to a place in front of me. 'No you don't.'

A glance over my shoulder told me I was getting absolute hate stares from the women directly behind me in the queue. Judy was chattering on, oblivious.

'It's ever so good, isn't it? Quite amazing how they do it. I don't usually like Shakespeare, but I always come to this.'

'They've cut lots of the words,' Ruth said with a sniff. 'Not the real play at all.'

'I suppose they want to keep it simple. The story is all there.' I was trying to be diplomatic. I was more inclined towards Judy's positivity than Ruth's criticism. I couldn't help doubting the intelligence we had about Judy. She spent so much time helping other people and she was relentlessly cheerful. Maybe she hadn't known what was going on with the vulnerable adults who passed through her home. I hadn't seen much of the son but he had none of his mother's bright-eyed charm. I could believe he might manipulate someone like Davy Bidwell.

I thought of the damage that had been done to Davy's poor frail body, and how he had died, and I hardened my heart. The important thing was finding out the truth, whether it exonerated Judy or not.

'Isn't Camilla excellent?' Judy again. 'And that's her boyfriend playing Oberon. He always used to be hanging around the place, but I haven't seen him in a while.'

'They broke up.' Ruth was up to speed, as I might have expected. Oberon was tall and handsome with a spiralling afro. I checked the programme.

'Isaac Dean.'

'That's the boy. He's got a twin – Elise. She's best friends with Camilla. But we never see either of them around any more, do we, Judy? And they only live in the next road over.'

'Is she in the play?' I was scanning the list of actors. 'Oh, she's in the backstage crew.'

'She's a quiet girl. Nice little thing. She helped make cakes for a bake sale once, do you remember, Ruth? Shame about Camilla and Isaac, though.' Judy nudged me. 'It can't always be Romeo and Juliet, can it? Not like you and your fella.'

'Um, no.' Given the ending of that particular play, I wasn't

188

sure I liked the comparison. 'I think the cubicle at the end is free.'

That distracted Ruth and a moment later a second one became available for Judy. I waited my turn, thinking about how a break-up could be the end of the world when you were a teenager.

Truth to tell, it wasn't all that great when you were an adult either.

'All right?' Derwent checked as I came back.

'Fine.' I rubbed my arms. 'It's actually getting chilly now, isn't it?'

'Did you bring a jumper?'

I shook my head.

'No. Why would you? You always get cold and you never plan ahead. Come here,' he said, resignedly.

So that was how I watched the second half of the play with Josh Derwent's arms wrapped around me, leaning back between his legs, my palms flat on his thighs, his mouth muffled in my hair. The broken night, the champagne, the dark sky above us and the warmth of his body: if I wasn't asleep, I certainly wasn't fully alert. I let my thoughts drift, running through the Dawoud case, considering the houses in Jellicoe Close and the secrets they held. On stage the lovers lost and found one another, Oberon forgave Titania, and all was resolved by marriage, but the real world wasn't like that. Happy ever after, I thought, didn't mean anything. Everything changed all the time. You could put your faith in money and legal commitments like Fleur or Cameron Dawoud, but that wouldn't save you from heartbreak. Yet opting out of relationships altogether would mean you were alone.

There were worse things than being alone, I reminded myself. I had tried to force myself into finding happiness with men who seemed to be perfect for me. They had wanted me, but I hadn't given much thought to how I felt about them. I'd merely gone along with it.

You couldn't just choose someone, anyone to love, I thought. You couldn't force it, any more than you could stop yourself from falling in love with exactly the wrong person at the wrong time.

Puck stepped forward for the final speech and I roused myself, sitting up, blinking against the night.

'If we shadows have offended . . .'

And then applause, the students coming forward to bow, dipping in an uneven line, awkward now that they were themselves again. The parents stood up and cheered, yelling approval for the teachers, the music, the actors, over and over again . . .

'Let's go home,' Derwent said in my ear, and I stood up, unsteady, as he threw the blanket over his shoulder and took my arm.

On the way back to the car, I looked across the lawns towards the old school building. Some of the students had gathered there, still in costume, talking and laughing. Camilla stood a little apart, with a girl all in black whose curls spiralled from her head in wild abandon: Elise Dean, at a guess. She was leaning forward, intent on Camilla, her face unhappy and tense. Whatever the girl was saying to her, Camilla wasn't listening. She turned her back, shrugging her off, and began to turn cartwheels, one after another, with the fluency of a trained gymnast. Her skirt fluttered as she rotated, head over heels, hair flying, pale limbs gleaming in the darkness.

26

I was setting up my laptop on the kitchen table the following morning when Derwent came in wearing black shorts and a T-shirt, his feet bare. In one hand he was carrying the football boots he'd borrowed from Brian Nolan. He frowned.

'What are you doing?'

'I have a video call with Georgia to talk about the Dawoud case.'

'But it's Saturday.'

'So? She's working.'

'Yes, but it's the football. It starts at ten. That only gives you half an hour.'

I was mystified. 'I don't actually need to go. I'm not the one playing.'

'You said you'd come and watch, that's all.' He sat on a stool at the kitchen island. 'Being supportive. It's what a real girlfriend would do.' He was fussing with the boots, adjusting the laces with great concentration.

'Oh, come off it. You're not serious.' I shook my head as I put my headphones on and connected to the call. Georgia appeared on screen, her make-up impeccable, her prettiness heightened by the camera in a most irritating way. I wasn't wearing any make-up at all and hadn't tamed my hair yet;

the contrast was considerable. I tried not to look at myself, focusing on her as she waved.

'Morning! How's everything going?'

'Not too bad,' I said, angling the monitor so Derwent was in the background. 'Say hi, Josh.'

He looked up briefly and was about to say something that probably wasn't hi, but a knock at the front door interrupted him. I leaned back in my chair, one earphone out, trying to work out who it was. Rhys Vonn's booming voice filled the hall and I winced.

'Here you go – socks and shirt. Sorry about the delay in getting that to you. All ready for today otherwise? Great, great. Good of you to help us out. We're going in a couple of minutes so we can get warmed up. Want me to knock for you when I'm heading over?'

'I think I can find it by myself.' Derwent at his driest. They were playing on the green area shared between the Admirals roads. I wondered if I should go along for a bit – but then, he was being such a *baby* about it . . .

'Sorry, Georgia,' I said, turning back to her. 'Josh has a football match this morning with the local five-a-side team. Where were we?'

'We hadn't really got started yet. Thanks for doing this on video. I just find it easier—' She broke off, her eyes wide, and I realised that she was staring past me to where Derwent was changing into the team strip. He had yanked his T-shirt off and was preparing to pull on a hideously striped football shirt, turning it around irritably. The expression on his face could stop a clock but neither of us was really focused on that. In the bright morning light every detail of his torso was clearly and beautifully defined, perfect as a statue in a museum. I knew he was physically fit, obviously, and the previous night I had been pressed against him at the play so I had *felt* the solid muscle that was now rippling in front of us, but somehow I hadn't thought about it. Because he was on screen and I

192

had my back to him, I could allow myself to stare uninhibitedly – not that he would have minded, I thought. He probably
knew we were gazing at him. He could have changed anywhere
else in the house if he'd wanted privacy.

'Holy shit,' Georgia breathed in my ears, which was fair
enough because it was a quasi-religious experience. I cleared
my throat.

'Well. As I was saying. Actually, you were saying.'

'Am I on speaker?' Belatedly Georgia was remembering the
lesson she'd learned the last time we spoke.

I shook my head, pointing to the headphones and she sagged
in her chair.

'I know I shouldn't be objectifying a colleague but I'm not
actually capable of speech at the moment.'

'Same,' I said, pretending to make a note on the page in
front of me.

Derwent pulled the shirt over his head and Georgia sighed
wistfully. 'Is there any way you could call me back after the
match when he's all sweaty?'

I bit the inside of my cheek to stop myself from laughing.
'Interesting. What else have you found out?'

'Um. Yes.' She started shuffling through the papers on her
desk, recovering her focus.

'You sent me the notes on your interview with the other
consultant – Stefanidis. He seems like a charmer.'

'He was a dick. He really hated Hassan Dawoud but he
was at another hospital the whole afternoon and evening on
the day Dawoud died. I checked – he was in surgery. No way
he could have been involved.'

'What did he tell you about the Arnold family?'

'He thought they had a case. He said he'd advised Dawoud
to get his insurance company to settle with them. Dawoud
wanted to fight it, which Stefanidis said was pure arrogance
because he didn't want to admit to himself that he was at
fault, whatever anyone else thought. Dawoud's barrister also

thought he should settle the case. That's what his liability insurance was for. Basically, the Arnolds were in a very strong position legally. It wasn't in their interests for Dawoud to die – quite the opposite.'

Derwent lifted one of my headphones and I jumped out of my skin, not having noticed him approaching. 'What is it?'

'I'm off.'

'OK. Good luck.'

'Break a leg,' Georgia said.

'Georgia says break a leg,' I relayed, and he bent down to give her a grade-A glower. I sighed. 'She didn't say it had to be *your* leg. But try not to put anyone in the hospital.'

'See you later.' He was heading out of the kitchen. 'Ask her about the drugs.'

'I will.' I looked back to see that Georgia was leaning forward conspiratorially, her eyes alight with mischief.

'How is it going with the two of you?'

'Fine. Absolutely fine. Nothing to report.' The front door slammed shut and I looked to make sure he was definitely gone.

'Really?' She looked sceptical. 'Nothing?'

'We're regarded as a very nice couple. We hold hands in public and enjoy each other's company,' I said primly.

'And you don't want to rip his clothes off?'

'I don't need to,' I pointed out. 'He's rarely fully dressed.'

'Oh my *God*,' she squeaked.

'Look, it's not like that.' I was laughing. 'We're here because we need to be, for professional reasons, and we're being professional about it. And speaking of being professional, did you find out anything about the Dawouds and drugs?'

'Yes, I asked Cameron about it. Definitely no drug use, and definitely no chem sex parties. He was annoyed that I even asked, but I really pushed him on it and he said Dawoud had a bad experience as a teenager when he was just starting to go to gay clubs. He had his drink spiked and it made him ill.

194

He was so sick that one of his friends took him home so nothing terrible happened, but it put him off the whole idea. He wasn't a drinker, and he wasn't into drugs, and neither was Cameron. He said they were always the sensible ones when they went out with friends, and that's what the friends said when I contacted them originally. Doctor Early said the tox screen came back negative for the usual drugs – cocaine, speed, that kind of thing.'

'Did you ask him about the WhatsApp message?'

'Yes.' She pulled a face. 'He was pretty upset. He said it wouldn't absolutely shock him if Dawoud had been seeing someone else, but that it couldn't have been serious. Dawoud enjoyed attention. He might have been flattered into an emotional affair.'

'Or a physical one?'

'Maybe. Cameron said their sex life had been a bit muted lately. He'd been busy at work so he hadn't really been home all that much. He said he was to blame if Dawoud got bored and looked elsewhere.'

'Poor guy.'

'I really like him.' Georgia was looking guilty. 'I know I shouldn't.'

'Just keep an open mind about whether you can trust him, that's all. You seem to have done a great job of persuading him to open up to you.'

She beamed. 'Thanks, Sarge.'

'Where would Dawoud find a boyfriend? At work?'

'Not according to Stefanidis.'

'Unless it was Stefanidis.' I raised my eyebrows. 'Plot twist.'

'Stefanidis is twenty years older than Dawoud and he is not my idea of someone who would send a message like that.'

'People can surprise you.'

Georgia pulled a face. 'Ugh. No.'

'OK. Maybe not him.' I checked my notes. 'What about the blanket?'

'The blanket is interesting. Cameron is absolutely sure that it's not theirs. He said they weren't into throws and blankets because Dawoud thought they looked untidy. Duvets on the beds, no extra covers. They didn't do picnics and Dawoud wouldn't have kept a blanket in the car for any other reason that Cameron could think of.'

I sat up. 'So it's possible it belonged to the killer or it came from wherever he was murdered.'

'I've let Kev know. It had already gone off for trace analysis, but he's put a special rush on it.'

'Good. And what about the WhatsApp message?'

'I've got to go back to the phone company. They're medium helpful but I haven't really made any more progress on it.'

I tapped the end of my pen on the desk, considering it. 'You know, I think if I wanted to kill my partner I might make it look as if they had a secret lover I didn't know about, so the police would waste a lot of time chasing someone who doesn't exist.'

'Cameron was shocked!'

'Or he's a good actor. Check with their insurance company. I want to know if he's keen to get his hands on the life insurance payout.'

She stuck out her bottom lip. 'He's my friend. Leave him alone.'

'He's not my friend,' I said, thinking of Derwent's take-it-or-leave-it attitude to people, 'and I'll leave him alone when I'm sure he's not a murderer.'

27

I hadn't been teasing Derwent; I'd forgotten promising to cheer him on. That he expected it from his 'girlfriend' amused me, but I thought he was right – the kind of girl who would choose to go out with him probably would feel obliged to watch him play, and she might even enjoy it. But what really made me decide to go was the exhausted look that had been on his face as he left to do something he really didn't want to do, for the sake of doing our job properly. The least I could do, I decided, was turn up and look pretty doing it.

Inspired by Georgia's example I took the time to put on make-up and changed into a fluttery little mini dress covered in tiny polka dots. I put on trainers and whistled for Pippin. It was a sultry morning, the sun hiding behind blue-grey clouds heavy with the promise of thunder, and I was already too hot as I walked down to the grass where the match was in progress.

Derwent didn't notice me at first, for the very good reason that he was engaged in a furious, jostling competition for the ball. With a fair amount of luck as well as skill he hooked it away to where Mike Knox was waiting on the wing, then darted forward so Knox could pass it back to him. In a single movement, while the defenders were still catching up, he volleyed it past the goalkeeper.

A cheer went up from the supporters as I joined them: they included a few strangers but also Nicola Vonn with her smaller daughter, Thea, Fleur Nolan, Alice Knox and her two sons, Judy and Ruth in deckchairs (somewhat inevitably, since nothing that happened in Jellicoe Close escaped their attention) and Alan, who was pacing up and down hurling advice and abuse in equal amounts. His face was brick-red and the back of his shirt had a damp patch in the shape of Africa between the shoulder blades. I hoped he wasn't going to keel over with a heart attack. I wasn't all that keen on the thought of doing mouth-to-mouth resuscitation if it involved Alan's wet, liver-coloured lips.

'That's one all,' Alice said to me in cut-glass tones. 'He's playing awfully well but they haven't had many chances so far.'

'Oh good,' I said, and waved at Derwent. He was walking back with his hands on his hips, his hair dark with sweat and the lurid football shirt sticking to his body. When he saw me he looked surprised and then a smile flashed across his face.

'Oh, that's sweet,' Judy said. 'Didn't he know you were coming?'

'I wasn't sure I'd be able to make it.'

'He'll be glad you saw him score a goal. That player on the other side isn't letting him get away with anything,' Alan said, furious, as if that wasn't the whole point. 'Keep little Pip on the lead, won't you? He'll be after the ball if he gets the chance.'

Derwent leaned in to say something to Rhys Vonn who nodded importantly.

'Four minutes left in this half,' Alice said, her voice clear and bell-like. Nicola Vonn was chewing her lip.

'What did you say?'

Alice repeated it with scant patience; I guessed she spent a lot of time recapping things she'd said for a dazed Nicola Vonn.

198

'I have to go and get things ready after halftime.' Nicola muttered it to herself, as if she was repeating an instruction she'd received. 'Twenty-five minutes in each half because it's five-a-side not a proper match. I'll need time to get everything ready.'

Ruth beckoned to me and I bent down so she could whisper in my ear. 'Rhys always invites all the players back to his house afterwards.'

'That's nice.'

'It's a lot of work,' she hissed, eyeing Nicola meaningfully. 'All the players and all the supporters. She does a buffet, all cold, but still.' She beckoned me closer. 'I've made a pavlova.'

'That's so good of you.'

'No trouble,' Ruth said, but she was pleased.

On the pitch, the players were shunting the ball around in what looked like desultory time-wasting. I remembered how boring amateur football was, and pushed my sunglasses up my nose since the heat was making them slide down, and wished I'd remembered to bring a drink, and then forgot all of that in sheer outrage as the large monobrowed player who had been marking Derwent lumbered forward and sent him flying.

'It's not *rugby*,' Alan cried as Derwent hit the grass with enough force to knock the air out of his lungs. He lay on his back, rolling gently from side to side as the referee bent over him. Vonn sprinted across to check on him, then turned and gave us a thumbs-up. I swallowed, genuinely relieved.

'Your boy will be fine,' Judy said. 'Don't you worry. He's just winded.'

He sat up eventually, wincing, and quite obviously took it easy until the whistle went for halftime a minute or two later. He jogged across towards the water bottles, one hand across his body, hugging himself as if he hurt.

I went to meet him. 'Are you OK?'

A brief nod as he drank most of the contents of the bottle

in one go. When he resurfaced, he whispered, 'I'm letting him think he's done my ribs.'

'And he hasn't?'

'Nope.' Derwent's eyes glittered. 'I'm going to tackle him so hard his kneecap'll pop off. That or a knee in the balls. I'll knock them into his tonsils.'

'Do you think that's a good idea?'

'Yes,' he said flatly. Then, 'Thanks for coming. Best-looking supporter by far.'

'That's more flattering if you haven't seen the competition,' I said, surveying the sidelines. 'But I'll take it. Are you going to the Vonns' house after the match?'

He groaned. 'Do I have to?'

'No, but I think I'll help Nicola set up.'

'Did Georgia have anything interesting to say?'

'Yes and no.' I filled him in, one eye on the others in case they got close enough to hear our conversation. At one point Mike Knox seemed to be thinking about coming over. I put my hand on Derwent's arm which made him go completely still and followed that up with a heavy-lidded look, as if I was overcome with desire. Mike veered away and I sighed.

'Sorry. Where was I?'

'I have totally forgotten.' He slid his other arm around my waist and pulled me close to him. I leaned away.

'Super-romantic but you are far too sweaty for this – no – Josh, I mean it!'

He laughed and let me go, and I knew my face was hot, and if that hadn't convinced Ruth and Judy that we were a proper couple I was no judge of people. They were staring at us with the same indulgent smile on their faces, their heads tilted at the same approving angle. If it helped Judy to believe in our cover story it was worth a red face.

The second half began and I stood next to Nicola Vonn, trying to catch the words she was mumbling under her breath. She looked strained, her eyes fixed on her husband as he sprinted around ineffectually, wasting energy on shouting. Derwent scored a second time, thanks to a beautiful cross from a player I didn't know, a balding man with glasses and a long, rangy stride. Derwent wasn't the best player on the pitch in technical terms but he was quick to take advantage of any opportunities and he had endless reserves of aggression to provide him with energy.

'One more for the hat-trick,' Alan roared and Derwent raised a hand in acknowledgement, but I knew he was more focused on stalking the player who'd fouled him. A few minutes later he found himself with the ball, unmarked, the goalkeeper in a flat-footed panic in front of him. Instead of trying for his third goal, he passed the ball carefully to Rhys Vonn, who kicked it in the right general direction. It hit the post but by an absolute fluke it rebounded across the line as the goalkeeper floundered.

'GOAL!' Alan roared. 'WELL PLAYED.' To me, he said, 'Your lad could have had that one.'

'I think Rhys was in a better position,' I said, one eye on Nicola Vonn, who was clapping wildly. Thea was jumping up and down, cheering. It was clearly a relief that Rhys had scored and I wondered what would have happened if he had missed, or if Derwent hadn't thought to pass to him.

'Well, I'd better go,' Nicola said vaguely, to no one in particular. 'Things to do.'

'I'll help.' I set off beside her, not offering her the chance to turn me down. I had already arranged that Alan would mind Pippin for the rest of the match, until Derwent was free to take over again. 'I can't believe you do so much for the team. Ruth said you organise a lunch after each match.'

'Rhys likes it.' She gave me an uncertain smile. 'It's no trouble really.'

'Just tell me what I can do to help.'

'Camilla is at home. She can give me a hand.'

'She'll be tired though, after last night. Wasn't it the most amazing performance?'

Nicola's thin face lit up. 'Oh, did you enjoy it?'

'Very much,' I said truthfully. 'And Camilla was terrific.'

'I was proud of her. She wants to act, you see. Rhys wants her to qualify as a lawyer or something first, but she's adamant. I think she was hoping to persuade him to take her seriously now that he can see what she's capable of.'

'Did it work?'

'I must think,' Nicola said, 'about what I need to do. I'm sorry, if you just give me a moment . . .'

I quite admired her vagueness; as a way of not answering questions while at the same time not causing offence, it was brilliant.

On the doorstep, Nicola's hands shook as she sorted through her keys.

'Is everything all right?'

'Yes. Of course. Why wouldn't it be?' A little laugh, more jangling metal. I was about to take the keys out of her hand and open the door myself when it swung open. Camilla stood there, her eyes bruised-looking with the remains of last night's make-up still clinging to her lashes.

'I thought I heard you.'

'This – er – friend has come to help us with the lunch,' Nicola said, gesturing to me, and I introduced myself cheerfully.

'My boyfriend is playing. And your dad just scored a goal.'

The teenager's sullen expression lifted for a moment. 'Did he? He'll be pleased.'

'Even if they don't win,' Nicola added, and then bit her lip as if she was worried she had said too much.

Is he violent?

Are you scared of him?

Do you want the number of a women's refuge?

I said none of it but followed them through to the most expensive kitchen I'd seen on the road so far: bookmatched marble on the island, a vast cooker with nine rings, bound in metal like a treasure chest, designer lighting and doors that disappeared into the walls to blur the boundaries between the kitchen and garden. It reminded me fleetingly of the Dawouds' house but it was even more expensive and ostentatious than theirs. A litter of laptops and iPads lay on the huge table, and one wall was taken up with an enormous artwork that was a tangle of neon tubes, currently switched off.

With an effort I focused on the job at hand. 'What can I do to help?'

Nicola had opened the fridge and was staring into it vacantly. It was Camilla who handed me a tablecloth and directed me to the long table in the garden where the buffet was going to be. She was busy taking out napkins and paper plates and disposable cutlery as her mother gave me bowls of salad and platters of sandwiches to lay out.

'It's too early to cut the bread.' Nicola rubbed her forehead with the back of her hand. 'What else?'

'Drinks?' I suggested diffidently.

'Oh God, yes.'

'Leave everything in the fridge, Mum. You know Dad hates it when the drinks are warm.' Camilla opened a cupboard and started taking out glasses, muttering under her breath. She was wearing leggings and an oversized T-shirt that had the effect of making her look fragile.

'You were fantastic last night,' I said, and Camilla lifted one shoulder as if she would like to block out my words. 'Is there going to be another performance so the rest of the school can see it?'

'We did it for the rest of the school already. It was the dress rehearsal.' Her voice was toneless. In person she had none of the wit and vibrancy that had been so hypnotic on stage. She had gloried in the attention on the previous night but now she was withdrawn. A humming sound made her jump and she slid her phone out of her back pocket with practised ease, her long nails tapping on the screen.

'Mum, can I go out?'

'Not for long. I need you. They'll be here soon.'

'I'll be back. I just need a second.'

'Just a second then.' Nicola dropped into a seat at the kitchen table, staring into space as her daughter swung out of the kitchen. On the way she slapped a light switch with the palm of her hand and over Nicola's head the neon artwork buzzed and flared into life so I could read what it said, in jagged pink writing:

WE COULD BE HAPPY . . . ?

I felt as if it was taunting the desolate shell of a woman sitting beneath it.

28

I couldn't bring myself to force Nicola Vonn to talk to me after her daughter left, and anyway I couldn't think of anything to say except, *Is your husband abusive or is he just a wanker?*

I muttered something about making sure everything was on the table and made my way out to the garden to stare at the buffet. The garden was full of toys, especially around the swing set, slide and trampoline at the end. Otherwise there was a startling quantity of abandoned sporting equipment: a cricket bat, a goal and balls of various shapes and sizes. If it had been tidy, the garden would have been nice enough, with a large seating area on the patio outside the back door. Most of the plants looked dehydrated or dead, though, and the ones that weren't neglected were coated in aphids. On the left the path ran down to the Holmwood, but the leylandii that grew along the wall hid it. There was something frenetic about the space – a commitment to Having Fun in capital letters so no one could possibly accuse the Vonns of being miserable. I was letting my negative opinion of Rhys Vonn influence my feelings about the house, I knew, but I couldn't help it. Instead of a home, it felt like a crime scene waiting to happen.

I checked the time: they would be finished soon. I hoped that the home team had won.

'You have to tell someone.' A low voice, just above a whisper, came from the path on the other side of the wall. I didn't recognise the speaker's voice but it was a girl. 'It's not right.'

'I can't.' High-pitched, on the verge of tears. 'There's nothing to say. Look, you need to go.'

'You can't let him hurt you like this.'

A sniff. 'It's complicated.'

'You don't love him and he doesn't love you.'

'He says he does.'

'Oh my God, Cam, he's lying. Haven't you worked that out yet?'

There was a sharp sound and a cry of pain: a slap.

Camilla, I thought, and ran down the side of the house to the gate. Whatever was going on, I couldn't stand there and listen to her get hurt.

They were twenty metres away, face to face. I saw immediately that I had been wrong about Camilla being the victim: it was Elise Dean who was sobbing, one hand to her cheek. She was wearing a baggy sweatshirt and an ankle-length skirt that swamped her. Camilla was glaring at her friend. Her hands were balled into fists at her sides and pink patches dappled her neck and face.

'Is everything all right?'

At the sound of my voice they both turned. Elise sniffed. 'Who are you?'

'A neighbour. Are you OK?'

'Mind your own business,' Camilla snapped.

'Whatever this conversation is about, you don't need to hit each other.' I took a step closer. 'Is there anything I can do to help?'

Matching expressions, a blend of outrage and dismissal. I had united them in loathing of me, if nothing else.

'Of course not.' Camilla shook out her hair and began to scrape it back into a high ponytail, affecting to be unconcerned. 'It's no big deal. Just a row about a boy.'

Elise glanced at her friend before looking away again, but I'd caught the expression on her face: surprise and doubt.

What was I doing, I wondered. This was what Derwent had warned me about. I was pushing myself into the middle of a teenagers' row and it was nothing to do with Judy Thwaites or Davy Bidwell.

'What's going on here?'

I looked over my shoulder to see Mike Knox, still in football kit but with an amateurish bandage wound around one knee. He limped forward, taking charge without waiting for me to explain what I was doing there. The two teenagers had fallen silent. The only sound was the whirring of crickets in the undergrowth and the drunken off-key drone of a bee flying past my face. Elise looked horrified and Camilla was wary, her face watchful.

'Camilla, you need to get home. Your dad will be back any minute. and you don't want to annoy him, do you?'

'We're allowed to be here,' Camilla said, attempting to stand her ground, but Elise ducked her head and walked away, as if the mention of Rhys had scared her too much to argue. Camilla shrugged and followed her. Mike waited for them to pass through the barriers, watching them go, his arms folded.

When they had disappeared, he turned back to me.

'It's a lot easier for me to tell them what to do. I've got dad power.'

'I noticed. Do you get that in the delivery room or is it something that develops over time?'

He grinned. 'You have to cultivate it. Start off with jokes and work up to stern disapproval.'

'Is the match over?'

'It was a draw.' He looked down. 'I came off a bit early. Grazed my knee. You can't play if you're bleeding. They had to manage with four players for the last few minutes.'

'What a shame.'

'Probably a fair result. Coming to Rhys's?'

'Sure,' I said, following him down the path. A low growl of thunder made me look up at the sky and I caught sight of a face in the window of number 5. Gillian Holding. I waved at her and she laid a hand on the glass in front of her. The window was misted with her breath and I couldn't see her clearly enough to read her expression.

'What are you looking at?' Mike had stopped to wait for me at the barriers. 'Is she in the window?'

'Mrs Holding? Yes, how did you know?'

'She's always there.' He frowned. 'She should be in a home.'

I gave a little gasp; it was practically the first opinion I'd heard him voice. He looked at me quickly, wary.

'It sounds like I'm not sympathetic, and I am, but she's not safe to have around here. You saw what happened the other night. It's only a matter of time before something terrible happens to her, or someone who's out looking for her. Ah, here are the rest of them.'

The footballers were making their way up the close, I saw as I stepped through the barriers, the supporters straggling after them. Derwent was right at the back carrying the deck-chairs, his head bent to listen to whatever Ruth was telling him. Alan and Judy were slightly ahead, walking with Tom Thwaites. I was sure that Tom hadn't been at the match; I would have noticed him. He made my skin crawl and this time it wasn't the late hour or the strain of searching for Gillian Holding or the fear that the faceless man had brought out in me. I would need to seek him out, I thought, so it was time to let go of my revulsion.

And speaking of revulsion, somewhere along the way Rhys had picked up Gary Holding, who was shambling along swinging a thin plastic bag. He had left his mother on her own . . . but she was fine. I'd just seen her.

Derwent saw me and raised his eyebrows, clearly wondering what I was doing there with Mike Knox. I shook my head very slightly, and then pinned on a cheerful smile for Rhys Vonn.

'I heard it was a draw.'

'Can't win 'em all.' He laughed. 'Josh was great. I'm thinking about injuring Toby again so he can't play next week. Quick shot to the kneecap, isn't that right, Brian?'

Brian gave him the kind of tepid half-smile that I recognised from my own interactions with people who thought every person with an Irish name loved IRA jokes.

'Come on, everyone.' Rhys led the way up the path. 'Grub's up. Let's eat.'

I hung back, because Derwent had diverted to leave the deckchairs in Alan's shed. When he came back he was moving stiffly. Pippin was looking up at him, concerned.

'How was that?'

'As I expected.' He winced. 'Never again.'

'Rhys wants you on the team permanently.'

'Rhys can fuck off.'

'Did you deal with the guy who tackled you?'

His expression lightened. 'In the last minute of the match. He thought he was safe.'

'Foolish,' I said.

'Very. What were you doing with Mike?'

'I'll tell you later. Are you coming to lunch?'

'No. I'm in too much pain. I'm not going to be able to move tomorrow.'

'You poor old thing,' I said, and got a glare. 'Go and have a bath. There are Epsom salts in the bathroom.'

He brightened. 'Where did they come from?'

'I bought them for you.' I patted his arm. 'Thought you might be a bit achey. I'll do the lunch.'

'I suppose you can't get in too much trouble at a lunch party.'

'Of course not. Everything will be fine,' I said.

As it happened, we were both wrong.

29

'Where's Josh?' was how Rhys Vonn greeted me, looking past me eagerly.

Thanks for making me feel special, Rhys.

'He's gone home, I'm afraid. It's just me for lunch.'

'Coward.' Vonn shook his head. 'All because I told him he had to down a yard of ale to mark his first game. Bit of a ritual we have for new players. Did he tell you about my goal?'

The most important moment of the match, clearly. 'I saw it.' I smiled. 'Very impressive.'

'Not at all, not at all. It was a fluke.' His face was a shade of pink that clashed heroically with his hair, and he smelled goatishly rank after fifty minutes of football in the heat.

I knew I was supposed to disagree with him about the goal being pure luck but the truth was that he had fluked it. I settled for another meaningless smile.

'Come and eat something, anyway.' He put a hand on my back and guided me through the house. His palm was hot through the light material of my dress and I had to constrain myself not to twist away from him. I imagined turning and grabbing his wrist, forcing his hand up between his shoulder blades until he begged for mercy. That was a pleasant enough fantasy to get me through the kitchen and out into the garden where there was a buzz of conversation and a surprising number of people under the bulging dark-grey clouds.

'Here's Maeve. Josh couldn't come after all,' he announced, and there was a murmur of polite welcome mixed with disappointment. I felt that Rhys had been waiting for Derwent with some trick in mind – something in the yard of ale to sabotage him, maybe, to make him feel humiliated in some way. A test of strength to prove, once and for all, who was the top dog. What would it be like, I wondered, to have to assert your dominance all the time? Was that what made Josh the way he was – that other men insisted on measuring themselves against him? Or did he simply like the fact that he could compete and win?

If I wanted, I could have you.

The memory slotted into my mind like a slide clicking through a projector: a calm statement of fact on his part. All swagger, I had thought at the time, and I still wasn't sure it was true, but now I understood that he believed it, and that generally, belief was enough. As with the football, it was his determination and self-confidence that got him whatever he wanted.

But he doesn't want you.

And of course you don't want him.

I blinked the thought away and with an almost physical effort focused on what was happening in front of me. Nicola was standing behind the table now, frowning in concentration as she watched people help themselves to food. Camilla was a little way behind her, arms folded across her narrow chest, ready to help if she was needed. There was nothing for me to do apart from accepting a drink from the lanky bespectacled man who had played so well. His name was Lee, he told me, and he lived in the next road over, next door to Elise and her brother, and he was married with two kids who happened to be in the same years as Rhys's children, and yes, he did play a lot of sport. Did I have any kids? Did I play any sport? It wasn't challenging conversation and I was free to scan the crowd, looking for Judy and her son. They were deep in conversation with Alan and I knew there was no point in rushing things, although I dearly wanted to talk to Tom Thwaites for the first time. I would never get a better opportunity.

Rhys Vonn moved through the group, playing the host, slapping the men on the back and kissing the women whether they wanted him to or not. He fetched up beside Mike Knox, who was forking up food industriously. Mike swallowed in a hurry, and turned his friend away from the crowd so he could murmur in his ear without anyone else overhearing. A prickle of unease ran over my skin as I watched his mouth move, and Rhys's sudden stillness. I looked across to see that Camilla had noticed them too. Her eyes were wide, her pupils dilated with fear. Both of us knew what he was saying.

I saw Camilla with Elise on the path . . .

They were arguing . . .

I told her to go home . . .

Rhys didn't say anything but the look on his face when he turned to look at his daughter was nothing short of murderous. He plunged across the garden and took her by the arm.

'No, Dad, really—'

'What did I tell you?' He was shaking her as he dragged her behind a bush, out of sight of the rest of the guests who were chattering and laughing, oblivious.

Not your business, Derwent would have said. Not *our* business. Concentrate on the job in hand.

Tom Thwaites was still listening to Alan, who was mid-anecdote and showing no signs of winding down.

I excused myself from the conversation with Lee and skirted the crowd until I could see Rhys and Camilla again. He was talking. I couldn't hear him but the tendons were standing out in his neck and his face was red. Camilla screwed up her face against a spray of saliva but she didn't try to argue with him, or even look at him. There was no hint of rebellion in her demeanour: it was all fear that I saw.

'Don't interfere.' I looked around to find Mike Knox at my shoulder.

'What did you tell him?'

'He doesn't want Camilla anywhere near Elise or Isaac. Especially Isaac.'

'She and Elise are friends.' My throat was tight. 'Camilla has to be allowed to talk to her friends.'

He shrugged, his attention still on the plate he held. 'I'd want to know if it was my daughter.'

'You don't have a daughter,' I snapped, and stalked across the garden. 'Rhys?'

He straightened up and let go of Camilla, trying to recover his usual heartiness. 'Yes – what is it?'

As I approached Camilla's expression was one of undiluted horror. The last thing I wanted was to make things worse for her, so I smiled.

'I was just thinking – it's Josh's birthday soon and I wondered if you could make any suggestions for what he might like.' I blinked a couple of times, channelling Georgia. *Remember, if in doubt, bat your eyelashes. It works every time* . . . 'You and he have so much in common so I think if you like something, he might like it too.'

'I think it's possible we have the same taste, yeah.' He was staring at me like a bear sizing up his dinner. Camilla slid past him and disappeared.

'It's really hard to know what to get him.' I tilted my head to one side. 'I was wondering about something sporty?'

'What about an experience?'

'You mean like skydiving?'

He pursed his lips, coming closer. 'Maybe. Maybe. Or something more . . . private. For the two of you.'

Oh bollocks. I was registering a little too late that I had

213

entered the part of the garden where no one else could see us, and that Rhys was set on making this conversation awkwardly sexual. I took a tiny step back, and another, trying to make it look as if I wasn't moving.

At that moment there was an enormous crash from the patio followed by a gasp of horror: a disaster for most people, a miracle for me. Rhys forgot about our conversation, shoving me out of his way as he stormed around to see what had happened. I followed, reprieved, and found Nicola standing in the middle of what looked like an asteroid strike, holding an empty platter with traces of cream on it. I covered my mouth in shock.

'My pavlova,' Ruth said to me with gallant composure. 'She dropped it.'

'I'm so sorry.' Nicola was shaking. She crouched and picked up a piece of meringue, holding it as if it could be rescued, dressed up with a little whipped cream and served to the guests.

'*Smashing*,' Rhys said, affecting to be cheerful in a completely unsettling way. 'A *cracking* get-together, Nic. Well done.'

'Rhys, please—'

'What else is there? Camilla, look in the freezer. See if there's anything else for the guests. Mind you, it's probably just as well. No one would want to eat something that fussy. Far too warm for anything but ice lollies, in my view – sorry, Ruth, but it is as hot as hell today. Get up, my love. What do you think you can do with that?' He took the meringue out of Nicola's fingers. A fine dust of powdered sugar drifted down to the ground as he closed his hand around it and crushed it.

By common consent, all of the guests began talking at once, plunging into conversation to cover the awkwardness of the moment. I turned and discovered I was standing beside Judy's son. No time like the present. I smiled at him brilliantly.

'We haven't met properly, have we? Maeve. I saw you the other night, when Mrs Holding went missing.'

'Tom.' He shook hands with me, his grip loose. His eyes were slightly unfocused and I wondered how many beers he'd had.

'I didn't see you at the match.'

'Didn't go.' He swigged from the bottle he was holding. 'It's not really my thing.'

'But parties are?'

'Free food, innit.' He belched. 'Scuse me.'

I smiled as if it was the most charming thing that had ever happened. 'Your mum is incredible, by the way. I hope I'm like her when I'm that age.'

He snorted. 'Any way in particular?'

'I hear she does amazing work for charity. Someone said she looked after people with special needs from time to time?'

'Respite care.' His mouth was tight and he was looking at me, his eyes suddenly shrewd. I'd wandered into dangerous territory and I guessed he was wondering if that was deliberate. 'Difficult people. Hard to place. Sometimes they need some-where to go between residential settings.'

'She's so kind. Where does she find them? I'd have thought the authorities would kick up a fuss about her age, even though she's obviously so able. You know what they're like.'

'It's all private.' He sniffed, forking food.

'Does she advertise? Only my mum would probably love to do something like that,' I said earnestly and untruthfully. 'The house is empty and she gets lonely. Like your mum, probably.'

'No, she doesn't advertise.' The idea seemed to strike him as funny. 'No, it's contacts. Personal.'

'Oh, I see.' I didn't. 'Friends of friends?'

'In a way.' He gave me another look from under heavy lids, one that assessed me and found me no threat. 'My wife is involved in the care sector.'

'Your wife – I didn't know you were married.' I managed

215

to get a hint of disappointment into my voice, which he took as his due. Yes, he was physically unattractive and unfit, but he had an expensive watch, a fairly new luxury car and considerable self-belief. Why wouldn't I think of him as a potential partner?

Because I had some self-respect. And a boyfriend, as far as he knew.

'Seven years married,' he said with some satisfaction. 'Which explains why I've got this terrible itch.'

I giggled. Then I tried, 'Why isn't your wife here with you?'

'She's too busy to come and visit my mum.'

'Working in the care sector. It's so demanding, isn't it? What does she do?'

'Manages a home.' He said it through a mouthful of food. 'It means she has to work shifts.'

'And do you come here when she's rostered on? You're here quite often, aren't you?'

'Who said that?'

'Um, Fleur, I think? She mentioned about your car?'

He muttered something absolutely filthy about Fleur. For a moment I wondered if I'd misheard. Then he laughed. 'You really are an innocent, aren't you?'

I pouted. 'I don't think I'm that much of an innocent.'

'Tell me, Mabel, does everyone around here gossip all the time?'

I let the name go uncorrected. 'There's nothing else to do. Don't get me wrong, it's lovely but I'd go mad if I was living here all the time.'

'Me too. I come and go. Get in late, go early.' He tipped the dregs of the beer down his throat and looked around as if a fresh beer might materialise in the middle of the lawn or under the slide. I was losing his interest and it made me risk a direct question.

'Is your mum going to have anyone staying with her soon?'

'We'll see.' His fingers tapped the neck of the bottle impatiently. 'Sorry, I don't mean to be rude but I'm parched. I need another drink.'

'Of course,' I said. 'I think there's more beer in the kitchen.'

He grunted and was about to set off in that direction when there was a flash of brilliant light followed a couple of seconds later by an incredibly long, loud peal of thunder and a gasp from the guests.

'Oh, that was close,' Judy called out. 'I think it's going to—'

Something hit the ground by my foot and I felt the water splash up my leg.

'Rain,' I said, and Tom nodded.

'Run for it.'

One drop multiplied to five, and a hundred, and then the rain began in earnest, drumming on the hard ground, so heavy that the end of the garden was barely visible behind a pale curtain of water. I ran along with everyone else, cramming into the kitchen in a confusion of wet limbs and soaked clothes. There was something hypnotic about the sheer force of the water. We stood and watched, enthralled, as it rattled down onto the remains of the buffet and flattened the lawn. It filled abandoned glasses and ran off empty plates. It tore leaves and petals off the bushes and made mud puddles at the base of the slide. It formed a pool on the patio, dissolving the fragments of meringue until there was no trace of the pavlova's tragic ruin.

30

'Some party,' was Derwent's comment. 'Glad I didn't go.'

'I could have done with you being there as a bodyguard,' I said, squeezing the water out of my hair. The thunderstorm was still circling the hills and the rain was constant. I had made a dash for home during what seemed to be a lull and I'd ended up soaked to the skin. The polka-dot minidress was glued to me, which my colleague was nobly pretending not to notice. 'What do you think about Rhys?'

'I think that if we weren't focusing on the Thwaites pair I'd like to find some reason to arrest him, and I don't think I'd have to look too hard.'

'His wife and kids are terrified of him. Doesn't anyone else notice? Why are they all so happy to let him get away with it?'

'Maybe they're not.' He was brooding. 'If Nicola doesn't want to leave him there isn't a lot anyone else can do.'

'She should go and not look back.'

'You know that's harder than it seems,' Derwent said gently, and I stuttered to silence as I grasped what he meant. It hadn't occurred to me to compare Nicola's situation with the violent relationship I'd been in. I remembered with a flare of shame that it had taken me a long time to realise what was going on, until it was almost too late, and my friends had seen the danger long before I did. 'Maybe people spend time with them because when he's happy he's nice to her.'

'Not noticeably today. He was vile.' Somehow I gathered my thoughts, feeling I needed to defend myself. 'But Josh, when I was in a bad relationship I was on my own. I only had myself to worry about. If I'd had responsibility for a child, or even two—'

'That doesn't make it any more straightforward,' he said curtly. 'Then you have think about how you can afford to look after them, and maintenance payments, and shared custody. You don't want to let them down by not being around for them. Children make everything more complicated.'

'But—'

'Trust me. They do. Now can you focus on the job in hand?'

'I am,' I protested. 'I was just about to tell you about Tom Thwaites.'

Derwent listened as I repeated our conversation and the impression I'd had of his arrogance.

'We need to trace the wife. I'll get someone working on that.' He clicked his tongue. 'No wonder this investigation didn't come to anything first time round. They didn't know about Tom, never mind the wife. Not exactly impressive. You'd think they'd have found a paper trail.'

'Assuming it was a proper wedding,' I said. 'It could have been an informal arrangement, like the one that has vulnerable adults handing over their benefits to him.'

Derwent nodded. 'It seems to me that it's worth spending some money to keep Tom under surveillance for a few days so we can house him and locate the wife. And get Colin to have a nose around to see if there are any other properties in his name, or Judy's, or the wife's once we know who she is.'

That would involve a considerable commitment of resources, but it was what we had promised Rula Jacques we would do.

Part of our job in West Idleford was to decide where to allo-
cate effort in the investigation, and so far Tom Thwaites was
looking like our most promising lead.

'And if we find where Davy Bidwell was living,' Derwent
said heavily, 'so much the better.'

The rest of Saturday was distinctly less exciting; I watched
TV and kept an eye on the road, and Derwent did the sort
of paperwork he only bothered with when he had absolutely
no choice, snarling about it every time I wandered into the
kitchen. Pippin politely declined to go for a walk in the pouring
rain, and no one else in the Close seemed to be keen on getting
wet either. The water running down the gutters was the only
movement I spotted from the bay window.

Around six the rain slackened and stopped. The sun came
out, slanting light that struck gold from every wet leaf, every
hanging droplet. Everything smelled fresh.

'I'll take the dog out,' I said, pulling on an anorak.

'I'll come too.' Derwent got up with a wince and stretched.

'There's no need. I think I can manage to walk the dog on
my own and everyone around here is now fully convinced
that we're a couple.'

'No harm in reinforcing the message.' He shrugged himself
into a jacket. 'Anyway, I want to go.'

'Is this because I said I wished you'd been at the lunch?'

'No. Not at all.'

'Liar,' I murmured, and he looked up quickly, his expression
guarded, moderating to a sheepish grin as he saw I was
laughing at him.

In the middle of the night I woke up with an agonising headache. A lazy needle of pain ran through my left eye, piercing
its way to the back of my brain. It was a legacy of the head
injury I'd sustained the previous summer, which was annoying
in itself. I didn't like to admit there were still any physical

consequences to that. I drew my knees up and curled into a ball while I considered the options. I could refuse to admit my head was aching until morning, but I wouldn't sleep, I knew. I needed water and painkillers and to my total vexation I had neither. I remembered Derwent pressing capsules out of a packet in the kitchen the previous night to take the edge off his muscle pain: I could picture the packet sitting on the kitchen island where he'd tossed it. Very slowly, with very bad grace, I peeled myself off the mattress and fumbled my way downstairs in the dark. The last thing I wanted was to wake Derwent up and discuss it with him. It was half past three, I saw by the oven clock when I made it into the kitchen, which made me feel even worse.

I found the painkillers and swallowed them with a few gulps of water, then staggered into the sitting room. I would go upstairs when I started to feel better, I assured myself, and lay down on one of the sofas to wait for that miracle to occur.

I had left the kitchen door open, but I only realised approximately one second after Pippin erupted on the sofa beside me.

'Oh God, please no.' I really couldn't cope with barking or hyperactivity in the middle of the night when I was feeling so rotten.

As if he understood, the little dog turned around fast, three times, and snuggled up against my stomach. The weight of his warm body was immensely comforting. I curled around him. There was a thin blanket on the back of the sofa; I dragged it over us both and closed my eyes. Twenty minutes until the painkillers started to work and then I would return Pippin to the kitchen and get back to bed.

I opened my eyes on daylight and Josh Derwent sitting a few inches away from me, preparing to put on his socks.

'Morning.'

221

'Oh – I wasn't going to sleep—' I shrank down under what proved to be a duvet. 'Where did this come from?'

'I got it for you in case you were cold.'

'It's not the one from my bed.'

'No, it's from mine.'

'Oh. Thanks. Pippin was keeping me warm.'

'He got bored and came to find me.' His voice was deceptively casual. 'Feeling OK?'

'It's just a headache.' I felt as if my brain was pressing against the inside of my skull.

'Get them often?'

'Now and then.' And you know that very well, I thought. You're only pretending to be unaware of it because I was so unhappy you'd noticed my PMT.

'Since the knock on the head?'

I nodded, and winced at the consequences of moving.

He slid some capsules across the coffee table. 'Here you go. Two for you and two for me. Get them down you.' He knocked his back with a swig from his water bottle.

'What are they?'

'Paracetamol. Definitely more than four hours since your last dose.'

'How do you know?' I frowned at him. 'You were awake?'

'I heard you go downstairs.'

'Sorry. I didn't mean to disturb you.' I closed my eyes again, wishing I was dead.

'Doesn't matter.' He stood up. 'If it's any consolation, I can barely walk today. We're a right pair.'

'I'll feel better by lunchtime.'

'I won't. And I have to go out later.'

'Out? Where?'

'Football team drinks to celebrate our draw yesterday.' He glowered as I laughed at him. 'Go on. Remind me that I should have said no in the first place.'

'Well, the heart wants what it wants. Or in this case the ego.'

'I've learned my lesson.'

'I doubt that. Are you going to be drinking?'

'I'll have to, I think. But I'll take it slowly. I'm not going to get drunk.'

'Of course not.'

He edged delicately past the table. 'Come on, Pippin. This walk is going to make your day. I don't even mind how long it takes you to sniff piss as long as I can stand still while you do it.'

I had been enjoying Josh's company far more than I'd expected to, but it was nice to have the house to myself after he had limped out of the house wearing dark jeans, a shirt that matched his eyes and a sulk you could see from space. I tidied up and did a load of laundry – by tacit agreement we had each kept our dirty clothes to ourselves. There were limits, I thought, and folding Josh Derwent's underwear fell very much outside mine.

I sat in the sitting room as the light faded, picking at a salad and listening to music while I read through the notes I had spent the rest of the day writing, on Tom Thwaites, his mother and the tiny scraps of information I had picked up from the other neighbours. I read it through twice, then sent it to Una Burt. She would want to know that we were actually working – and we were, I thought, a shade defensive, even to myself. Left to himself, Josh would undoubtedly have preferred to lounge around watching television, but he was out there, enduring an evening with Rhys Vonn and his crew so that we looked like part of the community.

At some point, seamlessly, enjoying my own company segued into looking forward to Derwent getting back. It got later and later still and I thought about texting him, just to know that he was all right. Everything in Jellicoe Close seemed safe but under the surface there was danger, jagged reefs under calm water.

I was being ridiculous.

But then, in my persona as Derwent's girlfriend I would definitely want to check up on him, so really it was just part of the cover story. I settled on sending him a jokey text (U OK HUN?) and got YES THANKS TREACLE in response, which was not particularly informative but at least reassuring.

I let Pippin into the garden for a late-night wee and stood looking up at the sky, at the stars I rarely saw from my flat, while the dog scuffled around in the bushes. I tried to imagine this being my life and wondered if I would like it, all things considered. Would it make me happy to live in the suburbs, with a dog and a house and a big garden?

And if it wouldn't make me happy, what would?

A clatter at the front door made me jump and sent Pippin into paroxysms of rage. He raced to the door where Derwent was sidling in, shutting the door behind him with the exaggerated care of the truly drunk.

'Well?' I closed the back door and locked it.

'Well.' He was squinting against the light as he made a beeline first for a glass, then the sink. 'Well what?'

'Did you have a nice time?'

'Yes.' He downed a pint of water in one long swallow. 'No, actually.'

'Go on.'

'Didn't say anything I shouldn't've. I was careful.'

'Good for you. Did anyone else?'

He frowned, swaying slightly. I'd seen him drunk before but this was on another level. 'I don't like Rhys.'

'I'm aware of that.'

'You don't know everything.' He was pronouncing everything very distinctly but his eyes refused to focus on me. 'You think you do.'

'Everything about what?' I was mystified. 'The case?'

'No.' He shook his head. 'No. Not saying. No comment.'

He had been so determined not to let anything slip when

he was out with the team that he had retained the need for secrecy without being able to recognise whether it was needed.

'Josh, you can say anything to me. You don't have to be careful.'

'Could be given in evidence against me.' He waved a finger at me, blinking. 'So no.'

'OK,' I said, frustrated. I could wait until the following day for a proper debrief, assuming he could remember anything by then.

He slid away from the kitchen counter and crossed the room to where I was standing, not quite managing to do it in a straight line. He put his arms on my shoulders and leaned his forehead against mine. 'The thing is, I can't.'

'Can't what?'

'You know.' He sighed and I leaned away.

'Do you mind? I'm not sure I'd be safe to drive with the amount of alcohol you just breathed on me.'

'Sorry, sorry.'

'I think it's time for bed.'

A long, slow shake of his head. 'We can't. Off limits. Absolutely not OK.'

I started to laugh. 'No . . . I meant bed for you, on your own.'

'S'for the best.' He blinked at me soulfully and I nodded.

'That's what I thought.'

'Goodnight.' He turned and shambled out, his head down, and I listened until the various thumps and curses from upstairs dwindled to silence.

'Wait until tomorrow morning,' I told Pippin. 'We'll see what he has to say for himself then.'

But the next day, when his hangover improved enough that he could speak, he came to find me in the kitchen.

'Did I say anything I shouldn't have last night?'

'Like what?'

He couldn't look at me. 'Anything . . . inappropriate.'

'No, nothing. You just went to bed,' I lied.

'I wasn't sure . . . did I really not say anything embarrassing?'

'Not a thing.'

He blew out a lungful of air. 'Not that I thought I had.'

'You'd never say anything inappropriate.' I smiled at him, all innocence. 'Who was there last night?'

'The team, but then we ran into Alan and Tom. There's only one decent pub in this place.' He started to laugh. 'I don't know which of them was having a worse time. Ruth and Judy had insisted they go out, apparently. They have the square root of fuck all in common, so they practically ran over to sit with us.'

'Did you talk to either of them?'

'I talked to everyone. Life and soul of the party, that was me.'

'And did you find out anything useful?'

'Tom invited me to go shooting with him in the autumn. He's got some land in a remote bit of Nottinghamshire.'

'*Does* he?'

'He has a farm. Some of it is set aside for rough shooting.'

'I'd like to know more about the farm,' I said. 'At least we have a county to search in. That helps. How did you get him to talk about it?'

'Flattery,' Derwent said morosely. 'And I bought him a fair few drinks.'

'I thought you might have been drinking quite heavily.'

He shuddered delicately. 'There were shots.'

'Of course there were.'

'Your pal Bundy was there. On a date.'

'Stephen Bollivant?'

'Him. Jealous?'

'No,' I said evenly. 'Were you?'

'She was nice-looking. You wouldn't climb out the bathroom window to get away.' He shrugged. 'Can't say there seemed to be much chemistry between them, but you never know.'

'Anyone else?'

'Not in the pub.' He snapped his fingers. 'But when we got back, guess who was wandering around in the dark?'

'Gary Holding?'

'How did you know?'

'I saw him. I was in the sitting room all evening.'

'That explains why he was standing outside the house trying to see in.'

I felt a chill prickle over my skin. 'Are you sure?'

Derwent shrugged. 'That's how it seemed to me. But you know he always looks guilty.'

'Did he say anything to you?'

'Not that I recall. He ran away home.' Derwent hesitated. 'And speaking of saying things, are you sure I didn't say anything weird to you last night?'

'Absolutely sure,' I said promptly.

He didn't look convinced, but it was enough reassurance to send him back to the sitting room where it was his turn to lie on the sofa all day, and my turn to dole out the pain-killers at regular intervals, which was fine by me. I definitely preferred being the one who didn't feel as if they were dying.

The pressure inside his head was intolerable. It was impossible to bear it, literally impossible, and yet somehow he had to. The alcohol decaying in his body wasn't helping, but it wasn't a hangover that was driving him crazy. He wandered around the house, unable to settle, unable to concentrate. This was frustration and anger, building up inside his skull like pressure building inside a volcano.

Was it too much to ask for Josh to be *bad* at something? To be humiliated, just a little? To be *grateful* for something? He had started to fantasise about it, about Josh looking at him with respect in his eyes, acknowledging him as superior, but every fantasy faltered because what was going to bring him to his knees?

It was all so effortless, that was the thing. So easy for him to turn up and take over. The hero, scoring two goals. Setting up the third as if it was nothing to him, as if it was his decision whether he took all the glory for himself or shared it out. And then he was so popular with everyone, so funny and easy-going, so careless about how people reacted to him.

And his bitch girlfriend watching him as if he was her lord and master. Fuck, it annoyed him! The whole situation annoyed him. She should recognise him as being made of the same metal, capable of the same as Josh if not more. Instead, she barely noticed he existed. Oh, she could be sweet when she wanted, but there was more to her than that. An edge. He'd have liked to dismiss her as an airhead, but there were flashes of competence, of *intelligence*, almost, you'd say, if she wasn't a woman. And *that* was annoying, that Josh had found someone who could be a partner to him instead

228

of dragging him down, holding him back, forcing him to limit himself and his potential.

It wasn't fair.

The thing that he needed was a plan, he decided. First things first. There was the awkward situation he had been trying to ignore, the Problem that needed to be dealt with. He had tried threats but it was clear that wasn't going to work any more. Fear could only take you so far. Then you had to act, to show that you meant what you said. You had to prove it, not just to the people around you but to yourself.

You had to believe in yourself or no one else would.

If he dealt with the Problem, everything else would fall into place, he thought.

Sometimes he felt as if he was standing on sand and every wave stole a little bit more out from him, unstoppably, catastrophically. Sometimes he felt helpless. He felt like giving up.

If he dealt with the Problem, he would be back on solid ground.

From then on everything would be easy.

31

The next week passed by without much actual excitement for us, while behind the scenes the efforts to trace Tom Thwaites's home and his wife escalated. All that we could do was watch and wait and engage the neighbours in inconsequential conversation while Judy pottered around her garden and waved to me when I was walking the dog. Tom Thwaites didn't show his face. The temperatures spiralled into a full, proper heatwave again, with searing days and oppressively hot nights. I slept badly and lost all interest in food. Derwent was on edge and inclined to be snappy. I was used to being under pressure, to urgent investigations and late nights at work. Leaving the investigation in other people's hands didn't suit me.

'You've got to have patience,' Derwent said, which made me snort.

'You are the least patient person I've ever met. Please don't tell me to follow your example.'

'Waiting for the right moment to intervene is everything. If we move and alert Tom to our interest, we'll give him a chance to cover his tracks. It's all about building a chain of evidence to prove that he had a hand in these vulnerable adults leaving their care settings and coming to West Idleford for a few weeks or months, and then that he played a key role in moving them on to wherever they've ended up. We don't know if it was one location or many. We don't know if Judy was aware of the plan. At some point, you'll need to talk to her. See what she has to say about Davy Bidwell. But again, it's worth waiting for the right moment. If we show our hand too early we won't get the evidence we need to put together a proper charge. I don't want to end up with CPS permission to charge some bullshit misdemeanour after all of this.'

It was a matter of holding our nerve, of watching and waiting and trying to keep in touch with the Dawoud investigation. I couldn't complain about the effort that Vidya and Georgia were putting into the case – I had efficient updates every day from both of them, with detailed explanations of what they had done and what they were planning to do. Vidya was a good influence on Georgia, I thought, giving her confidence but keeping her focused. If only I could focus. The Dawoud investigation still seemed murky to me, clouded with unknowns, bloated with facts of questionable relevance. I should have been using my time to get a firm grip on Hassan Dawoud's life and death, but somehow it floated away from me every time.

And back in London, though I didn't know it then, Una Burt was protecting us from the pressure she was under, with daily phone calls from Simon Grayton, who himself was bombarded with messages and calls from Rula Jacques. The pressure was building. Something, somewhere, was going to give.

Meanwhile everyone was preparing for the barbecue the following Saturday – the community's social event of the year. I had checked with Judy and Ruth that all we needed to contribute was some money towards the catering, and to bring some drinks.

'We did try all bringing food but you know how it is, you end up with five trifles and no rolls for the hot dogs,' Judy told me. 'Much better to let a couple of people organise everything.'

'Alan does the barbecue,' Ruth said happily. 'And Stephen is very good about setting things up.'

'Oh yes, he is. And Gary does the music.'

'Gary Holding?'

Judy nodded. 'He's an expert. All on the computer. He sets up a sound system.'

'He does lots of events around here,' Ruth said. 'The summer fete. The Christmas market. All of the summer parties and weddings and so forth. It's his main source of income.'

'This summer party sounds like quite a big deal,' I said.

'Oh, it is. Everyone makes an effort to come along.' Judy laughed. 'We'll be there, won't we Ruth?'

'And you and Josh are coming.' Ruth's face was anxious. 'Aren't you?'

'We wouldn't miss it,' I said truthfully.

The day of the barbecue, Saturday, the temperatures nudged up towards record-breaking: half a degree more, the radio informed me, and it would be an all-time high for July. The heat was a solid wall outside the house, and inside wasn't much better. The leaves were withering on the trees and the grass had turned brown, despite the thunderstorm the previous weekend; it was simply too hot to live, nature seemed to be saying. The birds had fallen silent and Pippin was lethargic, a profound relief to me since his walks had to be early in the morning and late at night, and I was chronically short on rest. I gave in and went back to bed after the morning walk, expecting that I would fail to doze off as usual. Instead I crashed into a dreamless sleep for a couple of hours. When I got up again the house was silent. I assumed Derwent had gone out. I showered, twisting my hair up into a knot on top of my head, and put on white shorts with a halter-neck top, both of which became limp with sweat immediately. The barbecue was at six, when it would be cooler, but I would need to change again for it, *and* put on make-up, I thought

with absolute loathing, my mood murderous. If only I had
been doing this surveillance with Chris Pettifer, who wouldn't
have minded how I looked, or Liv. We could have made a
wonderful and believable couple, and I wouldn't have needed
to put on eyeliner. But no, it had to be Josh Derwent with
his neanderthal attitude to women and his 'high standards'.

The kitchen was empty but I heard a splash from outside
and went to the back door to discover a large inflatable pool
had erupted in the garden, a sort of supersized paddling pool.
The garden hose was draped over the edge to fill it. Also in
the pool: Pippin, who was splashing around happily, Derwent
in nothing but a pair of shorts, and approximately ten thousand dead insects. Georgia would have dived straight in, I
thought, but I was not in the mood for the tiny corpses, not
to mention the six feet of rippling muscle, especially when it
was wrapped around such an infuriating personality.

'What is going on here?'

'I thought the dog would like it.'

'The dog,' I repeated, kicking off my sandals and stepping
into the water. 'Christ, that's freezing.'

'You get used to it.'

I eyed him. 'I suppose it helps that more of you is out of
the water than actually in it.'

'The problem is that if it's full enough for me to be
submerged, Pippin has to swim, and he gets tired.'

'Tired is good.'

'Drowned is bad,' Derwent said severely. He slid down
another inch or two, which meant that he was essentially lying
flat and taking up the entire pool, which I pointed out.

'My pool. I bought it. I blew it up.'

'For the dog.'

'Yeah, obviously.'

I nodded, then scuffed some water at him, getting him right
in the face. He surged up faster than I had anticipated, grabbed
me by the waist and pulled me down into the pool while I

233

shrieked and Pippin barked. The water was shockingly cold on my overheated skin.

'You started it.' He let go of me and sat back on his heels, which gave me a chance to sit up. I was laughing.

'That was so immature.'

'I'm glad you realise it was—' He broke off because I had put my thumb over the end of the hose and targeted the spray of water right at him. He lifted his arms to ward it off, spluttering and blinded, turning his head away. When I took pity on him and put the hose down again, he shook his head. 'Now why would you raise the stakes like that?'

'I'm not afraid of you.'

'You should be,' he said darkly, and lunged. I was too quick for him this time, scrambling out of the water and darting away, leaving nothing but wet footprints behind me.

'This isn't over,' he called after me, but it was too hot for revenge and he slid back below the surface.

In the heat, wearing wet clothes was a joy. I went into the kitchen and made lunch for us both by way of making amends, humming to myself. It was remarkable how a bit of stupid rough-and-tumble could ease the tension that had tightened my shoulders and knotted my stomach.

You wanted to know what would make you happy . . . well, this is happy.

The thought was unexpected and in its own way as shocking as the icy water I'd stepped into. I was quiet enough for the rest of the day that Derwent asked if I was all right.

'Fine,' I said. 'Just the heat.'

And then it was time to get ready for the barbecue so I could think about that instead.

We were early, or so I'd thought, but when we arrived on the green we found that things were well underway, with each family spreading a picnic rug and bringing coolers of drinks over to the table that was the bar. A short distance away the other

234

groups were gathering, five distinct knots of people brought together by the chance of which house they had purchased in one of the roads. The heat had eased slightly after the afternoon peak, and a breeze had sprung up that made it more comfortable to be outside. Gary Holding was standing under a small gazebo, peering at his laptop, and a group of children had gathered in front of him, dancing and singing along to the pop music he was playing. The barbecue was billowing smoke and Alan raised a pair of tongs in salute when he saw us.

'Welcome, welcome. I've done some chicken already – it's on that platter. You can be the first to try it.'

Derwent strolled over to chat to Alan and I saw him looking down at the platter. With a movement that was uncharacteristically clumsy, he knocked into the table. The platter slid off the edge, shedding chicken onto the grass.

'Oh shit, sorry.' He bent quickly to pick it up.

I handed Pippin's lead to Ruth to keep him well away from the food, then went across to help, crouching beside Derwent. The meat, I saw, was rosy pink where it wasn't charred black.

'If I don't help with the barbecue we're all going to die of food poisoning,' he said in my ear. 'Throw this stuff out in case anyone is crazy enough to eat it.'

'Won't Alan mind?'

'Leave him to me.'

And then an apologetic Derwent was putting on the spare apron and insisting that Alan (who was delighted) should teach him everything he knew about grilling meat. I smiled to myself as I turned back to the party and went to offer Judy some wine from our supply.

I hadn't expected to enjoy the barbecue but I found I was actually having a good time as the sun slid down towards the horizon and the shadows lengthened across the grass. The different roads had started to mingle. The older kids played a riotous game of football while the younger ones had a water pistol fight that ended when the smallest children needed to go home to bed. I talked to Stephen Bollivant about the giant mirror and whether it had survived its fall unscathed (it had) and about his dog, and managed to turn the conversation around to his date the previous weekend.

'I think I like her,' he said, concentrating on peeling the label off his beer bottle. 'She's an art historian. Dutch painters are her speciality and I've bought and sold a few minor interiors in my time. We had a lot in common.'

'Did you arrange to see her again?'

'I was going to . . .' He pulled a face, awkward.

'Stephen, you've got to strike while the iron's hot! Dating is a cut-throat business these days. Text her now.' I stood over him while he wrote the message, and read it before he sent it, and told him truthfully that it would make me want a second date.

'But what if she doesn't?'

'Then she's an idiot.'

He took a deep breath and sent the text, shaking his head. 'She won't reply.'

'Give her a chance to read it.'

On cue, his phone vibrated. He snatched it up to look at the screen. 'She says where and when.'

'Yay!' I clinked my glass against his bottle. 'Well done.'

He was red with pleasure. 'I wouldn't have done it without you.'

'Well, don't leave her hanging. Make your arrangements,' I said, and he headed off to compose his reply, a Cheshire-cat grin on his face.

I moved on to Alice and Mike, which meant a long discussion with Alice about Tip's end-of-year exam results. Mike stared into the middle distance, obviously bored, but I was in the mood to be amused by that rather than annoyed. I skirted Nicola and Rhys, not feeling strong enough to cope with them, and fetched up with my actual targets, Ruth and Judy, who were sitting in their deckchairs again. Pippin was sitting on Judy's lap, tongue lolling.

I dropped down at their feet so they didn't have to crane their necks staring up at me. 'This is lovely.'

'Isn't it?' Judy was resplendent in a fuchsia-pink dress covered in ruffles. 'Help yourself to some prosecco, dear.'

'I'm not sure how well it would go with the red wine.' Not that I was actually drinking it.

'You're having a good time, aren't you?' Ruth beamed at me. 'You look very pretty this evening.'

'Thank you. So do you two.' I looked around. 'Is your son here, Judy?'

'He was supposed to be but he got held up. He said he'd come later but who knows? He's very good to see as much of me as he does.' She stroked Pippin, smiling to herself, and I thought there was no way she knew what her son was up to. There was a child-like innocence about her that he was exploiting and it made me even more determined to bring Tom Thwaites to justice.

I hugged my knees and glanced across at Derwent to see if he was enjoying himself. He was flipping over burgers at top speed, watched by the younger Knox and Vonn children who were laughing at whatever he was saying. Alan had moved to a wholly supervisory role and was standing well back, holding forth about cricket to Mike Knox.

'He's very good, isn't he? Very kind to everyone,' Judy said. 'Alan?'

'Oh no, dear. Your Josh.'

I laughed. 'Well, he's on his best behaviour.'

'He's a darling.' The prosecco had gone to Ruth's head, I thought. She drained her glass and put it down unsteadily. 'We were watching the two of you, you know.'

'You were?' I felt a faint chill. We were supposed to be the ones doing the watching. Derwent was going to kill me if I'd given something away . . .

237

'Oh yes. We love watching people, don't we?' Judy giggled as she looked at Ruth, the two of them nodding significantly.

'And what did you notice about us?' I tried to sound light-hearted.

Judy leaned towards me, her manner confidential, her voice just above a whisper. 'When you look at him, you smile.'

I laughed. 'Well, that's not so bad.'

'Yes, but when he looks at you,' Ruth said, 'he looks sad.'

My smile faded. 'Does he? What does that mean?'

Judy put her hand on my shoulder and squeezed it, her nail varnish pearly in the light of the setting sun.

'It means you're going to break his heart.'

32

Derwent came to find me a little while later, not noticeably heartbroken to my eyes but a touch dishevelled. His T-shirt had a smear of ketchup on it and he was nursing a burn on his forearm.

'Ouch, that looks painful.' I turned his arm, examining the mark.

'I've had worse. It doesn't hurt.'

'That's because you've killed the nerve endings.'

'Then at least they can't complain.' He stretched. 'I've grilled every single burger, sausage and vegetarian skewer within a five-mile radius. My work here is done.'

I wrinkled my nose. 'You smell like a bonfire.'

'I feel like the inside of a deep fat fryer. Is it all right if I go home and have a shower? I'll be quick. I'll take Pippin home and feed him.'

'Of course,' I said, surprised that he'd asked, and he jogged away, the little dog running gamely beside him. I wandered through the crowd, noticing that Nicola had left, but that Camilla and her little sister Thea were sitting on the grass in a circle that included the two Knox boys and another two teenagers who, on closer inspection, turned out to be Isaac and Elise. They had run themselves ragged playing football and dancing, and now they were limp like tired puppies, sprawling with unselfconscious ease. Camilla was staring at her phone, her face bright with reflected light from the screen, and Isaac was leaning on one elbow, watching her. His sister sat beside him, in long sleeves and a long black skirt despite the heat. Elise looked exhausted and unhappy, her eyes flicking from her brother to her friend like the pendulum of a metronome.

'They'll sleep tonight.' Brian had come to stand beside me.

'I hope I do too. It's not easy when it's this hot.'

'We put air conditioning in our bedroom and it's the best thing we ever did. I can't stand the heat. I was brought up on Irish summers.'

'Me too. Where did you go?'

'Kerry. You?'

'Donegal or Roscommon, depending on which parent won.'

'Both renowned for their warm, sunny weather.'

'At least two days out of the three hundred and sixty-five,' I agreed, and he chuckled.

'Hi.' Fleur gave me her trademark hard stare as she looped her arm through her husband's. 'Can I borrow you, darling?'

'I was in the middle of talking to Maeve,' he said, his voice harsh. 'What is it?'

'Just a quick word.'

She led him away as he threw me an apologetic grimace, and I took myself off to the bar to get another drink. I hoped no one had noticed that I'd made one glass of wine last two hours. As I turned away I saw Brian and Fleur a hundred metres away in the shade of some tall trees, clearly in the middle of a flaming row.

'Is that your fault?'

I looked around at Alice, surprised. 'Brian and I were just talking.'

'Sometimes that's enough.' Her eyelids were drooping and it was taking her a long time to focus on me; I wondered how much she had had to drink.

'Is everything all right with them?'

Her mouth tightened. 'Hard to say. Brian isn't always such a nice guy.'

'What do you mean?'

'He's not exactly what he seems.' She tipped back the wine in her glass. 'Honestly, I would stay away from him if I were you. He's not worth the trouble.'

Mike Knox appeared beside her, his face taut. 'Alice, what are you saying?'

'Passing on some good advice.' She tried to drink again from the empty glass and peered at it in disappointment. 'Oh, fudge.'

'I think you've had enough.' He gave me a dirty look as he dragged her away, more or less implying I was the one who had got her drunk. I blinked; I wasn't even trying to cause trouble and yet I seemed to be doing a good job of it.

'Cheer up, I'm back.' Derwent put his arm around my waist and kissed my cheek. His hair was ruffled where he had given it a quick and violent towelling to dry it, and the bonfire smell had been replaced with his usual clean citrusy scent. The navy-blue polo shirt was back along with what I had come to recognise as his good jeans.

'That's better,' I said approvingly.

'I thought so.'

'You did a lot of cooking. Did you get anything to eat?'

'I'm all right, thanks.' He looked over my shoulder. 'I didn't know there was going to be dancing.'

We had reached the point in the evening when Gary switched to slow numbers, winding things down. Knowing what his audience would want, he was currently playing 'Eternal Flame' by the Bangles. The area in front of the gazebo had a few swaying couples on it: Ruth and Alan, revolving in a very slow, majestic waltz, and Judy performing something a bit like a tango with Lee the lanky footballer from the next road over, and Alice Knox in Rhys Vonn's arms as he mauled her.

Mike Knox was sitting back on one of the deckchairs, drinking, not taking his eyes off his friend and his wife. His expression was grim.

Derwent looked at me. 'Do you want to dance?'

'Why not?' I let him take my hand and we went closer to the others. Derwent swung me into his arms with a degree of panache, but once he had drawn me close to him he settled into a low-key sway in time to the music. I had danced with him before, at a wedding. His mood on that occasion had been simmering with troublemaking energy but tonight was different; he was quiet and remote, lost in his own thoughts. I let him lead, occasionally catching someone's eye to smile at them. Fleur and Brian arrived, both looking self-conscious but clearly having kissed and made up. Brian went for the traditional school-disco-shuffle approach to slow dancing. Fleur didn't seem to mind. Her mascara was smudged under her eyes and all of her lipstick had worn off.

The first notes of 'Time After Time' fell on the evening air, eighties synthesiser in full cry, and Derwent leaned back so he could see my face.

'All right?'

'Very.'

He pulled me back to him, even closer this time, and I allowed it, because we fitted together so well. He was exactly the right height for me, and he moved with understated confidence, so that it was a pleasure to dance with him. What would Georgia say, I wondered, and then stopped wondering about it, floating happily. It was getting late, the light dwindling as the sun set.

'Last song,' Gary announced, 'and appropriately enough it's Blur, with "To the End".'

I checked the time, surprised to discover it was almost half past nine.

'I had no idea it was so late.'

'Mm.'

Derwent wasn't in a conversational mood, I guessed, and so I took the hint, staying quiet until the music faded to silence. I made to step back and he held on to me for a moment before he released me. I looked at him, questioning, and he hesitated, on the brink of saying something.

'Are you all right to help with tidying up before it gets completely dark?' Rhys Vonn shattered the moment as effectively as any nightclub bouncer.

'Of course,' Derwent said with a savage smile that would have made me run and hide but Rhys was oblivious.

'If you could carry the chairs back for the old dears, that would be perfect.' He turned to me. 'You don't mind picking up some rubbish, do you?'

'Not at all.' I went and got a black bag, gathering up paper plates and napkins. Lee and Stephen were folding the tables. Mike Knox was dismantling the gazebo with great efficiency while his wife sat on the grass and stared at the sky, swaying slightly. I caught his eye and he grimaced.

Oh, get over yourself. At least she had fun. I hoped the thought didn't show on my face.

Fleur was also on rubbish duty and paused beside me. 'Sorry I was a bitch earlier.'

'Oh – it's fine.'

'Brian said I should apologise.'

'There's no need,' I said sweetly.

'I was having a moment.' Tears glittered in her eyes. 'I'm not usually like this, you know.'

'Really, it's fine. If there's anything I can do—'

'No.' She hesitated. 'But thanks.'

I didn't see a future of nights out drinking cocktails with Fleur, but I was pleased that she seemed to be making an effort to be nice. I could meet her halfway, I thought as I walked some distance away and bent to retrieve a plastic cup from where it had blown into the bushes. It was the least I could do—

The thought died as the dry grass crackled behind me: footsteps. I whirled around and found myself face to face with Rhys Vonn.

'What are you doing?'

'Just wanted to ask you something.' His eyes were bright. 'Are you faithful or do you play around?'

'What?'

He grabbed my arm and stroked the inside of my elbow with his thumb as he whispered, 'I keep thinking about how much I want to taste you.'

Hot breath on my ear. I twisted away in disgust but I wasn't strong enough to break his hold on me. I ran through the options for dealing with him physically and decided, with regret, that stamping on his foot would be too much like Detective Sergeant Maeve Kerrigan's response. I settled for a scornful, 'You're vile.'

Vonn chuckled, his face red from excitement rather than embarrassment. 'Can't you take a joke?'

'She can, but I don't have much of a sense of humour,' Derwent said from behind me. Vonn's grin faded.

'Just messing around, mate.'

He let go of me and Derwent took the opportunity to step between us, close to the other man. He said, quite quietly, 'If you touch her again – if you so much as think about touching her – I will break every bone in your face.'

'Understood.' A swallow; Vonn was genuinely terrified. 'I've had too much to drink. Sorry. Sorry, Maeve.'

'Don't speak to her. As far as you're concerned, she doesn't exist.' Derwent's face was stony. 'You can apologise to me.'

'I'm sorry. Very sorry. I – I shouldn't have done it.' All of his confidence seemed to have melted away.

'You've spoiled what could have been a lovely evening.'

'I know.'

'You're a twat, Vonn. An absolute wanker.' Derwent gave him a long look, then turned to me.

'We're going home.'

I was shaking. 'I was in the middle of clearing up.'

'You've helped enough.' He took the rubbish bag out of my hand and threw it at Vonn. 'Do something useful. Come on, Maeve.'

33

I followed him because I had no choice about it; he was holding on to my hand with a bone-crushing grip.

'I'm sorry that happened,' he said over his shoulder as we crossed the road towards Jellicoe Close. It was getting properly dark now, the sky a deep shade of blue, the streetlights casting shadows across the tarmac.

'It was nothing.'

'You didn't react like it was nothing.'

'Neither did you.' I dragged my hand free. 'Was that really necessary?'

'What?' He turned to look at me, eyebrows sky high.

'I could have handled it myself.' I was hugging myself for comfort. 'It's not the first time something like that has happened. I didn't need you to intervene.'

His face went blank. 'You were upset. You're trembling.'

'I'm shaking because I'm absolutely livid,' I hissed.

'With *me*?'

'You sounded as if he'd dented your bumper – as if he'd damaged your prize possession.' I imitated his macho delivery: '"You can apologise to me." What the fuck, Josh?'

'What were you going to do, arrest him?' He took a step closer. 'I talked to him the way he would understand. That's all. You weren't in a position to handle it by yourself, because that's not what we're doing here. Nine times out of ten you would have been fine and I'd have left you to it. This was the tenth time.'

'You made me feel worse than he did.'

The words seemed to have more weight than I'd intended; Derwent actually took a step back. A muscle tightened in his jaw and it was one of the signs I knew to look for when he lost his temper. *Good*, I thought, quailing a fraction.

But what he said was, 'Look, I'm not having this conversation. Not here in the middle of the road.'

'Is that it? *That's* your response?'

'Shut up,' he said through gritted teeth.

I was angry enough and unwise enough to snap back. 'Make me.'

Something flickered in his eyes and I knew what he was going to do before he did it: a stride as smooth as a dance step, his fingers caught in my hair, his mouth on mine. Inevitable.

I asked for that, I thought, stuck to the spot like a moth with a pin through it.

It had been bad temper that made him kiss me, but I could tell the moment his anger faded. His mouth curved against mine, and I knew he was laughing at me because I wouldn't kiss him back. *So what are you going to do now?*

What I was going to do was nothing. I turned away from him when he let me go and walked back to the house with him silent by my side. He had anticipated anger, outrage: what I was prepared to give him was nothing more than professional composure. My lips were tingling which annoyed me even more.

He stopped in the porch, spinning the keys around his finger. 'Maeve.' His voice was low, warm, shaken with amusement. 'Come off it.'

Inside the house, Pippin set up his usual racket, which saved me from answering. I waited for Derwent to open the front door, then stalked past him into the kitchen where I took up

247

a position near the sink. He tipped some food into Pippin's bowl before he moved over to the other side of the room and leaned against the table, folding his arms, defensive but still with a glint in his eye that spoke of mischief.

'Before you say anything, there was someone right behind us. I had to shut you up in case you gave us away.'

'Is that it? *That's* the reason you crossed that particular line?'

A one-shouldered shrug, amusement fading to be replaced with boredom. Criticism never sat well with him. 'Look, I've had closer moments with the dog. Do we really have to make it into a big deal?'

'No. Of course. Why would we?' My vision blurred and something wet streaked down my face. I blinked fiercely and he came back into focus.

'Are you crying?'

'No.'

'You are. Why? Because of that kiss?'

'No,' I said again, and sniffed. 'Well, not exactly.'

His face tightened, as if he was bracing for something that was going to hurt him badly. 'Explain it to me.'

I considered brushing the question off with something dismissive, but he sounded as if he really wanted to know.

'Ever since I was attacked . . . I haven't been myself.'

'I've noticed.' He shifted his weight, restless.

'Yes, of course. You notice everything.' I caught myself: this wasn't the time to start sniping at one another. 'I don't mean at work. I mean everywhere. In every way. I don't *feel* anything. It's not even that I don't want to be touched. I've tried. That part of me – it's like something died.'

'That doesn't surprise. You couldn't really expect anything else. You went through something terrible. Of course it affected you.' He paused, weighing his words carefully. 'I've been through a few bad experiences. The only time I ever had counselling that helped, the therapist told me you remember pain in your body as well as your mind. The two aren't separate. You have to fix both of them before you can move on. You've been telling yourself you're OK now, but that's not what your body thinks. You can't hurry this. You need to find someone you trust and then give it time.'

'You know me better than that. I find it hard to trust people.'

One side of his mouth curled up. 'Understatement.'

'It took me a long time to find someone else after Rob left, and it didn't exactly work out as I'd imagined. But the difference was that I wanted to find someone. Now it's worse. I just wonder—' My voice was wobbling and I stopped, mastering myself. 'I don't think I'll ever want anyone again.'

He laughed. 'Of course you will.'

'I'm glad you're so confident,' I spat, thoroughly nettled that he was making light of it. 'Can I remind you that you kissed me and it had no effect whatsoever.'

'Yeah, well, I wasn't really trying.'

'Of course not. But we're here pretending to be madly in love all day, every day, and you're supposed to be the expert at sweeping women off their feet, and there should have been *something*. Some kind of spark.'

'Come on.' He tilted his head back, considering me with lazy interest. 'I wouldn't even have to cross the room.'

'You are so *arrogant*.'

'No, accurate.'

I fully intended to argue with him – I had already decided what I was going to say – but I made the mistake of looking at him first. I wasn't prepared for the expression on his face. It was a look I'd accidentally intercepted once before, the look that said I *want you, right here, right now,* and I felt a wave of heat sweep through me, instantly, making my anger evaporate like mist.

He raised his eyebrows. 'See?'

'That's not fair,' I said flatly.

It made him laugh again. 'Look, Maeve, I'm not trying to

wind you up, but I don't think things are as dire as all that. You have to be patient.'

'I'm bad at that.'

'I'm well aware.' He stood up and walked over to me. 'Come here.'

I allowed him to draw me into a hug, his arms tight around me. Without thinking I turned my head towards him instead of away, my face pressed against the angle of his neck and shoulder. I shut my eyes and let myself relax, comforted by the warmth of his body, and the familiar smell of him, and the slow rhythm of his breathing.

I don't think he intended for anything else to happen any more than I did, and I couldn't precisely pin down when that changed, or how – a shift in his weight, a tiny movement of his hips that brought us a fraction closer, and called to mind something that was quite distinct from an innocent hug – but suddenly I was aware of him in a totally different way. His hands moved and he said my name, a soft, barely audible sigh that brought my head up so I could look at him. As a rule these days he kept himself under tight control, all of his emotions and desires hidden from me except in brief, revealing flashes. Now I had the sense that he was allowing the reins to slip through his hands, reckless of the consequences.

Two key things about our conversation had brought us to this point: I had found him a problem to solve, and I had dented his ego. Add that to the fact that we were on our own, far from home, and that as he had proved there was heat between us that could be coaxed into a flame with very little encouragement, and it was no wonder we were in new territory.

He slid a hand up, his palm against my cheek, his fingers tangling in my hair. 'It's all right. Just stop thinking,' he said softly. He was completely sure of himself.

'It's not that easy.'

He tilted his head, studying me. 'Isn't it?'

No. This was a bad idea and boundaries had been blurred already and we had a professional relationship to think about and he was in a relationship, and even though no one would know anything happened, that didn't mean there wouldn't be serious fallout, and the *sensible* course of action—

'What would help?' He took a step forward, moving me backwards, until I collided with the kitchen counter and had nowhere to go. 'What about this?'

Dismay was a lead weight in the pit of my stomach. This was a test I was going to fail. I was drearily familiar with the grinding, or hair-pulling, or grabbing – the whole violent repertoire of all-out assault to overwhelm my reservations that other men had tried at other times.

But this was Josh Derwent, and I should have known better.

He put his left hand on the counter, between my arm and my hip as he closed the distance between us. The whole length of his right thigh pressed against the outside of my leg and I realised he had neatly trapped me, squeezing me into a smaller space. As my knees pressed together, the heat started to build between my legs. Even though it was the opposite of aggressive, it wasn't what I'd been prepared for. Confusion spiralled through my mind, clouding every other feeling. I looked at him, uncertain, and bit my lip.

'No.' He frowned in disapproval, put his thumb under my mouth and drew downwards gently so my lip pulled free.

He leaned in and I waited for him to kiss me, but instead he trailed the thumb down from my mouth to the hollow at the base of my throat. His fingers spread out slowly inside my dress, his fingertips resting along my left collarbone. They grazed my skin with the lightest possible touch, and it wasn't an area I had previously considered to be particularly exciting but the skin was so thin there that every point of contact tingled, and I felt my stomach flip over as I stared into his eyes. The heel of his hand was over my heart; I assumed he could feel it thumping.

I'd always known he could cast a spell over women, but

I'd never understood how he did it before. The seconds dragged past, the delay intolerable now, and I tried to move towards him, to reach his mouth with mine, but he held me back gently, the tiniest increase in pressure from his hand telegraphing: *No, wait, don't rush it, trust me.* He was barely touching me and I was dizzy with wanting more.

It was a clever trick, the tiny part of my mind that was still functioning informed me. He was using almost no force and yet he had total control of me. He was the cliff edge, the sheer drop, the high mountain, the North Pole: a bad idea and an irresistible challenge. No one in their right minds would, but you had to, you couldn't stop yourself, you'd die if you did and die if you didn't. You'd give everything up to him and be glad when he took it . . .

I moved then, arching my back so our bodies were touching everywhere they could. As I pressed against him his eyes went inky dark, want driving out thought. His hand slid up to the back of my head, drawing me to him. Knee to knee, hip to hip, his chest against mine, closer, tighter, and with a rush I remembered what it was like to be desired, and to desire. Nothing else mattered. I *needed* him. I was back to how I used to be, except that this wasn't like anything I'd felt before: this was a sharper hunger.

The distance between us narrowed until I could feel his breath on my mouth.

The next second, the room exploded with noise and I came back to earth so fast it winded me.

'What the—?'

Derwent was already wrenching open the back door. Pippin danced around his feet, keeping up the volley of ear-splitting barks that had interrupted us. As he stepped out past the dog, Derwent caught hold of his collar and pushed him back, shutting him in.

He disappeared into the night, and left me with Pippin, on our own.

34

I was on my own again the next morning, I discovered, standing by the kitchen table reading the note that Derwent had left me.

> I've got to go home for a couple of days. Sorry, it's unavoidable.
>
> I've walked Pippin and fed him, but he'll tell you I didn't. Ignore him.
>
> Don't get into any trouble while I'm gone. I mean it.

I turned the page over and found the other side was blank. 'Is that it? Typical.'

I made myself some breakfast that I didn't really want, ignoring Pippin's quivering dejection. I was caught between anger and relief. So he was gone, without so much as an apology or an opportunity to have something like a conversation about what had happened the night before.

What had almost happened, I corrected myself, squirming with shame.

What I had wanted to happen.

But actually, it was possible to go back to a normal working relationship if we just cleared the air like grown-ups instead of running away from the situation we'd created. I found my phone and called him. A light, straightforward conversation and then we would be back to where we needed to be: colleagues, friends, whatever term fitted best in the moment . . . It rang twice, and then there was a click.

'You have *reached*. The voicemail of. Oh, seven, seven—'

I cut off the cooing robot without leaving a message. I could just picture him glancing at his phone and rejecting the call. It was infuriating and childish of him and I needed someone to agree with me about that.

'What's wrong?' Liv sounded as if she was out and about.

'Nothing. Everything's fine.'

'You're ringing me at ten to eight on a Sunday morning, completely out of the blue, because you feel like a chat?'

I sighed. 'No. Obviously not. Can you talk?'

'I'd love to. I've been up since five and I'm walking around the park with Sonny like a zombie. What's going on? How are things with Josh?'

'Things are *without* Josh, currently. He's gone off for a couple of days, according to the note he left me.'

'He didn't tell you he was going? I'm parking the buggy for this one.' I waited while she arranged herself on a bench. 'What happened?'

I gave her a quick run-down of what had been going on since we arrived, ending with a fairly detailed description of the barbecue – and the dancing – from the previous day.

'Uh-oh. I think I can guess where this is going.'

'I didn't,' I confessed.

'Well, there's a shock.' She chuckled. 'You're incredibly slow on the uptake sometimes.'

'That's not fair. Anyway, it didn't happen the way you think. And what you think happened didn't. Not really.'

'I love it when you're mysterious. Go on.'

I told her about the argument and how it had ended temporarily when he kissed me.

'NO. He DIDN'T. Please tell me you're wearing his bollocks as earrings.'

'It was nothing. A joke.'

'You mean it didn't rock your world? Despite everything?' She sighed. 'Being straight must be so disappointing. You should report him for false advertising.'

'He wasn't trying, he said.'

'Oh, sure. A likely story.'

'Actually, I believe him,' I said carefully.

A pause, because Liv was good at listening to what people said and what they didn't say. 'What are you not telling me?'

Slowly, painfully, I ran through the conversation we had had when we got back to the house. It was the first time I'd talked to Liv about the numbness that had afflicted me since the previous year and her response was instant compassion.

'No one would just bounce back, Maeve. No one. It's completely understandable that there would be a physical effect on you as well as a mental one.'

'That's what Josh said.'

'I suppose he suggested fixing the problem with his magic cock.'

Silence.

'Oh Maeve, you *didn't*. He has a girlfriend.'

'No, we didn't. It wasn't like that.' I leaned my forehead on my hand and rocked gently on my chair. 'He didn't even kiss me again. He only touched my neck.'

'Your *neck*,' Liv repeated, deadpan. 'Wow.'

'Look, it was – he . . .' I gave an involuntary shiver of pleasure at the memory of it. 'I really don't think he thought anything was going to happen except that he was going to win the argument about whether he could make me want him.'

'And you didn't take the opportunity to climb him like a tree.'

255

I draped my hand over my eyes, as if that would stop me replaying what I'd done. 'We didn't even kiss.' Honesty compelled me to add, 'We might have, but the dog went mental, barking at the back door. There was someone in the back garden, watching us.'

'Seriously?'

'It was pitch dark out there so neither of us saw him properly, but it was definitely a man. Josh ran out and tried to catch him but the guy went over the fence at the back of the garden and disappeared. Josh was out looking for an hour. No sign of him. And by the time he came back . . .'

'You had to talk about the voyeur, so neither of you brought up what happened before the dog barked, which was a huge relief because you could trot off to bed on your own and pretend nothing had happened.'

'Exactly. I thought we could talk about it today.'

'But he fucked off and left you on your own.' She clicked her tongue, irritated. 'And I suppose it didn't occur to him that you might be in danger.'

'He told me to stay out of trouble.'

'Oh, brilliant. What the fuck is he thinking?'

'I don't know. He hasn't given me much to work with.' I hesitated. 'Someone was following me around the other night. Maybe the same person who was watching us.'

'Right. This is ridiculous. Leave it with me.'

'What are you going to do?'

'Fix this.'

To give Liv her due, she was good at dealing with awkward people. Within twenty minutes, my phone was ringing. I snatched it up to discover Una Burt's number flashing on the screen, which I had neither wanted nor expected.

'Maeve? Josh rang me. I understand he's had to leave West Idleford for personal reasons.'

That's one way of putting it . . .

'He doesn't want you to be on your own and I must say I agree with him. I'm going to send someone down to stay with you until he gets back in a couple of days.'

'Who?'

'I haven't decided yet. It will depend on workload and who volunteers.'

Fucking fuck; I would rather be alone than stuck with Pete Belcott.

'Ma'am—' I began, but she cut me off.

'Josh wanted to let me know what a good job you've been doing. He's been very impressed with your hard work and positive attitude.'

I bit back what I wanted to say about my positive attitude. 'Well. That's kind of him.'

She hesitated. 'He wouldn't have left if he didn't have to go, Maeve.'

'Is that what he told you?'

'I know him well enough to be sure of it.'

Nice words, but she didn't know him at all.

I spent that Sunday cleaning the house in readiness for the new arrival, working out my feelings by scrubbing surfaces and shoving the vacuum cleaner around.

'And he left me to do all of this by myself,' I said to a demoralised Pippin, who was sitting in his basket. 'This is his mess too.'

A mess in every way, I thought, miserable about it. Everything was up in the air, resisting neat solutions and easy answers. I had a headache and my brain seemed fogged so even the simplest tasks took too much concentration. We were wasting time in West Idleford to please the bosses, and that had a cost, whether it was to the Dawoud investigation or my peace of mind.

Derwent's bedroom door was closed and I hesitated before going in, to discover the bed neatly made and the room empty of his belongings. I sat on the edge of the bed and ran my hand over the duvet, thinking about how he had brought it downstairs when I wasn't feeling well. There was the faintest hint in the air of the citrus smell I associated with him, that I noticed when I was close to him. It was the only sign he'd ever been there.

I was close to him a lot, I thought. Not just during this investigation, with the slow dancing and cuddling on the sofa and rubbing up against him in the kitchen for the benefit of onlookers. It was all of the other times – the arm around my shoulder, for comfort or mockery. The tight spaces. The crushing hugs when I was falling apart. The swerves into my personal space, diving across my desk for a snack or a pen or to annoy me. The job cars on late nights. Those moments of being alone together in the lift at work – the way he always took the stairs unless he was with me. The times he'd stepped in and saved me. The times I'd done the same for him. The conversations I didn't have with anyone else. The things I couldn't say to anyone else.

The slow drift from not liking him, to tolerating him, to enjoying his company, to needing him.

Needing was the wrong word. I stood up with decision. I did not need him.

I was just used to having him around, that was all.

A car parked outside the house in the late afternoon. I looked up from my position on the sofa, saw who it was, and gave a deep sigh. Of course. It would be.

I went out, squinting in the bright sunshine. 'Hello, stranger.'

'So this is where you're staying.' Georgia dropped a straw sunhat onto her head and turned around to admire Jellicoe Close from under the shade of the brim. 'Very nice. You should come over and hug me.'

I went and put my arms around her for a brief squeeze, almost asphyxiating in a cloud of perfume. Before I let go, I murmured, 'What's the cover story?'

'I'm your best friend. We haven't seen each other in ages. I'm keeping you company while Josh is on a work trip.' She grinned. 'Pretty close to reality.'

'Sorry for the last-minute notice.'

'I really didn't mind. It gave me a chance to wear my new dress.' A pirouette so I could admire it, which I did. The dress was sky-blue cotton heavily embroidered with white stitching, pulled in at the waist but flaring out to mid-thigh, where it ended. Her shoulders were bare and tanned to golden glory. Instagram perfection had come to Jellicoe Close.

The whir of a bicycle's wheels made me start: Rhys Vonn, coming back on his own from a long, hot ride. His Lycra suit was unzipped to the waist. He glanced at Georgia but there was no reaction behind his expensive sunglasses, and he didn't even acknowledge me.

'That's a bit disappointing.' Georgia looked down at herself. 'You'd think I'd get a good afternoon.'

'He's too scared to say anything. I'll tell you why later.' I watched Alan emerge from his front garden, scuttling faster than I'd ever seen him move before, his expression gleeful. 'This should be a bit more reassuring.'

Alan was delighted with Georgia, and with her dress. He was ecstatic that I had a friend staying – 'two lovely ladies' – and there was no suggestion he wasn't convinced by the story. He offered to carry Georgia's bags into the house and invited us round for tea – 'Ruth won't mind' – and warned us that the weather was 'on the turn' despite the warmth of the afternoon sun, and generally did his chivalrous best to make Georgia feel welcome. I put him off gently and we managed at last to go inside the house, sans Alan, where Georgia put her sunhat on the newel post.

'This is so nice. It's like a little holiday.' She bent to stroke Pippin. 'Hello, cutie.'

'I need to brief you on this case,' I said repressively. 'And then we need to walk Pippin. After dinner we can talk about the Dawoud case.'

If she had been a dog, her ears would have drooped, but she nodded. 'That's fine. I brought the file.'

'On the other hand, since it's such a nice evening and you've had such a long drive, we could go to the pub.'

'Really?'

'Sure. As long as you're happy to stick to soft drinks.'

Her face lit up. 'This is going to be so much fun.'

The Dawoud file remained unopened that night; we talked it over but it was an easy discussion rather than hammering our way through the evidence. I'd had worse evenings than sitting outside a pub on a clear summer night with a little dog curled up against my leg, running through the houses in Jellicoe Close and what we had found out about them in the previous weeks. Georgia attracted enough attention that she was happy, but she brushed off all of the offers of drinks and dates.

'Do you have a boyfriend now?'

'Do you remember the director at that clinic we went to last year? The bus murder?'

'I remember him, he's cute.'

'We've been together ever since. It's changed everything.' She was glowing. 'It's long-distance, which should be a deal-breaker, but I don't mind.'

'You seem happier.'

'I am. It's not that he fixes all of my problems. He just gives me the space to be me.' She shrugged. 'I've never really had that before.'

I thought about that while she was at the bar. Was that what Derwent had offered me the night before? The space to be me? It had felt more like a challenge.

Georgia was a fun person to be around, I discovered that night, but despite her chatter I still felt lonely.

*

When we got back to the house, I made a snap decision. 'Why don't you take the bigger bedroom? It's really lovely in the mornings when the sun rises. Make sure you close the curtains or Alan will have his binoculars out.'

'I liked Alan.'

'And he liked you.'

She caught the sardonic undertone. 'Oh. Is Alan a bit like that?'

'He is indeed.'

'Oh.'

'But he's quite nice too. You just have to avoid wearing anything revealing. Or short. Or tight.'

She looked down at herself. 'Everything I've packed is short or tight. Or both.'

'Then Alan's in luck.'

I said goodnight to her and dived into the bathroom, anticipating that Georgia was not going to be quick (wholly accurate; it would be a full forty-five minutes before she finished her bedtime routine in there). Scrubbed and pyjama-clad, I tiptoed down the hall to the other bedroom. I climbed into the bed, tucking the duvet around me, and felt comforted for no reason at all.

35

Overnight the weather changed, as the forecast and Alan had predicted. I looked out at flat grey skies, the trees dipping and swaying in a sharp breeze, and decided Pippin could wait for his walk until later, something that he seemed to agree with. He was still despondent.

'Are you all right?' I bent to stroke his head. 'Missing him?'

Pippin blinked up at me, huge-eyed.

'He'll be back.' At which point I would murder him, but the little dog didn't need to know that.

When Georgia got up we had breakfast together. I found I preferred the make-up-free, sleep-creased version of my detective constable. She was unguarded in a way that I rarely saw at work, where she tried to second-guess what I wanted to hear all of the time.

At least, I preferred her honesty until she turned the conversation to me.

'So you know you barely mentioned Josh last night.' She bit the corner off a piece of toast. 'Was everything OK between you?'

'Don't speak with your mouth full.'

Eye roll. 'Yes, Mum. But why did he go away so suddenly? I got the impression you didn't know he was going.'

'I didn't. Maybe he got a message or something. Nothing dramatic happened.' I buried my face in my mug so she didn't read my thoughts: nothing dramatic except a moment of sheer and absolute desire that was the height of folly. I didn't blame him for running away. I slightly wished I'd thought of it. 'While he's away and you're here, let's go through the Dawoud case. We can talk about it in the sitting room and keep an eye on Judy Thwaites and her son that way.'

'What if something happens with them while I'm here and he's not?'

'Then we do our jobs, Georgia. You're capable of arresting people, aren't you?'

'Don't you want to wait for Josh to come back?'

'If he misses it, that's his problem. He made his choices.'

'You're so hard-hearted,' Georgia said appreciatively, and I smiled, wishing it was true.

In the sitting room, she flung herself on one sofa, bare feet propped on the arm. 'I'll watch television while you read the file so it doesn't look suss. To be completely honest, I think I forwarded you most of it, or we talked about it already. I don't think there's all that much that's new.'

'You never know what will jump out on a second read,' I said, leafing through what she'd brought with her. It was neatly tabulated, as I'd taught her: witness statements, forensic reports, the notes from the post-mortem, phone records and downloads from Hassan Dawoud's laptop. There was a separate book of photographs and I started there, flicking through them: the house, the car, the body in situ, stomach-churning shots of the injuries taken at the post-mortem, in bright light, after Dawoud's hair was shaved away. It was hard on people when their loved ones became evidence, I knew. We needed to see the damage that had been inflicted on him, but the murderer had left him looking relatively untouched. It was the scalpel of the pathologist that had carved lines in his body and the razor that had taken his hair, unmaking the man to reconstruct the story of what had happened to him before and after he died. Dr Early had tried to minimise the effects of the post-mortem but Dawoud looked monstrously unlike the handsome man in the photos we had of him. Faces and hands were what mattered to loved ones, I thought, and was reminded to look at Dawoud's hands. He had a neat manicure that told me a lot about who he had been in life and what had mattered to him.

'Whoever killed him, he trusted them,' I commented. 'He'd turned his back on them.'

'Or he underrated them.'

Georgia was channel-hopping and the one-second bursts of random noise were driving me mad.

'Can you find something to watch and stick with it?'

She gave me a wounded look. Click. Click. Click. 'Hey, *Traffic Cops*.'

'Not that.' My voice was sharp and Georgia sat up on her elbows.

'Are you all right?'

'Yes. Just – that would be distracting.'

'OK.' More clicking. 'Ooh, *Grand Designs*.'

'Better.' I was reading the contents of the laptop tab. 'What's RoomBoom?'

'Budget Airbnb imitator.'

'I've never heard of them.'

'They're new. The USP is that you can rent a room or apartment by the hour.'

I snorted. 'I can't see that being used for any illegal purposes, can you?'

From: ZBraine@rbcustomerservice.co.uk
To: DawoudH@mymail.co.uk
Subject: re: Excessive Penalty Charges

Hi Hassan,

We are so sorry that your RoomBoom experience was unsatisfactory. We do have a strict policy about our charging, where staying later than you've booked incurs a penalty fee. This is clearly explained on our website and in the terms and conditions on the booking form.

We want you to be happy with RoomBoom so we would like to offer you a £30 credit for your use in the next three months on a full-price apartment.* This will be added to your RoomBoom account 183309.

Regards,
Zeb
RoomBoom Customer Satisfaction Team

*minimum reservation three hours, excludes weekends and bank holidays.

'Where was this email?'

'The RoomBoom one? In the Trash.'

'Did you check out his account?'

'Yes. He used it three times, three different apartments. The reservations were all after work – six or seven in the evening – and all between the hospital and his house. An hour at a time, except that one time that it was longer and that's when he got the penalty charge he complained about.'

'Close to home.'

'*Really* close. Unfortunately there wasn't any more information about how many people used the places he rented or what they did. This company totally knows what it's doing and they are discreet about clients and CCTV and so forth.'

'Presumably they have a cleaner on standby to turn the flats around after each stay. Could we talk to the cleaners who went into each of these places after they were used? See if they saw or found anything that might be relevant to us?'

Georgia blinked. 'I'll check.'

'Since it's a murder investigation.'

'Yeah. I don't know why I didn't think of it.'

'Well, that's why I'm here.'

I went back to the file, skimming the pathologist's report and the forensics, which were still frustratingly unhelpful.

'Dawoud had eaten very little the day he died.'

'He was fasting.'

'For religious reasons?'

'No, weight. He was obsessed with how he looked. He was doing a programme that involved sixteen hours of fasting. He hadn't consumed anything solid since ten the previous evening.'

'Fun. Maybe he got hangry and said the wrong thing to the wrong person.'

'A spur-of-the-moment kind of thing, you think.'

'Maybe?' I shrugged, helpless. 'I think it's obvious this wasn't a stranger murder. They killed him somewhere and put him at his place of work. There has to be some significance to that. His husband was elsewhere. He'd booked time off work for some unknown reason and he was booking rooms by the hour and he had a message on his phone from an unknown person which strongly implies he was having an affair. He was ruinously handsome and we know he was both arrogant and vain, in work and out of it. I think we've dealt with the professional questions – there was one complaint outstanding against him and there was no reason for the family to take matters into their hands at that stage.'

'The Arnolds were really nice people,' Georgia said. 'I felt so sorry for them. Their mother's death ripped the heart out of their family. They have absolutely no connection with crime, no records, wouldn't know where to start with commissioning someone to murder Dawoud, even if that had been what they wanted. They were clear in every communication with the hospital that their goal was to stop him from causing the same pain to another family, and they took the complaint forward so they could be taken seriously.'

'So let's rule them out. There was no love lost between him and his colleagues but again, it was low-level stuff. Everyone has colleagues that annoy them but you need something more to commit murder. Something personal.'

'Yeah, and like I said, there's no way that Dmitri Stefanidis was involved with Dawoud romantically in any way.'

'But putting him at the hospital must have served some purpose.' I tapped my pen against my mouth, considering it. 'We got someone on CCTV purely because they moved his car with the body on the back seat. Then they had to transfer Dawoud to the driver's seat without being seen. It's massively high-risk, all of it, when they could have left him parked in a side street or even in his garage.'

'What are you thinking?'

'I don't know. It's just the detail that keeps tripping me up.'

'Maybe the lover met Dawoud at work. Maybe he works at the hospital in a different department.'

I groaned. 'How many people work in that hospital? A thousand? Two thousand?'

'If I look at people who would have been coming to work around the time that the car drove through the barriers, that might help. And only men, presumably.'

'Yeah, why not. The only thing we know for sure about the man in the CCTV is that he was at the hospital, and what time he arrived. We don't know where he started from, and we don't know where he ended up, but we can be sure he drove in, moved the body, and walked out through that gate.' I was working through it slowly, for myself as much as for Georgia. 'We've been assuming he walked away but what if we're wrong about that? What about taxis near the hospital? And ride-sharing apps? Did we look into them?'

'If he got a taxi, we haven't been able to track down the driver.'

'So maybe you're right and he never left. We have no proof that he did. He could have gone in another gate and then into the buildings. Have we got CCTV from the hospital?'

'About a million hours of it.'

We looked at one another and said in unison: 'Colin.'

'He'll be *delighted.*'

'It'll have to include all the entrances and exits of all the buildings.' I winced, thinking of the sprawling hospital complex with its collection of buildings from various eras, in various styles. 'Not a small job.'

'No, I wish I'd thought of it sooner.' She swung her feet off the sofa and jumped up, energised. 'I'll go and email him.'

I turned my attention to the witness statements, reading through them with care. The pain radiated through Cameron Dawoud's account of what had happened – how he had said goodbye, how he had spoken to his husband two or three times while he was in Wales. How he didn't think they had any problems in their marriage. The secret lover had come as a bolt from the blue for him. He had trusted Hassan, completely, and he had been wrong about that.

It was like losing him twice over, I thought, skimming through the neighbour's statement about finding the body and finding I wasn't as interested in her domestic difficulties as she seemed to think I should be. There was more detail about the parking machine being out of order than about her discovery of the body. I kept thinking about Cameron. Dawoud was gone, but so was the memory of the man Cameron had loved. How did you begin to mourn for someone who had lied to you? Which did you deal with first – the betrayal or the grief?

The last thing I did was to read through Kev Cox's reports on the house, the car and the body. There was something bothering me about what he'd found, or hadn't found, but I couldn't quite work out what it was. The smudge of blood on the back door. The blanket, new and unhelpful, a cashmere blend, the source of three fibres from something like sportswear that Kev hadn't been able to match to anything in the car or on the victim's body. The footprint on the garage floor. Something or nothing. It was one of those cases where every step forward took you in a different direction, and every new direction seemed to lead to another dead end.

Frustrating, but there was no point in giving up, I chided myself. Cameron Dawoud deserved answers about what had happened to his husband, and I wasn't finished yet. I turned back to the start of the file and began to read through it one more time.

A disaster. A total, overwhelming disaster, the kind you didn't come back from easily, if at all.

First of all, and worst of all: he had given himself away. He had made them aware that someone was watching them. Whatever about walking up and down the street or behind the houses, there was no excuse for being in the actual garden. He had been right up by the doors, staring in like some sort of basic pervert, oblivious to everything except the throbbing in his cock and what he hoped was about to happen. The fact that he was the reason they had stopped what they were doing – the fact that he had robbed himself of exactly what he wanted – felt like the worst sort of irony.

He burned, knowing what they would think: a peeping tom, staring through windows for his own gratification. A laughing stock. A punchline. He didn't like seeing himself through their eyes. He was allowed to look, wasn't he? If they hadn't wanted to be seen, they could have gone somewhere else, somewhere that was actually private. Sometimes, he almost managed to convince himself that they had known he was there all along, that they had been putting on a show for his pleasure. But then he remembered the way they had reacted – the instant, aggressive response that he had triggered.

Third: he had run away with his tail between his legs as soon as the shitty little dog started barking at him. There was no dignity in that. There was nothing brave about that, nothing that reinforced his own image of himself as a secretly powerful figure, forceful and impressive. He had sprinted for the fence, his heart thudding, his stomach in knots. He had actually vomited, once he was sure he was safe. If there had been a lower moment in his life, he wasn't sure that he could recall it – spewing into some nettles, his hands on his thighs, everything in his guts forcing itself out under high pressure. There had been the awful fear that someone would come along, too, and see him like that, reeking and humiliated. He hadn't really been able to eat since Saturday night, his throat tight, his stomach clenched like a fist under his ribs. He had blamed it on the food at the barbecue – which, again, led him back to Josh Fucking Derham, convincing everyone to do things his way. People trusted him. They listened when he talked. There was nothing fake about Josh, nothing hollow.

He, on the other hand, felt like a shell of a man. There was nothing inside him except rage, burning him from the inside like a tree struck by lightning, heartwood charring away inside the bark. Nothing could have made him angrier than being treated like an empty threat. Nothing. He could tell that they hadn't taken the incident the other night seriously, because there she was, on her own, or as good as. Yes, the other woman had come to stay, for company, he assumed, but what use would she be if he made his way into the house? Josh had fucked off and left his girlfriend unprotected, as if he was sure no one would dare to touch her. It was like leaving his car unlocked with the keys in the ignition. Essentially the other man had thrown down a challenge. Now it echoed through his thoughts, all the time.

Here's your opportunity. If you're not going to make a move now, when will you decide it's the right time?

Or is it that there's no substance to the promises you make yourself?

Is it time to admit you're lying to yourself, all the time, about what you can do and what you want?

He wasn't sleeping, of course. He got up in the middle of the night and locked himself in the bathroom, staring at his red-rimmed eyes in the mirror, trying to guess what people thought of him.

271

Did they talk about him? Did they even notice he was there? Sometimes he felt as if no one could hear him when he spoke, as if his words dissolved before they left his mouth.

It made him cruel, when he knew he had someone's attention. He was merciless when he had the upper hand. He did things that seemed right in the moment but afterwards he was ashamed – him! He felt uncomfortable about his own behaviour, which wasn't the feeling he wanted.

Somehow that was Josh's fault as well.

The entire situation was becoming unmanageable, he thought. He needed to take control, while the other man was out of the area. He needed to execute the plan he had made to deal with the Problem.

What was stopping him?

Fear, came the answer. He would have liked to think there was some other explanation but it rang with truth that was undeniable, and that seared his soul. He was scared to do what he needed to do – what he had to do.

He had to prove that he was more than a shadow of a man.

36

When Georgia discovered we were out of milk on Monday evening, it seemed like an inconvenience rather than a catastrophe. She straightened up from the fridge and shook the plastic container at me, the last drops rattling around inside it.

'Should I get some more? We'll need it for breakfast.'

I chewed my lip. Derwent would never have let us run out of milk, which was of course the one and only reason I missed him. 'It's getting late.'

She cast a look at the sky. 'It's not dark yet.'

'It will be soon, though. Has it stopped raining?'

'Just about.'

I had a sink full of soapy water and a stack of saucepans to wash up. 'I could come with you, if you wait a minute.'

'The shops aren't far.' She was already putting on her jacket. 'Really, I don't mind. I'll run there. I'd go in London and my manor is well dodgy after dark.'

'I know it seems as if we're safe here and nothing bad could possibly be going on, but you know better than that.'

'I'll be careful.' She smiled at me as she picked up a shopping bag. 'What's the worst that could happen?'

'Don't say that,' I said automatically, and she laughed.

'I'll keep my wits about me, I promise.'

I let her go, feeling responsible for her safety. I had always thought Derwent was overbearing and overprotective, but I was starting to understand it. Watching a junior officer potentially careening into danger was no fun.

I finished the washing-up, made a mug of tea with the last of the milk and opened my laptop to check my email. A couple of messages had come in and I dealt with them briskly. The sluggish way I had been working in the office was a thing of the past. It had done me good to get away. Derwent had been right.

Derwent again. All thoughts led back to him. All roads led to Rome.

Without really thinking about it, I was keeping a rough track of where Georgia was likely to be. I checked the time. Not quite at the shops yet, but soon. The house was quiet without her, and still. I glanced down at Pippin's basket and frowned. Empty. That wasn't like him.

'Pip?'

No tick-tock of claws on the floor. No excited terrier-yelp of acknowledgement.

I got up, suddenly on edge. Maybe she had taken him with her, that would explain it – but the lead and harness were looped over their hook in the hall. A cold breeze lifted the hair on my arms and I saw the front door was ajar. Georgia had banged it behind her but the latch hadn't caught, and neither of us had noticed.

Pippin had noticed, clearly.

All of the warnings we had had that he was an escape artist, that he had no recall, that he couldn't be trusted . . . Vanessa would kill me if anything happened to him, and rightly so. He was my responsibility, not Georgia's. This was on me, although if I had had Georgia in front of me at that moment I would have said a number of things at full volume. It was so inevitable that she had cocked up, so completely

274

predictable. She was careless, fundamentally, and that wasn't something that was ever going to change.

It occurred to me with a sickening, guilty lurch that I hadn't warned her about the front door lock.

This was my fault, too.

I ran to the porch and called Pippin, looking up and down Jellicoe Close, seeing nothing.

Back in the kitchen I grabbed my jacket, aware even then that I was conducting a conversation with Derwent in my head: *Look, I am capable of planning and I do notice the weather conditions and I don't need you.* As I dragged the jacket off the back of the chair I turned to go, not realising that I had caught hold of the tablecloth as well. There was a crash as my laptop slid off the table along with the mug, which smashed. Tea splattered across the kitchen; I had been at enough crime scenes to know that high-velocity liquid went everywhere. I picked up the laptop and checked it: one corner badly dented, the screen flecked with droplets but functioning. Rattled and thoroughly furious with myself I left everything else where it had fallen and rushed outside, slamming the door behind me before I thought to check my pockets.

No keys.

No phone.

No lead; if I found Pippin I would have to carry him.

What an amazing job you're doing. Really impressive, Maeve.

The light was fading fast, the day drawing to a close not with a spectacular sunset but creeping greyness thanks to the low flat clouds. I hesitated on the doorstep for a moment, then set off towards the Holmwood. It was Pippin's favourite destination, after all. If he had gone the other way, Georgia would run into him on her way back from the shops, and I thought she might recognise him, given that she had spent all day cooing over how handsome he was. The Holmwood, though, was a wonderland of strange smells and small animals.

Pippin would be beside himself to be alone in there, unleashed, unsupervised. I would have to hope he was dashing around barking and generally making himself obvious so I could find him.

If I got him back – when I got him back, I corrected myself – he was going on a full categoryA prisoner security regime.

'All right, love?' Alan, putting out his bin for the following morning, watching me with his usual speculative interest.

'I've lost Pippin. The front door was open and I didn't know.'

'Oh blimey.' Alan rubbed his head, looking around him. 'I haven't seen him, I'm afraid. When did he get out?'

'Twenty minutes ago?'

'He could be miles away by now.'

Thank you for the reassurance. 'I hope not. I'm going to look in the woods. He likes it there.'

'I'll wait out here in case he's wandering around the houses. If he comes back, I'll grab him for you.'

'That's really kind, thank you.' I was already turning away to jog down the lane to the Holmwood. I was in leggings and trainers having been too lazy to change after a YouTube yoga practice that afternoon. At the time I had congratulated myself on making the best of Derwent's absence. There was no chance I would have dared to attempt a downward-facing dog in the living room in front of him. I zipped up my jacket against the chill in the air and thanked my lucky stars I wasn't wearing a tiny skirt or brief shorts or any of the other girlfriend-appropriate attire I had been forced into during the heatwave.

The path down to the Holmwood was gloomy and deserted. In ordinary circumstances I would have thought twice about going down there by myself at that time of day. At least I could see there was no one lurking on the path, although halfway along there was a patch of dried vomit that I had to hurdle. Someone had been lavishly sick, I thought, eyeing the splashes that were stuck to the wall. A drunk, or someone stressed, or someone who had run with lung-bursting effort. The memory returned: a figure in dark clothes leaping the fence at the back of our house, disappearing into the night, too quick for Derwent even though he was faster than most. It probably wasn't anything to do with the voyeur, I informed myself, hurrying on, but the lane's resemblance to a crime scene was ever more unsettling. My heart was thumping as I slid through the gate.

It was dark under the trees and I looked around warily. I would have liked to set off running straight away but I made myself stop to listen to the sounds of the woods, straining to pick out Pippin's surprisingly deep bark, the one that he reserved for squirrels. There was nothing but the rustle of leaves and the whirring flight of late birds fluttering their way home. The sliding scale of an alarm call sounded from a blackbird as I began to jog down the path, careful about where I placed my feet. I called the dog as I went, whistling for him, hoping it might remind him that he was actually a small domestic pet rather than the wolf he so clearly imagined himself to be.

I was aware that I was making quite a lot of noise – it was deliberate, after all – but as I reached the bottom of the hill I began to wish I wasn't drawing so much attention to myself. The woods pressed around me and I felt a tingle of fear, something instinctive and primal. Someone was watching me, I thought with a flare of panic, but when I looked around I couldn't see anyone. I shook it off – of course I was on edge, in the circumstances, but there was nothing to be scared of except what was in my imagination, and no reason to think anyone was doing anything like following me, especially since they couldn't have known I was going to be in the Holmwood.

Unless someone had *taken* Pippin. Unless he was bait in a trap, and I was blundering right into it.

Ridiculous, I told myself, and tried not to think about the man who had been lurking in the back garden. The more I told myself to forget about him, the less I could manage it.

Left or right. I took the path that led away from the lake. I didn't know that end of the woods as well as the area near the water but I knew the Holmwood was shaped like a long teardrop and that the lake was in the rounded lower part. The section I was exploring was a narrow spit of land with long paths cutting it into slivers. The hot weather had dried out the trees and some of them had already begun to shed their leaves in a weird kind of seasonal confusion. As I walked, the rustling of my movements drowned out any other sounds around me. It seemed at times as if there was an echo of my footsteps and I stopped sharply once or twice, my eyes wide, scanning my surroundings for a threat, seeing nothing, hearing nothing but the thumping of my heart.

If I was in danger, instead of just being paranoid, I had made it easy for them by leaving my torch and my phone behind. The uneven ground caught at my feet and I stumbled a couple of times. I wished I could tell Georgia where to find me. Would she realise what had happened when she got back? It occurred to me that she might think I had taken Pippin for his evening walk as usual, that she might not realise that his harness was still on the hook. She wasn't as familiar with the routine as Derwent had been.

Oh Josh, I wish you were here.

I swallowed the lump in my throat and gave myself a shake. So he wasn't here. I could cope. I peered into the hollows by the path, looking for Pippin's bright white chest and paws, and called him in a voice that was strangely muffled by the dense forest that surrounded me. The Holmwood had its boundary fence and I knew if I kept going for long enough I would reach it, but that was reason and the part of me that was operating on pure instinct felt as if the woods had become infinite, repeating endlessly, and I was going to be lost there forever.

He wasn't anywhere in the area I was searching, I concluded as I reached the narrow point of the woods at long last. I could go back up the other side of the long V, and I would arrive back at the lake in due course, but that path was narrow and significantly muddier. I looked along it, hesitating, and heard a branch crack as if someone had put an unwary foot on it.

Silence followed, but a *breathing* silence. Forget imagination, forget intuition, I *knew* there was someone in the woods with me – a human presence, not an animal, but by no means tame. They were standing still, close to me, waiting to see if I reacted. Waiting to see if I carried on down the path in all innocence, defenceless, oblivious to harm.

Don't go down there. It's not safe. A fundamental reflex that had been keeping humans out of harm's way since long before history had a record of them.

The memory of Derwent frowning at me. *You have good instincts, as a rule. It's just a shame that it doesn't stop you blundering into trouble.*

I took one last look at the path, and turned, and ran back the way I had come as if I was being pursued by the hounds of hell instead of being the one who was hunting in the woods that night.

37

It wasn't a long walk to the shops and back again; it passed fairly quickly even though Georgia didn't allow herself to listen to music. She stayed alert, in touch with her surroundings. This wasn't an area she knew, and these weren't people she could trust, as Maeve had warned her. The shop was small but crammed with shelves and late customers on a similar mission. The aisles were too narrow to push past anyone with a basket so Georgia found herself joining the end of a long, shuffling queue that went at the speed of the person at the top of it, which was not fast. It took forever to work her way around to the tiny refrigerator where there were about eighteen different kinds of milk: almond, soy, goat, sheep, full fat, skimmed, organic . . .

'All I want is a litre of semi-skimmed,' Georgia said out loud, and the man behind her laughed.

'Bottom shelf. They hide it away.'

'Very helpful of them.' She flicked him a look and, deciding he seemed pleasant, a smile. In the old days, she might have been tempted to make conversation with him: he was acceptably attractive despite thinning hair, and he had an appreciative glint in his eye when he looked at her. But that was the old version of her, the one that had depended on other people's positive opinions to shore up her self-confidence.

She didn't need his admiration now. What she needed was milk, and nothing more.

On the way back, she set herself a challenge: to hit a particular walking speed and maintain it, all the way. Her breathing came faster, and her blood sang in her ears. Being fit, being fast – these were not things she took for granted. She spent considerable time on her fitness as well as her appearance. Not for her the annual worry about the police fitness test—

The blare of a horn interrupted her thoughts and she registered that a car was crawling along the kerb beside her. Instant outrage, just as instantly moderated as she bent to see the driver. DI Derwent had put down the passenger window to talk to her.

'What's going on?'

'You're back!' But of course he knew that already; she was the one who was surprised. Georgia gathered her thoughts. 'We weren't expecting you tonight. Maeve wasn't sure when you'd turn up. I told her you'd let us know when you were on your way.' But you didn't, she almost added.

'Why are you wandering around at this time of night?'

She held up the shopping bag. 'Out of milk.'

'Typical. Where's Maeve?'

'She's back at the house.'

He nodded and drove away without any further attempt at conversation, leaving Georgia flat-footed on the pavement.

'Yes, I would actually have liked a lift. Thank you.'

The attractions of the evening stroll suddenly felt very limited. Georgia checked the time. Ten minutes until she was back in Jellicoe Close, at her best pace. If Josh Derwent was back, did that mean she had to leave straight away? And why was he in such a hurry that he drove off without her? It was rude, Georgia thought.

Or maybe it was just that he wanted to speak to Maeve without Georgia overhearing. The way he'd left, with no warning, there was clearly more to the situation than either of them was prepared to admit.

A smile spread across Georgia's face as she thought about it. If that was the case, she didn't mind hanging back. In fact, she might even dawdle a bit on the way.

The car swung into the road at a respectable speed, not too fast, not hanging about, and swooped across to pull in outside number 3. The driver parked behind Georgia's car, got out and stretched, as if the journey had been a long one and he hadn't wanted to stop on the way.

'Josh.' Alan waved from his front garden. 'Just a minute, I—'

The other man sketched a salute in Alan's direction and jogged up the drive, clearly preoccupied. It would have taken a very keen observer to notice his hesitation prior to sliding his key into the lock, and how he squared his shoulders before he pushed the door open and went inside, as if he was bracing himself for what awaited him.

Alan, of course, was that observer. He stood with his arms folded, waiting. If he was any judge of character, Josh would be back in three . . . two . . . one . . .

Inside the house he stopped short, as if he'd walked into a wall.

It was quiet – too quiet, he thought, yanked out of his previous distraction by the hunch that something was wrong. He tilted his head, listening to the ticking of a clock in the living room. He let his eyes roam around the hall and what he could see of the other rooms, looking for the detail that was out of place – for proof that the tingle at the back of his neck was fully justified.

'Maeve?'

His own voice echoed back to him. No sound from the bathroom or bedrooms upstairs. He walked slowly down the hall, past the hooks, noticing the lead hanging down, the harness limp and empty.

'Pippin?'

In the kitchen he paused by the door, taking it all in: the

disarray, the spilt liquid on the floor, the smashed mug. He crouched to rest the back of his hand against the largest piece of china and found it still retained the ghost of warmth; whatever had happened, it hadn't been long before. His gaze passed over the computer then snapped back to it as he registered the damage that hadn't been there the last time he'd seen it. She had left it open, flung to one side, carelessly abandoned. Her keys were on the worktop by the cooker. The tablecloth hung askew where she hadn't taken the time to straighten it and a chair was shoved back as if she had jumped out of it. Everything in the room spoke of hurry, of panic, of needing to get out.

Moving carefully, as if through a crime scene, he went to the back door and tried it. Locked, and the key was in its usual place in a bowl on a side table.

That was one thing, he thought, swallowing. No one had come in from the garden to hurt her. No one had chased her away. It was all right, it would be fine – he was taking out his phone and scrolling to her number with the half-thinking fluency of someone doing something so familiar, so habitual that it is more or less automatic – and all he needed to do was find out where she was—

Quiet ringing, persistent and unhelpful, interrupted his train of thought. He left the call connected while he searched, running the phone to earth on one of the chairs under the table. He picked it up and weighed it in his hand, fighting to control the fear that was drowning out every other thought, except one.

I shouldn't have left her.

The front door of number 3 slammed open and Josh came down the steps at speed. Even from across the road, even in the blue-grey of dusk, his face was pale.

'Everything all right?' Alan couldn't keep a hint of smugness out of his voice, but then he didn't try very hard.

'Did something happen? Where's Maeve?'

'I saw her earlier. Goodness me, she was in a bit of a flap, but I reassured her – not that I can say for sure it will all work out and I don't blame her for being upset, given the circumstances.' Alan settled himself in for a nice comfortable chat. 'What I said to her was that it was only to be expected. I mean, I had warned her before that Ruth and I worried about it, so it's not as if she didn't know.'

'Know what?' Clenched teeth made a threat of the question. *Get on with it.*

Alan looked at him properly, a little shocked. 'Well, about Pippin. He got out, you see. She wasn't sure when, or how. It's a big responsibility, looking after a dog like that. Ruth and I had told Vanessa we couldn't do it any more, which of course Maeve knew.'

'When was this?'

'Last year after Christmas. Some time in January, as I recall. She wasn't happy but then what can you do?'

A tiny pause. When Josh spoke, Alan had the impression that he was striving very hard to sound calm. 'No, I meant when did you see Maeve tonight?'

'Oh, about fifteen minutes ago,' Alan ventured, having no precise idea. He had been pottering in the front garden where there was just enough light to see the weeds and grub them up, but he didn't like to mention that to Josh when he was in such a state. It was as if he was really worried about her – or about the dog, Alan reminded himself. They were there to look after the dog, when all was said and done. Vanessa would be beside herself if anything happened to Pippin.

'Where did she go? Which way?'

'Down to the woods. She said it was Pippin's favourite place, which is probably true now that I come to think about it.' Alan gave an awkward little chuckle. 'As long as he doesn't end up on the railway line like Gillian Holding he should be all right, shouldn't he?'

Josh began to speak, his voice low and clipped as he issued

284

orders. 'Do you know Georgia, who's staying here? You do? She's on her way back from the shops. When she gets here, tell her what's happened. Tell her to check the lane behind the houses and the embankment in case he's found his way there. She should be here very soon so you shouldn't have to wait out here for too long. Have you got that?'

'Yes, I have, but can't you tell her?' It was a lot of pressure, Alan felt, vaguely resentful. Yes, he had offered to help Maeve if he saw Pippin, but that was different from having orders barked in his face by this thin-lipped, ashen stranger who had abandoned the easy-going manner he had come to associate with Josh Derham. Funny how being upset brings out the worst in some people, he imagined himself saying to Ruth later on, when all of this was over. He would have a cup of tea and tell her all about it.

As if Josh knew what he was thinking, he managed a sort of smile. 'I'm sorry. I can't stay to do it myself. I've got to go after Maeve.'

And before Alan could even discuss it, he was gone, sprinting down towards the Holmwood 'like his life depended on it', Alan told his wife when he was eventually back indoors in his favourite armchair, halfway through a milky cup of Earl Grey with a Rich Tea biscuit on the saucer. 'Or hers, I suppose.'

Ruth was counting stitches, whispering under her breath. When she got to the end of her row she looked at Alan over her glasses. 'Well, you know why, don't you?'

'I suppose you're going to tell me.'

Ruth smiled at him serenely. 'He was worried about her because he loves her.'

'That's no reason to be rude to me.'

'I think it's a very good reason,' she said, and stared away into the distance, lost in her thoughts. She was distracted for so long that when she came back to her knitting she had to count the stitches all over again, which, Alan thought, served her right.

38

My wild flight took me back towards the foot of the path I had taken down into the Holmwood. When it came into view I slowed down, getting my breath back, unzipping my jacket and tugging my top away from my skin where it had glued itself to me. I had a decision to make. No one would blame me for heading back up the path to safety. I could return with Georgia and, more importantly, my torch, to search the remainder of the woods, if Pippin was even still missing. He might have gone home already; I had no way of knowing. It was foolhardy to keep searching as darkness descended on the woods. If I slipped and twisted my ankle, there would have to be another rescue party. I imagined myself having to accept a fireman's lift from Rhys Vonn and shuddered.

It made sense to turn away from the lake and climb up the hill.

And yet.

I was reluctant to go down to the lake because I was afraid of what I might find, or more properly of what might find me. I could tell myself it was sensible to leave Pippin to his fate but really it was cowardice on my part. I would kick myself if something happened to him when I had the opportunity to save him. So I should go down to the lake.

If I genuinely thought someone was stalking me through the woods, it was insanity to stay there instead of turning for home.

I had seen no one, I reminded myself, doubting my own recollection of it. Maybe I had just spooked myself in unfamiliar territory, knowing that the night was coming on. I stood still, at a loss.

As I hesitated, I heard a noise. No subtle sound this one: someone was sprinting down the hill with scant care for their own safety. I could see a figure flickering through the trees, cutting corners, on the verge of a catastrophic loss of balance but with enough athleticism to defy gravity every time it clawed at his heels. With a slither and a well-timed jump he reached the flat ground at the bottom of the hill and skidded to a halt to get his bearings.

I knew who it was, of course. Only one person moved like that. What Josh was doing there, why he had come back – none of that occurred to me at that moment. He turned his head and saw me, and I raised a hand. I had been angry with him, and frustrated, and hurt, but all I felt was happiness that he was back.

It was so dim by now that although my eyes were used to the dusk I could only see his face when he was a few strides away from me: relief uppermost, and strain, and something else that I had never seen before – because he usually took care not to let me see it, I realised, in the moment before he reached me, and caught hold of me.

Since he'd left I'd spent a lot of time berating myself for letting things go as far as they had. I had reminded myself that he was in a relationship, and my colleague, and that I was fundamentally a good person who followed rules and had clearly defined boundaries. There were things you did, and things you did not do, and one of them was getting involved with a colleague who was already committed to another woman. All of those pious thoughts fell away the second he touched me. His heart was thudding and he was breathless from his sprint down the hill, and I turned my face up to his, waiting for him to recover, because this *had* to happen, whether it was the right thing to do or not . . .

His grip loosened and he took a step back, leaving inches of air between us that might as well have been a million miles. He cleared his throat. 'Maeve—'

The light of a torch bouncing towards us made us spring further apart. I shaded my eyes and blinked at Stephen Bollivant.

'Sorry – I didn't mean to startle you.'

'You didn't.' I was surprised that I sounded normal.

'Alan told me the dog was missing?'

'Yes, he got out. I came down here to look for him but I forgot my torch.'

'And your phone.' Derwent's voice was dry.

'And my keys.' I gave an awkward shrug. 'I just ran out of the house as soon as I realised he was gone.'

'I don't blame you.' Stephen turned and shone the torch into the woods, catching a flare of light from some pairs of eyes that were far too small and close together to belong to Pippin. They blinked out of sight immediately. 'I didn't bring Klaus in case he scared the little dog, but I've got some treats and a spare lead and my whistle.'

'Is Pippin trained to respond to it?' Derwent was completely composed now that he had got his breath back, I thought, which was in itself infuriating when I couldn't seem to drag enough air into my lungs. I had thought – but perhaps he hadn't noticed—

Focus.

'Pippin isn't trained at all. Vanessa started doing classes with him but she was terrible at it. She could never discipline him. He knew he was in charge.'

'Well, he's certainly got the upper paw at the moment,' I said bitterly. 'I knew this would happen.'

'Where have you searched?' Stephen asked me, and I blinked at him, wondering if Derwent had known he was there and had been setting the scene for him, nurturing the myth of our romance as he came back to me.

In which case I had misunderstood to a simply staggering extent.

'Maeve?' Derwent said, and I snapped back to full attention.

'I went down to that end of the woods. No sign of him anywhere.'

'He's more likely to have headed for the lake. He likes hunting the ducks that nest in the reeds.' Stephen's face was tense in the light that reflected back from the torch. 'Vanessa always worried about him getting tangled in the reeds and drowning.'

I shivered. 'If anything happens to him—'

'He'll be fine,' Derwent said, without much conviction it seemed to me.

Stephen Bollivant said nothing.

Without any further discussion the three of us set off in the direction of the lake.

In the near-darkness, the water was opaque and hard, like a sheet of metal. The trees around it were barely visible, flat black shapes as unreal as the stage scenery from the school play. Tiny biting insects swarmed around me and I pulled my sleeves down over my hands to protect my skin. Their bodies whirled wildly in the light of the torch.

'Do you want to stick together or split up?' Stephen asked. 'I can go round one way if you two head in the other direction.'

'I want to check the boathouse,' Derwent said. 'He might have gone in there.'

'We can start there.'

I trailed the two men towards the wooden structure that

extended over the water. It looked ramshackle, as if their weight might cause the planks to splinter. Their voices echoed from inside it as the torchlight stabbed through the window, the door, across the lake . . .

'Josh?'

He came to the door instantly.

I was straining my eyes in a desperate attempt to see through the darkness. 'I thought I saw something in the water on the left. Something white. The beam of the torch just caught it . . .'

'Show me where.'

I pointed and he ducked back inside to confer with Stephen. I heard the rattle as the window opened.

'There, she said – look, by the reeds.'

'Definitely something.' Stephen Bollivant sounded grim. 'I can't see if it's the dog.'

'Could be a bag or something.'

It wasn't a bag, I thought. The tension was making me tremble; it was unbearable. As I began to run I heard them coming out of the boathouse and Derwent saying my name, but I wasn't prepared to wait. I needed to know the worst, if it was Pippin in the water. The path that ran around the lake was well worn and wide, smooth under my feet, and even though they were both faster runners than me I had the benefit of a head start. I got to the sloping bit of bank just as they caught up with me. I had to stop short, almost over-balancing, and I put an arm out to stop either of them from coming forward.

'There are marks here. Footprints.'

Stephen shone the torch down at my feet. Deep ruts scarred the soft black mud at the edge of the lake, and flat swathes where something had been dragged, and indentations that looked like a place where someone had stood.

'Is it the dog?'

'I don't know,' I said.

Derwent, further up the slope and taller than me anyway, had a better view through the reeds. 'Shine the torch on the water, mate.'

Stephen did as he said, and there was a split second of silence. Then Derwent was swearing as he dragged off his shoes. He threw his phone to me, and his car keys, and I fielded them instinctively. He went along the bank, a few feet away from where I stood, and waded into the water at speed.

Stephen was on his heels but paused to give me the torch. 'What is it?'

'I think it's a person.' His expression was set as he splashed into the lake, trying to find a path through the reeds. 'Careful, Josh. It's not safe to swim here.'

The deep, cold water, the tangling weeds, the distance to where the white patch floated: I was scared of all of these things. The object in the water swayed with the ripples that raced across the lake as the men struggled to make any progress, but otherwise there was no movement. There was a lifebelt by the boathouse, I remembered, but I couldn't make myself go and get it, as if the only thing that was keeping them safe was the very fact that I was watching. Something brushed against my ankle and I almost screamed before I realised it was a small, quaking body: Pippin, tunnelling between my feet, his outsized ears trembling. I scooped him up and held him, for my comfort as much as his.

Derwent reached the white object first and turned it over. He slid an arm under it and hauled one end out of the water, cradling it against his chest as a tangle of hair streamed down over his arm.

'Is she—' Stephen, out of breath, battling to reach his side.

'I can't find a pulse.' His fingers probed under her jaw. He had his head bent over her face so I couldn't see it in the wavering light of the torch that I was trying to train on them.

'There's a gap in the reeds down there, on the left.' I had noticed it while walking around the lake with the dog, on

291

pleasant mornings and fine clear evenings that were not like this one. 'It might be easier to get her out of the water there.'

Together the two men dragged her free from the grasses that had held her, then half-floated, half-carried her to the place I had indicated, where the bank was sheer rather than sloping. She didn't weigh much, I thought, my throat tight as they lifted her together and laid her on the ground. It was awkward to lift her and she landed hard but there was no reaction, no cough or twitch that I could see. Derwent levered himself up out of the water, knelt beside her and tilted her head back.

I remembered that I was holding his phone. I put Pippin down so I could use it, my hands shaking, and spoke to a soft-voiced woman who promised she knew where we were and that she would be able to get the emergency services to us as soon as possible.

'Ambulance and fire brigade are on their way.'

'And police,' I said, because there were enough alarm bells ringing for me to know they would be needed. 'It's a police matter too.'

39

Even though I knew from first-aid training that most efforts at resuscitation fail, and even though I had seen the marks that suggested this wasn't a straightforward case of drowning, I still found it hard to keep my composure when the paramedics sat back and shook their heads. Gillian Holding's body lay between them, her nightdress in disarray thanks to the efforts they had made to bring her back. One of the paramedics reached out and drew the skirt down over her knees, a small gesture of kindness and respect that made me choke up.

Beside me, Derwent sighed. His clothes were clinging to him, damp and cold, and he looked exhausted.

'You did everything you could.'

'They'll have to get CID here.' He mumbled it, his words inaudible to anyone except me. It was uniformed response officers who had come to the woods and secured the scene but even now one of them was on his radio, reporting to the control room that it was a possible murder. 'This is going to be tricky.'

'Not necessarily. Do they need to know who we are?'

'Whoever's running this case will need to be told. But you don't think there's a connection with our job, do you?'

I shook my head. 'Unless I'm missing something. Do you think she was murdered?'

'Toss-up. There's a clump of hair missing from the back of her head and a mark on the back of her neck that could be a bruise. I'd be treating it as a murder.'

'Oh no.' I had been prepared for him to say it, and I was used to murder, but his words still hit me hard.

His face softened. 'It's different when it's someone you know. I'll call Una and let her know she needs to reach out to the OIC.'

'It's late.' I checked my watch. 'Not office hours.'

'That's why she gets paid the big bucks.'

'Josh, someone will need to tell Gary about his mother.'

'Not your job.' He moved away to make his call and I stood with Pippin, shivering, until one of the PCs came over to take my name and address.

'You all right to give a statement to the detectives?' He was a hearty kind of man, big and defaulting to cheerful when he didn't remember to be grave.

I nodded, trying to work out how a civilian would respond to what was going on. 'Is it – do they think it's suspicious?'

'We've got to treat it as if it was a murder unless we're told not to. They're sending out the pathologist and SOCOs.' He looked back at the body. 'I know it looks upsetting to leave her there like that, on the ground, but that's all evidence now. If we took her away we might lose something important.'

'I understand.'

'Did you know her?'

'I'd met her a couple of times. She had dementia.'

'Might explain how she ended up here.'

'It's possible,' I said politely, but if CID took that approach I was going to have to disagree.

'It's a good thing you didn't go down the bank where she went in,' he went on. 'The crime scene techs will be pleased.'

Yes, why had I been so focused on preserving the evidence

294

when I wasn't a police officer, and particularly not a murder detective? I hadn't been thinking about giving myself away but I couldn't have done a better job of drawing attention to myself. 'It was easier to take a different route,' I said lamely.

To my right, well within earshot, Stephen Bollivant was frowning. I knew he was thinking about how I had stopped him and Derwent from obliterating the marks that might provide the answer to what had happened to Gillian Holding. And Stephen was the last person to gossip with the neighbours, but who knew what he might say? The slightest hint of doubt could influence Judy and her son to play it safe, and we'd end up with nothing.

Shit-shit-shit, I thought and put a trembling hand to my head. I didn't have to try too hard to look distressed. 'The whole thing is so awful. I've never seen anything like this before.'

The police officer snapped his notebook shut. 'I don't think it matters if you see it all the time, you never get used to it. If you want to head home they'll come and speak to you when they're ready. It's going to get a bit crowded around here.'

The three of us were silent as we walked back up the hill in the dark, past the police officer who as scene guard was entitled to stop anyone from trying to enter the Holmwood through the green gate. We gave him our names and watched him tick them off his list.

I had clipped Stephen's lead to Pippin's collar and he trotted ahead of us along the path.

'He wants to get home, doesn't he?' Stephen observed.

'Don't we all?' Derwent said. His jaw was clenched to stop his teeth from chattering.

'You must both be freezing.' The paramedics had given them foil blankets to ward off the chill but both of them had been standing around getting cold while we waited for the emergency services to give us permission to leave.

'I'll warm up. Have a shower, have a hot drink.' Stephen shrugged. 'It's funny, I wouldn't have minded if we'd been able to save her.'

'You did everything you could,' Derwent said.

'You too.'

'If you hadn't had the torch, we might not have found her until morning.'

If I had gone to the lake instead of touring the other end of the woods, I might have found her in time. I didn't say anything but Derwent glanced sideways at me, mind-reading as usual.

'If you'd seen her first, Maeve, on your own, what would you have done? Jumped in? You wouldn't have been able to get her free from the weeds – it took the two of us to do it and we're both bigger and stronger than you. Then you wouldn't have been able to get her out of the water by yourself. You wouldn't have been able to call for help because you didn't have your phone. It wouldn't have made a blind bit of difference if you'd gone right instead of left when you got to the woods. In fact, more than likely we'd have been dragging two bodies out of the water.'

Stephen was nodding. 'He's right.'

I felt a sting of tears at their kindness, and didn't want them to see it. I let Pippin tow me to the other end of the path so that I was a little ahead of them when I moved through the barriers. I should have been expecting a reception committee – I'd left Alan on high alert when it was only the dog that was missing, and now there were emergency vehicles parked up along the Close. Genuine excitement, in a road where the bin men coming early caused a scandal. Someone had taped off the area directly in front of the barriers, but on the other side of the tape most of the residents seemed to be standing around, arms folded, and when they saw me there was a murmur. I hesitated, suddenly unsure of myself, self-conscious now that I was the focus for everyone's attention.

Gary Holding ducked under the tape and came towards me. I froze as for the second time that night a man grabbed hold of me before I'd realised what his intention was. He draped his arms over me and hung off my shoulders, moaning in my ear.

'She's gone . . . they told me she was gone. You saw her, didn't you? You found her again . . . but this time you couldn't save her. I never thought this day would come.' He was sniffing and gasping as he spoke, and I felt the wetness of tears against my neck which was repellent, obviously, but made me feel he was sincerely devastated. If I'd been feeling sorry for him I stopped when he made a couple of convulsive movements that felt a lot like he was taking the opportunity to rub his skinny frame against me. I forced a hand up between us and shoved him away.

'I'm sorry, Gary. There was nothing we could do.'

A police officer materialised beside him and helped him away, to my eternal relief and gratitude. I picked up the dog and ducked under the cordon, pushing through the crowd, ignoring everyone who tried to speak to me. I went straight to the house where I remembered I didn't have any keys. The bell echoed in the empty house when I rang it: Georgia wasn't back yet. I leaned my chin on Pippin's soft, warm head as we waited for Derwent to catch up with us, which he did eventually, stopping at the car to retrieve his bag before he came up the drive at a slow saunter.

'Thank you for your help with getting Gary off me,' I snapped once we were inside the house.

'I thought you liked to deal with these situations by yourself.'

That drawl. Maddening. And back to normal. He would never change, I thought, glaring at him as he grinned cheerfully. He was as annoying as ever.

'But you came back.'

A clatter at the front door stopped him from answering: Georgia, letting herself back in.

'Oh my God, what a crazy thing to happen. Did you actually have to jump into the lake?'

Derwent looked down at his wrinkled and filthy clothes. 'What makes you say that?' To me, he said, 'Una just texted. She's had a chat with the superintendent who's running this one. He doesn't see any reason to tell his detectives who we are, so remember to sound like a civilian when they come round to take a statement.'

'Got it.'

'Is it suspicious?' Georgia asked, eyes wide.

'Yes. But not connected with our case,' I said.

'Are you sure it's not?'

'How could it be?' I heard the edge in my voice and regretted it; I shouldn't take my feelings out on Georgia just because it was easy. 'I've been trying to work out if there would be any reason for Judy Thwaites or her son to want to kill Gillian Holding and I can't put it together.'

'Same here,' Derwent said. 'Even if she knew what they were up to, she wouldn't be able to give evidence against them.'

'The neighbours were saying she was prone to wander.' Georgia looked from him to me. 'Are you sure it wasn't an accident?'

'She had bruises on her neck,' I said. 'So I'm fairly sure.'

'Who could have done that?'

'Her son?' Derwent looked at me, eyebrows raised. 'Gary would be my top pick.'

'I'm even more pleased that you made no effort to get him off me,' I said acidly. 'But I don't agree. She was scared of someone. She had seen something from her window. Whatever about giving evidence, she could have made people suspicious of someone for some behaviour that we don't know about. Maybe she saw the wrong thing and someone felt they needed to shut her up.'

'Which means that your suspects could be implicated,' Georgia said. 'Doesn't it?'

'All the evidence suggests that Judy was kind to the people who stayed with her. The theft of benefits and depriving them of their liberty – that was behind closed doors. Gillian saw something that upset her. Someone harming a girl.' I shook my head. 'Tom Thwaites might well be capable of murder but if he did this my guess is it was because of a different crime that we don't know about yet.'

'At least it's not our case. I'm going to get changed,' Derwent said. 'Put the kettle on, would you, Georgia? I could do with a brew to keep me awake. The local CID will probably take a while to get to us.'

Derwent was wrong about that: half an hour later, thankfully after he had showered and changed, he was shut in the sitting room with one detective and I was in the kitchen with another. Georgia took herself off upstairs and I concentrated on the decidedly novel experience of being interviewed. DC Jones was in her fifties and said, 'O-kay,' at the start of every sentence, which began to grate after a while. I was tired, I found, and I had to focus on giving her the information she would need.

No, I wasn't usually resident in Jellicoe Close. No, it wasn't my dog that had disappeared but the one I was looking after. No, I had not known Mrs Holding was missing. No, I had not known she was in the lake. No, it wasn't usual for me to be in the woods late at night. No, I hadn't seen anyone else there until first my boyfriend came to find me, and then my neighbour. No, my boyfriend couldn't have been in the woods before he found me; I had seen him running down the hill. No, I didn't know about Stephen Bollivant. No, I hadn't seen where he had been before he joined us. No, I didn't know him well. No, I didn't have any reason to think he would wish me or anyone else harm. No, I hadn't gone into the water myself. No, I didn't really know why I had stopped the others from walking on the footprints I'd noticed.

'I watch too much television, I think.'

'Good thing for us.' DC Jones smiled comfortably. 'O-kay . . .'

After the detectives had gone, I went into the sitting room where Derwent was leaning back on the sofa, the heels of his hands pressed against his eye sockets, every line of his body speaking of exhaustion.

'They had a go at suggesting we might have done it.'

'Awkward,' I said, picking up a cushion to hold as I sat down with one leg tucked under me.

'I presume their boss will head off that line of enquiry.'

'I hated being interviewed. I've never been so thoroughly not believed.'

'My one sniffed constantly.' He glanced at me. 'Do you think people feel like this after we've interviewed them?'

'No, I think they're bowled over by our insight and intelligence.'

'Mine, maybe.'

I threw the cushion at him. 'Be serious for a minute. Do you really think Gary killed her?'

'It's the obvious answer. Who had most to gain?'

'He did, but—'

'He'll get the house and now he doesn't have to worry about her getting lost or needing to go into a home.' Derwent stretched. 'If it wasn't him, he's got to be pleased about it.'

'I keep thinking about the man who followed me the night she went missing, the one I tried to catch. I think we can assume he was the one who was in the garden the other night.' I said it levelly. I wasn't prepared to let embarrassment stop me from bringing it up.

'Did you mention him to the cops?'

I nodded. 'You?'

'Yeah.' Derwent looked away. 'I'm sorry I left you on your own.'

'Was that an apology? Seriously?' I blinked. 'I don't even know where to start.'

'Don't push it.' A warning glower. 'I needed to talk to Melissa. It was unavoidable, or I wouldn't have gone.'

'And?' I was trembling, I discovered.

'And I did.' He wouldn't look at me again. He had almost kissed me, and then he had gone to seek forgiveness from his girlfriend, and on his return he had made it very clear that we were friends. The other night had been an aberration, a moment of madness.

It was what I had been telling myself, but I felt unaccountably disappointed that he'd reached the same conclusion.

He was focused on something else. 'I don't think you should go out on your own from now on. Not even during the day. Not until they find out who killed Gillian Holding. If it is the creep who was hanging around here, he's got some experience now and I don't like the idea that he's focused on you.'

'That doesn't rule Gary out, it seems to me.'

'I thought that too.'

I shivered. 'It's late. We should go to sleep.'

There was a creak from upstairs and he looked up at the ceiling. 'Is Georgia in my room?'

'No. I was sleeping in your bed.' It was an unfortunate choice of words but I didn't realise that until I'd already said it. I wished I still had the cushion to hide behind.

'Well.' For once he seemed to be lost for words. 'Doesn't make much difference, does it? I'm still on the sofa.'

'If you don't mind.'

'I'll cope.' He yawned. 'I'll get rid of Georgia tomorrow. There's no reason for her to stay.'

Only as a chaperone. I hoped that his mind-reading equipment was switched off for the night. 'It was a good idea to send her here though.'

'I can't take the credit. Una organised it.'

'After you rang her.' I hesitated. 'Did Liv call you? What did she say to you?'

He pulled a face. 'Nothing I can repeat. I deserved it.'

'Josh, I—'

'We'll talk.' He looked up at the ceiling again and I remembered how very poor the soundproofing was between the sitting room and the large bedroom. 'But not now.'

What it reminded him of was the first time he'd had sex. Not because it was exciting, although it was, and not because he couldn't believe people didn't see what he had done on his face, although he couldn't. He felt changed, completely: a new man. It seemed incredible that no one else noticed the difference in him, as if the sky had turned black and no one cared. He hadn't got a thrill out of killing the old woman in a sexual way – that would have been disgusting – but there was something very special about having that kind of power over another human being. He was the one who had decided she should die, and he had made it happen. He had coaxed her out of her house and followed her down the path into the woods. He had shadowed her as she moved under the trees, nudging her in the direction he needed her to go. And when she had turned with those huge, watery eyes and asked him what he wanted, he had smiled.

Just to take you for a little walk.

I don't like you.

I know.

Of course it had been risky to take her into the woods rather than dealing with her in the house where there was no possibility of anyone seeing them, but he wanted her in the open where forensic evidence would be limited. They had taken a little-used path that was choked with brambles and thick with nettles, and he had stayed in the overgrown, less popular part of the woods where the trees grew so close together you had to be on top of someone before you knew they were there, until he was ready to walk her into the lake.

It had been a last-minute decision to knock her down and push her face into the water instead of trusting that the lake would do his work for him, but he was glad he had done it. Her body had felt so delicate under his hands, so alive – until he held her under the surface and the life struggled out of her. One minute she had been a sentient human being (well, more or less) and the next she had been limp, a loose collection of bones and butcher's bits in a bag of sagging, clammy skin. How he had enjoyed letting her slip away from him into the reeds.

It sounded stupid but he hadn't realised how intimate murder could be.

Just like the first time he had had sex, he had been worried he wouldn't be able to do it – that something would go wrong and it wouldn't work. And just like sex, now that he had done it once, it was all he could think about. The ache was close to hunger, and as much of a torment. As he had walked away from the lake he had already been imagining the ways he could have improved the experience for himself.

Number one: choice of victim, obviously. That was unfortunate but, look, it was a wholly functional murder, necessary for his peace of mind and safety. If he had been killing for fun he would have arranged it so that he had a sexual connection with the victim, so he could enjoy her first – that had been out of the question. He would have punched anyone who suggested he had even thought about the old woman in that way.

Number two: he would have found some way of taking his time. It had all been such a rush. He had been hasty and it was all over almost before he realised he was going to do it. What he liked to imagine was going slowly. Tightening his grip and then releasing it. Taking her to the edge and letting her look over before he pulled her back, a few times, until he was bored or allowed himself to lose control.

(Was it really losing control? It was more unleashing himself. Losing control sounded sloppy and desperate and he was neither.)

Number three: he would have spent longer with her after she

304

was dead. Something was gone from her, some spark of vitality – her soul, he supposed – and he wished he had been able to sit with the empty shell, exploring the difference between a living woman and a dead one. He hadn't wanted to explore her physically. The thought of delving into her withered, sexless body made him want to be sick. But if it was another kind of body – a fresh one, with firm limbs and soft, springy flesh – well, that would be different. It would have grieved him to lose one like that to the lake water. He would have had to find some way around it.

For all its flaws, he was content with his murder. It had been perfectly executed, if he might be allowed a small pun. (He allowed it.)

His first time.

Not the last.

40

Georgia left the next morning, after breakfast, having taken an extravagant amount of time to pack her things.

'How long did she stay for?'

'Two nights,' I said.

'She seems to have spent the entire time strewing her personal belongings around the house,' Derwent said crossly, kicking a sock out from under the sofa in the kitchen.

'She dropped everything to be here.'

'Fine, but she could have stopped dropping things when she got here.' A blusher brush joined the sock.

'You sound like her dad.'

That made him go quiet and retreat to the garden and a long overdue date with the lawnmower. I ran upstairs with the things he'd found and tapped on the bedroom door.

'Need a hand?'

'Ugh, don't tell me you found more stuff.'

'Josh did.'

She folded the sock into her bag and tucked the brush into a side pocket. 'At least it wasn't a pair of knickers.'

'He would have been a perfect gentleman about it,' I said. 'He shows off in public but he wouldn't embarrass you when you were here on your own with him. He knows it's strange to be in a house instead of the office. The rules are different.'

'Are you going to be all right together?' Georgia was fighting the zip of her bag which bulged on all sides.

'Yes, why wouldn't we be?' I helped to hold it taut and she pulled the zip home.

'Just – I know there was some reason for him to leave.'

'Honestly, Georgia, nothing happened. Don't get carried away with imagining some sort of argument. He has respon-sibilities elsewhere. He did warn me that he might have to go at short notice, and he went.'

'When he came back he wanted to talk to you without me being there.'

'Did he say that?' I asked, a little too quickly.

She gave a one-shouldered shrug. 'I worked it out.'

'Yes, but your speciality is two plus two equals five million.'

'I'm not *always* wrong.'

'On this occasion, you're mistaken.' I picked up an over-flowing carrier bag. 'How on earth do you have so much stuff? I swear you didn't have this much when you got here.'

She bit her lip. 'I have no idea. It's like it just . . . expanded.'

At long last Georgia's car was fully loaded, in that not another thing was going to fit in it. Georgia shoved her jacket on top of the pile and quickly slammed the boot shut as everything tipped forward to rest against the back windscreen. A muscle tightened in Derwent's jaw when he saw it and I grinned at him. I knew an untidy car was one of his triggers.

'At least it's all in there.'

'It had better be. If she's left anything behind it's going in the bin.'

Oblivious, Georgia turned around, dusting off her hands. 'It's been so much fun. I'll see you when you're back in London.'

'Yes, we should go out for drinks,' I said quickly, aware

307

that Alan and Ruth were in their front garden and Alice Knox was walking past carrying a bunch of chrysanthemums which she laid outside the Holdings' house, where an unofficial memorial had sprung up. At least Georgia hadn't actually said 'in the office'. I hugged her tightly. 'Thanks for coming. I'm sorry it was a bit more exciting than I'd imagined.'

'I'm glad I was here for you. Stay safe.'

'See you, Georgia.' Derwent sketched an unenthusiastic wave. She threw her arms around his neck and kissed him on the cheek.

'See you soon, you big grouch.'

He grabbed her upper arms and walked her backwards to the car where he reached around her and opened the driver's door.

'In. Engine on. Go.'

'You'll miss me.' She grinned up at him, her tongue caught between her teeth, looking adorably cute. He stepped back to let her close the door, stony-faced. You could never tell what would work on him, but Georgia never gave up.

As she drove out of Jellicoe Close, a silver BMW turned in. Derwent had come back to stand beside me on the kerb.

'What's this now?'

The car pulled in outside number 7, Judy's house. A woman got out and stood for a second beside the car, writing a message on her phone, long pink nails tapping. Her mouth was plump, the lips taut and overlined which suggested to me that she was waiting for her latest round of filler to settle. Her figure was top-heavy, her red hair tumbling down her back in a waterfall of expensive extensions. She gave me a brisk once-over, lingered on Derwent for three times as long, then clip-clopped briskly up the drive and let herself into the house.

'Tom's wife?' I murmured to Derwent, who had turned to head into the house.

'I should think so. Worth running the plate through the box.'

'Do you think she's here to set up the next victim?'

He glanced back at me, his eyes bright. 'It's a possibility, isn't it?'

An hour later we were sitting in the kitchen, Derwent's phone between us, on a conference call with Una Burt, Chris Pettifer and Vidya Long.

'That plate comes back to an address in Cheltenham,' Chris said. 'Myra Ivanova. She's currently working as the manager of the Abbey Home. It's a private residential home for adults with intellectual disabilities.'

'Bingo,' Derwent said. 'Is she married to Tom Thwaites?'

'They were married in Belarus eight years ago.' Vidya's voice was breathy, as if she was nervous. 'All properly registered in this country but they don't live together and it looks as if they never have, and she doesn't use his surname, so we didn't identify her until now. She lives on site in the nursing home. It sounds grand but it's tiny – it's literally a house. They have a small staff and no more than five residents at any time. She's the one who started the nursing home, incidentally, two years ago. And get this, she was the assistant manager at Davy Bidwell's previous long-term residence. She and Davy got on like a house on fire. When he left the previous place, he went to Abbey Home.'

'Strange that she didn't mention it when the cops went looking to see who gave him the idea to move out.' Derwent was sounding grim. 'So she's running a proper business looking after vulnerable people, presumably at vast expense since it's private, and using it as a way to find new targets.'

'The council pay for some of the residents.' Vidya again. 'For what it's worth, it has a high approval rating and the residents seem happy. Three of them have been there since it opened.'

'Davy Bidwell was there for six months,' Una Burt said. 'Placed there by the council, at his request, after his previous placement failed.'

'Did his family know?' I asked.

'There was some breakdown in communication. Someone thought that Davy didn't have any family, possibly because his parents had both died in quick succession. No one seems to have known he had a brother,' Una said.

'And they didn't know the brother was Rula Jacques' husband,' Derwent said. 'He looked like an easy target, didn't he? Physically healthy, mentally vulnerable. He was probably highly suggestible.'

'We don't know where he went after he left Abbey Home, but two weeks later he was registering Judy Thwaites as his official carer and using her address for his benefits,' Chris Pettifer said. 'And when the police came and asked her about it, she said she had looked after him for a while but he'd moved on and she had assumed her address was no longer used for him. She played the sweet, confused little old lady and it worked.'

'Or she really was confused,' I said.

'That's a possibility,' Derwent said, quite kindly. 'But we should assume she knew.'

'So this Myra identifies residents who don't have families or any other visitors and if they're physically viable she moves them to Judy's house. What's the purpose of that?' Pettifer said.

'To see if anyone raises the alarm?' I suggested. 'It would be easy enough to pass it off as a long holiday or some respite care if a family member did turn up. If the gang weren't so greedy they wouldn't claim the extra benefits, but I suppose someone vulnerable disappearing is more likely to provoke suspicion than a change of address.'

'It breaks the chain,' Derwent said. 'It makes it that bit harder to work out where they've gone after Jellicoe Close.'

'Ah, well, as to that,' Pettifer said with some satisfaction. 'You wanted a farm in Nottinghamshire owned by Tom Thwaites and I have found it. It's in the middle of nowhere.

The nearest town is Newark, but it's not what you'd call *close*.'

'What does he farm?' I asked.

'All sorts. Various crops. Various types of livestock. Eggs. Ducks. He used to qualify for some pretty decent EU subsidies.'

'And all of this is legit?' Derwent checked.

'As far as I can tell. But labour intensive. He's got a farm manager who lives there all the time, and Mr Thwaites comes and goes.'

'Shuttling between Cheltenham and West Idleford and the farm,' I said. 'Which makes sense because this is probably a good place to stop off and break the journey.'

'You'd never put it all together unless you were having a damn good look at him and his movements.' Derwent shook his head. 'Clever.'

'Evil.' Una Burt sounded genuinely upset. 'I'm going to tell Mrs Jacques and Mr Bidwell what we've found out so far.'

'You might want to wait until we've decided what to do next,' I said, alarmed. 'Do we swoop in and search the farm? Arrest everyone and hope the CPS lets us charge them? What if we don't find any of the other vulnerable people? We can't link Davy Bidwell to the farm yet. We don't know how he got from there – if he was there at all – to London. We don't know if he was living rough or if he just looked as if he was because he was receiving such poor care. All we have so far is a theory.'

'We badly need some evidence,' Derwent said, flicking me a warning look. *Don't piss Una off. Leave that to me.* 'Can we send a covert team to look at the farm? I'm assuming money is still no object on this investigation.'

'We can. I'll request it.'

'I want to keep a low profile until we know for certain that we have a case. And then I think we need to watch the woman and Tom. Get some surveillance in place so we know where they are and what they're doing.'

'And what about Judy?' Una said. 'What are you planning to do with her?'

'I'll talk to her,' I said, feeling like a traitor. 'She likes me.'

'That's why you're here,' Derwent said. 'Catnip for old ladies.'

'I want you watching her,' Una Burt ordered. 'I don't want any gap in the schedule where a defence barrister could introduce some doubt. If she ends up on trial, we'll need to know where she's been and what she's been doing.'

'Of course,' I said. 'Can we find out if there's anyone suitable in the home in Cheltenham at the moment? Talk to the social workers in charge of placements there, maybe? Myra turning up here makes me think they're planning a new run at this. As far as they're concerned, Davy Bidwell is done and dusted.'

'And that might be making them more confident about trying it again, not less,' Derwent point out. 'Tom Thwaites is an arrogant man. He's greedy and he's not the type to play it safe when there's money to be made.'

'That's how we'll get them in the end.' Una managed to sound completely confident, which I quite admired. She would need all of her bravado when she explained to Rula Jacques that the sum total of our achievements so far was one mysterious death, a few weeks of dog-walking, a big draw in a minor football match and the possible destruction of what had been a pretty decent and effective working relationship.

After he ended the call, Derwent stood with his phone in his hand. He was looking at me.

'What is it?'

'Just wondering if you were OK. You seem to be on edge.'

I laughed. 'Why wouldn't I be? Gillian Holding was murdered, Josh. Someone was spying on us.' That was enough on its own, but I found myself going on with what was really bothering me. 'And you and I – we haven't even talked about what happened the other night. You said we would and we haven't.'

'Because I don't think it's important.'

I blinked. 'I do.'

'It was nothing much, and it was over before it started,' he said, dismissing it.

'I want to talk about it. We need to clear the air and get things back on a professional footing.'

'Who says it's not on a professional footing already?'

'But – in the woods, when you came back—'

'Stephen Bollivant was watching.' He got up and went to fill the kettle, saying over his shoulder, 'Presumably you knew that. Do you want a cup of tea?'

If I had wanted to save face he was offering me the chance, and it was tempting to take it. In the old days, I might have done that, but I didn't want to be anything other than honest. This felt too important.

'No, I don't want any tea. And no, I didn't know he was there. I thought you were picking up where we had left off.'

'And how did you feel about that?' His tone was absolutely neutral, his back unhelpfully turned towards me so I couldn't read his expression. All I had left was the truth.

'Confused.'

His shoulders dropped a millimetre or two before he turned to face me. His face was rueful, which was unusual. He generally didn't bother with regret. 'I don't blame you. It was confusing, and that's my fault. I'm sorry.'

'I think that's the first time you've ever sounded sincere when you apologised to me.'

'Well, it's the first time I've ever really needed to apologise.' That was debatable, but he was going on. 'I had no right to do what I did the other night. I'm your boss, and I shouldn't have done it.'

'That's what I was thinking while you were gone.'

He winced. 'And worse, I imagine.'

'I was angry that you left without telling me you were going,' I said levelly. 'But I wasn't angry about what happened here.'

He shook his head. 'You should have been. It wasn't appropriate.'

'You were trying to help me.'

'That was part of it.'

'What was the rest?' I couldn't help asking and he grinned.

'Sheer self-indulgence. As I said, I'm sorry.'

'I could have said no.'

'I didn't really give you the chance to think about it. In fact, I told you not to think about it.'

'Yeah, but you tell me lots of things that I ignore.' I folded my arms, nerving myself to go on. 'Look, Josh, I thought about it a lot while you were away. I thought about how you made me feel and what that meant and I decided when you came back I'd tell you that it was a one-off, late-night mistake that we should both forget about. And then when I saw you in the woods, I forgot all of that.'

He was leaning against the cupboards, his legs crossed at the ankle, outwardly relaxed, but his hands were gripping the edge of the countertop so hard that his knuckles flared white. 'Maeve—'

'I know, OK? I know it would be a disaster.'

'It would be the best thing that ever happened to you,' Derwent said icily, with a flash of arrogance that was more of a reflex than anything else. He paused for a moment, then went on, 'but you're right. It would have consequences that go far beyond the two of us. I take full responsibility.'

'You weren't the one who wanted it to happen again,' I said softly.

'I wouldn't say that.' His eyes were steady on mine. *Help.* It wasn't fair – *he* wasn't being fair . . . 'I think we both know that if we hadn't been interrupted—'

'We don't know what would have happened, and we never will. I think we'd have come to our senses before too long.'

He raised his eyebrows. 'Really?'

I felt myself blushing. I had to shut this down, and quickly,

314

or we would have to stop working together. If we couldn't manage to behave in a professional way behind closed doors we would be finished as colleagues. 'You proved my point when you called a halt in the woods. I should thank you for backing off the way you did.'

'I still need to apologise for what I did before. You know me. I try, but I don't always do the right thing.'

'You've almost always done what was right for me.' I tried to smile. 'It's OK, Josh. It's not a disciplinary matter. We're both grown-ups. It was a moment, that's all. And it passed. All in all, you handled it better than I did.'

'Yeah, well, it's not just about that.' He shoved his hands in his pockets, uneasy now. 'I left you here on your own so I could go and talk to Melissa. You were in danger. I made a serious error of judgement and you could have paid the price. If something had happened to you in the woods last night . . .'

I held up a hand. 'You don't need to say any more.' There was something I had to ask him, though. 'Did you tell Melissa what happened between us?'

He looked horrified. 'No. I needed to talk to her about something else. Nothing to do with you. She doesn't need to know, does she?'

'I don't think so. The only thing that comforted me was that no one else could ever find out.'

'Except Liv, who you told.'

'Oh dear. Did she give you a bollocking?'

'A monumental one.' He smiled with that disarming sweetness I saw so rarely. 'But she said there was no way we were going to get out of this without something like that happening.'

'I didn't see it coming.'

'No, you didn't. I'm used to being in your blind spot.'

Before I could think of something to say, he went to the table and opened his laptop: end of discussion, clearly.

'Una should keep us in the loop on the Holding investigation. If they find out anything dodgy about any of the neighbours, I want us to know about it. And I don't want you wandering around on your own until they've made an arrest. No early morning dog walks or late-night jaunts to the shop. We go out together or you go out in the car.'

'House arrest,' I said bitterly.

'Yeah, but it's better than being dead.' He frowned. 'It's strange when it's someone who lives down the road from you, isn't it? I don't get spooked easily when I turn up at a crime scene but this murder has me properly paranoid.'

'I'm glad you're back,' I said. 'And not just for my safety, but for Pippin. He missed you.'

'You missed me too.'

'I did,' I admitted. 'But I'm not entirely sure why.'

41

The subject line on the email that pinged into my inbox was Hassan DAWOUD: Developments, and there were attachments. I felt my heart rate rise, excited that we were making progress at last. I wanted answers, to prove to myself that I still had what it took to do my job. As soon as I saw the images Georgia had emailed me, I picked up my phone.

'Where did these come from?'

She sounded perky. 'Colin struck gold with the hospital CCTV. The driver doubled back and went into the buildings. He went up to a disabled toilet just outside one of the stroke wards on the third floor of the Hodginson building – the big one behind A&E – and got changed.'

'He looks totally different. Much older.'

'Doesn't he? That jacket is Ralph Lauren, and the jeans and trainers look expensive. You honestly wouldn't know it was the same person.'

'Well, I suppose that was the point.' I was clicking through the images. 'Are these the best stills we have?'

'Unfortunately. He remembered to put on a different cap. But I think we can be sure that he's white – the hair that's coming out from the back looks fair.'

'Where did he go after this?'

'He left the hospital, so it doesn't appear he worked there – or at least, he wasn't starting a shift. We're checking to see if we can find him on the street CCTV and circulating the new image around the local taxi companies in case anyone picked him up.'

'Show them to Cameron in case he recognises this guy. And also once you get hold of the cleaner from RoomBoom, see if she saw anyone who looked like this with Hassan at the flat he rented. It would be so neat if he was the secret lover who sent the WhatsApp message.'

'Ugh, I've had huge hassle with RoomBoom.'

I could imagine Georgia rolling her eyes and I found myself grinning. 'They've earned that one star for customer service on Trustpilot.'

'If there was a lower rating than one star, they'd have it. I've spent the last three days on the phone to them. Basically, they won't give me the information on their cleaner at the moment. I'm going to have to get a warrant to check their records if they won't give in. My feeling is that they're paying her off the books so they don't have to make the proper employee contributions or bother giving her anything like minimum wage, and now they're stalling me until they can put the fear of God into her.'

'Don't give up.'

'I'm not.'

'When you get the cleaner, make it clear to her that we're not interested in her immigration status, just in case that's an issue. Try to get her to trust you before you show her the picture. RoomBoom might tell her not to say anything, given that they sell discretion as well as rooms by the hour, but I want to tie this guy together with Hassan if I can. We need a motive for the jury, assuming we ever get that far, and a lovers' quarrel would fit the bill.'

'No problemo.' Georgia shuffled papers. 'Are you OK? I hear they're treating the neighbour's death as suspicious. Una told me. Do you wish you were investigating it or not?'

318

'I'm glad it's not me,' I said frankly. 'From where I'm standing it looks as if they're making a mess of it. They keep bringing the son in for interview. It's probably where I would start too, but I'm worried they're not looking for anyone else.'

'He's the obvious choice.'

'Yes and no. He could have let her fade away. She could have died of dehydration during the hot weather and no one would have thought it was suspicious. Or she could have had an accident – a fall in the house. Much easier than taking her out to the lake.'

'Could that have been an accident, though? She drowned, didn't she?'

'Yes, but someone made sure of it – they found some pretty significant bruising when they did the post-mortem. The theory is that someone knelt on her body while they forced her head under the water. I presume we were supposed to think she wandered off and went for a swim, then drowned accidentally, but whoever killed her lost control and left marks on her body.'

'Do you think she fought back?'

'I don't know. I keep thinking about how scared she was when I met her first. She must have been terrified when he walked her down to the water.'

'Oh Maeve, that's tough.'

My throat tightened and I ran a knuckle under my eyes to stop the tears that were welling out. 'I just hope it was quick, in the end.'

'I wish I could give you a hug. At least you have Josh for that.'

I managed a shaky laugh. 'Josh is busy doing surveillance on the house across the road. He doesn't have time for a hug. We've spent the last three days staring at number 7, trying to be subtle about it.'

'I heard I missed the daughter-in-law by seconds! What are the chances? I must have driven past her on my way out.'

319

'She came and went. I gather from Ruth that Judy is not a fan.'

'Well, mothers.'

'Yeah.' I sniffed, still trying to shake off the unexpected wave of emotion. 'Listen, Georgia, I'd better go.'

We said goodbye and I put the phone down. Something – a noise, a disturbance of the air – made me turn around to find Derwent standing in the doorway.

I put a hand to my chest to stop my heart from bursting out of it. 'Jesus, you scared me.'

'I heard my name.'

'It wasn't intended to summon you. I didn't even say it three times or recite the incantation.'

He half-smiled but his eyes were full of concern. 'Were you crying?'

'Just telling Georgia about Gillian Holding's post-mortem.'

'Oh.' I had the impression that he was disappointed. 'Well, for the record, I'm not too busy for a hug. If you need one.'

'I'll let you know.'

He looked past me, his focus shifting to what was happening outside the house. 'Judy. Go.'

She was getting into her car, I saw. I jumped up and hurled myself out of the front door, jogging across the road a little bit faster than I would have preferred. It didn't look casual enough for my liking, but she had been keeping a low profile for the last three days and Derwent was desperate for me to find out what I could about Myra.

'Hey, Judy.'

She was reaching to close her car door but she stopped. 'Hello, love. Are you all right?'

'I just wanted to check in with you to see how you're doing after what happened.' I looked at Gillian's house meaningfully and shuddered, which wasn't totally fake. There was something grim about the house: it looked more dirty and neglected than ever and the curtains were drawn all the time.

The flowers that people had left straggled along the pavement, wilting for lack of water. No one knew what to do with them now. Gary was unlikely to take them in, but it wasn't anyone else's place to interfere, Ruth had told me. It was typical that her shock about what had happened to her friend had sublimated to worry about the way Jellicoe Close looked. Appearances were everything. Chaos and despair could be kept at bay with a little light weeding and a power hose.

'I'm fine, darling.' Judy flashed a wide smile at me. 'Just getting on with things. I'm going to the hairdressers.'

'Oh, lovely. Nice to get a bit of pampering, isn't it?'

'You could come with me.' Her eyes skimmed over my hair and I put a hand to it, unsettled. 'You know they have treatments these days that can do wonders for curly hair.'

'I think it's beyond help,' I said with a little laugh. Maybe Judy wasn't all that nice after all. 'You know if you need anything, Josh and I are right across the road. If you're worried about your safety or you want some company . . .'

'I know. You're a good girl.' She patted my hand where it was holding on to her car door. 'I don't mind telling you, it's given me a shock. It's not fun being alone when something like that happens.'

'I thought you had someone staying with you. Was that your daughter?'

'Daughter-in-law.' Her mouth puckered like a drawstring bag. 'Myra.'

'Lovely name.'

'If you say so, my love. If you say so. It's not her real name. She picked it herself. I think it suits her because she's all fake, isn't she? Fake nails, fake eyelashes, fake hair. All she thinks about is how she looks. I don't know what Tom sees in her. We have nothing in common, unfortunately. She's a superficial little madam.'

Judy was wearing a highly coordinated navy and white

outfit with scarlet nails and lipstick. I thought Tom had been drawn to someone who was as high maintenance as his mother, and the problem with Myra was probably that she was too similar to Judy rather than too different.

'It's a shame when it's hard to get on with people like that, isn't it?' I gave her the head tilt of sympathy. 'My brother's wife is like that. But we're stuck with her. He likes her and that's what matters.'

'Well, if he'd asked me before they got married, I'd have told him to run a mile.' Judy's usual sunniness had gone behind a very dark cloud at the thought of Myra.

'At least she came to see you,' I offered.

'She comes to see me when she wants something. Not otherwise.'

'Oh Judy, that's sad.'

'It's life, darling.'

'What did she want? Not money, surely. My aunt's daughter-in-law borrowed thousands from her to get a business up and running,' I confided, 'but then it turned out there was no business. It broke her heart.'

'No, nothing like that. She wants me to put someone up for a few nights.' Judy was looking out through the windscreen, thinking about it. Her face had fallen into wrinkles that I'd never seen before. 'I think I'll do it this once. As a favour. And I don't mind having company with what happened to Gillian. But next time I'll say no.'

From: georgia.shaw@met.police.uk
To: maeve.kerrigan@met.police.uk
Subject: re: Hassan DAWOUD: Developments

I've hit two snags. One is that the cleaner has gone back to Nigeria for a 'holiday' according to RoomBoom and they can't get in touch with her. I've been to her address and her belongings are still there. From what her housemates

322

said, she's expected back this week. I don't think she's done a runner – it was her sister's wedding and a planned trip.

And the other news is that Cameron Dawoud has gone into rehab for addiction to diet pills, painkillers and the odd toot of cocaine. So much for Mr Clean Living! He doesn't have access to his emails or phone, obviously, and the doctor in charge of his treatment basically begged me to leave him alone unless it was super-urgent. He also pointed out that we might want Cameron to be clean before we talk to him again, which sort of makes sense. My feeling is that since we're waiting for the Nigerian lady anyway we might have to put up with a bit of a delay. What do you think? Should I insist? Reading between the lines, Cameron was in a bit of a mess when he landed at the clinic.

Georgia

From: maeve.kerrigan@met.police.uk
To: georgia.shaw@met.police.uk
Subject: re: re: Hassan DAWOUD: Developments

ARGH that is so frustrating. (I'm also *very* frustrated by the fact that Josh is being unspeakably smug about Cameron and his drug-taking. How did he know? Also, how did we miss it?)

I'm going to say we should sit on the pictures until you can get hold of the cleaner and Cameron. I know the temptation is to share it far and wide but we don't want to tip him off that we're on his trail. This man looks like the sort of person who has considerable resources, at least in the second set of images, and I don't want him to decide to make a run to a country that doesn't like extraditing criminals to the UK. With any luck he thinks he's home and dry at this point, given that we haven't got close to him so far in the investigation. He may be aware we were looking for someone quite different, based on the tracksuit pictures. I want him confidently going about his everyday business in the belief that he's got away with murder. With any luck we will be able to ruin his day once we get a positive ID from Cameron. If he doesn't recognise him, we can start taking the image to Dawoud's wider circle of colleagues and friends. Someone must know him.

42

I closed my laptop and looked out of the front window, a movement that had become a reflex over the past few days. Telling Georgia about it had made me realise how much more edgy we were than for the previous weeks we had been in West Idleford, even the first one when we had been settling in. It was harder to remember to look innocent – to look like civilians, with reasonable levels of curiosity about our neighbours' lives. Everything in me was screaming to pay attention, to watch out, to miss nothing. There was a very real danger that something we did or didn't do could end up destroying our case, and if we were the reason for it to fall apart, there would be consequences all the way up the chain to Simon Grayton, the assistant commissioner, if not beyond to the mayor. Una Burt was in contact with us daily, often more than once, and it was torture for Derwent. I got used to hearing his slow, colourless updates on the phone, his patience worn thinner than a shadow.

'No. Still nothing new. I'll let you know if there are any developments.'

And in the meantime we received clips of video footage: Myra going for pedicures and hair appointments, her heels ever higher, and Tom moving around outside an old farmhouse with trees growing out of the gutters and damp patches in swags on the outer walls. A team from the council did a snap inspection at the care home and reported five clients in residence, three male, two female, aged between twenty-four and fifty. They were all healthy and happy; full marks, Myra.

I had expected that it would be awkward to be back in the house on my own with Derwent, but in fact we barely saw one another. One or both of us had to be on duty all the time, either in the sitting room behaving as if everything was normal to allay anyone's suspicions about us, or in the front bedroom, curtains drawn to hide the surveillance set-up we had installed there, with a camera and night-vision binoculars. We took it in turns to sleep and eat, and in Derwent's case to go out for walks with Pippin, or for errands, or running. I was still stuck in the house since we couldn't both go out at the same time and I wasn't allowed out alone. It felt increasingly unfair as the days dragged by.

'This is like being a second-class citizen. I should be able to go for a run without needing a male companion for safety.'

Derwent was watching Judy's house through the viewfinder of the camera, one eye closed. He didn't even look around. 'I know. It's not fair. You're still not going.'

'It's broad daylight.'

'Gillian Holding was taken from her home in daylight, they think, while Gary was having a nap in the sitting room. It was audacious and high-risk. Her killer took her through the woods at a time of day when it might have been busy with dog walkers and runners. He was lucky as hell that no one was around to see him walking her down there, and even more lucky that no one saw him drown her. There was rain that afternoon which probably made people change their plans to go out and he took advantage of it. He must have decided to act at the last possible minute when he saw his opportunity.' He was still staring through the viewfinder. 'I'll be honest with you, Maeve, I'm scared of this guy and what he might do next.'

I shifted, restless. 'It just seems all wrong that he's done something terrible and I'm the one who's locked up.'

'Yeah, it stinks. And so does the timing. If we weren't doing this proper surveillance we could go out together, like before.'

'I don't like running with you.' I sounded sulky, even to myself. 'You go too fast and then you say encouraging things that make me want to murder you myself.'

'I know. We call that motivation.' He glanced at me. 'Why don't you see if any of the neighbours want to start a running club? The women, I mean. You can go out together.'

'That's not a terrible idea.'

'I know.'

Slightly to my surprise, Fleur agreed to it, as did Alice Knox. (Nicola Vonn was an instant no.) We ended up agreeing to go out every other day for a half hour. We didn't go far, or fast, but I was so happy to be outside in the fresh air that I didn't care. Fleur was defensive about her running until she discovered she had better stamina than Alice, at which point she became gracious and even kind, pretending she needed to slow down or stop to re-tie her laces when Alice was red-faced and gasping.

The company mattered to me almost as much as the exercise, I discovered to my surprise. I was lonely during the long hours of watching nothing happen across the road. I missed going out for walks with Derwent and Pippin, and watching television on the sofa, and cooking dinner as we bickered over which saucepan to use or how long pasta took to boil. The fun had gone out of our domestic arrangements; it was all grim practicality now.

It was, in short, work, which was what it had always been.

It just hadn't felt like that to me.

Eight days after we found Gillian Holding's body – eight endless days – the surveillance team at the farm sent us footage that was grainy and shot from slightly too far away to be

327

detailed. What it showed, however, was clear; the farm manager, a bull of a man named Nevis Anderson, with his dog, pinning three men up against the wall of a derelict building in the remotest part of the farm. The dog jumped and the men flinched, terrified. Their hands were over their faces. They all looked thin, and one of them had a bad limp. The last thing that happened before the men disappeared inside the building was that Anderson punched one of them in the face, so hard that he would have fallen if the bigger man hadn't been holding him steady.

'Those poor bastards,' Derwent said, unblinking, as he watched the footage again and again. 'It's raining, it must be cold and he's wearing a nice warm jacket. They're in T-shirts.'

'Davy Bidwell all over again.'

'Not this time, if we have anything to do with it.' He rang Una Burt. 'They'll have to make a move on the farm. Nothing is happening here. We can't wait any longer.'

'I was going to say the same to you.' Una's voice was always penetrating but it was even harsher on speaker, and Derwent winced at it. 'It's a safety issue, isn't it? Officially, there's no one living full-time on the farm, but they clearly are. No one knows about them. The local police have heard rumours about the place over the years but they haven't had anything concrete to go on. Thwaites is regarded as intimidating locally and no one wants to get in his way. This is the first real evidence anyone has seen that they're abusing people there.'

'Slave labour,' Derwent said. 'In this day and age. Working them to death.'

'Doesn't bear thinking about.' She sounded more cheerful. 'Glad to have your buy-in on this. Hopefully we'll find paperwork at the farm. Our victims might be able to help as witnesses. This isn't over.'

After he ended the call, though, Derwent and I sat in silence. The action was going to happen elsewhere; what we had been doing was a dead end, as far as the investigation went. It wasn't uncommon for weeks of work to end up with nothing to show for it, but I felt we deserved more this time.

The raid on the farm was scheduled for dawn two days later, the earliest possible moment that the specialist officers with expertise in human trafficking and modern slavery could be available for it. Derwent had an invitation to go, but when I asked him when he was leaving, he looked offended.

'I'm not.'

'Don't you want to be there?'

He shook his head. 'Not my arrest.'

'You were the one who found out the farm existed.'

'I pointed someone else in the right direction. A bit of research at the Land Registry would have done that for us.' He was in a bad mood, brooding on the case, spending hours poring over maps of the farm and the local area. It bothered him that he wasn't in charge, I thought.

We were both in the kitchen when I heard the car, around half past six that evening. It was Derwent's turn to monitor Judy's house but I would seize any excuse to stop cooking. I put my knife down in the ruins of the pepper I'd been chopping up. 'I'll go.'

It was raining – not heavily, but the miserable drizzle of a wet, cool summer day. The street was slick and there was no one around, except for the men getting out of the Ford Focus parked at Judy's front door. It wasn't Tom Thwaites's usual car, although he was the driver, and it wasn't his usual kind of companion. The other man was young, his posture stooped although he moved with a rangy kind of energy. He had a shock of fair hair sticking out from under the hood of an anorak but I couldn't see his face in any detail thanks to the shadow of the hood. Tom went to the boot of the car and took out a bulging holdall. He slung it over his shoulder with an effort. I had hooked out my phone and started filming them for want of any better equipment, hiding behind the curtain as much as possible, although I thought the rain would do a decent enough job of screening me. Tom gave a cursory look around as he went to the front door of his mother's house, but he saw nothing to alarm him as he ushered the younger man inside. The door closed behind them and I stared across at the blank, uninformative outside of the house, wondering what was taking place inside.

'Josh?'

He was in the room already. 'What is it?'

'Tom has come. With a friend.'

'What kind of friend?'

I handed him my phone. 'Someone who looks young and strong and exactly their type. We need to share that with the Cheltenham surveillance team. Find out if he's usually one of the residents of the home.'

'Why didn't they spot him leaving, if he is one of the residents?'

'I don't know, but that's probably a hire car Tom's driving.'

'They're learning,' Derwent said grimly. 'They're hiding their tracks better. If we weren't here, who would know this lad had come here, or where he'd come from?'

'It's wicked, isn't it?'

'Absolutely.' He was watching the short clip I'd recorded, on repeat. 'Up there with murder.'

'It *was* murder in Davy's case,' I said. 'Just a long, slow death.'

'We don't know what's going on in there.' He frowned across at the house. 'Best to play it safe.'

'And wait?' I said it sharply, tension making my voice crack.

'For now. There's no evidence that Davy or anyone else came to harm in Judy's house. I'll let Una know.'

'What if we're wrong?'

He shrugged. To me he appeared completely detached, but I knew it was his reaction to extreme stress. The worse a situation was, the calmer he got. It was a reflex on his part and yet I found it comforting. I tried to imagine handling this situation with Georgia in Derwent's absence, and what I would be doing if I was the one who had to make the decisions, and once again I was glad he was back.

I was less glad the following morning, when he was rapping on my bedroom door.

'Maeve? You up?'

'Yes,' I said, although I wasn't. Six in the morning, and I had been too wired to get to sleep the previous night, so I was managing on four or five hours of sleep, at best. I stumbled to the door and opened it. Derwent was looking about as rough as I felt.

'Get dressed,' he said, without preamble. 'I have to walk the dog so you're in charge. If Judy comes out, I want you to go and talk to her. See if she mentions her house guest. Whatever she does – whether she talks about him or not – it's evidence.'

I rubbed my eyes. 'Did you spend all night thinking about this?'

'Just about.' He snapped his fingers. 'Come on. Time is wasting.'

He had gone, taking the dog and his excess of nervous tension with him, and I was sitting on the sofa with a mug of tea when the front door of Judy's house opened and she came out. She was filling the bird feeders, which I knew would take her a few minutes. I gathered my wits and my house keys and wandered across the road, carrying my mug.

'Morning.'

'You're up early, dear, aren't you?'

'Josh has taken the dog out already.' I stifled a yawn which wasn't actually feigned. 'I didn't sleep well last night.'

'I never sleep well.' She was still bright-eyed, though, her make-up on and her hair neatly curled. 'I'm used to it now.

I take advantage of the extra time. Read my library books, clear out cupboards. No one to disturb, most of the time.'

'Unless you have a house guest.' I sipped my tea, looking at the bird feeders dreamily.

'Then I have to remember to behave myself, you're right.' She gave a little chuckle. No constraint, no worry, no hint of guilt. 'Tom's here but he won't be up for ages.'

'I saw him arrive last night.' I shrugged. 'I suppose I'm jumpy at the moment. I heard the car and looked out.'

'We're all jumpy.' She looked up at Gillian Holding's house and shivered. 'Hard to believe she's gone.'

'You know they think it's murder.'

'Well. The police don't always know what they're looking at, do they? They'll *say* murder but it will turn out to be an accident.'

I smiled. 'It doesn't sound as if you're much of a fan of the police, Judy.'

'I've had nothing to do with them, really.' She shuddered theatrically. 'But the stories you hear.'

Nothing to do with them apart from the interviews about Davy Bidwell, I thought. You can't have forgotten Davy.

And just like that, I felt my own guilt melt away. Judy was nice to me, but that didn't mean she was a good person. If she knew what was happening to the young men who passed through her house, she needed to be locked up, and if she hadn't known, she would have been outraged and traumatised by her interaction with the police. Pretending she'd never had anything to do with them was a lie – a lie delivered so fluently that I almost believed it in spite of knowing the truth. Judy lied and I needed to bear that in mind.

I looked around casually. 'That's not Tom's car, is it?'

'It's in for a service. Courtesy car.' She gave another wheezy laugh. 'He's spitting feathers about it. Not up to his standards. He's here with a friend. I'd better go back in and make them some breakfast.'

332

'What a good hostess. They should be looking after you, not the other way round.'

'I don't mind. Doesn't take long to fry some bacon and eggs, but I'd better get on with it.' She collected up the nuts and seeds, moving fast now, and scuttled away into the house. I turned back to go home, and it was only then that I noticed, with a prickle of unease, that two of the feeders still swung half-empty.

43

'I'm sorry,' I said to Derwent as he shut the door behind him, out of breath from sprinting back to the house. 'I had to call you.'

'You did the right thing.' He filled Pippin's water bowl. 'What do you think spooked her?'

'I don't know. Maybe the fact that I saw Tom arrive so I knew he wasn't on his own? Maybe I was too obvious about noticing the car.'

'I'm not angry about it.' He pulled his T-shirt off over his head and bent to yank off his trainers. 'Lighting a fire under them feels like the right thing to do. I'm fed up with waiting around. I want them to start making mistakes, like lying to you.'

'What do we do now?' I kept my eyes on his face. So nothing that had happened between us made him feel that he shouldn't wander around half-naked. Interesting.

'Watch them. I'll get ready. If they make a move, I'll follow them – we don't have time to get another surveillance team in place so I'll track them until someone else can take over. With any luck it will take them longer to get organised than it'll take me to change.'

'Well, get a move on.' I made shooing motions and he jogged up the stairs to the bathroom. I went into the sitting room and perched on the edge of the sofa with a book, not reading it. My attention was half on the house across the road and half on the noises from upstairs where Derwent was performing his usual quick-change act. He came down and sat on the sofa beside me to put on his shoes.

'Are you going to wait until they come out? Won't they spot you following them?'

'No. I'll go and plot up in one of the other roads. When you see them leaving, you'll let me know. With any luck I can hang back and they won't even know I'm there.'

'And I just stay here?'

He nodded. 'Keep an eye on Judy.'

'In case what?' I put the book down. 'She's not going anywhere. I should come with you. What if they notice you're behind them? What if you end up in a car chase, or Tom calls up reinforcements?'

'They won't know I'm there. And you need to stay here. Too bad. Boring, I know.'

'Boring and frustrating.'

He put his hand on my arm. 'Quite seriously, Maeve, I like it when your life is boring. When it's interesting, I start to worry.'

He was gone a matter of ten or fifteen minutes when Tom Thwaites came out of the house, pulling on his jacket. He looked around and I felt my breath hitch as his eyes seemed to linger on Vanessa's house, where I was sitting in the bay window of the bedroom. I hoped I was invisible. Apparently satisfied that no one was watching, he leaned back into the house and came out holding the younger man by the arm. I was filming so I concentrated on making sure the image was pin-sharp, and tried not to think about the obvious terror on the man's face – he was little more than a boy, really – or how bewildered he seemed, or how sharply Tom Thwaites spoke to him. Judy was in the hall but she would

335

be little more than a shadow on the footage, hanging back, out of sight.

Tom only needed one hand to control the other man, shoving him against the car with enough violence that the young man cried out. Tom opened the car door and shovelled him into the passenger seat, leaning in to put the seat belt across him. I saw two short, vicious movements from his arm that suggested he was punching the man, and I realised I was clenching my teeth so hard that my skull ached. Glancing down at my phone for a split second at a time, I sent a message to Derwent.

They're on the move.

I got a thumbs-up back; he was in position, waiting. That was comforting, that and the fact that Una Burt had back-up speeding towards us to take care of the surveillance, and that the plans for the farm were far enough advanced that they could swoop in as soon as Thwaites was arrested and rescue the men we'd seen on the footage.

But at the moment, no one was under arrest and the man in front of me was in helpless, awful misery, and there was nothing I could do but watch.

Tom got into the driver's seat with a nod to his mother, whose response was to shut the front door. No big farewell here. He reversed out of the drive and drove cautiously down to the end of the road. I craned to see and was rewarded with a flash of sunlight on the back windscreen as the car turned left.

I rang Derwent. 'They've gone left.'

'I've got them. They've just passed the end of this road.'

I could hear the engine noises as Derwent followed them. 'Perfect. Two cars between me and them. My best guess is they're heading for the motorway.'

'Don't get too close.'

'I have done this before.' He sounded relaxed and almost

excited, the hunter at work, a natural at it. 'I'll be in touch if I lose them or when I hand them over. One or the other.'

He ended the call and I sat in the empty house, listening to the creaks and rattles that I didn't usually hear. Pippin was fast asleep in the kitchen, exhausted by his run that morning. It felt strange to be on my own.

What if Gillian Holding's killer saw Derwent outside and took advantage of his unexpected absence?

Paranoia, I scolded myself, even as I checked over my shoulder, my eyes wide, my heart in my throat. I was tense enough about what was actually happening without inventing new fears.

And speaking of fear, I was imagining what might be taking place in Judy's house. I stared at the windows, wishing I could see what was going on inside.

To move or not to move.

To intervene or let it play out.

If Derwent got it wrong, he would be left to take responsibility for it. He had known that would be the outcome all along, I realised with a belated flash of insight. That was why he had warned Rula Jacques not to expect too much despite Una Burt's promises. It wasn't reckless disagreement with a superior officer; it was a badly needed dose of realism. All of a sudden I understood why he hadn't been worried about what might happen between us when we went back to work. If it all went wrong, he wouldn't be coming back. And how would I cope with that?

Before I could answer that very uncomfortable question, I saw something that made me sit up straight. The front door of Judy's house came open and Judy emerged, dragging a large black rubbish sack. She hauled it to the end of the drive and propped it up against her bin. Too heavy for her to lift, I guessed, and I wondered what was in it. She looked into the bag, then double-knotted it firmly. She walked back into the house, her head high, not a care in the world. Tomorrow was bin day; whatever was in there, it would be gone in the morning.

And meanwhile, her son's car was speeding across England, heading north, while the machinery of the legal system was turning to close a trap around him, and her, and anyone else involved in their conspiracy.

The surveillance teams took over from Derwent about fifty miles from Newark, and he rang me.

'The plan is for them to shadow him to the farm. We'll wait until then to send the team into the farm itself.'

'We,' I repeated. 'Are you going up there?'

'I thought I would. Is that all right?'

'Of course.'

'Great.' He had stopped at services to fill up the car and the roar of the motorway almost drowned out his words. 'They're going to coordinate the raid on the farm and the nursing home. I've asked for a team to pick up Judy at the same time.'

'I don't think she's much of a flight risk.'

'You never know,' Derwent said darkly. 'Plan for the worst, hope for the best.'

'You missed your calling as a football manager,' I said. 'All of these helpful little aphorisms.'

'At the end of the day, it's a game of two halves.' I could hear from his voice that he was grinning. 'See you in a while. Stay out of trouble.'

'I don't have much choice.'

Time seemed to drag even more, knowing that other officers were out there, preparing to make arrests. All I could do was wait, my thoughts skittering from Judy Thwaites to the Dawoud case, from Gillian Holding to Nicola Vonn, from Josh Derwent to what I wanted out of life, and back again.

I had expected to get a courtesy call from someone to tell me what was happening, even if Derwent was fully occupied with running the operation at the farm, but in fact I was almost as surprised as anyone else to see a police car turning into the street, late that afternoon.

I left my post and hurried down the stairs. Across the road, two uniformed officers were making their way up Judy's drive, not hurrying, one stocky and male, one slight and female. I let them go, knowing that they would be more than capable of making the arrest without my input.

Inevitably, there seemed to be lots of people about: Alan was gardening with Ruth's assistance, and both of them turned to watch when the police rang the doorbell. They looked worried, to give them their due, and I supposed it was more likely that the police would have bad news to deliver than that they were there to arrest an elderly lady. Stephen Bollivant had just returned in his little van and he stayed in the driver's seat, staring out at what was going on. Gary Holding walked past with his head down and maybe it was that he'd had enough of the police lately, or maybe it was that he was too sunk in misery to notice them, but he seemed oblivious.

I let myself out of the house, my wallet tucked into the back pocket of my jeans for the first time since I'd arrived in Jellicoe Close. I walked across the road to where the two police officers were guiding Judy down the drive. She was trembling, barely able to walk, and the contrast to the spritely woman I'd seen earlier was painful.

'Oh . . . Maeve . . .'

'It's all right,' the male PC said to me. 'We're taking this lady to the station.'

'Thanks,' I said, and hooked out my wallet to flash my warrant card at them. They must have been briefed to expect me, but from the look of surprise on his face he had been imagining a very different-looking detective sergeant. 'Has she been cautioned?'

They both nodded.

'Maeve?' Judy was stock-still. 'You're one of them?'

'I'm afraid so. Can I look in here, Judy?' I had gone to the bin bag she'd left at the gate earlier.

'I don't think – why? It's only some things my son left . . . I suppose it's all right . . .'

I bent over the bag and untied it, peering inside with the help of the torch Fleur had at last returned. Men's clothes, and a wallet that I would have loved to look at but I had no gloves, I discovered. The female PC came to the rescue, taking it out gingerly and flipping it open, holding it so I could see. A photo ID for a rail card was the first thing in the wallet and I spotted the fair hair of the man I'd seen with Tom Thwaites.

'Laurence Dixon,' I said. 'Does that ring a bell, Judy? Your house guest from this morning, isn't it?'

'I don't know.'

'Don't you think he might need his wallet?'

'I didn't know what was in the bag,' she began, and I thought of how I'd watched her inspect the contents before she knotted it up, and how that was on video and how she was lying to me all over again.

'We can talk at the station,' I said, and smiled at her to hide my true feelings. The two officers carefully inserted her into the back seat of the car.

'Do you want a lift?' the male officer said. 'I can get someone to pick you up.'

I shook my head. 'I'm going to join the search team to go through the house first. I'll hang on here and catch up with you later.'

They duly drove away, Judy's small head bobbing as the car went down the road. I thought she was in tears and I suppressed the pity that was my first reaction. Laurence Dixon had probably cried too, but no one had cared.

The car turned onto the main road and Judy disappeared from view. Then, and only then, did I allow myself to make eye contact with the neighbours. Their expressions ranged from shock all the way through to betrayal. I suppressed the urge to shrug at them, and turned to go into Judy's house, feeling obscurely guilty myself.

44

At ten the following morning I was sitting in an interview room in the local police station, balancing a notebook on my knee, across the table from Judy Thwaites and her lawyer. We had been in no rush to interview our suspects, even though the custody clock was running and we only had twenty-four hours from their arrest until they had to be charged. Search teams had gone into the addresses we had for them, gathering evidence, collecting anything that might prove to be important in constructing the case against them. Una Burt came from London to contribute little more than her presence but for once I was pleased that she was there, and that she was happy with us. She was almost giddy with relief that we had made arrests. I recognised the feeling, and if I'd had time to think about it I might have felt the same way.

Instead, there were updates from the farm, where three men were rescued from conditions of the utmost squalor and taken straight to hospital. Derwent's voice broke when he was talking to me about it late that night, on the phone.

'The officers from the task force took the lead and thank Christ for that because I wouldn't have known where to start. They're like skeletons, the three of them – barely able to talk. Filthy. And the place they were sleeping was a shed. They had nothing. No comforts at all. Not even blankets. How anyone could treat another human being like that is beyond me.'

'Were they working on the farm?'

'Yes. One of them thinks he's been there five years. He was the most communicative one. None of them has any family. They were terrified to talk to us. They trust Tom and the farm manager – can you believe that?'

'Well, they've probably been told they can't trust anyone else.'

'Exactly that. They've lived through a nightmare.'

'Did they remember Davy?'

'The chatty one did. He said he didn't escape. Tom was the one who took him away when he got sick.'

'*Did* he? What did Tom say about that?'

'Nothing yet. But I'll get him to talk.' There was a grim note to Derwent's voice that made me believe him.

Now I was sitting opposite Judy herself, preparing to persuade her to tell me everything. Without her make-up she looked far older and less glamorous, her eyes cloudy like smoked glass, her whole personality shrunken. Everyone had agreed that I should interview her, along with a sweetly pretty officer from the task force. Neither of us looked threatening. She could trust us, I tried to convey with a smile that felt forced and fake.

'This is strange. You being here like this.' She shivered. 'Me being here. At my age. I never thought it would come to this. How's the boy who was staying with me?'

'Lawrence? I think he's OK.'

'He's a nice kid. He didn't deserve what they were planning to do to him. I tried to tell Tom that, but he wouldn't listen. He never listens to me.' She looked up and held my gaze. 'I know my son is going to prison for what he's done, and I'm sorry about it. I've got to tell you the truth even if it gets him in trouble. What can I say, he fell in with the wrong crowd. It was never his idea, any of it. That harpy he married came up with the plan, her and his friend Nevis. I want them punished. They bullied me, and they lied, and they deserve to be locked up.'

'Mrs Thwaites,' her solicitor said quietly, and she jumped.

'Sorry. I forgot.'

I was trying to forget too, specifically the large number of people who were watching a live feed of this interview, in the building and elsewhere. I had reminded Judy that she was under caution. I was playing it by the book.

'Do you understand why you're here, Judy?'

She nodded. 'Because of the men.'

'Which men?'

A long sigh. 'The ones my son brought to stay with me. The ones he put to work on his farm. Nevis – his friend, you know – said there was a good income in it. He said we should keep it small and no one would notice. Choose men who could work and who didn't have any family.'

'Why do you think it mattered that they didn't have any family?'

'I thought it was because they needed looking after?' Judy whispered. 'But that wasn't what happened, was it?'

'What happened to the men once they came to stay with you?'

'Nothing. I minded them.'

'Did you take their money? Their passports or other ID?'

'No.'

'But you threw away Lawrence's belongings, Judy. I found his wallet in the bin bag you took out of your house.'

'That was an accident,' she said vaguely. 'I wasn't sure if he was finished with it.'

'When we arrested you, you told me that you didn't know what was in the bag.'

'No, that's right.'

'But you did know about the wallet.'

'No.'

'You just said you weren't sure if he was finished with it.'

She shook her head. 'I don't know. You're putting me on the spot.'

That's the idea. 'How did your son find these men?'

This was safer ground. 'His wife. She runs a care home. She looks for anyone who doesn't have family or friends who would interfere. The ones who have nowhere to go and no one to help them.' Judy blinked. 'Nothing to do with me, really it wasn't. I told you, Maeve, that woman is poison. It was all her idea.'

'When did it start?'

'The first one was a few years ago. They did one and then I got cold feet.' She gave an uneasy little smile. 'I was worried about getting found out. I wouldn't touch the money they gave me.'

'How much did you get?'

'Two thousand pounds.' She whispered it, her eyes wide at the unimaginable wealth it represented.

'And you kept it?'

'Yes, but I didn't use it.'

'How much did you make altogether?'

'Six thousand pounds. It's in my attic.'

I leaned across the table. 'What about the forty thousand in your freezer, Judy? Cash. Used notes. Where did that come from?'

Her whole face tightened, a hundred new wrinkles appearing. I had found the money, frozen in ziplock bags inside Tupperware containers full of dry-looking casseroles.

'You hid it well, but not well enough.'

'I didn't know it was there. What did you say? Forty thousand? I had no idea.'

'Where did it come from if you didn't put it there?'

'Someone must have put it there.'

I raised my eyebrows. 'And made casseroles to cover it? And you didn't notice? Come off it, Judy. You hid it there.'

'It wasn't mine,' she said. 'Tom asked me to keep it for him.'

'So you did know it was there.'

A small, uncertain nod. 'You're confusing me.'

'I'm sorry you're confused. We can take it slowly. I just need to find out a few things, you see.' I changed tack again, smoothly. It was unsettling for her, interrupting her every time she found her groove. 'Do you know what happened to the men after they left your house?'

'No.' Her response was a shade too quick. 'They worked. I don't know what the work was.' She started to fidget. 'I don't know. You'll have to ask Tom. I was only a helper. No one paid attention to me.'

I took my time in leading her through the events that led up to the first man arriving and his disappearance, and then moved on to the second. It was the places where her story went murky that interested me, because she was specific and helpful when it implicated anyone else in wrongdoing but her whole narrative was designed to make me think she was helpless, in Tom Thwaites's thrall. When she became vague, my attention sharpened.

'Let's talk about Davy.'

'Who?' Judy turned to her lawyer. 'Is there any chance we could take a break? I'm very tired.'

'I only have a few more questions,' I said sweetly. 'Davy Bidwell. Two years ago.'

'Davy. Yes. Could I have a cup of tea?'

'We'll have a break in a minute. Davy was how old?'

'Thirty-ish, I think.'

'And you met him how?'

'My son brought him here.'

'To your house, as usual. You had it all worked out – the same routine, the same result. But it all went wrong, didn't it? Because Davy wasn't strong, and he got sick. He ended up in London and his body was discovered in a derelict house.

345

And then it went wrong again because he wasn't completely alone in the world, was he? His brother is married to Rula Jacques, the Mayor of London's assistant.'

Panic flared briefly in her eyes. She turned to her solicitor. 'I don't know anything about this.'

'You were interviewed about it, Judy. You said you didn't know anything about Davy, but you had his bank card in your house, between two books, on a shelf in your study. We found it a few hours ago.'

'I don't know how that came to be there.' Her face was sullen.

'No? When the police came asking questions about what happened to him – because they did try to find out how he had ended up where he was – you were ready to sell a sad story of an old woman who had just wanted to help people, when all you wanted was to make money off the most vulnerable kind of person imaginable. You were very convincing and you persuaded them there was nothing left to investigate.'

Judy said nothing, her fingers plucking at the blanket that was draped over her knees.

'You know, if you hadn't tried to do it again, you might have got away with it.'

'That wasn't my idea. I wanted to leave it.' She shook her head. 'They wouldn't listen to me or Tom. They bullied us.'

I closed my notebook. 'Would it surprise you, Judy, to hear that Tom says you thought these men deserved it. He said it was all your idea, all along, and you kept half of the money because it was your idea and your house and you were the one who was the last official point of contact for them so you said you had the biggest risk.'

'He said what?' Judy's face was shrivelled, her eyes blank with rage.

'He said he hopes you end your days in prison.' I smiled at her as I reached out to end the recording. 'Something to think about, isn't it?'

346

'He's trying to put the blame on me,' she said to her solicitor, who was trying in vain to shush her. 'I'm not having it.'

I paused, my finger on the button. 'If you have anything to add . . .'

'I do. I'll tell you about Davy. I'll tell you about Tom and Myra taking him to London and shutting him up in an empty house. Myra called it letting nature take its course. They wanted him gone. They dumped him.'

'We can't prove that,' I said.

'I can.' She was trembling. 'Myra used to live on the road behind that house, didn't you know that? She was the one who suggested putting him there. She said he'd die of natural causes and no one would ever come looking for us because there was nothing to connect his death with us. But she was wrong. She picked the wrong victim. And Tom made the same mistake when he tried to pin all of this on me.'

After the interview I walked straight into DC Jones, as if she had been waiting for me. Without preamble, she said, 'We didn't know about you being police.'

'No, I know.' I smiled. 'It was a bit awkward for us too, given that you had to treat us as potential suspects, but we were operating in strict secrecy.'

'So I hear.' There was a hostility to her expression. 'I suppose you've been thinking you could do a better job on Gillian Holding.'

'No, not at all.' I had forgotten to allow for the county forces and their dislike of the Met; we were viewed as arrogant and over-confident, inclined to dismiss our colleagues in other parts of the country. 'We were impressed. Really.'

'What were we impressed about?' Arrogant and over-confident to his core, and inclined to dismiss just about everyone, Derwent strolled into the hall at precisely the wrong moment.

'The investigation into Gillian Holding's murder.' I made

eye contact with him, hoping he could read my thoughts. *Be nice. Don't be an arsehole.*

'Oh. Yes. Maeve said how much she admired your inter-viewing technique, actually,' he said smoothly.

DC Jones coloured with pleasure. 'Really?'

'Absolutely. Very instructive for us to be on the other side for once.'

'Oh, well, I'm glad it was all right.' Her manner had warmed up considerably. I tried to put myself in her shoes – interviewing senior officers without knowing who they were or what they did – and I thought I might have been prickly about it too.

'It was a fascinating experience,' I said truthfully, and she beamed.

'Our superintendent was wondering if the two of you would like to come and see the incident room we have up and running for Gillian Holding. Meet the team properly.'

'The thing is,' Derwent said slowly – I cringed, hoping he wasn't going to brush off the offer because we were too busy, for which they would hear 'too important' – 'Maeve and I didn't want to intrude on your investigation.'

'Oh, it wouldn't be an intrusion. We'd be delighted.'

'If you're sure.'

Charmed, she led us down the corridor. A glance showed me that Derwent was smiling to himself.

It was surprisingly nice to be back in a murder investigation again, in an incident room full of people who were keen to show their absolute dedication to solving Gillian Holding's murder. The superintendent was a grey, worried man, who was pleased by the compliments we paid him on his team and their work. Derwent engaged him in conversation about the murder rate locally and I wandered over to look at the board on the wall, the at-a-glance guide to the investigation that was so useful for a quick catch-up. Gillian's picture was in the centre. It was an old headshot, from before she was ill, and she smiled into the room with quiet confidence.

'Is it strange that you knew her and now she's the subject of an investigation?' The question came from one of the younger detective constables, a bright-eyed twenty-something Black woman who wore her hair in hundreds of braids.

'A little. I was just thinking that I never knew this Gillian Holding. I wouldn't have recognised her.'

'Dementia will do that.'

'She was so scared,' I said softly. 'She knew someone wanted to hurt her. I wish I'd managed to find out who she meant.'

'Maybe she didn't know.'

'I think she knew something, but she couldn't put it into words.' The devil who smiled at her. Something she saw from her window. Someone who knew the area, who was confident enough to go into her house and take her into the woods. The tiny fragments of knowledge I possessed spun around and around, like a kaleidoscope that refused to fall into a pattern. 'I know you were looking at her son, but he seemed loyal. Dutiful. He's not the most appealing person but I can't see him killing her – not in a public place, anyway.'

'He's still on the list, but further down. We're looking at all of the local sex offenders, obviously, given your evidence that she seemed to be concerned about a young girl's welfare, and burglary suspects in case it was a break-in that went wrong. I don't think that's it myself, but we have to start somewhere.' She glanced at me. 'Don't say I said that. But I wanted you to know.'

'I appreciate it.' I sighed. 'If you want to know how this feels, I hate it. I missed an opportunity to help her and now her killer is laughing at us.'

'We're not giving up,' the young detective said, folding her arms and staring at the board as if the answer was on it, somewhere. 'We'll find him.'

'Thank you,' I said, and meant it.

45

Of course, after locking up Judy and her son, there was no reason for us to stay in Jellicoe Close any more. Number 7 was empty, the curtains drawn, the contents ransacked by a determined POLSA team that had swept the place after our initial search. There was still Pippin to look after, but Derwent had news about that, from Una Burt.

'The usual dog-sitter is available again. She can start on Saturday. Vanessa is happy for her to take over from us for the next few weeks, until she gets back. Pippin knows this woman and likes her.'

'What about the dog-sitter's mother?'

'She's made an excellent recovery, apparently. Out of hospital, doing well.' Derwent looked up from his phone. 'So we get to go home.'

'Great.' I tried to sound as if I was pleased about that, but something told me he knew I was experiencing mixed emotions. Of course we couldn't remain in Jellicoe Close, in fake domestic bliss – I knew that – but there was something brutal about being jerked out of the world we'd been inhabiting, and at such short notice.

What Derwent felt about it, I couldn't tell. He was generally brisk and businesslike, fully occupied with coordinating the investigation into Tom Thwaites's illegal activities. He was delighted to hear I'd discovered Judy's share of the profits.

'I love it when they lie. Always a fun moment in court when the evidence contradicts what they said in interview.'

'It makes me feel better about locking her up.'

'She deserves it.' He was in the middle of an email but he stopped to look at me. 'It's nice of you to care about the horrible old witch.'

'It's not so much her I'm worried about. Haven't you noticed the looks we've been getting from the neighbours?' I pulled a face. 'They are not happy with us. I suppose we did lie to them for the last few weeks.'

'Maybe you should do some outreach work. Go and explain we were doing our jobs.'

'Do I have to?'

He had returned to his email. 'Well, we're leaving in two days' time when the dog-sitter gets here. You have to say goodbye. You might as well make it count.'

I wasn't quite prepared to go around knocking on people's doors to explain myself, but I managed to run into a few of the neighbours before Saturday came. I saw Stephen Bollivant at the shops that afternoon. He gave me a shy smile and said he hadn't guessed, and it was none of his business, but he was glad it had all worked out. A knock on the door was Brian with a misdelivered parcel for Vanessa, and I invited him in for a cup of tea.

'Ah, I'd better not. Fleur is cooking dinner.' He wouldn't meet my eyes.

'Fair enough,' I said levelly. 'I understand.'

He started to walk away, then wheeled around and addressed me from halfway down the drive. 'You had us all fooled, didn't you?'

'That was sort of the point.'

'Do you not have any conscience about it?'

351

'I was doing it for the right reasons. I can't tell you anything about Judy or what was going on here, but it was the sort of thing that can't be ignored.'

He looked me up and down. 'A police officer. I would have had no idea.'

'Again, that was the point.'

'It's a bit transgressive, isn't it? A nice Irish girl being in a position of authority in an English police force?'

I recognised the needling tone. I had heard this kind of line so often before that I wasn't going to rise to it. 'There are a few of us around.'

'What do your family think about it?'

'They're proud of me.'

'All of them? What about the extended family back in Ireland?'

'Well, there are always pricks who have an opinion about the job I do,' I said pleasantly. 'But I've learned to ignore them.'

He gave a shout of laughter. 'I deserved that. Sorry.'

'Keep probing for a weak spot. I'm enjoying it.'

'I wouldn't dare.' He hesitated for a second. 'We all liked you, you know, you and Josh. Before we found out you weren't who you said you were, we were talking about how we could convince you to stay. You could have lived in number 1. Tidy it up a bit and bob's your uncle.'

'That would have been lovely.' I sounded far too wistful; I looked over my shoulder to be sure Derwent was safely out of earshot.

'Look, I'm sure everyone will forgive you in time. Except for Ruth.'

'Ruth? Why is she angry? Because I arrested her best friend?'

'Not sure. But she's very upset. Alan said she won't even knit or bake anything. She's just sitting in her chair.'

It really hurt that Ruth was upset, I discovered – hurt to the point that I felt it physically as a weight on my chest. 'I wondered why he kept glaring at me. Thank you for letting me know.'

'Any time.' He began to walk away again, then came back. 'Are you any good for traffic tickets?'

'Fuck off, Brian.'

He laughed all the way back to his house.

Alice Knox came around later on, in running kit, and asked if I wanted to go for a jog with her. I was surprised but pleased, and said so when we set off, heading towards the common rather than the Holmwood. I hadn't been back since I found Gillian Holding's body there.

'I wanted to let you know that we're keeping the running club going,' Alice said after we had settled into a comfortable pace. 'It's a really nice thing to do and we have you to thank for it.'

'That was Josh's idea,' I said. 'He has his moments.'

'I'm trying to persuade Camilla to join us. She could do with getting some fresh air.'

'Teenagers. I don't think I left my bedroom for about three years.' I hesitated. There was something that had been bothering me for weeks and I'd never get another opportunity to ask about it. 'What happened with Camilla last year? Ruth said something about her going missing.'

'She disappeared for a couple of days. Do you know, it was Mike who actually found her in the middle of London and brought her back.' Alice was smiling to herself, proud of her family. 'Tip told me where she was and Mike persuaded her to come home.'

'How did Tip know where she was?'

'I don't know. He and Camilla have always been close though. She broke up with her boyfriend Isaac afterwards. Wouldn't talk to his sister Elise either. Usually with that kind of drama it all comes back to me eventually but neither of my two would talk about it.'

353

'Did you talk to Nicola about it?'

Alice snorted. 'She wouldn't have known anything. She barely pays any attention to her children. Far too busy worrying about what her husband is doing.'

My attention sharpened. 'And what would that be?'

'I don't suppose it matters if you're leaving. I can tell you. Rhys had an affair.'

'That doesn't exactly shock me, Alice.'

'With Fleur.'

'What?' I actually stopped running, I was so surprised. '*Fleur*?'

'Briefly. I think she realised it was a mistake as soon as it started. Rhys took advantage of Fleur when she was at a real low point, when she'd found out she was the reason they were having trouble conceiving.' She pulled a face. 'I've always got on with Rhys, don't get me wrong, but I don't bring out that side of him. When he sees an opportunity, he goes for it. But he's never gone for me.'

'Probably just as well, given that he's so friendly with Mike.'

'You know, Gillian didn't like him. I've been wondering about that lately.' She said it in a rush, as if she had been holding the words back for too long. 'I remember standing talking to her and Gary one day and Rhys cycled past with Mike. She stared and stared at them. Then she told me he wanted to kill her.'

'*Rhys* wanted to?'

'That's what she said.'

'Did you tell the police this? When did she say it?'

'It was months ago. I – I didn't like to. She was very wild that day. She wasn't making sense about anything. Gary told me she was paranoid. She was barely sleeping at the time.'

I would pass it on, I thought, for what it was worth.

'Please don't say anything to Fleur. She knows that I know about her and Rhys. No one else does. I'm glad she and Brian stayed together. I told her, you can't run away from your past

354

but you can learn from it.' Alice ducked her head. 'Sorry. That makes me sound very prissy.'

'No, it doesn't. I think I needed to hear that.'

She looked surprised, but she didn't push me to elaborate, and we ran on together.

If we had stayed longer, I thought, in this alternate reality, Alice and I could have been friends.

46

I had expected a polite 'thank you but no thank you' from the local CID in response to passing on Alice's information, but I was wrong. They were more desperate than I had thought, I realised, as they dragged a protesting Rhys out of his house very early the following morning. He was wearing sagging boxer shorts and a T-shirt that rode up so far too much pale skin was on display for my liking. He complained about the way he was being treated and how tight the handcuffs were and how ridiculous it was to be arrested for something like this. Nicola watched from an upstairs window, her face distraught. Thea stood by her side with her face pressed against her mother's arm, unable to look. I felt sorry for them, and tired, and I hoped there was more evidence than Alice's uncertain recollection of something Gillian might have said. The question of why Camilla had run away scratched at the back of my mind like a starving cat trying to get in. It felt significant, somehow, and connected, and I couldn't make sense of it.

'This is getting to be a habit,' Brian said to me, strolling up to me in slippers, a hoodie thrown over his pyjamas. 'Seeing the neighbours being carted away, I mean.'

'Déjà vu all over again.'

We both watched as the police van lurched away, carrying its furious burden.

'I take it this has something to do with you.'

'Me? No. Not really.' I gestured at my own nightwear. 'I don't go to work like this.'

'Did he kill her?'

'I don't know. I'm not involved with the investigation.' I glanced at him. 'But would it surprise you if he had?'

He shook his head slowly. 'I think he's capable of anything.'

I had Alice's words about learning from mistakes in mind when I knocked on the door of number 6 a couple of hours later. Nicola dragged the door open. She stared at me blankly, without a hint of recognition. I didn't blame her entirely; I had reverted to the jeans and T-shirt that I would have chosen to wear if I hadn't been undercover, and I knew it changed how people saw me. Nicola would have struggled even if I'd been wearing a name badge, though. I wondered whether there was any point in trying to talk to her if she was lost in a chemical haze.

'It's you. The policewoman.'

'That's me. You can call me Maeve though. May I come in?'

She turned and walked away. I followed her into the kitchen.

'Would you like a coffee?'

'Just a glass of water, please.' I watched her moving around the kitchen like a sleepwalker, taking a glass from a cupboard and holding it in both hands as she crossed to the fridge. The ice-maker in the door rumbled and two pellets fell into the glass. A slice of lime from a covered bowl kept in the fridge. Water, at last, from a filtered tap. It made me uneasy that she was taking such care over the simplest thing, as if someone had taught her to expect the worst if she didn't try her best.

By contrast, she made herself a mug of instant coffee, the boiling-water tap sputtering dangerously. She caught her breath as it splashed her and I went towards her, wanting to help.

'Careful.'

'Oh.' She shook her hand where the water had scalded it. 'I keep meaning to get that fixed.'

'Have you heard from Rhys?'

'No.' She was trembling. 'They said not to expect him back for a few hours.'

The house felt empty. 'And the kids?'

'All at school for another couple of weeks.'

'Come and sit down.' I drew out a chair for her at the table, under the neon artwork.

'What do you want?' She said it to her mug rather than to me, drawing her elbows in, taking up as little space as possible. The question wasn't confrontational. It was a prey animal's awareness of threat. She was used to reading ulterior motives and she knew I had a goal in mind.

'It's not official business.' I sipped my water. 'It's about you. Your safety.'

'My safety,' she repeated. 'I'm safe.'

'Are you? That's not how it looks to me, Nicola.'

'Rhys.' She smiled bitterly, not meeting my eyes. 'You're worried about me because you think Rhys is dangerous.'

'Am I wrong? I've met men like him before. I've arrested men like him before.' I turned the glass around, a half turn. 'Don't be fooled, Nicola. You're not safe. He's been taken in for questioning but he's not the kind to break, is he? Unless they have enough evidence to charge him, he'll be back. And I think he might hurt you. I think he hurts you a lot of the time.'

She gave a little gasp, shocked. 'He's just very confident.'

'He humiliated you at that lunch party when you dropped the pavlova.'

She flinched, still not looking at me.

'Does he hit you?'

358

A shake of her head.

'Are you too scared to be honest with me?'

Silence apart from the ticking of a large clock on the wall. I felt as if it was saying, *you're running out of time.*

'I don't want him to be sent to prison,' Nicola whispered.

'No. I can understand that.'

'Can you?' She looked at me for the first time since we'd sat down. 'I don't think you can.'

'You'd be surprised.' I gave her a couple of seconds. Then I asked again, 'Does he hit you, Nicola?'

'Not often.'

'It should be never.'

She folded her arms across herself. 'It's only when I get things wrong. When I annoy him. Sometimes when I argue with him. You don't know because you only see me like this, but I have a temper – I can be infuriating when I get into a mood with him. I give as good as I get. Sometimes he needs to stop me from going on and on at him and it's the only thing he can do to shut me up.'

'Is that what he tells you?'

'It's my fault. Once or twice a year. That's not much.'

'But when he's not hitting you, you're scared that he will. Once or twice a year is enough to make you afraid of him all the time. Nicola, I want to help you. I've seen him belittle you. And it's not just you in the house, is it? Your daughters walk on eggshells.'

She flinched. 'That's – I don't think they notice.'

'I promise you, they do. He's starting to treat Camilla the same way as you. She ran away from him, didn't she?'

'I – I don't know.'

'He's a controlling man and he wants to manipulate all of you. It won't be long before it starts to affect Thea too.'

'It's complicated.' I had lost her somewhere along the way. She was picking at her fingernails, her expression hard. 'You wouldn't understand.'

359

'I know it's hard when you have kids.' Derwent had said as much to me, I remembered, with a strange kind of intensity in his voice. His girlfriend Melissa had fled her violent husband, Thomas in tow, and all of Derwent's protective instincts had kicked in. 'I'm not saying it's easy.'

'What *are* you saying?' She shifted in her chair, on edge. I needed to win her over.

You can't run away from your past, Alice had said. But you could use it, when you needed to.

'My last boyfriend hit me. He broke my cheekbone. He broke my collarbone.' I lifted my hair. 'He gave me this scar on my forehead.'

Nicola Vonn was staring at me. 'You? He hit you? Even though you're a police officer?'

'I think that made it better for him,' I said, and I hadn't voiced that thought before. 'I think he got a thrill out of it *because* I was a police officer.'

'What happened?'

'First he cut me off from my friends and my family. Then he sapped my confidence by telling me I wasn't good enough for him. He kept changing the rules so I didn't know when I was doing the right thing – unless he told me I was. I lived for his praise because I couldn't stand his disapproval.' I swallowed, aware of a bitter taste in my mouth as my stomach tightened. 'He said he loved me. And the first time he hit me, I thought it was my fault.'

'And then?'

'Then he nearly killed me. And I was so ashamed of myself for mistaking him for a good person that I almost let him.'

'What happened to him?'

'He went to prison. I gave evidence against him. It was the hardest thing I've ever done. I didn't want to admit what was happening, even to myself. I didn't want to admit I'd been a fool to trust him. But it wasn't my fault that he hit me, and it's not your fault that Rhys hurts you.'

360

'It's the same. Just the same.' Her eyes were brimming. 'The first time was before we were married and I wish – I wish I'd gone then, before we had the children. I wish I hadn't believed him when he said it wouldn't happen again.'

'You want to believe the best of them,' I said quietly. 'They use that.'

'People think I'm lucky. People envy me this house. Our money. That Rhys has retired, at his age, so he can piss about on his bike and pretend he's an athlete. But it's all a lie. The evil seeps out. Look at the garden.' She twisted in her seat, staring out. 'I tried to plant things, when we moved here. I planted vegetables. Herbs. Flowers. Everything died. Nothing good can grow in poisoned ground. I should have remembered that.'

'More people realise what he is than you know. Everyone wants you to be safe and happy, Nicola.' I put my hand on the other woman's arm. 'It could be any of us, any time. It's not our fault. It's theirs. But you don't have to put up with it.'

'He said I'd lose the house. He told me I'd lose everything.'

'A house is just some walls. You can be happy in a smaller house, if you feel safe.'

She nodded, still dazed, still uncertain. 'But the kids. He told me I'd never get custody. I'd fail a drugs test.'

'And he wouldn't?' I hesitated. 'Look, I'm not here officially. I'm aware that Rhys likes cocaine. I don't know what you take and I'm not going to ask, but if I were you I would get myself straightened out. Stop taking whatever it is that means you find it hard to walk in a straight line. Stop drinking. Get some good legal and financial advice, find out everything you need to know about his assets, and then get away from him.'

She nodded, slowly. 'I will.'

'If he hits you again, call 999. Domestic violence is a priority. The police will listen to you and they will help you. If nothing else, this arrest might scare him into leaving you alone until you're ready to leave him.'

'It's the first time I've felt there was a way out. I haven't been able to think of anything I could do up to now,' Nicola said. 'I just felt trapped.'

'I'm not saying it's easy, but it's possible. You deserve to be happy, not scared. You deserve a better life than this.' I gave her a piece of paper with my number on it. 'Put this in your phone. Put it in under "plumber" or something. You can call me if you need help, and I'll help you.'

47

Our last full day slid by and Rhys Vonn returned to his house, not meeting anyone's eye, and no one could say for certain if he had killed Gillian Holding or not. It wasn't my investigation, and it wasn't my problem, and I could think of little else, except that I was running out of time.

The one person that I didn't see was Ruth, until the following morning, Saturday, when we were packing to leave. The house was almost silent as we gathered our things. I had woken up with an ache in my throat that got worse during breakfast (the last breakfast), and didn't improve during the brief conversations we had about what we needed to do before we departed. Ridiculous; I had known it was coming. It felt like grief, but I couldn't mourn for a life that wasn't mine, that had never been mine. I overcompensated with cheerful remarks about the weather, which was bright and sunny, and the dog, who was down in the mouth, and the West Idleford annual summer fete that was happening on the big green, where we had had our barbecue.

'Do you think we should drop by the fete before we go? It's a fundraiser for the children's hospice. Good cause. They have rides and animals and a vegetable-growing competition and a cake sale. I'll pay for you to have a go on the merry-go-round.'

'No thanks.'

If I was excessively cheerful, Derwent had gone the other way. He barely spoke to me, focused on making sure we left nothing behind and on cleaning the house before we left. I thought he was exhausted from the constant strain of the case, and oppressed by his forthcoming parting from Pippin, who was following him around the house anxiously. I heard him talking to the dog a couple of times, though he went quiet when I walked into the room. Eventually I got fed up, tracked him down and asked, 'Are you all right? Because you're behaving as if I did something terrible to you and I really can't think what it could be.'

I got the force ten glower as a reply. 'Have you packed the car?'

'I'm just going.'

I went outside with two bags and a feeling that even if I got everything into the boot Derwent would find some reason to take it all out again and repack it. That was when I ran into Alan carrying a cake box with a handle in each hand, and Ruth with a tray of tiny, very elaborate pastries. When she saw me crossing the road, Ruth tried to reverse so she could retreat to the safety of the house, but the danger to her pastries rooted her to the spot.

'Can I help?' I lifted the tray out of her hands and helped Alan put it into their car. 'These look amazing. Are you taking them to the fete?'

'Yes. I always bake something for it.' She was trembling but her manner was dignified: never less than a lady but clearly outraged.

'Ruth, I'm so sorry you're upset. It wasn't what I wanted but we had to arrest Judy. I can't give you all the details but it's a serious case. When it comes to trial, you'll understand.'

'I just feel like a fool.'

'Because she misled you? She tricked a lot of people. She almost convinced me and I knew what was going on.'

Her face worked. 'No, not Judy. Though that was a shock. No, it was the two of you.'

'We couldn't tell people we were undercover, even if we wanted to,' I began, but she shook her head.

'I thought you *loved* each other, you and Josh. The way you behaved around one another – the way you talked about one another . . .'

'Er, no. Friends. Colleagues.' I was floundering badly. 'He's one of my best friends. I mean, we're very close.' Still no closer to a definition of what we were to one another, I acknowledged. Ruth put her finger on what we *weren't*.

'But you're not in a relationship. Romantically.'

'Well.' I cleared my throat, looking at Alan for help. He was whistling soundlessly and not catching my eye. 'The thing is—'

'The thing is, you were right, Ruth.' Derwent had come out of Vanessa's house and crossed the road without any of us noticing. I jumped a foot in the air as his arm went around my shoulders. 'You saw things that no one else did. Maeve is very special to me. I've never felt about anyone the way I feel about her.'

I couldn't look at him. I didn't want him to lie to Ruth, but I didn't want to let her down either. He sounded as if he meant what he was saying, but then that was his gift; he always said what women wanted to hear. He was completely committed to Melissa, and that was that.

And if he wasn't?

His hand tightened on my shoulder as if he could tell what I was thinking.

'We had to lie about some things, Ruth, because of our jobs. But not the important stuff. We couldn't have fooled you. You were spot on.'

Ruth glowed gently as she said goodbye and sat carefully in the car, her faith in romance completely restored.

'Will we see you at the fete?' Alan asked.

'I shouldn't think so. We'll need to head off.' Derwent shook hands with him. 'Look after yourself, and Ruth.'

'Of course, of course. Goodbye, my dear.' Alan swooped in and pressed a kiss on my lips before I had time to realise what he was intending.

'I feel violated,' I said through the smile I had pinned to my face as their car stuttered to life and began to reverse.

'Oh get over it. He's had a lot to put up with in the last few days. Anyway, you should be used to being kissed in the middle of this particular road.'

That shut me up as comprehensively as his mouth on mine. The memory of it made my face burn. He waved as Alan drove away. Ruth was blowing kisses at us.

'Don't you feel bad for lying to her?'

He gave me a cold look. 'Is that what you heard?'

'I don't – I assumed—'

'The important thing is that she believed it.' As soon as the car was out of sight, he dropped his arm from my shoulders and stalked back into the house. I blinked, more confused than ever.

Ruth had looked at him as if he'd hung the moon for her, and he was treating me as if I'd shot it down.

He moved through the crowds in a haze of happiness, the sounds and sights blurred for him. He was on another level to these people with their meagre concerns, their pathetic screams as a ride flung them around like a doll, their greed as they consumed fast food. Fake food. Fake risk. Pretend danger. He understood the real thing. He *was* the real thing.

It had been a bad couple of days. He had really suffered when he found out the truth about Josh and Maeve. Liars. All Coppers Are Bastards. He had wanted to scream it to the night, to spray it on their fence or their car. He had imagined a hundred little revenges, small to big, all the way up to petrol through the letterbox and a conflagration while they slept. Vanessa had betrayed everyone

366

in Jellicoe Close and he intended to punish her for that when she came back. He imagined her screams if she found Pippin pegged out on the lawn in the back garden – that shitty little noisemaker that had ruined his night when he had been watching them.

How close his escape.

How unfortunate he would have been to be caught then, before he had been able to take Gillian Holding's life. He would have been a half-person, a sketch of what he was becoming. Unrealised. Immature. He would have missed out on so much.

What had nurtured his spirit in the last couple of days was the thought that Josh had been too slow to catch him, despite his training and experience, and that neither of them had been remotely suspicious of him afterwards. They had been friendly, amenable, unsuspecting. His cover was perfect.

He was perfect.

And now they were going, taking the whole show with them. Life would go back to normal without them. He would be free to do what he wanted, when he wanted. The local police were no problem. They were easy to out-think, out-play, out-manoeuvre. It was clear that no one had the least idea why Gillian Holding had to die. She hadn't managed to tell anyone what she'd seen, not in terms that they could understand. The only other person who knew was no risk. Not now. Not after Gillian's death had proved he was serious.

All in all, his mood couldn't have been better. He felt all-powerful.

He felt as if he could do anything.

By lunchtime, we were ready to go. I did a last check around the house, peering under beds and in drawers. The rooms looked just as they had when we arrived. I would miss it, I thought – even the pornographic artwork had a strange sort of nostalgic appeal now.

The doorbell rang and downstairs I heard Derwent greeting someone. In the kitchen Pippin was barking with high excitement. The dog-sitter, I guessed. She was half an hour early, which I found unreasonably annoying. In practical terms we were ready to go; emotionally I was far from it. I went down the stairs and found them in the kitchen. I said what I hoped were all the right things to the dog-sitter, who was short and blonde and endlessly enthusiastic. Pippin kept dashing off to find a toy to throw into her lap.

'I missed him so much! But it's brilliant that you were able to look after him.'

'We enjoyed it. How's your mum getting on? I heard she wasn't well.'

The dog-sitter launched into a lengthy account of her mother's illness while I nodded and smiled and tried not to look at Derwent. He was standing with his arms folded, waiting for me. He seemed detached, indifferent.

'We should go,' I said eventually, and he nodded.

'See you later, Pippin.' He walked out of the house calmly enough and got into the car, leaving me to say a final farewell to the dog-sitter and the dog, handing over my keys with what, in the end, was a sense of release.

We had done it. It was over.

'Back to reality,' I said as I got into the car.

Derwent gave me a look that I couldn't read, but that mainly seemed to be contemptuous, and started the engine.

'What is your problem?' I snapped, smiling and waving out the window at Pippin as the dog-sitter waggled his front paw at us.

'Nothing.'

'Oh, come off it.' The familiar houses slid past us as he drove down to the junction. It seemed so strange that I hadn't known anyone there a few weeks earlier and now I felt a connection with them. It was impossible to imagine never going back. Sideswiped by sorrow again, and glad to hide it with irritation, I cleared my throat. 'You've been miserable today. Absolutely horrible.'

A brief glower in my direction. 'You think I have been miserable.'

'Yes,' I insisted. 'The only time you perked up was when you were talking to Ruth, and you lied to her.'

All his focus was on the road. His hands were tight on the wheel and his jaw was clenched. It made me furious, all of a sudden, that we had spent weeks in perfect harmony and now we were leaving he was punishing me for something I didn't know I'd done. I folded my arms and looked out of the window, trying not to cry. I'd left the window down and the warm air blasted into the car, blowing my hair. It reminded me of arriving in West Idleford, nervous but full of resolve. We hadn't known what to expect, I thought. I hadn't known what lay ahead.

If I had known, what would I have done differently?

Clearly, he hadn't intended to do anything at the fete. He was there because it was what the local community expected; he had done his share of throwing money around and talking with the neighbours. He had ticked every box, crossed every t, dotted the i. No one would think twice about his behaviour, which was the point. He wasn't acting as if he felt guilty, like a murderer might. He wasn't arousing anyone's suspicion. His mood was excellent – because he was glad he had killed Gillian. If anything, he was more pleasant and popular now than before.

But there were so many of them, these girls. Flitting around from stall to stall in groups, like flocks of tiny, brightly coloured birds. The clothes they wore – the midriff-baring tops, the cut-off denims, the running shorts cut high on the thigh so their spindly little legs looked endless. The suggestive T-shirts. The make-up, inexpertly applied, to advertise that they thought they were all grown up.

It wasn't his fault that they were there, available to him.

It wasn't his fault either that he was turned on by them – their shoulder blades arched through the skimpy tops, their soft skin, their newness, their perfection, their trust in goodness. He had come to realise that the earlier you got them the better – there was no point in waiting until they were cynical and bitter. Everywhere he looked he saw them, as if someone was nudging them into his path, as if it was meant to be that he should take one of them.

As if it was a gift to him.

And even then, he might have turned away if one hadn't smiled at him in recognition.

'Hello there.'

'Hi.' There was a trace of uncertainty in her voice. She was a confident girl, he knew that, but she could be shy around people she didn't know well, and he supposed he fell into that category. But she would have seen him talking to her parents. She had grown up knowing who he was. He could warm her up.

'Are you having a good time?'

'Amazing. It's such a cool fete this year. I've just had some candy floss and now I'm going to queue for a slushie.' She held out a hand full of sticky coins. 'Do I have enough?'

'Let me see. Not quite.'

Her face fell. 'But I don't know where Mummy is.'

He jangled the coins in his pockets, looking past her as if he was lost in thought rather than scoping out the territory. One: neither of her parents was in sight, and no one nearby looked familiar. Two: her friends were distracted, chattering to one another, oblivious to him.

Everything had fallen into place. He hadn't even had to try.

The green was on our left, a chaos of colour and noise, the fete in full swing.

Derwent swore under his breath, viciously, and turned the car into the makeshift car park, bumping across the grass to where there was a space right at the end. A fence made of bamboo canes and string marked the border of the car park. Beyond that fragile boundary, to the right of our car, people wandered, laughing and talking, tending to children, queuing for rides. It felt as if I was watching them from a great distance as I looked past Derwent, wishing I had nothing more on my

370

mind than whether I wanted a hot dog or a ride on the Ferris wheel next.

He turned to face me, propping one elbow on the wheel. 'I wasn't going to do this.'

'Do what?'

'Talk to you about this.' He took a deep breath. 'Look, Maeve, I know this hasn't been an easy job. I wanted you here for two reasons. One, you needed it. You were disappearing in London. You know what I mean, don't you?'

I nodded.

'I'd have done anything to bring the old you back,' he said softly. 'I thought if you took some time off you might find yourself again. And you did.'

Emotion was making my throat tight. I managed to ask, 'What's the second reason?'

'The second reason . . . the second reason was for me. I needed a break too. I wanted to know what a different life might feel like.' He half-smiled. 'I thought it would help me get over what I couldn't stop myself from wanting.'

'And what is that?'

Instead of answering me, he looked away with a tiny shake of his head.

That is none of your business.

And he was right, it wasn't anything to do with me. I fixed my eyes on the area of the fete that I could see over his shoulder, the people a brightly coloured blur. It was a quiet stretch of stalls near the back of the fete, away from the great press of people who were crowded around the main attractions. Four little girls had gathered in the gap between the stalls and I watched them whispering together. I wondered what scandal or tragedy they were discussing and whether it was more easily resolved than mine.

'I'm sorry. I shouldn't have asked you that.'

'No, don't worry.' He winced. 'The one thing I didn't want was for things to be awkward between us.'

371

'It's fine. Everything is fine.' The first thing was to get out of the conversation; the second was to escape from the car. I swallowed, hard, and watched the girls. They were arguing, one shaking her head, one on the verge of tears.

'The whole time we've been here, I had to keep reminding myself it was work, and we were playing a part.'

'Me too.'

He sighed, and his voice was heavy when he spoke again. 'But it was just a job, Maeve.'

I was beginning to see where he was going with this.

It's not your fault, it's just that it wasn't real, even if it felt like it was.

I have a life already.

You really should have given that a bit more thought.

But since you didn't, I don't think we can work together any more.

We can't go on like this.

The little girls' heads turned as if they'd been jerked with a string and my focus switched from idle interest to something much sharper. They were looking back, between the tents, and I couldn't tell what was worrying them. Derwent was still talking but my attention was now wholly absorbed, as with one purpose they turned to run away. From what? The answer came as one stopped, yanked backwards with main force, her face terrified.

He moved into view then, holding on to her arm as she squirmed and tried to get free, up on her toes.

Rhys Vonn. A man who had no business to be going anywhere with a little girl that didn't belong to him – a man whose expression was a giveaway that he was up to no good.

I had the car door open before I'd consciously decided to go, jumping the string, running full tilt across the tussocky grass towards them. I didn't breathe, I didn't blink, I didn't think. All of my focus was on moving as fast as possible, to get there in time to stop him.

48

He saw me coming, of course, but he didn't let go of the little girl. She was seven or eight, fine-boned. Her hair was tied up with a rainbow scrunchie and her T-shirt had a sequined unicorn on it. She was sobbing desperately; I could hear her as I got closer.

'Please, leave me alone. Mr Vonn, please.'

He dragged her closer to him, his eyes fixed on me, his face drained of colour. Caught red-handed, and what would he do? Try to take her hostage? She was too fragile, too vulnerable for me to play games with him.

'Let her go,' I said, skidding to a halt a few paces away from him. We were outside the fortune teller's tent but the flap was closed; she was on a break. No one else was around. The noises of the fair seemed surreal around us – how could people fail to notice what was going on?

'You. It would be you.' He gave a horrible, cracked laugh. 'You got me arrested, didn't you?'

'I did. I'm about to do it again. Let that little girl go.'

'Bella? But I need her.' His hand tightened on her arm and she cried out in pain. 'You don't understand.'

'I understand enough. Let her go. I'm not going to let you do this.'

'Bella's *helping* me. She's Thea's friend.' He shook her, hard enough that the little girl overbalanced and would have fallen if it wasn't for his hand gripping her. 'Tell her.'

'I can't,' Bella wailed.

'Let her go!' The other three girls were standing together, holding on to one another. 'She's telling you the truth.'

'Please, Rhys.' I took a step closer. 'You're making this worse.'

'*I'm* making it worse? Christ . . .' He shoved Bella away from him, so she staggered, off balance, before sprawling on the grass, and that was what I'd wanted even though it left him free to deal with me. We were starting to attract attention, I noticed out of the corner of my eye – the gaps between the tents were filling with curious faces. But I didn't dare look away from Rhys to take it in properly. He glowered at me, his head down like a bull about to charge. 'Why is it always you? Why do you always get in the way?' And then, louder, 'What gives you the fucking right?'

I reached into my back pocket and took out my wallet, flipping it open so he could see my warrant card. 'This, mainly, since you ask.'

'I've got to go.' He looked away from me, his eyes red-rimmed. 'I don't have time for this.'

'You know who I am and what I do, and you know I can't let you walk away from me.'

'I've got more important things on my mind.'

'More important than being arrested for attempting to abduct this girl?'

He sneered. 'I'd like to see you try, you interfering bitch.'

'Have a go,' I said. 'See what happens.'

His hands balled into fists and he charged towards me, getting close enough that I felt a breeze as Derwent connected with him, his shoulder driving into the other man's midriff. The air left Rhys's body with an audible whoop. He went down as if he'd been hit by a train. On the way to the ground, his head collided with a metal sign that was advertising the fortune teller's prices. He lay on the grass, his body slack, his eyes unfocused. Derwent slowly got to his feet and inspected him for a few seconds.

'Yeah, I think he's done for the day. That's proper concussion.'

'You took your time,' I observed. 'I was wondering if you were ever going to show up.'

'I think you mean my timing was impeccable. I was getting into position.' He glanced at me as he rubbed his shoulder. 'He didn't even touch you.'

Bella was still sobbing hysterically, as were her friends. I went to pick her up and calm them down, moving them away from the immediate vicinity of Rhys Vonn, who was making confused noises. Two uniformed officers were hurrying towards him, but Derwent could deal with them, and with the paramedics who would need to treat him. It was a shame Vonn had been concussed; it added a layer of difficulty to arresting him. He would need to be checked carefully before he was interviewed and charged. I held Bella's sticky little hand as we searched through the crowds for her parents, a comet's tail of her woebegone friends trailing after us, and once we found her mum and dad I had to try to explain what had happened while Bella wailed and her friends all talked at once.

'Thea's dad—'

'He was so angry.'

'He wouldn't let her go!'

'We told him she wasn't lying.'

'I never lie,' Bella sobbed into her mother's hair. She was clinging to her like a monkey, her legs wrapped around her waist and her arms half-strangling the poor woman.

In the end I took Bella's dad to one side and explained what had happened, keeping it brief.

'And you arrested him,' he checked. He was stocky and

naturally cheerful, but shock combined with his daughter's distress had made him sombre.

'Yes. He'll be on his way to custody.' Via the hospital, probably, but Bella's father didn't need to know that.

'I can't believe it. I thought Rhys was a good bloke.' He shook his head. 'You never really know people, do you?'

I was about to agree when I became aware of two teenage girls hovering beside me. I looked around to find Camilla Vonn and her friend Elise at my elbow. Both of them looked upset. Elise was in her customary goth attire, no concession made to the bright sunshine. Camilla wore a green dress with massive white trainers and her glorious hair loose, like an updated pre-Raphaelite painting.

'Is it true? Did you arrest Dad?'

I nodded. 'We had to.'

'Why?'

'He tried to abduct a young girl.'

'*He* tried to abduct a girl? Are you sure?' She looked past me to where Bella was still sobbing with her little ring of acolytes. 'Her?'

'I saw him.'

'Are you sure?'

'Very,' I said, wanting to shake her for her misplaced loyalty. *Your dad is a shit, Camilla, in case you haven't noticed.*

'Why did he want to abduct her?' Elise asked.

'I don't know exactly what he was planning to do, but I stopped him.'

'They're all Thea's friends.' Camilla was staring at them, her face so pale that every freckle stood out on her skin, gold sequins on white silk. 'That's Bella, her best friend.'

The seconds seemed to stretch as a sudden realisation hit me.

Thea's friends.

No Thea.

Bella's helping me, Rhys had said, and I'd ignored him.

Camilla had been surprised, not by the abduction, but the identity of the abductor. Someone was dangerous around here, and she knew it, but it wasn't her father.

'Camilla, what's going on?'

'N-nothing.' She looked at Elise and some unspoken message passed between them. Elise turned to face me.

'We have to go.'

'Wait a second. Camilla, who else would have tried to abduct a little girl?'

'I can't,' Camilla said desperately. 'I can't tell you.'

I looked at the little group that had gathered around Bella. 'All of Thea's friends . . . but Thea's not there. Your dad was looking for her, wasn't he?'

'I need to find her.' Camilla's eyes were wide and fearful. Beside her, Elise looked petrified.

'Do you think someone has taken her?' My mind was racing. If Rhys hadn't been trying to kidnap Bella . . . if he had been asking her for help . . . If Rhys wasn't the predator I needed to worry about, then who . . . ?

The answer came as loudly as if Camilla had shouted it: a man who had been in plain sight all along.

'It's Mike Knox, isn't it? I thought it was your dad, but it was Mike who scared Gillian. It was Mike she saw with you. She tried to tell people but they didn't listen. *I* didn't listen.' I was remembering him, intent at the play as he watched the teenagers, surly in the alleyway as Camilla defied him, solicitous on the railway line when Gillian was terrified.

Elise took Camilla's hand. 'It's OK. You can say.'

'No. Maybe not. I don't know.' She looked at me and bit her lip. 'I can't.'

'Come with me,' I said, making up my mind. The two girls followed as I hurried across to Bella. 'Can I ask you something, sweetie? Just quickly? It's important.'

Bella's dad leaned in. 'It's all right, darling. You can talk to her. She's here to help.'

377

Help? I had made a huge mistake, a mistake that might have unthinkable consequences. I tried to smile as Bella twisted around to look at me. She hadn't let go of her mother yet.

'You know how Mr Vonn was holding on to you?'

Bella's mother bristled. 'Is this really necessary?'

'Yes,' I snapped. 'Can you remember for me, Bella, what did he tell you he wanted?'

'I don't think—' Bella's father began, but his daughter was speaking, her voice clear and precise.

'He was looking for Thea. But we hadn't seen her. She went off with the other man.'

'And what did the other man look like?'

I wasn't expecting much from her – she was only a child, and even adult witnesses were notoriously unreliable, but Bella solemnly described the man in every detail, from his shoes to his beard. Mike Knox.

The teenagers were both crying when I turned back to them.

'Camilla, I need you to be brave. I need you to be honest with me about Mike. I need you to forget any loyalty you think you have to him, or anything that might stop you from being honest.'

They had both stopped blinking. I thought they might have stopped breathing.

'Last year, Camilla, you went missing. It was Mike who found you and brought you home, wasn't it?' I waited for a response but none came. They were as still as a painting, an allegory, a myth. One of my father's favourite poems came to mind, in his slow, lovely voice: *two girls . . . both beautiful, one a gazelle . . .*

'But he didn't have to find you. He knew where you were. He had sent you away himself.'

A single tear rolled down her cheek.

'And you were a child, Camilla. You *are* a child. You didn't do anything wrong. Whatever he told you – however he threatened you – he was lying. I'm going to arrest Mike, and

378

I'm going to make sure he can never hurt you again, OK? But first we have to help Thea. Your dad tried and I got in the way so now it's my job.'

She nodded, once.

'Where is he, Camilla?'

'I don't know.' A whisper.

'He's taken Thea somewhere. It will be somewhere he feels safe.' I kept my eyes locked on hers. 'Where did he take you?'

'Different places.'

'Narrow it down for me. Where was his favourite?'

'The boathouse in the Holmwood.'

I thought of it: damp, musty, dark and silent among the trees, the lake water oily around its base.

'Great. Thank you.'

'But he won't be in the boathouse,' Elise said. I had almost forgotten she was there. 'It's too busy at this time of day. Too risky. He wouldn't use it now. He wouldn't want to be interrupted.'

'So where?'

Another look passed between the two of them.

'The first time,' Camilla said, 'he took me to the empty house. Number 1.'

Elise nodded. 'Me too. The empty house. Upstairs. There's a mattress.'

Camilla nodded. 'The back bedroom.'

Both of them. I was so tired, I thought, so tired of this tide of harm that seemed to roll, unstoppable, over the weak and the vulnerable.

But there was still a chance for Thea. I pushed my feelings to one side. 'Let's go.'

49

The house brooded in the sunshine, the weeds in the front garden shiny with honeydew. The windows were blank, boarded up with plywood. Behind me, Jellicoe Close was silent. No one was around, and nothing moved except for the three of us. The teenage girls were, like me, out of breath from racing across the green. We faltered to a halt and looked up at the house. It was giving nothing away.

'You stay here,' I said, gulping air. I handed Elise my phone. 'I've called for back-up. They're a couple of minutes away. If that rings, answer it. They might need more details from you.'

A nod. Her hands were shaking but her eyes were steady. I trusted Elise to do what needed to be done.

'If DI Derwent – Josh – calls, tell him where I am.' His phone had been engaged when I tried it, and I hadn't bothered with voicemail. He would see that I'd called; he would call back. He was probably tied up, anyway, with Rhys – I didn't even know if he was still at the fete or miles away, en route to the hospital with his prisoner.

'Camilla, you're not coming in either.'

'But—'

'I'll send Thea out to you, if she is in the house. You need to be waiting here for her.' *I don't want you anywhere near Mike Knox if I can keep you apart.*

'What are you going to do?'

'Go in. Get Thea. Arrest Mike.'

'On your own?'

I flashed a grin at her. 'No problem.'

It was a problem, obviously. I didn't have a choice about it. Two minutes, the control room had promised me, but that could be more like five, and Knox was ahead of us by who knew how much? Anything could have happened inside the house. Anything could be happening at that very moment.

Get on with it, Maeve.

No one had been through the front door, I could see at a glance: undisturbed spiders' webs hung across it. And I knew that Mike knew his way around the back gardens. The figure on the path, the man in our garden: that shadow had a face now. I couldn't prove it was him but I thought he was the sort of person who was constantly looking for titillation and thrills, wherever he could find them. He must have been walking behind us when Derwent kissed me after the barbecue, not far from where I was standing at that moment. He had seen an opportunity. He had wanted to watch us. He had taken too great a risk, drawn Pippin's attention and interrupted us but if he hadn't . . . I shook my head. *Concentrate.*

I ran lightly around the side of the house, trying not to make any noise, skirting some old panels of wood and metal poles. Brambles had taken over the back garden, great swathes of them, the fruit still hard and pale among the leaves. The air smelled dank and earthy.

I found a crowbar leaning up against the back door and paint flecks on the ground from where the lock was splintered. Someone had done me a favour there; the girls had told me Mike had a key and I'd expected that I would have to break in. The door opened when I tried it, sliding open silently. I had anticipated a shriek of hinges, but of course Mike Knox had wanted a discreet way to come and go when he used it. I slipped into the dim kitchen, leaving the door open so there was some light. The crowbar was reassuringly heavy in my hand, a lot better than nothing. The kitchen smelled of mice and mould and pipes that had been dry for too long. I gagged, the back of my hand pressed against my mouth to muffle the sound.

Upstairs, the girls had said. The back bedroom. I moved through the hall, my ears straining for any sound, my eyes wide as I passed the doorway that led into the sitting room. Nothing moved. A floorboard creaked, as if someone had moved upstairs. A murmur from behind a closed door followed, and a high-pitched wail that stopped at a snapped command.

Shit. I flew up the stairs, my trainers as silent as I could manage on the uncarpeted treads. The door to the back bedroom was shut. I tried it gently – locked. But it was a rotten door, the panels cracked, daylight showing through gaps around the handle. I wedged the tip of the crowbar between the door and the jamb and leaned into it, snapping the lock out of the old rotting wood in a shower of splinters.

The door came open, juddering back, and I took in the scene in a single second as if I'd snapped a photograph: Thea Vonn standing in the corner of the room with her finger in her mouth, unsure, her face flushed, a mattress on the floor, and Mike Knox frozen, staring at me with his hand inside his unbuttoned jeans. He was surprised, that much was clear: he had been fully occupied with Thea and he hadn't heard me coming.

I took advantage of his surprise to lunge at him, swinging the crowbar, aiming for his knee. The idea was that he would be incapacitated by the first blow and in too much pain to fight back. He was a fraction of a second too fast for me, turning and bending so I hit him on the muscle of the thigh rather than the knee joint itself. Momentum carried me forward and I cannoned into him. He went down onto the

382

bare, dusty floorboards with a grunt of pain. His reactions were faster than I'd expected again; he started squirming around, getting a hand free despite my best efforts, his fingers stretching for my face, my throat.

'You're under . . . arrest . . .' I managed to gasp, and he kneed me viciously in the stomach, then pushed my shoulder down to the floor so I rolled onto my back, helpless. He was far stronger than me, and far more aggressive despite the deep, burning anger I felt, and all my training, and all the time I'd spent imagining myself at some man's mercy again, and what I would do to them. I fought, desperate now, as he swung a leg across me and pinned me down. He would strangle me, I thought, or just punch me until I was unconscious, which was infuriating. He grinned down at me, enjoying himself, utterly confident.

'Get . . . off . . .'

'No chance,' he hissed. His eyes were bright. 'You wouldn't believe how much time I've spent thinking about this. I'm going to enjoy the next few minutes, even if you're not.'

I kept my eyes on him, not wanting to betray by the slightest flicker of my focus that the odds had just changed in my favour as a figure loomed into view behind him. Without warning Knox hit me in the face with his closed fist, a short, sharp punch that made my head ring and threw stars across my field of vision. My nose started to bleed immediately. I put the pain to one side and got a hand to his jaw and pushed up, so his head reared back, and Camilla, wonderful Camilla, who had ignored what I'd told her about staying outside – Camilla, who had wanted to take the fight to Knox as much as I did – hit him on the side of the head with one of the metal poles from the garden. He went down like a felled ox, instantly and completely unconscious. I was peripherally aware of Camilla dropping the pole and running to her sister, which I completely understood, but blood from my nose was coursing into my throat and pooling there. I couldn't move, or breathe, and Knox was a dead weight, and I was in serious trouble as I made weaker and weaker attempts to get free. He wasn't even awake and he was going to win this fight . . . Derwent would be *furious* . . .

Knox moved an inch, and then another, sliding down my body in jerks. I raised my head and saw Elise was dragging him off me, heavy though he was, two hands locked around one of his ankles. She was sobbing, but she was determined. I wriggled, and she pulled, and I got out from under him so I could sit up and try to breathe as the blood ran down and soaked my top. My throat was full of it still, and I felt as if I was choking. I leaned forward with my head between my knees and coin-sized drops of blood splattered on the floor-boards, faster than I could count. I used my sleeve to stem the bleeding as I put my other arm around Elise, who had fallen to her knees beside me. I checked back over my shoulder to where Camilla was holding Thea, so I could be sure that I was right when I said, 'It's OK. Everything is going to be all right.'

'Is he dead?' It was Thea who asked, her little face peering anxiously over her sister's shoulder.

I pressed my fingers into Knox's throat and felt his pulse, slow and steady. 'No. Just unconscious.'

'That's a shame.'

I couldn't help it; I started to laugh. Elise buried her face in her arms, her shoulders shaking and Thea managed a watery giggle. It was proper, old-fashioned hysteria. Only the sight of Camilla's pale face in the corner of the shadowy room made me come back to myself. No laughter there; she looked distraught. I would need to talk to her, I thought, when I got the chance.

I rolled Knox into the recovery position. That was the training. Personally I would have been happy to let him die then and there.

*

I stepped carefully out of the ambulance and looked around. Camilla and Elise were sitting on the edge of the pavement, their arms wrapped around their knees. Circling them, the standard parade of police cars and ambulances and forensic vans: all the paraphernalia of the emergency services ruining the peace of Jellicoe Close once more. I walked across to them and sat down beside Elise.

'I thought we could have a chat.'

'Is your nose still bleeding?'

'A bit,' I admitted. I felt light-headed but the ice pack I was holding against the bridge of my nose had to be helping to slow the flow. 'I'm OK though.'

'You were brave,' Camilla said, shivering.

'We couldn't let you do it on your own.' Elise was looking guilty. 'I know you said to stay outside but we thought he'd be too strong for you.'

'You were right about that, but I couldn't wait.'

'No,' Camilla said. 'I think we were just in time. Thea didn't really know what he wanted to do to her.'

'Hopefully she won't work it out for a while. She's too young for that kind of memory.'

Camilla looked down. 'She should never have been in that situation. I should have stopped him a long time ago.'

'You did what you could, when you could.' I sniffed, tasting metal. I really wished the blood would dry up but it kept seeping out, even if it was slower than it had been. 'They're going to want a statement from both of you.'

They nodded, upset.

'The best thing you can do is tell the truth.'

'I'm scared,' Camilla whispered.

'Of him? He's locked up.'

Elise shook her head at me, a quick warning. I thought about it for a second.

'Did he tell you you'd get in trouble?'

'He said I'd go to prison for what I did.' Camilla risked a look at me and I laughed.

'He's a piece of work, isn't he? Look, I can't tell you that everything will go away if you talk about it, but I do know the CPS and how they feel about charging minors with crimes – especially ones who have a cast-iron duress defence. He abused you, Camilla. Whatever you did, he did worse. And he needs to be locked up for it. He's tried to keep you quiet because that suited him but it's time to speak up now. It's the last thing he wants you to do, and the best thing you can do for yourself.'

She dropped her head into her hands. 'I haven't told anyone yet.'

'Tell us now.' It was Elise who said it. 'It'll get easier and easier. Say it now, here.'

Camilla looked at me. I spread my hands. 'You're not under caution. No solicitor present. No responsible adult. You can say what you want and all I'll do is listen.'

The girls were gone, whisked away to the police station with their mothers by their sides. Nicola had made eye contact with me as she climbed into the car, a silent message of thanks that was also a promise. She was alert, attentive – a new woman, just in time. The girls would be looked after, I knew, but I felt protective of them. I was sitting in the open doorway of the ambulance, on my second ice pack.

'If that one doesn't work, I'm taking you to hospital.' The paramedic was fair and tanned with bright blue eyes and a cheeky grin. I found myself wondering idly if he had a girlfriend, which made me think I might be on the mend, at long last. He looked as if he would be fun, and I needed some fun, badly.

'I really think it's stopping.'

'Five more minutes, then.' He looked past me. 'Can I help you?'

'I just want a word with my DS.'

386

At Derwent's voice I looked up. He was a silhouette with the sun behind him. I shaded my eyes. 'Hey.'

'All right, slugger?'

'I've been better.'

'You've looked better too.' He sat down beside me. 'What did I miss?'

'I bet you know already.'

He shrugged. 'I've had the headlines. Mike Knox.'

'He's a very bad person,' I said soberly, trying to hold the ice pack so I could look at him. My arm was starting to ache. 'Camilla's been telling me what he did to her.'

'Give me that.' He held the ice pack in place, one hand bracing the back of my head so he could press it against the bridge of my nose. 'Talk.'

'He started a relationship with Camilla last year, when she was fourteen.'

Derwent grimaced.

'He had already seduced Elise Dean, but she only had two or three meetings with him. The first was in the empty house. The others were in his car. She managed to avoid him after that. She blocked his number on her phone. Camilla wasn't so clever, or lucky, I suppose. She said she was flattered by his attention. He was kind to her, at first. He helped out with the drama productions at her school, and she loved acting. He seems to have used the plays as a way to audition potential girlfriends. She said he told her she wasn't his first girlfriend from the school. He said she was his favourite.'

'She didn't stand a chance, did she? He would have known her parents were no use. She was an easy target for anyone who would show her some affection.'

'He knew exactly what he was doing. Camilla broke up with Isaac. She didn't know then about Elise and Knox, and Elise didn't tell her the truth, but when she tried to warn her to stay away from Knox, Camilla thought she was intervening on her brother's behalf. She was madly in love with Knox.

387

She said she would have done anything for him. After a few months she found out she was pregnant. Knox arranged for her to "disappear" and have an abortion, at his expense. He managed to convince her parents and everyone else that she had run away and he was the one who had tracked her down – the hero, in fact, instead of the villain. From that point on, he changed. He was cold with Camilla, testing her loyalty. He could be cruel. He started forcing her to take chances. On one occasion, she said, he made her have sex with him on the path that leads down to the Holmwood. She said they both realised that Gillian Holding was watching them from her house, and Knox became worried that she was going to give them away. He threatened Gillian but of course she was unreliable. She could blurt out the truth at any minute, and indeed she did try to tell someone about him.'

'Alice.'

'And Alice thought it was Rhys Vonn, which I can't blame her for, because I thought the same. I suppose Alice never dreamed Gillian was talking about her husband. When Gillian fainted on the railway line, Knox was running towards us. She knew who he was and she was going to find someone to tell at some stage. He couldn't be sure she would stay silent because she was scared of him. Her inhibitions were evaporating as her dementia got worse. He couldn't frighten her into silence. He could only silence her permanently.'

'Circumstantial.'

'You're right,' I said. 'It's a motive, that's all. But what isn't circumstantial is that Camilla is prepared to give evidence saying that he murdered Mrs Holding.'

'And how does she know that?' Derwent asked.

'She watched him do it.'

He winced. My head was aching. The adrenalin had worn off, leaving only sadness.

'We all wondered how he persuaded Gillian to leave her house when she was so scared of him. He used Camilla. She went into the house. She asked Gillian to come with her. She said – as he told her to – that she was afraid to go out on her own. Gillian wanted to help Camilla, from the start. She trusted her. She walked out of her house and into Mike Knox's hands, which is why there was no trace of his DNA in her home, or any signs of a struggle. He made Camilla walk with her down to the lake, in case anyone saw them. He hung back until he was sure there was no one else around to watch him murder her. And when he'd killed her, he told Camilla that she would be next if she said anything to anyone about it.'

'But you got her to talk.'

'Because he's in custody. She feels safe now that he's locked up. And because I saved Thea, I suppose.' I shifted my weight, my bones aching from tiredness. 'Elise can back her up on a lot of it. Camilla remembers where she went for the abortion and the hotel where they stayed. There will be details they can corroborate.'

'Is she credible?'

'I believe her,' I said simply. 'I don't know about a jury. I think they'll feel sorry for her.'

He lifted the ice pack away. 'Has it stopped?'

'Maybe.' I was cautious. 'It stopped before but then it started again. It's not broken, as far as they can tell, but he hit it pretty hard.'

'You should have called me. I wouldn't have let him do that to you.' He was careful not to sound hurt, but I knew it mattered to him.

'I had to prioritise back-up. Anyway, you had your hands full with Rhys.'

'It's not funny, Maeve. What would I do if anything happened to you?'

'Sorry to interrupt.' The paramedic again. He occupied himself with a series of checks while Derwent wandered a short distance away, his hands in his pockets.

'It was a good thing you didn't hang around, for Thea's sake,' he admitted.

'Mm,' I said.

'Do you think he was going to kill her afterwards?'

The paramedic's head snapped up, his eyes wide with shock. Derwent had sounded casual, but I knew he was anything but.

'I was wondering about that. I think he'd have had to. Whatever he was planning to do to her, she was old enough to tell someone. She was too young to fall for the girlfriend line and he couldn't be sure he could frighten her into silence. She knew who he was. She would have given him away.'

'And he'd killed once. The second time would have been easier.'

'That's looking good, actually,' the paramedic said. 'I think you're going to be OK.'

'I think so too,' I said.

50

'I hear solving one crime's not enough for you.' Chris Pettifer leaned back in his chair and grinned at me as I put my bag down by my desk the following Monday. 'You found yourself another murderer.'

'I told her not to bother.' Derwent was standing in the doorway to Una Burt's office and I hadn't even noticed him. He looked very different from the off-duty version I'd come to know, his suit dark, his shirt bright white. 'I thought we had enough on our plates without looking for more trouble.'

'I was just lucky.' I sat down.

'Better hope you're lucky again, then.' Derwent came to stand by my desk and tapped the Dawoud file meaningfully. 'Or do you think you've done enough and this should be someone else's problem?'

'You're never happy,' Chris Pettifer said. 'Don't listen to him, Maeve.'

'He's right though.' I sighed. 'I don't know why I can't get to grips with Hassan Dawoud.'

'You haven't given yourself a chance.' He moved behind me and drew my chair back. 'Come on.'

'What's happening?'

'You're going to spend the next couple of hours on your own with the file. Up you get. Take it with you.'

I picked up the file and followed him to the meeting room, trying to look unruffled.

'How's your nose?'

'Bruised.' I had two black eyes as well, but they were fuzzy and undefined, so I just looked as if I hadn't slept for a week. Coincidentally, that was exactly how I felt.

'Shut the door. Rula Jacques is coming in today and I don't want her to sneak up on me. They've allowed three hours for the meeting. I think they should call it an interrogation.'

That explained the good suit. I made sure the door was closed and he sat down, flipping the file open. After the briefest of hesitations, I sat down too, leaving one chair vacant between us.

'Like that, is it?' He wasn't even looking at me, but I blushed.

'Everything's back to normal.'

'Of course it is.'

It was a good thing we'd had a day apart, I thought. It helped to meet this professional, hard-edged Derwent in the office, instead of Josh with his unpredictable acts of kindness and unguarded honesty and occasional nudity.

'Are you hungry? Thirsty? Need the bathroom?'

'I'm fine,' I said, wary. 'Why?'

'The only thing you need is time alone with this file. If you actually sit down and think about Hassan Dawoud, you'll work out what happened to him.' He got up and looked through the glass of the door. 'There's Rula now. Wish me luck.'

'Good luck,' I said automatically. 'But you won't need it. She must think you're wonderful now.'

'That might be more trouble than when she hated me.' He tucked in his shirt and straightened his tie. 'How do I look?'

'You look fine,' I said, and he went out of the room, whistling, cheerful as could be as he locked the door behind him.

*

Two hours later, he came back. I was sitting on the window-sill, looking out at the street below. He leaned in through the door.

'Well?'

'I know who did it. And I know how to prove it.'

'Told you. How long did it take?'

'About twenty minutes,' I said, getting down. 'Don't ever lock me into a room again.'

'It was for your own good.'

I stopped beside him and glared at him. 'One of these days, Josh, we're going to have a talk about what you need to do for *your* own good.'

'I'm looking forward to that.'

'Not as much as I am.'

The interview room looked dingier than ever when Liz St John walked into it. She was perfectly turned out in a white silk T-shirt half-tucked into pearl-grey jeans. She had all of the attributes of the wealthy young mother: wedge-heeled sandals, an armload of gold bangles, a pendant on a long gold chain, a designer handbag. And the most important accessory of all, even if she didn't realise it yet: Jeremy Greene, her lawyer. He was balding and slightly sweaty but his suit was superbly cut and his briefcase came from Smythson.

'I don't know why on earth you want to talk to me *here*.'

'As I explained on the phone,' Georgia said, 'we need to show you some evidence and it's easier to do it here. Some of it is video. Some of it is photographic.'

'I still don't see why you couldn't have come to me. It's not convenient at all.'

'This shouldn't take too long,' the lawyer said, holding her chair out for her. She sat in it with a pout of disgust.

'She's not happy about this,' Derwent said from beside me. We were watching the live feed from the interview room in a space that was little bigger than a broom cupboard, squashed

393

together on two vilely uncomfortable upright chairs I was leaning sideways to maintain some space between us. 'Are you sure it's a good idea for Georgia to do this?'

I nodded, hoping I looked confident. 'I think she needs this.'

'You're sure you don't want to do it?'

'She's got Chris. Nothing is going to go wrong.'

Derwent looked down at the foot I was swinging compulsively. 'Yeah, you seem relaxed about it.'

I stilled my foot, with an effort. 'Give her a chance. I think she'll do fine.'

Chris Pettifer set up the tape. 'Now you understand this interview is under caution and we're recording it.'

'Yes, but I don't understand why,' Liz said, irritated.

He nodded to Georgia. 'My colleague will just run through the statement you wrote about the day you found Hassan Dawoud's body.'

Georgia did exactly that, pausing so Liz could agree every so often. 'I don't see the point in this,' she said at the end. 'I could have done this on the phone.'

'I have a photograph to show you. It's a still from some CCTV we collected.' Georgia flipped open her folder and took out a black-and-white picture, the clearest one that we had of the man in his Ralph Lauren jacket. 'Do you know this person? Look at it carefully. Take your time.'

Liz's hand trembled as she drew the picture towards her. 'I don't think – I'm not sure.'

'You don't recognise that man? Look again.'

'No. I don't.' She pushed it back with an air of finality.

'That's odd,' Georgia said brightly. 'Because it took Cameron Dawoud about a second to recognise your husband.'

'That's what I thought. I thought it was Hughie.' She looked up, agonised. 'But it can't be.'

'Does your husband own a Ralph Lauren jacket like this one?'

'Yes, but—'

'And could he have been at the hospital that night?'

'Only if he left the children on their own.'

'Would he do that?'

'I would have said no. But then I would have said there was no way he could be involved in anything illegal.'

'Why do you assume he's doing something illegal?' Georgia asked.

'But – the context – you made me think it was the hospital. You made me think it was something to do with Hassan's death.'

'Now she's confused,' I said softly.

'You jumped straight to the conclusion that he was there, and that he was there for some illegal purpose. What did you think he was doing at the hospital?'

'I don't know.' Her hands were clenched in her lap.

'Could he have been disposing of Hassan Dawoud's body?'

'I don't know.'

'You do know.' Georgia started laying photos out in front of her. 'This is your husband driving Hassan's car into the car park. Hassan is on the back seat under a blanket that I suggest came from your house. Forensic analysis will confirm that. Here's your husband pretending to leave the hospital. Here's your husband doubling back . . . and going into the disabled toilet . . . here he is having changed his clothes – see how we can trace his movements?'

'I had no idea.' She looked from Georgia to Pettifer. 'Why would he want to dump Hassan's body? Did he – could he have *killed* him?'

'What sort of relationship did they have?'

The lawyer stirred. 'You should ask Hugh St John about that, not my client.'

'I want your client's impression of their relationship,' Georgia flashed back.

'Good girl,' Derwent said. He stretched and I smiled to myself; tension was knotting his muscles if mine were anything to go by. 'She's learned a lot, hasn't she?'

'I taught her everything she knows.'

'They were friendly enough.' Liz was rooting in her bag for a tissue. A plastic dragon fell out onto the table along with a half-eaten biscuit. 'Oh God.'

'They were more than friendly, actually.' Georgia showed her the email correspondence about the flat, and the statement she had taken from the cleaner who also recognised the man in our CCTV image as the man who had been arguing with Hassan Dawoud – arguing so fervently that they had overrun their allotted time.

'Your husband was in love with Hassan Dawoud, Mrs St John. He wanted Hassan to leave Cameron, and he wanted to leave you. He spoke to an estate agent about selling your house. He viewed a penthouse apartment in central London and said he would be living there with his partner.' Georgia leaned forward. 'And you found out, because the estate agent called you.'

'That was a mistake,' Liz said sulkily. 'How did you know about that?'

'We recovered a deleted text message from Hassan Dawoud's phone. It came from a number that also sent intimate messages to a WhatsApp conversation between Dawoud and your husband.'

'I don't think that can be true. Hughie wouldn't.'

'We know he did,' Pettifer said idly. 'And we know you knew.'

She hesitated for a second. 'So what? I was furious with him but shit happens, and I forgave him. He had to get it out of his system. We're a good couple. I wasn't going to let him go over a stupid little fling. That wouldn't give him a reason to murder Hassan.'

'No, but it gave you an excellent motive.' Georgia was smooth, totally unflappable. 'You just said it. You wouldn't let him go. But that was what he wanted, not your forgiveness. The fact is, Hassan was horrified. He didn't want to leave Cameron. He knew he'd made a mistake with Hugh.'

'And Hugh killed him because he was so distraught? I can't believe it.'

'Oh, tears.' Derwent checked the time. 'We should have had a sweepstake on how long it would take her to turn on the waterworks.'

'That's not what happened.' Georgia smiled at her. 'Do you remember us asking you about deliveries the day Hassan died? He missed a delivery, at six minutes past three. The delivery guy said he left a card, and he said he left the parcel with the next-door neighbour. He remembers it well, incidentally.'

'You made quite the impression on him, Mrs St John,' Pettifer said heavily. 'He wasn't expecting to hear language like that from a lady.'

'Hassan was getting changed to go for a run, we think, based on what he was wearing when he died. Maybe he didn't get to the door in time. We think he went to pick up the parcel. He left his phone behind which makes us think he wasn't expecting to be out for very long. He took the card with him. It wasn't in the house when we searched it.' Georgia took out another photo and slid it across the table. 'Did you know that the company who supplies your alarm system and video doorbell keeps a record of every movement at your front door on their own server? They keep it for three months. They were very helpful when we approached them. You'd deleted it from your own home system but when they looked, they found it.'

She had gone completely still.

'I think we should bring this interview to a close,' Jeremy Green said heavily.

'I think you should shut up,' his client snapped.

'I wish,' Derwent said, 'I'd remembered to bring popcorn.'

I elbowed him. 'Shut up. We're not home yet.'

'Go on. Is that all?' Liz St John sniffed. 'It's not much.'

'This is the delivery note.' Georgia circled it with the end of her pen. 'This is Hassan. And this is when you answered

397

the door and invited him in.' She paused. 'You know, his husband told us that he was killed because someone hated what he was, and I think he was right, even though he meant something else entirely. Hassan was an arrogant man, Mrs St John, and he didn't like being criticised. You lost your temper with him and he argued back. He wasn't afraid of you or anyone. He didn't care that you were going to tell Cameron about the affair. He knew Cameron would forgive him. And he wouldn't promise to leave your husband alone.'

'That's not . . . that's not what happened.'

'Do you remember that the box was falling apart? It was too weak to hold the contents. The delivery man remembered that.' Georgia flattened out a piece of paper in front of them.

'That's the delivery notice,' I told Derwent. 'One kettlebell, weight sixteen kilos.'

'I think you must have scratched yourself – maybe on the cardboard – when you picked up the kettlebell and swung it into Hassan's head. His blood went everywhere, but it happened in your house. Your spotless home, which you cleaned obsessively. And then you tried to out-think us.' Georgia folded her arms. 'You decided that you would put him in his car and take him to the hospital, and that you would have to be there too so you could legitimately touch him, and his car, and be the person who raised the alarm.'

'That's not true.'

'You went and got his car from the garage. You parked it in front of the house. The door camera is movement-triggered. It recorded you carrying him out over your shoulder, wrapped in a blanket – he wasn't a big man and you lift weights, don't you, Mrs St John? I talked to your personal trainer. He was very complimentary about your strength training.

'You cleaned up so there wasn't a trace of him anywhere. You checked his house for anything that might incriminate you. Then you took a knife and cut yourself deliberately so that you had a bleeding injury to your hand and you created an opportunity to transfer the blood in an explainable way, in case there was DNA from you on Hassan's body. You got your husband to help with moving the car while you were in A&E drawing attention to yourself. You had your alibi because you couldn't have been moving the body if you were in A&E, and you alleged that he was here with the children – but they were asleep, on their own. Still, it was a good enough alibi for him, especially since your husband swore no one else knew about the affair. We weren't suspicious at all.'

'You're insane,' Liz said. 'This is insane.'

Derwent dropped his arm on the back of my chair. Both of us were leaning forward now, focused on the screen in front of us. I for one had forgotten all about keeping a distance between us. 'Here we go.'

'Even though your house is very, very clean, and you bleached everything, I bet our forensics expert will find another splash or two, when we look. Your shoe size matches the half print on the garage floor. And you – only you – saw a notice on the parking machine at the hospital. No one else mentioned it. The machine was in full working order, all night. The hospital takes the car park very seriously – they can't function properly if it's not working, they told us. If the machine had been broken, there would have been a repairman there within an hour. But there wasn't even a request for someone to come and look at the machine.'

'I saw a note.' She sounded sulky now.

'You wanted Hassan to be away from the house to make us think he didn't die here. You told us that he was argumentative and that you had heard his husband beating him up so that we would focus on Cameron Dawoud instead of you, but you were the only person we spoke to who said that they had problems in their relationship. You were pushing a different line from everyone else. Again, if you'd done nothing, we might not have considered you as a suspect. But we did.'

Georgia closed her folder. 'You came up with a reason for everything that might have triggered our suspicions, and that was enough to make us suspicious. You killed him, and we can prove it.'

'I need to talk to my client.' Jeremy Green's complexion was living up to his surname. 'We're going to need some time.'

'You beauty.' Derwent put his hand on the top of my head and he dragged me towards him so he could kiss my cheek. I half-turned my head, surprised at the movement, and the kiss landed on the corner of my mouth. Flustered, I almost overbalanced and had to brace a hand on his leg. We were inches apart, staring at each other.

'Georgia did it, not me,' I managed to say.

'You worked it out. The old Maeve, back in action. Lethal as ever.'

'Was there ever any doubt?'

He grinned. 'Not in my mind. Plenty in yours.'

'Anyway, she still had to do the hard part.' Under my palm the muscles of his thigh were taut. I didn't want to move, in case it broke the spell. He was staring into my eyes, and then, deliberately, his gaze dropped to my mouth. I was instantly, totally lost, and to hide it I gabbled, 'Didn't she do well? I'll never doubt her again.'

'Don't go that far.' Una Burt from the doorway behind us, her voice exceedingly dry. Derwent lowered his arm and sat up and I shifted so far to my left that I almost fell off my chair. All too easy to imagine how it had looked to her.

'Well done, anyway.' She waited for a beat, and when neither of us said anything she nodded and walked away. I gathered my things hastily.

'I'm going to talk to Georgia and Chris.'

'Yeah, I have to do some paperwork.'

The two of us went our separate ways, just a little too late to salvage our reputations.

51

Derwent was in the meeting room when I went looking for him a few hours later, a stack of files in front of him. I shut the door behind me and slid my folder onto the table. 'Her lawyer is still talking to her. They're going to give us a prepared statement but they're taking their time about it.'

'What's your betting? Manslaughter?'

'I'm going to say self-defence. She'll try to suggest that Hassan desperately wanted Hugh to leave her and attacked her when she tried to explain that wasn't going to happen. She lashed out, terrified. The rest is a detailed conspiracy with her husband to get away with what looks a lot like murder but definitely isn't.'

'Good luck to her.' Derwent leaned back, locking his hands behind his head. 'You can go home, if you want.'

'I'm going. But there's one thing I wanted to ask you first.'

He looked, if possible, even more relaxed. 'What is it?'

'I had plenty of time to think earlier, when you locked me in here, and there's one thing you never told me.'

'What?' He was warier now. He would be expecting me to pick up the conversation we had had in the car – or almost had – and another time I might have, but there was something I needed to know.

'What did you need to ask Melissa, when you ran away and left me?'

He sat up, the warm easy manner gone as if I'd imagined it. 'I told you it wasn't about you.'

'I know that,' I said calmly. 'I still want to know what it was about.'

He considered the question. Then, 'Why?'

'I know you're not happy. I know you want a different life. I know you took the chance to go away and get over it. You thought you'd find out everything would be much the same, so you could forget about what you want and can't have.' I had reached the point where there was no going back. 'But I think you found out how unhappy you really are. Maybe you're not made to be domesticated, or maybe you're with the wrong person, but you can't lie to yourself about it any more.'

He was withdrawing from me the way he used to, using anger to warn me off, his face grim, his eyes hooded. 'Leave it.'

'No. What did you ask her?' I softened my tone. 'You might as well tell me.'

He couldn't look at me. 'I asked her if she'd let me see Thomas if we broke up.'

'And she said no.'

'She said no.'

'And you'll never leave Thomas.'

'No. I made him a promise that I would always be there for him. That comes before everything else.'

'His happiness matters more than yours.'

A flash of anger as he looked up at me. 'Of course it does. It's the most important thing.'

I sat down beside him and leaned my chin on my hand. 'I had no idea you were so unhappy.'

'No. I didn't want you to know.'

'Is it bad?'

402

'Depends on how you define bad. She's not happy. She blames me for that. She's probably right. I'm not good at making people happy.'

'Well, that's not true.' He raised his eyebrows at that, but some instinct told me to make light of it. 'For instance, you made Pippin very happy.'

He actually laughed, and then sighed.

'What are you going to do?' I asked.

'Nothing.'

'But—'

'No. Thomas needs me. I made a commitment to him.'

'There has to be another way.'

'If there was, I would have thought of it already.' He looked at me. 'I prefer it when we talk about your problems.'

'I bet you do.'

'Look, Maeve, I can cope.'

'I know, but isn't there more to life than just coping? Isn't that what you'd say to me?'

'I'm going to pick myself up and go on, like you did when you got knocked down. I'm going to make the best of what I've got. We lock up the bad people, and we do our best to live a good life, because it's the only one we've got.' He checked the time. 'Now I'm going home and I suggest you do the same.'

I could do that, I thought. I could let him continue on his lonely way, and not interfere. I could let him have his privacy and keep our relationship on strictly professional terms, the way he never did with me. I could take advantage of the next moment when he looked at me the way he had earlier, and that might distract both of us from our problems for a while. Or I could be the friend he so desperately needed. He might be ready to give up on his happiness, but I wasn't.

He was already at the door when I spoke. 'I think we should go for a drink first to celebrate the end of the case. We could see if anyone else wants to come along. I saw Chris Pettifer at his desk when I came back – he's usually thirsty.'

He paused, and I thought he was going to say no. 'I could go for a drink. One drink. Because I need to get home.'

Chris Pettifer *was* thirsty, it transpired, and so were Vidya and Georgia, and, to my disappointment, Pete Belcott. As we got ready to leave, I noticed that Derwent's shoulders had come down from around his ears, that he was wandering around with a hint of his old swagger, and I smiled to myself. I waited until he was near my desk.

'I was thinking, you could get a dog.'

He groaned. 'Yes, because what I need is another commitment.'

'Thomas would like it. You would like it.'

'Maeve—'

'I know you're going to miss Pippin. What about a Jack Russell cross?'

There was a glint in his eye that I recognised as he sat down on the edge of my desk. 'What about an Irish setter?'

'Why would you suggest that?'

'It just popped into my mind for some reason. How much would you say you have in common with them?' His phone was in his hand. 'Let's have a look, shall we?'

'I am nothing at all like an Irish setter,' I said with dignity.

'I beg to differ. Deep chest, small waist, slender hindquarters,' he read off the screen. 'Affectionate, independent, playful, companionable. It doesn't say intelligent here, but don't take that to heart.'

'Fine, don't get a dog.'

'Apparently I don't need a dog if I've got you.' He glanced at me. 'I've got bad news about your life span.'

'Keep this up,' I said sweetly, getting up, 'and there'll be bad news about yours.'

He was about to reply when his phone vibrated with a new message. He glanced at the screen and then stopped to read it properly.

'Something wrong?'

'No. It's fine.' He looked around. 'Are we ready yet? How can this possibly take so long?'

It was late and the building had emptied out, so the lift came almost immediately. We crowded in together. Derwent was near the front and I was at the back, behind Vidya who was telling Georgia an endless story about an arrest she had once made. Pettifer and Belcott were having a low-level argument about football. I watched Derwent, troubled for him. His head was bent as he looked at the screen of his phone, tapping out a message. As soon as he sent it, another message hummed back. I saw him flinch.

And then the lift arrived at the ground floor. We piled out into the lobby, sorting ourselves out. I made my way to Derwent's side.

'Is everything OK?'

He dropped his phone in his pocket. 'Yeah, but I have to go.'

'Are you sure?' I was looking at him closely, noting the muscles tightening around his eyes and around his mouth: a quiet kind of misery. The harder Melissa tried to hold on to him, the further she was pushing him away, and it was tearing him apart.

'Another time.' He raised his voice. 'Sorry, gang. I can't stay.'

There was a chorus of disappointment and good-natured jeering as we all spilled out onto the street, the warm fug of evening air a surprise after the chill of the office air conditioning. He nodded to me and walked away, in a hurry, preoccupied. I turned to go the other way and found myself face to face with Pete and Chris.

'So?' Pete demanded.

'So what?'

Chris took the lead. 'Did anything happen between you and Josh when you were away?'

'Nope.'

'Sure?'

'I think I would remember.'

Chris held out his hand to Pete, grinning. 'Told you so.'

Pete took out his wallet with an expression of total disgust on his face. 'I'm not sure I believe her.'

'Georgia can back me up. She was there.'

'Yeah, I would have picked up on something but there was absolutely nothing going on there.' She shrugged. 'No romance. No shagging. All totally asexual and above board.'

Pete handed Chris a twenty-pound note as I kept my face completely neutral and memories flashed through my mind.

Holding his hand.

His mouth curving against mine.

I've never felt about anyone the way I feel about her, he'd said to Ruth.

The way he'd looked at me.

The way he'd touched me.

'Let's get a move on,' I said.

Georgia sighed. 'I was so sure something would happen.'

'We're friends,' I said. 'Just friends. Nothing more to it than that.'

As we walked down the street, I wondered if I was trying to convince them or myself.

Acknowledgements

Creating a book is hard work, not necessarily for the author, but for many people behind the scenes. My first thanks must go to my super-editor, Julia Wisdom, who made sure that *The Close* was a proper crime novel, and my wonderful agent, Ariella Feiner, who campaigned hard for more romance. Between the two of them, I think we came up with a perfect balance.

I am very grateful to everyone at HarperCollins, particularly Kimberley Young, Kate Elton, Kathryn Cheshire, Angel Belsey, Lizz Burrell, Fliss Denham, Susanna Peden, Amber Ivatt, Amy Winchester, Maddy Marshall and Hannah O'Brien among many more. I would also like to thank the team at United Agents who look after me so well, especially Amber Garvey who is unfailingly helpful and Jennifer Thomas, a genuine miracle-worker.

I would like to thank David Higham Associates for granting me permission to use a line from Robert MacFarlane's beautiful book *Underland* and I wish to acknowledge the epigraph here:

Quotation from *Underland* © Robert Macfarlane, published by Penguin Books.

I am so fortunate to be part of the wonderful gang of writers at work currently, in what is surely the second golden age of crime fiction. Special thanks to Liz Nugent and Sinéad Crowley who are as essential to everyday happiness as my morning cup of tea, Catherine Ryan Howard for vital cocktails and conversations, Sarah Hilary for her beautiful friendship and thoughtfulness, Erin Kelly for being a perpetual joy, Colin Scott who never seeks the limelight but always knows exactly what to say, and Cressy McLaughlin for her dedication, enthusiasm and all-round loveliness while I was writing this book. I'd also like to thank the readers who have waited so patiently for this book, and for *something* to happen! I hope you'll let me know what you think.

Authors are terrible people to have as friends – we disappear for months when we have a deadline, we're vague about commitments and we drift off into our own world regularly. I'm so fortunate to have people like Claire Graham, Sarah Desmond, Alison Gleeson and Sarah Law in my life. This book is dedicated to Sarah Law, who makes me laugh more than anyone and spends her spare time helping people through her voluntary work which I admire so much. She makes life better for everyone she knows.

My father died while I was writing this book, just a year after my mother, who he missed terribly. He retained his love for literature into his nineties, particularly Shakespeare, who he quoted often and accurately. I think he would have enjoyed the play in this book (possibly more than the time he sat through *Hamlet* performed in Romanian). My sister and I were so lucky to have him in our lives. I think of him and miss him every day.

I'd like to thank Kerry Holland and Philippa Charles for their constant support and weekly conversations during these difficult years, and Edward and Patrick for respecting the sanctity of the writing shed most of the time. And of course James, for everything, always.